Chest of Souls

Book One

By Michelle Erickson

Acknowledgements:
I have a firm belief that Gratitude goes a long way.
I humbly recognize my Father in Heaven for gifting me with the ability to write in the first place and staying by my side, opening doors and bringing so many talented people into my life so my dreams could come true.
My editor: Thanks doesn't cover it. You know how important the first time through is, thanks for your patience, support, chocolate, and conversation while we plowed through a manuscript littered by computer generated semi-colons and endless 'levels'

Praise for Chest of Souls Book One

A new series sure to please the pickiest fantasy readers..,
<u>Readers Favorite "Book Reviews and Award Contest"</u> - Reviewed by Anne B. for Readers Favorite

"Michelle Erickson has created a new series sure to please the pickiest fantasy readers. [She] does exactly what all authors should do...begin the book with a dynamic, attention grabbing scene. However, she doesn't stop there; she continues with one heart pounding scene after another. Her talent for description brought to life the strange creatures previously only seen in her mind's eye. There are plenty monsters to fear and battle in Chest of Souls... This is the first book in a new series; I can hardly wait to see what our two heroes face in the next book."

Wonderful start to a great series!, By <u>T. K. Arispe</u>
"Chest of Souls epic starts off with a bang! The first book of Michelle Erickson's magnum opus explodes with colorful, engaging, dynamic characters, an immense and intricately crafted world and its history, a tightly woven narrative that is as complex as it is suspenseful, and of course plenty of action and adventure. I must give due praise to the author's skill in writing children--the child characters in this book are so utterly endearing and sympathetic that they strike a chord within your heart that will continue to resonate as they grow older."

Praise for Klaus

I highly recommend Klaus for the whole family,
By <u>Readers Favorite "Book Reviews and Award Contest"</u> Reviewed by Anne B. for Readers Favorite
"...Erickson combines romance, adventure, suspense and humor to create one of the best Christmas tales I've ever read... This book will become a family favorite. I can see this tale making it to TV as a Christmas special..."

Praise for Pic Jump

First rate story with a unique plot,
By <u>Readers Favorite "Book Reviews and Award Contest"</u>
Reviewed by Alice D. for Readers Favorite

"Pictarine Nebbie loved her parents but not her name; she...meets the most marvelous man, Mason Jump, and marry weeks after meeting. ..their wedding car is sideswiped, Pic suffers massive head injuries and lies in a coma!

Though badly injured, she is given an out-of-body ability to transfer from one pair of eyes to another. [She] lands as a little girl's Barbie doll's eyes. The little girl, Emma, and her mother and father [get on] a plane with a terrorist on board. Pic, Emma, and Emma's mother flee for their lives... with one of the terrorist's comrades coming after them...

This is a really first rate story with a unique plot that flows well from beginning to end of story. It offers romance and then adventure that will keep the reader enthralled until story's ending. It is well-edited, extremely well-written, with believable characters who hold true throughout the story. A wide number of readers will enjoy this...."

Dedicated to:

My husband, I love you, Heart and Soul, 4-ever, thanks for always believing in me, for encouragement, both listening ears, and the snake trip.

My children, Thanks for the role-playing-until-midnight and endless flow of ideas and enthusiasm that brought our family closer together. You kept me going long after I'd had enough. I love you all.

My mom, a single mother, who read to me in the first place and then bought me books, even when she couldn't afford to.

My dad who could have been a great writer, but chose to stay in the background on the green.

My aunt, for laughing and crying in all the right places and cheering me on. You gave me a rare gift that all author's should receive that at least once – a firsthand reaction to every page.

To all those who read the book in its rawest form and every time after, giving me hope that I had a story worth reading.

Illustration Copyright 2010 StravenLite
Copyright 2010 Michelle Erickson
ISBN Softcover: 978-0-557-68002-3

Books by this author

5 Blanks

*Klaus

*Pic Jump

CHEST OF SOULS SERIES

*Chest of Souls

Lend me Your Mind

Aftermath

Sacrifice of Souls

Traps

Stone Dreams

Division of Souls

Storm

Walking in Lightning

*Won Readers Favorite awards 2011

2011 Whitney award nominee

Prologue

Chapters

Prologue

It was time to summon the Chest of Souls.

The light was dim inside the cave, the Guardian noted with disapproval. Even then it wasn't a steady glow, but the dancing flickering light that came from torches held by those in front of him as they descended the stairs.

The faces of those with him, four Sons of Ammon, and four women, were shaded and appeared altered or grotesque as the uneven flames fought the draft coming from below. In respectful silence, seven of the others took their positions near the sacrificial pool. He noticed they did not meet his eyes when he looked at them – except one man; his best friend. He wished he hadn't. The pity there was almost too much.

He clenched his jaw and took his place near a mammoth-size block of stone that had been wood eons before. Sitting on the stone was the sacrifice, a tall woman dressed in pristine white. Her face was tight with anxiety and her slender hands were clasped tightly together in her lap. He gently laid a massive hand on her shoulder and contemplated the task before him. He had objected to what was to take place in no uncertain terms. He even threatened some of those present with physical harm, but it boiled down to one fact: They had a chance to destroy the city of Sogo and they must take it, no matter the cost. He found it ironic that he had been the one to say those very words. He hadn't known the cost; could not have, or he would never have said them.

The price was one soul - hers.

"You don't have to do this," he whispered. "Let me."

"I have the strength to do this one thing," she said with fearful determination. "You have the strength for the rest."

They anxiously watched the Poolseer gracefully kneel beside the sandpool. She was no ordinary Poolseer. She was also a Mage.

She lightly touched the surface of the sand with her right hand. The sand hardened like stone, returned to granular form, and then flashed the full spectrum of purples, ending with the richest of all..

The surface of the sandpool awakened and spun faster and faster until wisps of color-filled sand smoked up from its surface.

"I summon the Chest of Souls," said the Poolseer firmly. Then she looked right at him with now-purple eyes, "Whatever happens, don't let her go or she'll kill everyone in this room."

The willing sacrifice rose, her hands in fists. The Guardian grudgingly put his massive arms around her from behind, then clasped them over her arms as the sandpool turned white and the screaming began.

Chapter 1: Run!

On his ninth birthday, Talon Ryhawk woke to the startling sensation of flying through pre-dawn dark. All that registered was the fact it was cold, and all he wore were his underclothes. He landed with a bounce. His air left him with a solid whufff when he connected with the hard-packed dirt outside the cottage and he rolled over the uneven ground, coming to rest on his stomach.

Dazed by the jolt, Talon looked through the curtain of his sun-streaked brown hair back at the doorway where his father, Tasut, stood. His massive arms were folded against his thick chest, his dark brown eyes unreadable. His father looked real enough - tall as a mountain and nearly as strong, in Talon's estimation. He fought rising panic. *Have we been attacked again?*

Their cottage was near the biggest and only red leafed tree in the Rahazi Forest; a place known for harboring the dregs of society. In the few months they had been here, they had been attacked twice. Both times, he had been told to run to the stable and stay with Harcour, his father's stallion. During the last attack, there were sounds of a ferocious battle. Later, he helped bury the men that attacked. One of them died just outside the stable. Talon hated how his eyes always settled on that spot and in his mind, he could still see the dark patch of earth where blood had soaked the ground.

Right now, he couldn't hear any signs of attack and as unfeeling as his father was, he doubted Tasut would just stand in place while strangers killed his son. Talon struggled to breathe as yellow motes flew in front of his vision, swimming on a blue-black background.

Gradually the motes stopped spinning long enough to form into sky and the gargantuan red-leaved tree in their front yard. Talon pushed himself up from the ground to a sitting position and looked toward the cottage. *It's too quiet for an ambush.* When he caught his breath, his father pointed at the forest and spoke one word: "Run."

There was only one place to run and that was the Village.

Talon didn't point out his meager clothing, the bleeding scrape on his leg, or the burning sensation on his back. Dream or not, he got up off the ground and sprinted in the direction Tasut pointed, not questioning his father's orders. *Maybe the enemy is near and he's sending me away.*

Tasut Ryhawk was formed like a wedge of granite and had to duck to enter most houses. He was a man of few words and a person's health depended on listening well the first time. Talon knew if he was dreaming, it would end and he would wake up in his bed. If it were real, then it would be in his best interest to obey his father without hesitation. In his nine-year-old world, obedience meant survival.

He was unaware his father watched him enter the forest, unaware Tasut signaled his men to be alert by shooting an arrow into a nearby tree. He didn't hear his father murmur into the quiet, "It begins."

*

It was early summer, but the Rahazi Forest hadn't noticed. Heavy frost stubbornly bit the edges of leafs and plants covering the edges of the dirt road. As Talon puffed tearfully along the pathway through the woods, small clouds of steam came from his mouth and he tried, without success, to jog his memory in search of any offense he might have committed so he could avoid it in the future.

His normal days were occupied by various chores. He was confident he finished all of them yesterday, but his mind followed the riverbed of his chores anyway, in search of neglect.

From the time he was six years old, he was to rise and milk the cow when dawn touched the window of his room. Gathering eggs and mucking out the stable followed. During this time, Tasut always rode Harcour into the Village. *Is he going to meet me there? Does he know an attack is coming?* Upon returning from the Village, Tasut would throw Harcour's reins to Talon and head to the cottage to make breakfast. Talon would spend that time avoiding the large blunt teeth of the stallion. The last pre-breakfast chore was a strenuous set of exercises called forms, something he'd been doing since he was three. When Talon finished, he was supposed to meditate while Tasut performed the more advanced forms. Most of the time Talon peeked through his lashes and watched his father. He knew when Tasut finished because they'd meditate until Tasut declared it was time to eat.

Talon shuddered as dawn breathed life into the world. The chill air seemed colder as the sun peeked over the canopy of trees seeking to pierce their protective shade. Puffs of white erupted from his mouth as he ran. Within an hour of leaving the cottage, there was a coppery taste in his mouth, like blood, and the taste was stronger now. He tried not to think how unpleasant the Rahazi Forest was in the early morning when you were barefoot and nearly naked. He still hadn't figured out *why*.

Yesterday after a hearty breakfast, Talon was sent to harvest the herbs Tasut wanted. He'd returned to the cottage with the poisonous plants and watched as his father painted different combinations on star-shaped weapons called quills. They came from the city of Sogo, a place Talon had never seen, but very much wanted to visit. When he'd told his father this, his father had given him a long hard stare and said, "No." He hadn't asked again.

He'd been sure to take the proper dosage of the poisons to build up immunity. Tasut was very strict about that. Some of the poisons were bitter, but Talon never dared complain; his father drank even more of them.

More than the cold, he was concerned that Tasut had waited to discipline him. He had never done so before. Talon wasn't sure if he had the courage to ask his father what he had done wrong. Once, he had seen Tasut pick up a peddler and shake him hard, slamming him up against a wall just for mentioning Laysha, Talon's mother.

The deeper into the forest he ran, the deeper the shade became. He couldn't even see the sun and the cold bit deeper as his nose caught a strong wet smell. Talon jumped over the small creek that meandered through the forest and stopped to kneel by its side. Gratefully, he dipped his hands in and slaked his thirst. The icy chill made his hands and head throb. He took a moment to wash off the dried blood that still clung to the scrapes on his leg and chest. There wasn't anything to be done for the stinging on his back. He stood and his stomach grumbled as loud as the gurgling water.

A sharp uneasiness filled his mind as he stared into the grey shadows. Every story he'd heard about the Rahazi Forest came to mind with disturbing clarity. In particular, a story concerning man-eating dogs repeated itself.

He anxiously turned back to the path, but his thoughts returned home. He'd cleaned the cottage, checked the traps for game and cleaned and tanned the hides as quickly as possible. *What did I do wrong?* His tired legs stumbled over a root and he flew into a rut that had been iced over. The ice broke under his weight and the cold water took his breath away.

He struggled to get to his feet. His side ached and his bare feet were pink, stinging with the cold. As he moved forward, awkwardly examining marks that would grow into bruises, reality slapped him again. This time his toes connected painfully with a good sized stone a wagon wheel had turned over in the road. He could feel the scrapes on his back sting more fiercely after his fall and his young body ached with the cold. Tears of frustration came to his eyes.

He no longer tried to run with his arms wrapped around his upper torso. It made his movements more awkward and uneven. He was a mile outside the Village when his skin prickled as if eyes watched him. *Maybe it's animals.* His feet slapped faster against the frosty dirt paths. He kept looking back over his shoulder. It didn't feel like animals. This feeling stayed and got stronger. He tried not to panic, but control wasn't working as effectively as imagination.

His legs stretched harder and he pushed himself to get out of the forest. There was eerie silence around him except for his hoarse ragged breathing. At the pace he was running, he could hear his own heartbeat thundering in his ears. He knew he couldn't keep his stride. *I'll slow down when I see the houses, and then I'll be safe.* He slowed to a walk as he crested the small rise and could see smoke rising from chimneys. His legs shook with the effort of his sprint and he felt light-headed with relief.

Then he heard the solid 'Thock!' of an arrow slamming into a tree behind him. He spurred himself forward, ducking off the path and turning the corner of the first building he saw.

The Village was hardly worth the name. It was a small non-descript gathering of sad hovels. Its people were dark-haired and had dark eyes. He stood out among them with his blue eyes and light brown hair. He was outside so much the sun had twisted its fingers through it enough to leave its mark. It was lighter than Tasut's even in deepest winter. Tasut once mentioned he had his mother's coloring.

Talon didn't remember his mother. That hadn't stopped Talon from wondering about her and what happened. *Did she die in an accident?* Sometimes he wondered if Tasut even knew how she died or if Tasut had driven her away. In moments of despair over his unsuccessful efforts to please his father, he had the unholy thought that maybe Tasut had done something to her.

Common sense laughed at such a thought. Tasut was big and brutal, but not a murderer. However, his fear was loud enough to drowned out common sense. All he could do was cling to hope that when all was said and done, his fear would be proven wrong.

Chapter 2: Nyk

The sleeping Baker was a man with forearms like hams and hands that the wise avoided shaking, even in friendship. He went by the name of Jon. Like most folk in the Village it wasn't his real name, but it suited him.

He was a widower until recently. His new wife, Shar, was rosy-cheeked, loving, and if truth be told, not the brightest apple in the basket. However, in Jon's opinion, she was the shiniest of the bunch. Shar was born and bred in Utak, so no one expected her to be anything other than beautiful. The irony of his married life was that Shar could not cook.

He had been alone for five years when he met Shar at the annual Utakian Harvest Festival. He discovered she could talk faster than birds could fly. His friend, the Smith, bluntly pointed out, 'Your wife is beautiful, Jon, but I've met flocks of sheep with more sense. Watch her.'

He did so with pleasure. Each morning, she was the first person to greet their customers. She would hurry them into the warm sweet-smelling shop with a pleasant smile and an endless flow of words from the time they entered to the time they left.

In the charismatic weave of her endless chatter, she sold whatever he could bake. It wasn't because she tried to sell anything to anyone, she just had a gift with people. He thought giving samples to the customers was a terrible waste of money and refused to believe it would do anything but put them in the poor house.

She insisted in her jovial manner, "C'mon Jon, we'll try it for one day. If it doesn't work, you'll hear no more about it." They sold out before noon. From that time forward, he let her handle the customers and he did the baking.

Jon frowned upon waking. Today was the day Tasut would be testing his son. Shar didn't know about Tasut or the boy. He yawned, stretched and winced, his shoulder was stiff and complained. He rolled it back and forward until it loosened. It was feeling the effects of an encounter with a heavy pan that struck him the evening before.

Oddly enough, the pan fell from the overhead cage where it had been hanging on its nail for as long as he owned the bakery. He was puzzled over the accident because, upon investigation, the head of the nail was sawn off. *Who would pull such a stupid prank?* Moreover, who would have access to his kitchen without being observed?

He seriously doubted his wife's ability to think of such a prank much less know what tool would be required to saw metal. He stood under that pan every single day. He frowned in thought and pulled on his boot. He hadn't gone anywhere during the previous evening and he would have heard anyone coming in. The only people in the store, at that time, were a boy and a man.

The man was quiet, middle aged, thin, and of average height with a weak chin and disposition. He'd been staying the past two days at the Mast, the local inn, or at least, what served as an Inn for the rare traveler in these parts.

The little boy was Shugahauzian. Most people called them 'Hauzians for short. This boy might have been half-bred because his skin wasn't the ebony of the natives. It was more the color of the sweet cocoa drink his wife served on frosty cold mornings like today. The boy's eyes were a startling pale almond color instead of the near black of his people. The only reason he remembered the boy's eyes was because his wife commented on how unusual they were the night before.

The boy, like most boys, was hungry and simply wanted the free samples. The energetic youngster never went near the kitchen because the Baker had chased him away, threatening to remove some of the boys quick fingers if he didn't stay out of the shop. Shar had gotten after him about that. She liked the boy and enjoyed his stream of chatter, accent and all. The boy had been ordered to stay with Cal, the Blacksmith, for the last two days. He would be leaving today, with Tasut's son.

The Baker with both boots on now, stood and frowned. There was just something about the falling pan that made him feel out of sorts. His mind played at it like a cat with a mouse. *Something isn't right.* He could hear his wife's chatter. She was serving the man that stayed at the Mast.

The Baker wanted to crawl back in bed, but knew he couldn't. *Painful or not, the dough must be punched.* On the bright side, working the dough might ease his frustration. *First things first*, he told himself.

The Smith was very observant. It was a habit learned in the last war the Sogoian government had called a conflict. Naturally, the Council of Nine hadn't been the ones dying or watching their comrades hewn down by the hundreds nor had they seen or smelled the carnage that accompanied the 'conflict.'

At that time, the Smith was a General in the regular army. The Baker had been his Captain and the company's cook. Of their thousand men, four survived because the Smith was observant and noticed things other men did not, like the fact there was a series of root cages out in the forest where men could hide; if they knew what to look for. The Baker nodded to himself. Yes, if anyone had seen anything out of the ordinary, it would be the Smith. He finished dressing by putting on his large Bakers' apron and went into the kitchen.

"...contest in my city," came a man's voice, "We always look for new blood to make the sport more exciting."

"I never heard of anyone like that," his wife was saying cheerfully. "If there were any men that tall around here, I'd be blind not to notice." She took the man his usual order of three seasoned twisties. "Course, I'm new here," she nodded her pretty head and bustled back to the counter.

When the Baker peeked around the corner, he could see the man looked faintly disappointed.

"Are there any folks in these parts? I mean other than those in this village? I'm thinkin' I may find somethin' out of the way, maybe a farm where they grow their boys big and strong."

The Baker didn't like the direction the question seemed to be taking. His heart nearly fell out of his chest when he heard his pretty wife say, "Interesting you put it that way. I haven't thought on it for awhile, but I heard from the innkeeper's nephew there's a place way out in the wood. He might have been teasing. Only a fool'd live in the Rahazi."

The Baker froze at the information his wife had just unknowingly divulged. It hadn't occurred to him to warn her to never mention the cottage out in the woods because she wasn't supposed to know. *Tasut is going to kill me!*

*

With the sunrise, the people in the Village were just waking. Thankfully, few were out and about. The scent of freshly baked bread spiced the air with such a delicious aroma that Talon's mouth watered. He was ashamed at his state of undress and felt pitifully weak and lightheaded as he avoided steaming piles of horse offal. Gnawing hunger mixed with a newer feeling. Anger.

He wasn't paying attention to anything except putting one foot in front of the other and was startled to hear a voice announce, "I'll run with you."

He hadn't heard the pounding of an approaching runner until the last moment. He looked to his right and running beside him was a 'Hauzian boy with striking pale bronze eyes. To Talon's surprise, the runner was wearing bright blue underclothes. The runner's smile was broad and white as he spoke, "My name is Nyk Taym." He looked expectantly at Talon.

'Don't speak to strangers' was Tasut's first and most clearly understood rule. Talon wasn't about to break it. This rule was followed by: 'Lie if you must, but get away at all costs' Usually attached to that was: 'Do not give them our names' Most disturbing was something new: 'If there comes a time when I don't come back, go to the Smith or the Baker in the Village and tell them' It was one of Tasut's longest speeches.

Yet, Nyk had introduced himself. To his knowledge, Tasut had never covered that topic. *Now what?*

Nyk looked a few years older and reached Talon's shoulder in height. His chest had none of the definition that marked Talon's. Nyk was long-legged and slender, but wiry. If it came down to it, Talon was sure he would win Nyk in a fight - as long as he didn't have to chase him. Just the thought of running longer made Talon feel rubber-legged. He was very close to the end of his strength. The boy beside him started running backward, spun and ran forward, and switched again. *Show off* Talon thought unkindly. *He hasn't run twelve miles either.* Talon knew he had no energy left to run away no matter what Tasut ordered. Nyk would easily catch up with him. He would save what strength he had until there was no choice except to fight or run. Having made the decision to conserve some energy, Talon slowed to a stumbling walk.

"What's your name?" Nyk seemed to smile a lot. He didn't even seem to mind the silence that Talon kept. "What do they call this place?"

Talon remained silent although this question had a simple answer. A few of the businesses had names like the Bakery and the Blacksmith. There was also a small building across from the Bakery that had a wood sign that squeaked in the breeze proclaiming it as The Mast.

Talon marked the location of the Bakery and Smithy with his eyes as he held his side and winced as he took another breath.

Nyk watched this action, smile intact, and said, "Cough, it helps sometimes"

Talon decided he didn't care if Nyk was a stranger. Nyk wasn't out of breath and he looked confident in what he said. Talon decided to try coughing.

"Harder than that," Nyk encouraged, "or it won't work."

What does he want from me? Talon tried coughing harder, a difficult feat when breathing in hurt like someone was pinching his side with blacksmith tongs. He concentrated, took in a quick, deep breath and coughed like he wanted to see his toes emerge from his mouth. It worked. The stitch was gone. He was so surprised that he stopped in mid-stride and looked at Nyk whose great white smile broadened.

"There's a Bakery at the end of the street," Nyk's eyes glittered with excitement. "His wife gives samples away of the best twisties and seed-bread I've ever tasted."

Talon's salivary glands worked overtime. He put a hand to the corner of his mouth, embarrassed to find he was drooling.

The door opened to the Bakery. Talon watched as a large man with a limp called back into the shop, "I'm going to get some liniment, Shar, be back soon." He barely glanced their direction as he limped over to the Blacksmith's across the street.

"What's your name?" Nyk asked again with a friendly smile.

Talon remained silent, watching the Baker greet the Smith.

"If you won't tell me your name, I'll call you turtle. I never met anyone slower than you."

Talon just looked at him, made his decision, and walked away from Nyk and toward the Bakery.

"So," Nyk laughed, "you decided to get some twisties?"

Talon decided shaking his head wasn't talking, so he shook it. He wished Nyk would go away.

"I'll go get enough for both of us," Nyk whooped and ran to the Bakery, across the street.

*

The Blacksmith had turned from pumping the great bellows and wiped his brow in time to see Nyk run into the Bakery. He silently cursed. *The Vael-brained idiot!* Nyk had been told to run with Talon, period. Still, Talon was in sight so, what harm could come? Obviously, Tasut's son was smart enough to obey even if Nyk wasn't.

"Trouble Jon?" the Smith asked, sticking a raw piece of metal into the fire to let it become hot enough to pound a plowshare from its mass. The Baker frowned and began relating his dagger-sharp suspicions about the stranger who had been staying at The Mast.

*

Talon felt he would throw up if he didn't eat soon and it was a long way home. His mind finally registered the idea the Baker was now over at the Smith's shop. What good would it do to enter a place when the man he'd been told was okay to talk with wasn't there? He altered his path and headed for the Smith's shop. He was desperate and felt hollow, but needed water even more than food. The Baker stopped talking to the Smith as soon as Talon got within hearing distance.

"Hello boy," the Smith boomed, "what do you need?"

Talon dryly swallowed the dust that had built up at the back of his parched throat, "Water," his voice cracked. The Smith nodded his head toward the water pitcher near the door that led into his home. Talon drank deeply and drained the glass. He refilled it with shaking hands

"Looks like you can use some liniment," the Smith observed.

"And some food," the Baker said, his eyes flickering over Talon's form.

Talon froze with the second glass of water at his lips. He had forgotten about the scratches. Still, Tasut had told him to go to the

Blacksmiths if he had trouble. Dying of thirst was enough trouble to make him go there.

"Thank you," he said with a nod toward the Baker and to the Smith he added, "And thanks for the water."

The Smith nodded, his ham-like fist rising to his chest in a salute that Talon had seen before. The familiar movement clicked in his memory. The Smith was the peddler who came to their cottage, the one Tasut had slammed against a wall. He gave Tasut that same salute each time he finished his business dealings.

The door to the Baker's shop banging open diverted Talon's attention. Nyk erupted from it like a rock from a sling, eyes wide with fright, and panic-driven legs pumping toward the Smithy.

"Run!" Nyk yelled at Talon.

"Stop! Thief!" A thin man with a dark cloak was on Nyk's heels. He caught Nyk by his hair, turned him around, and slapped his face hard enough to knock him to the ground.

One fact stood out in Talon's mind that screamed of Nyk's innocence: Nyk's hands were empty. There was no way to hide anything in what little he was wearing.

The angry man had straddled Nyk and was strangling him. Nyk was frantically trying to pull the man's hands away from his throat.

"Tell me where it is!" he demanded of Nyk, "and I'll let you live."

Talon didn't stop to think. He ran right at the man's back and launched himself into the stranger, feeling a solid connection. It broke the hold the angry man had on Nyk. The man fell and the two boys scrambled to their feet, Nyk held a hand to his throat as he gasped for breath. Talon grabbed Nyk around the waist and pulled him along, but Nyk broke away and together, the two boys took off at a dead run into the Rahazi Forest.

Chapter 3: Disposal

When the boys disappeared into the woods, a brief nod from the Smith to the Baker had them roughly helping the chinless man to his feet.

"Who is the boy that hit me? Tell me!" the stranger hotly demanded. They calmly looked at each other and the man lost his temper completely. "Fools!" he yelled at them, pulling away from their helpful hands.

"Come to my shop, good sir," said the Baker solicitously. "I assure you that I'll do all in my power to compensate you for what was done and get you on your way." The Baker noted the greedy look in the man's eye and the hackles on the man smoothed down somewhat at his offer of compensation.

"Come with us," the Baker said to the Smith, "You're a witness to the crime."

The Smith frowned and said, "It'll take a horse to catch them now."

"Yes!" agreed the man feverishly, "I must get my things and leave."

The Baker and Smith exchanged dark looks as they followed the irate man into the Bakery. The Smith closed the curtain on the front door, signaling business was closed for the day and smiled at the Baker's pretty wife who saw the closed curtain and frowned at him.

"Shar, will you please go and fetch the Magistrate?" asked the Baker.

She looked startled, but left the bakery.

"Rest yourself while we make plans to give you justice," insisted the Smith.

"Just give me your horse and I'll be gone!" The man insisted as he stuffed his waiting saddlebag with the breads the Baker's wife had left.

He turned to find his way blocked by both men. "Out of my way you fools! I must get that boy!" insisted the irate little man.

The Baker stood in front of the door, arms crossed and his eyes flat. For the first time, the dawn of his true predicament finally crashed in on the man's consciousness and his eyes widened.

The Smith shook his head, laying a heavy hand on the man's shoulder. "You won't be going anywhere – Feesha."

After they finished burying the broken corpse, the Baker wiped the sweat from his brow. "Thank Father of All the Assassins Guild sent less than their best."

"I'm not so sure the Guild sent him," the Smith said with a grim, tight look in his eyes. "At least we know who sawed off the nail in your shop. I'll ride to Tasut's," offered the Smith, "Lyon is there and between them, we'll get answers."

The Baker nodded his agreement. Lyon would have answers and Tasut would order the action; whether they stayed put or packed up and left. For now, he needed to return to his insatiably curious wife. She would want to know why he had given her the pre-arranged sentence that would require her to leave without question and not return until he came for her.

In her ignorance, Shar nearly got Talon killed. He needed to fill her in on Tasut, and tell her that the Village was no more than a place for Tasut to house those who could help protect his son. Most importantly, that Tasut would kill whoever failed him without question or mercy.

Sometimes the line between enough and too much was the edge of a blade and in this Village they all walked a very fine edge. Most were connected to Tasut through battle and war and served with him and General Monus. You couldn't serve under such men and not feel an obligation. Tasut was an extraordinary man with keen intellect, though the first thing you noticed was his height topped by the dead look in his dark eyes.

With courage bred of confidence, Tasut had forged a brilliant alliance between assassins and warriors. Lyon Tybar was that link, and they had reason to be grateful he was on the same side.

He went into his shop to wash his hands. They didn't need Lyon to tell them why the Feesha was here. He was obviously searching for Tasut. What they needed from Lyon was information. Specifically, who sent the Feesha and who he may have contacted about it.

*

The two boys ran pell-mell through the forest, heedless of their surroundings. It was a headlong flight of fear and panic. Talon didn't see the root he tripped over, but keenly felt the thud of his head hitting the ground for the second time that day.

"You stay here," Nyk helped him up and pulled him into the shrubbery at the edge of the path. "You're too slow, turtle. He can't catch me. I'll lead him away from here and come back and get you."

Talon grew stubborn. "I'll walk, you go ahead. I'll catch up." Talon would not surrender.

Nyk pressed his lips together, "If you hear riders or footsteps, get off the path. The man that follows us is a Feesha."

Talon's breath caught. *Feesha. One of the damned.* Their brutality was legendary. The nicest thing said about them was that they peeled their victims. In his imagination, they all looked like they wanted to peel you slowly; like Tasut. This man had appeared old, weak, and too thin. He looked like he'd have trouble peeling an apple much less a human.

Nyk picked up the pace and in an amazingly short time, he was out of sight. Talon's strength had played out. In hindsight, he wished he had stayed to get help from the Smith or the Baker. At least at the Baker's he would have had twisties, whatever they were.

A mile later he was stumbling over the uneven path. He felt everlastingly hungry and drier than fire seeds left too long in the sun.

Nyk was going to come back for him. *But why should he? Why should I trust him? He's a stranger.* He knew his father would want to know about the Feesha. If his father knew the Blacksmith and Baker well enough to tell Talon to go to them for help, they must have been trustworthy. He should return to the village and wait there for Tasut.

He had turned back when Nyk reappeared, roughly pushed him off the path into the bushes, and shushed him by putting his hand over Talon's mouth, fear in his own eyes. Talon nodded to indicate that he would remain quiet. Nyk removed his hand and neither said a word. Nyk listened with his eyes shut and his lips pressed together. Talon could hear hoof-beats that got stronger and then passed. Nyk opened his eyes and dug into a weathered bag. Smiling, Nyk handed him a strip of dried meat.

"I ran back to the Village and got my rucksack," Nyk said as he held up a weather-worn leather sack.

Talon didn't care where he got it. He was ravenous and tore into the meat, unsure when he would get another meal.

As of this morning, a day meant to celebrate his ninth year of life, his world had turned upside-down, but his stomach reminded him that life went on even if nothing he thought to be secure really was. Nyk sat nearby listening intently and watching the road. When Talon finished eating, Nyk put his finger to his lips to maintain their quiet and waved at Talon to follow him. They started at a walk and Talon was grateful for the reprieve from certain death at the hands of the Feesha.

"Did you see who rode by?" Talon asked quietly, feeling renewed strength flow into his limbs from the small breakfast he had just consumed.

Nyk shook his head and scanned the forest with his eyes. Talon went quiet as well. He was content for the moment to let the food he had eaten make its presence known to his brain so it could function. Part of him felt shame that he had run away. Yet, there wasn't another option. He had no weapons.

"What do you think the Feesha wanted?" he asked Nyk, who shrugged in answer. He had the feeling Nyk knew, but didn't want to say. Maybe he felt as uncomfortable as Talon; the world was less safe than when he had started on his run. But life was good. Better somehow, because Nyk had saved his life and stayed with him although he didn't have to. Talon felt obliged to call him friend no matter what Tasut thought.

*

As the Smith rode through the forest, his battle-trained eyes spotted the two boys as they ducked into the foliage, but had no time to stop and reassure them they were safe. He knew his former Commander well enough to report immediately and whipped his horse to a mile-eating gallop. He rode about five miles when his horse skidded to a stop, nearly sitting in its effort to do so. Puzzled, he tried to kick it into action, but it balked, taking the bit in its teeth as it backed away with a terrified whinny. He knew then that something was terribly wrong, and when he relaxed enough to listen, he heard it: clicking, a consistent thrum of it.

He knew the drums of death were beating for him as dread filled his heart. He looked to either side of the path. It looked like the shrubs were roiling with what was commonly called the plague. He roughly pulled the reins to turn the horse. It needed no further urging to thunder away from an inescapable death. In his heart, he knew it was too late for them, but he had to try and save the boys. Father of All willing, he wanted to survive long enough to accomplish that much.

He desperately ignored the fact that the bushes in front and to the sides of him were occupied. He knew it would take a miracle to make it back to the boys, but he believed in miracles. He believed that whatever happened was in the grand design, whether he understood it or not. He only hoped that being able to warn the boys in time to save their lives was part of that design.

He knew the end was near when he felt his horse get hit more than once. It was dead, but it didn't know it though he could feel its life draining away as it ran. In the distance ahead, he could see the two boys. His horse ran about fifty more feet and dropped. He leaped from its back and hit the ground running as if Mayhem were at his heels repeatedly shouting, "Run! To the trees!", knowing it was the last thing he would ever do.

Chapter 4: Infestation

Talon's legs shook with the effort of simply walking. *Something doesn't feel right.* He looked off to either side of the path, took a quick peek over his own shoulder and tried to shrug off the feeling of being watched.

"You aren't a runner," was Nyk's honest observation.

Talon, sore and shaky, bit back a nasty reply.

"But I could teach your feet to fly. Neff Tally taught me how to run," Nyk said with a proud smile.

"Who?" Talon asked, more to keep going than to indicate real interest.

Nyk looked dumbfounded, "He was the greatest runner in all of the world. He told me that the day I bested him in a race, I'd be ready for..."

They both looked up at the sound of a man's voice raised in warning. In the distance ahead they saw the Smith running hard and fast toward them repeatedly shouting "Run! To the trees!" Behind the Smith, his horse had collapsed to the ground. Talon looked at Nyk who went unbelievably pale beneath his dark skin.

Talon didn't wait. Tasut had named the man as trustworthy. Talon headed for the nearest tree. In their weakened condition, his limbs shook in protest at the exertion. He felt strong arms throw him up to the closest over-hanging branch. He looked down in time to see something small and white hit the Smith in the neck. To his complete revulsion, he saw a ridge of flesh rise from the place where the thing had hit the man and watched as it burrowed under the skin of Smith's neck and up his face at astonishing speed.

Talon looked into brown eyes and read there that the Smith knew he was a dead man. With his hand on the place where the white thing had hit him, the Smith staggered back. His body convulsed as more white things sprang from a foamy puddle on the ground and burrowed into his flesh. His body fell into the shrubs at the side of the path. For a few moments, the bushes shook as his body thrashed. Then all was still except for the sounds of shear-like claws clicking together. Talon retched and the little he had eaten decorated the ground below. Instantly hordes of crabs swarmed from the bushes.

"Higher!" Nyk screamed from the tree next to his. "Higher!" Nyk insisted from his perch, ten feet higher than Talon's. Talon needed no urging.

*

Tasut sat on a log sharpening an axe with a rasping file. He had counted in his mind and the time had come and gone when his son and Nyk should have returned. With Tasut were Lyon Tybar, his wife Marianna (who went by Mari) and their six-year-old daughter Brenna.

Lyon was tall, but still only reached Tasut's shoulder. He had ropy, wiry muscle and a lithe grace that was denied Tasut. His full head of sun-streaked brunette hair was the envy of many men and his grey eyes were heavily lashed. Laysha had commented on his good looks once, Tasut recalled. Though Lyon was handsome in a way that he never would be, he had no cause to worry. Lyon was a one-woman man.

Mari, with her long golden-brown hair and bi-colored eyes was Lyon's equal. Many affluent men, including at least four of the Council of Nine members, wanted her, but Lyon and Mari married the night they met. It was a good match.

Their daughter Brenna would be even more beautiful than her mother. Even using cold logic, Brenna was the most beautiful little girl Tasut had ever seen. Lyon doted on her and Mari wasn't much better. Brenna stood about ten feet away, looking at him with huge blue eyes that were rimmed in long dark lashes and a curious look on her beautiful face. Something in her eyes, the way she carried herself, spoke of the power within; enough power to save or destroy the world.

Tasut shifted on his seat and ignored her until she left. She did not like him and made no secret of it. In his opinion, Brenna was beautiful, courageous, and spoiled.

Three of Lyon's men were hiding in the nearby woods. That had been expected. Lyon was a careful man and when his family was concerned, he took no chances. *Especially after yesterdays attack.* Tasut didn't blame Lyon for the extra protection. He would have thought him foolish if he hadn't brought them. Besides, on a professional level, it was an excellent, even rare training exercise.

As for Talon, something had gone wrong. He knew from experience that Nyk was as fast as Lyon claimed. In all likelihood, Talon, with no previous experience in distance running, was the one who dictated the pace. Tasut continued to work on his axe until one of his men came into the clearing with something close to panic on his face. He instantly saluted and said, "There's a crab infestation in the forest and two of our men are dead. The boys are heading right for them!"

"The Smith?" Tasut put the rasping file away and gave the man his full attention.

"Riding this direction."

Tasut remained calm and tested the edge of the axe with his finger. "Pull the men out."

The man saluted, turned, shot an arrow into the forest, and then turned back to his Commander. He opened his mouth for one moment, looking as if he would like to ask a question, but thought better of it, and faded into the shade of the Rahazi.

Lyon and Mari exchanged looks. "The Smith?" Lyon asked Tasut.

"Dead if he tried to come here. The crabs are on this side of the forest."

A child-like voice piped up and a small, squirrel-like head rose from the circle of fur around Brenna's neck. "Crab?"

The voice belonged to a Shee, a rare and intelligent creature that normally lived in the Rahazi. This particular Shee was like no other before her. Brenna had accidentally modified it. Her fur was whiter than snow with pale orange stripes running diagonally through it and her blue eyes more human in their placement and size. She was stunning compared to the average brown and grey forest Shees. The animal had named herself Mee.

Mee's small voice grew more insistent and she held Brenna's face between her paws, desperation colored her tone as she asked, "Crab?"

Tasut noted that her insistence didn't surprise the Tybars who had been forced to study what little was known about the shy forest dwellers. All he knew was the Rahazi was the only known place to contain wild Shees.

"It would be suicide for her to go." Tasut told them.

"Shees are invulnerable to the larvae the crabs produce," Lyon corrected, looking to reassure their daughter, who hugged the white Shee close and scowled at Tasut.

Tasut merely glanced at Mee, Mari, and finally Lyon, for a long moment. He picked up the leather belt that held his sword and began to rub oil into the leather to waterproof it.

Mari's slender jaw tightened and she knelt in front of her daughter. She looked at the beautiful animal that was now standing on Brenna's lap, with tufted ears twitching.

"You have been very obedient Mee. You deserve a reward."

The ends of her ears twitched. "Mee get crab?"

"For protecting Brenna yesterday and being good today, you can have many crabs."

"Much fat crab?" the sheer excitement at these words made Mee's plush tail bush out and her blue eyes glitter.

Mari nodded. "Enough to feed many Shees."

Mee needed no more encouragement. Leaping off Brenna's lap, she became a white blur streaking toward the forest.

Tasut listened closely and could hear the Shee saying "Crab!" each time her paws touched the ground. In a few minutes a strange 'Woo-Woo-Woo' sound echoed back to them.

From the corner of his eye, Tasut knew that Mari was glaring at him, but Lyon reached out and put a hand on her shoulder when she opened her mouth.

*

Talon stopped counting plague crabs after he reached fifty and put all he had left into the act of climbing. With his heart pounding, his chest, arms, and legs scratched from the roughness of the bark, he looked down from his lofty perch.

The crabs were about the size of one of Tasut's boots, bright green, and scuttled around on white legs with red tips. Their shells were smooth as glass with three grey and milky-white stripes that blazed diagonally across the green expanse. They had long thin pincers that were straight and sharp as a sword rather than curved like a normal crab. They clicked these together like a pair of large, unwieldy shears as they moved. There were so many crabs, the forest was filled with the clicking noise.

Talon's hair stood on end as a dozen or so of the crabs scuttled to the bottom of their trees and their bodies began to quiver. When they stopped shaking, from their maws gushed grey-white slime that was deposited at the bottom of the trees. From the slime, small projectiles erupted, popping upward to surprising heights in efforts to reach them. For the first time, Talon could see that the small, white things that had hit the Smith were like maggots and sprang from the slime the crabs had spewed. He shivered and began shimmying farther up the trunk. He flinched away from the sight as if they could climb up after him. *If the Smith hadn't picked me up and thrown me...* He shuddered, but couldn't turn his eyes away. The crabs waited below. He glanced at Nyk who was still pale under his skin. He too crawled farther up. *How are we going to get down?* He'd rather sit in the tree for the rest of his life than suffer the fate of the Smith. He studiously avoided looking at the low growing bushes where the Smith fell.

A half-hour later, Talon faintly heard someone calling, "Woo-Woo-Woo". He looked at Nyk who remained staring at the crabs. The call wasn't repeated and he figured it wasn't anything to worry about. One good thing that had come of the crabs' presence: he no longer had an appetite. Food was the last thing he wanted now, but his thirst was becoming a trial of measurable proportion. Then he distinctly heard what he thought was a child's voice and his heart froze inside of him.

"Crab!" said a voice.

"Crab?" asked a few more voices.

"Crab!" this time it was an entire chorus.

More and more voices called from all around him. He looked at Nyk who was standing on a thick branch looking back at him. Talon shakily pushed his way to his feet. They both saw what looked like a herd of squirrels, led by a white one, converging on the crabs.

"Its Mee!" Nyk yelled.

Brenna's pet? Talon craned his neck to look closer. Then he looked at Nyk. *How did he know Mee?*

The crabs below universally emitted a high pitched whistling sound that vibrated their shells just before the Shees attacked. What ensued was a feeding frenzy accompanied by graphic ripping, crunching, and snapping of crab limbs. The Shees grabbed the crabs and ripped off their tops with little effort, then stripped out the pale green and yellow flesh and stuffed it into already-full cheeks, gorging themselves.

Talon began to retch again, dry heaves making his fatigued muscles clench.

Nyk swallowed hard and then urged, "Let's go!"

They quietly made their way down their respective trees, carefully looking and listening for the monstrous crabs. Once down from his tree Talon felt as if his feet were made of stone and his legs of sand. He followed Nyk blindly and after a few minutes, he found they were headed not to the Village, as he had originally thought, but toward the cottage.

"What were those things?" Talon asked. He knew the obvious answer, but thought perhaps there was more to it. He badly wanted an explanation of what he had just seen; a logical word for the nightmare he had witnessed.

"Plague crabs," Nyk shuddered.

"Aren't crabs supposed to be red?" Talon felt the familiar word 'crab' didn't apply to the monsters. Even "plague" seemed too tame.

"Not these," Nyk shook his head and turned into the trees, following a deer track that would lead home. Talon felt uneasy leaving the regular path and voiced his fear.

"What if there are more of them?" Talon looked around. His nerves were taut as a bowstring ready to release. "Have you seen them before?"

"Yes." Nyk looked serious for the first time and slowed his pace. Talon had no idea how to get home from where they were, but he was grateful he didn't see any crabs. He was beyond tired, beyond the rush of adrenaline. He just wanted to get home.

"When I was younger, Neff took a group of boys into the part of the Rahazi that touches Shugahauze to study plant life. My people did not know of these crabs." Nyk went silent in remembrance.

"What happened?" Talon welcomed anything that would take his mind off his fatigue.

"Neff adopted me to train as a special favor to my parents. I was five years old so he carried me on his shoulders. We came to a place where there were huge rocks to sit on while we ate lunch." Nyk hopped over the small creek that Talon knew would lead home. While Talon was grateful that he knew the general direction they were heading, he was now buzzing with curiosity and grateful for something other than his exhaustion to contemplate.

"Neff loved to teach," Nyk smiled sadly. "Just as we finished our lunch, a doe jumped into the clearing and began to jerk and tremble...then we heard the clicking. Neff yelled at the class to follow him. He picked me up just as the deer hit the ground and the crabs came."

The hair was standing up on Talon's neck as he thought back to the scene just minutes before.

"No one but Neff and me got away."

They could still hear the Shee's voices in the distance but, thankfully, no more clicking of sharp pincers.

Nyk seemed to shrug it off. "Only some bones and the clothes were left. The parents blamed wolves and said Neff was lying. He tried to tell them about the crabs, but no one believed him."

Talon frowned, his thoughts tugging him forward to a place he did not want to go. "What happened to him?"

"In Shugahauze, if you're a murderer, you're stoned." Nyk's full lips grew tight, "My parents tried to intercede, when that didn't work, they tried to help him escape. They were put in prison."

Talon felt the bitterness of his new friend. He knew that nothing he said could change it. He thought back to the Smith who sacrificed his own life for Talon's. There wasn't anything the Smith could have done. *He chose to save me like Neff chose to save Nyk.*

They walked onward, lost in their own dark thoughts. Nyk seemed to perk up when the branches overhead thinned enough to let in some light. Talon tried to ignore the effervescent Nyk who now was running to the left and right of the path, forward and back. Just when Talon thought Nyk had run home, he appeared again.

"I found the path," Nyk beamed a great smile.

"What about the crabs?" Talon looked behind them, "Will they follow us?" Crabs inside the Rahazi were bad enough, he didn't want them near his home.

"I think we can outrun them." Nyk looked at Talon, re-assessing, "Well, I can. Maybe you should stay here in a tree and I can bring help."

Talon stubbornly shook his head, wondering how fast Nyk really was. It didn't matter. No matter what Nyk said, he was going home. Now.

"The crabs looked pretty slow," Nyk gauged Talon's physical condition, "but so are you. I'll scout around and see if there are more so I can warn you if you need to head for the trees."

Talon was sure that the path they were on led back to the original dirt road where he had been earlier. He wasn't sure about the time. Time had no meaning in the shade and shadow of the Rahazi, especially when there were droves of carnivorous crabs hiding in the bushes.

He felt a light breeze come up, lifting bumps on his bare skin. His spirits rose. He knew that they were getting closer to the cottage because he smelled bacon and caught the scent of fresh made bread. His stomach knotted with hunger. *It won't be long now.* He held that thought close as his stomach refused to hold its temper and yelled its complaint so loudly that Nyk looked at him with an understanding smile.

With the cottage close enough to smell the food, his thoughts returned to Tasut. Perhaps his father would explain why he had been thrown out of the bed this morning. Even as the thought formed he knew, with a dark sense of injustice, that his father never offered explanations.

The very last thing he remembered doing the previous night was meditation, a part of their normal routine and usually the most peaceful. Together, they had sat on the wood floor of their cottage and crossed their legs, clearing their minds and communing with Father of All, the one and only Being that Tasut recognized as all-powerful. Talon had been unable to focus; instead, his mind re-played the attack that had occurred just hours before.

Is that what I did wrong? It was true that the Tybar's little girl, Brenna, had been in great danger. *Or was it because I only killed* one *of the creatures that tried to kill her?*

It was no use to try and figure it out. He had to concentrate now just to keep one foot in front of the other. His thoughts returned to the present and Nyk.

"Where you from?" Talon asked, avoiding eye contact. It still felt odd to speak. He was tired beyond any kind of tired that he had felt before. Even his tongue was tired, but he felt he needed to know more about Nyk in case Tasut asked, plus he was interested in his new friend.

"Obviously, I'm 'Hauzian by birth," Nyk smiled. "After Neff was killed, I decided to be an Achaite."

Talon ran out of conversation. His thoughts turned inward. *Is Tasut waiting?* That thought goaded him. Pulling energy from somewhere within him, he began to run again. Nyk easily kept pace. *I wonder if Nyk has eaten?* Talon was sure there would be enough for the two of them at the cottage. Arranging his thoughts was difficult. Which should he tell Tasut first? Which would be the most important for Tasut to know? Should he talk about the crabs or the Feesha who tried to kill Nyk?

The crab infestation might not be important by now. He pictured the eating frenzy that must still be taking place in the Rahazi. Though unlikely, because of the crabs, the Feesha could still be following them. He desperately hoped the crabs made a meal of him. Talon heard Feesha were very nimble and clever, even if the one he'd seen didn't appear to be.

Talon tried to picture Tasut eagerly awaiting his return. He failed conjuring anything but the stern visage of his father sitting in front of the cottage with a sack of the special fletching he ordered from Rykett near his side, attaching the black feathers to his specially made arrows.

Will he let me eat? The thought was a sobering one. He had never had to consider that Tasut might withhold food. However, Tasut was a man that you didn't want to keep waiting. *And I'm late.*

"You need to pace yourself," Nyk said into the quiet.

Talon looked at his running partner. Nyk looked as if he had nothing better to do than run for the rest of the day and wouldn't be tired if he did.

Instead of pacing himself, Talon stubbornly pumped his legs faster, trying to leave Nyk behind. No matter how hard he tried, he couldn't get ahead of him.

They reached the edge of a meadow that marked the halfway point home. Neither boy offered conversation. Talon jumped when he heard a small animal cry somewhere in the forest behind them.

He thought he saw a man in a tree at one point, but when he glanced up again, whatever he saw was gone. He didn't dare spend more time looking up when it was all too easy to trip. He was grateful the noise he heard wasn't clicking. He'd probably have nightmares about that sound and worse, in his dreams he would be looking into the Smith's brown eyes knowing there wasn't anything he could do to save him.

Chapter 5: Beware Beauty

"The idea was to train the boy, Tasut, not kill him!" Lyon's thick head of hair framed his furious face and his hands clenched with the effort of controlling his urge to run into the forest and save the two boys himself.

Mari grabbed her husband's shirt as he headed for the forest, "You don't know where they are, Lyon, and there are still crabs or Mee would be back."

He wasn't in the mood for logic. What he wanted to do was strangle Tasut if for no other reason than to feel a sense of satisfaction.

Tasut had risen from the chopping block, turned, and deeply embedded the axe into its surface. He stepped into the cottage to take his spot by the front door. Lyon followed him in, knowing better than to hope that his presence would irritate Tasut to the point he'd agree to save his son, but doing it anyway just to feel like he was taking action. They all knew why the crabs were called a plague.

It sickened him that Mari was right. It was better to wait for Mee to return. He was not built for waiting; he preferred the heart-stopping thick of things where he felt he could control the outcome.

The boys were in grave danger and he was helpless to do anything. He looked out the window, time and again, as if by watching for them they would appear. Every now and then, he would go out to the enormous red-leafed tree that stood near the place they expected the boys to emerge from the forest. Inevitably, Lyon returned to the house to pace.

*

Tasut briefly studied the tall, slender man who moved around the small cottage like an agitated panther. Lyon Tybar was a powerful man, even a man to fear...if one was permitted the luxury of that emotion. He admired Lyon despite the fact the man was the best assassin that ever served the Council of Nine. The Council thought Lyon was dead. He would hate to have to kill him. If he could. That was it, really, he wasn't sure he could kill him and that was unusual for Tasut. Lyon had earned his respect - so far.

There was no love lost between himself and Lyon's wife, Mari. He knew from painful experience that she was more perilous than her husband, and far more dangerous than the Council of Nine suspected. One or more of the Nine had perceived her as a threat and ordered her assassination years ago based on what little the Council thought they knew then. In Tasut's opinion, this was a remarkably accurate assessment for the power mongers that ruled Sogo, although Mari wasn't a threat for the reasons they claimed.

Mari's heritage was never misunderstood. She was a great beauty even among Utakians. Tasut acknowledged her beauty with an old adage about flowers that was specifically applied to Utakian women that read:

> "Beware all beauty
> For the rose that is bright,
> May look tender
> But possess thorns bite"

Physically, Mari could well be the epitome of why Royalty persisted in trying to find its way into the enchanted land of Utak. Many had and would surrender kingdoms to have Utakian women for wives and Tasut was man enough to appreciate it. Yes, Mari was beautiful to behold, but it was there the likeness between her and most Utakian women ended, and so did his trust.

Mari was a well-known Poolseer in Dyman before her 'death' and a woman that harbored many secrets. He only knew one of her secrets with any degree of certainty: Mari was a Mage.

Such a calling in life was a pre-ordained situation and extremely rare among women. Within the slender frame and in addition to flawless beauty, she possessed power enough to stop his heart from beating. And right at the moment, the look she gave him was winter-chilled, her body was stiff with bubbling anger as she finished preparing the meal for Talon's return. She chopped the vegetables in front of her with precision and a good deal of anger, all of it, he knew, was directed at him. He could live with it. She was Lyon's problem and he had every confidence in Lyon's abilities. He looked at Lyon and nodded. The message was clear: Deal with Mari.

*

Catching Tasut's nod, Lyon's mood soured. He didn't have Tasut's confidence. He'd worked off the worst of his own anger, but he was in tune with his wife's moods and she was gearing up to release the dam that held her fury. He knew Tasut would be receiving double helpings when it burst. He fervently prayed the boys would return prior to that point.

Tasut only thought he knew what Mari was like when she was in a rage. Wordlessly, Lyon helped her with the meal preparation by putting plates on the table while gauging the tempest he knew could become a hurricane if not checked soon.

She wasn't to the point he would need to gently place his hand on her shoulder, or ask her to step into the other room with him, yet. He inwardly winced. He wanted to avoid letting it get that far. Normally, she was a happy woman and possessed a deep-seated belief that anything was possible. If someone was Vael-brained enough to let her fire turn to ice, they'd be worse off than a cursed wave breaker; better off at the bottom of the sea.

He finished setting the table and went out of the house. Hopefully, one of his men would come to report to him soon; Tasut's didn't share information. Not that he blamed them. Failing Tasut was not an option if you wanted to remain alive.

Tasut probably spotted Lyon's men already. It wasn't much of a secret because he hadn't meant it to be. One of his men came out of the woods, signaling wordlessly what he had seen. Lyon felt a choking swell of anger, gave the shaken man a brief nod, and signaled for them to return to Cress City.

Lyon stayed by the enormous tree, breathing deeply, trying to get his emotions under control. According to the report, Nyk was in good shape and could probably outrun the crabs if he really wanted to, but Talon couldn't, his feet were a mess.

His hope for Talon's survival was based on Mee, who was completely reliable when it came to crabs. The mere mention of the word was enough for her to become glittery-eyed and bushy tailed. *Mee will take care of them, with a little help.* He only hoped she didn't kill any of the other Shees who wanted some. *It's no use. I have to try to talk some sense into Tasut.* He was too angry to muster diplomacy, but his conscience would not let him wait and Tasut had the thickest skin of any man that lived.

*

Tasut didn't even let Talon eat before he sent him out! Mari huffed to herself. Of course that was just one of the offenses Tasut had given today and the tally was growing at the same pace that time stretched without sign of the two little boys. She wasn't really worried about Nyk. *Well, perhaps just a bit.* However, Nyk had grown up on the streets of large cities and had the cunning necessary to see him through. *Nyk is a survivor.* He'd proven it many times in the past. Mari's sister Loni had found him half-starved on the streets of Dyman a few years ago outside one of the brothels that infested the city and taken him in.

Talon, on the other hand, had been raised in the wilderness. He had not been trained to run. She bit her tongue to remain silent, but her emotional state was loudly punctuated with the banging of pans and dishes. Thankfully, this activity had the benefit of skimming the suds off her anger.

Her husband leaned up against the doorframe facing Tasut, to watch for the boys. Mari could feel his concern and understand his nervous energy. She glanced over at the immovable mask of the man she no longer knew. At one time, Tasut had been a man of great passion. He had laughed easily and often with Lyon. He had not genuinely laughed for seven years, nor smiled. *He knew the price. He knew it and Laysha knew it.*

Tasut's hours were consumed by a purpose greater than he was, and that same purpose had them all resolutely headed in a steadfast direction.

But this Tasut was a dangerous man; incredibly strong, deceptively intelligent, and terribly, appallingly, empty. He was half-a-soul minus the softening influence of his beloved wife, Laysha. Without her, Tasut had become a rather impossible man with little soul left for anyone to make appeals to. Yet she knew Lyon would try - for Brenna's sake. Their daughter's happiness depended on it.

*

Brenna was quietly helping her mother, and doing her best to stay out of the way of the man her parents called Tasut, but whom she privately thought of as "the grumpy giant."

Brenna didn't like Tasut. If her parents were mad at him, she would be too. Following her mother's example she sent many icy looks his way, usually when he wasn't looking. After all, he was enormous even sitting down. Tasut was in a large chair sitting in the corner by the window.

Her father had been leaning against the door, his jaw was tight like he had his teeth clenched. The grumpy giant moved away from the doorway and now sat at the table, pulling black feathers from a bag and with careful precision, tying them on the end of arrow shafts. Her father turned to look at Tasut and the tightness in his face that told her he was very angry.

"He's your son!" her father shouted as he slammed the table with his fists.

Startled, Brenna jumped and frowned at Tasut. She looked at her mother, who also frowned, but Brenna thought her mother looked rather pleased with her father.

"He could die out there!" The fury in his dark grey eyes spoke volumes, but was tightly contained when he looked down at the rough table and back up into Tasut's face, his jaw was clenched in an effort to get himself under control. "The boy's hands and feet are bloody!"

The hot anger left her father in a rush, replaced by a bewildered whisper, "By all that is holy, where is your mercy?"

"There is no time for mercy," Tasut's voice rumbled through the cottage and he looked at Lyon and then Mari, stood up and moved back to the chair by the window.

Brenna fretted about Talon's hands and feet. Talon was the best, bravest boy in the whole world and she was going to marry him someday. *Why does his father hate him? What if Talon dies?*

She sent Tasut yet another icy look, this time he was looking, and she refused to look away. What she felt wasn't fear, it was anger and she continued to glare at the grumpy giant, feeling her fingertips tingle with heat and race up her back to settle right at the base of her skull.

*

"Brenna, go outside and fetch some kindling," Mari ordered, reading the look on her husband's face. Once Brenna went out Mari was the first to speak, "You can teach him to kill, after all, it's your forte now." She swiped a fly off the table as she looked at him to see if her statement stung him at all. Tasut didn't flinch, but she hadn't driven her point home yet, she stepped over to the window and looked out, then at him and softly asked, "But who will teach him to love?"

"He can't have both," Tasut said tonelessly, looking at Mari and back out the window, "Love or life."

"You didn't always believe that," Lyon entered the conversation, gazing sadly at the man in the corner.

"I'm not the man you remember," Tasut now locked eyes with Lyon. "I made a choice seven years ago. What I am is a reflection of that choice."

Mari had made her point and went back to the table to finish getting the meal ready. She knew Lyon was at the end of his patience. She exchanged looks with him and gave him a brief nod, indicating to pull out all stops.

Lyon plunked down on the threshold and bleakly looked up at Tasut, his voice deceptively soft, "You have a son whose destiny is to help save us all and yet you never tell him why he has no friends and you show him no love or give him praise when he does well." Lyon couldn't sit still and he rose to his feet, scrubbing his hand through his hair. When he passed by Mari, she raised her bi-colored eyes to him, giving him her silent support.

Lyon took a deep breath and turned once again to Tasut. "Even you, my friend," he pointed at Tasut, "did not survive becoming Guardian alone."

There was still no response from the giant man so many feared. Mari knew from the set of her husband's jaw that it was the last straw when Tasut ignored him.

"By all that holds together what's left of your soul, he's a boy doing a man's work! Have mercy! Let me go get them!"

Tasut's face tightened and with eyes cold as death, his voice went off in the silence of the small cottage like a cannon blast, "There's no time for mercy! He must be the best! He must!" His voice lowered, but was still a growl and his large finger came up like a thick dagger to point at Lyon, "And you, of all men, know it!"

Tasut silently rose from the chair and came to the table to look at the food.

"You mean to tell me, Tasut Ryhawk," Mari felt the bite of her temper, "that you have no intention of going out and finding your nine-year-old son?" Her patience hit the wall of his stubbornness. Her normally well-disguised temper was becoming rage.

"He is my son," Tasut acknowledged the fact without emotion. "I will do with him as I please. It isn't any of your business." He chose a small apple and bit into it as he returned to his corner.

"That's where you're wrong," she flared. "He is my business because he will be our daughter's champion. If nothing else, Talon deserves to be loved even more than other children." Mari's voice lowered, but was just as intense as if she screamed in his face, "You *know* what he is to be and what that will mean to her!" She pointed out in the yard at Brenna, whose small arms were full of kindling. "Talon has always been more than **Just. Your. Son!**"

Tasut's eyes went flat. "Exactly my point." He tossed the apple core into the fire, opened a drawer, and drew out a quill pouch. "I'm training him to win Cubes."

Mari felt she would drown in her emotions. She put her hands on her hips, looking out at the forest, her voice dripping with disdain, "Yet you expect him, untrained, to run as well as Nyk, who was trained by the greatest runner of our time and has done little else his entire life!" Her temper flared hotter and she stood in front of Tasut, jabbing his chest with her finger to emphasize each point. "You ordered your men to pull back yet left your son and Nyk to the crabs!" Her eyes burned and she felt Lyon gently put his hand on her shoulder. She shrugged it off.

"He's going to hate you!" she hissed, moving away from him with fists clenched.

"That will be his choice," Tasut replied.

Mari's left eyebrow rose and her eyes narrowed. "Choice!" You're not giving him a *choice* you great brute!" She grabbed the closest thing to her, an apple, and threw it at Tasut's head. Lyon diplomatically stepped between her and Tasut, who added insult to injury by neatly catching the fruit and taking a large bite.

"I will make him a Champion," Tasut said calmly as he impudently took another huge bite out of the apple. This statement seemed to enrage her further.

"Mari," Lyon said in a warning voice as Mari grabbed at the next nearest thing, a paring knife. "That won't help Talon or Brenna."

Mari's bi-colored eyes lost their fire, but her face was etched with anger and her jaw was tight as she grit her teeth. She felt herself shaking with unreleased power and glared at Tasut.

Lyon removed the knife from her hand and moved behind her while she regained enough control to bank her power. His hands lightly kneaded her shoulders as if reminding her that destroying Tasut wasn't an option.

Ignoring her, Tasut laid the quill pouch down and went to his herb cabinet. He gathered several colored vials with steady hands and faced her fury, his face and voice carefully blank, "Father of All is in charge. It is His will I follow. He can – and has – asked everything of me.

"The price I paid the last time the Chest of Souls was summoned was my wife and with her, my heart. That sacrifice taught me this much: the whole world can rage against me, hate me, or try to kill me. If I'm not appointed to die, it won't happen."

Tasut continued speaking, his dark eyes boring into Mari and then Lyon, "You both know the powers of the Council of Nine extend to every government but Utak's. You know what the Book of Benamii says about this time we live in. Do you want less than a Champion? Less than I can and will provide to keep your daughter alive?"

They remained silent as he gathered his vials and quill pouch. Point made, he walked out the front door and into the yard where Brenna stood looking at him, her pretty face wearing a black scowl.

"You better not hurt my Talon," she warned, looking up at him with strange intensity.

He ignored her and spoke to her parents. "Talon will be the best of all the men I've ever trained. He'll survive this, and he'll survive becoming Guardian." He pulled up a shorter, wide log beside the chopping block and sat his vials and pouch on it.

Mari and Lyon had followed him outside. "Brenna, go in the house and put the wood in the box by the stove," Mari watched as a defiant Brenna stomped into the cottage.

She turned on Tasut. "You're too hard on him!" Mari hissed. "He's only nine years old! Many never make it past the first floor; much less survive to compete in Cubes!"

Tasut almost smiled. "For the last seven years, I've been Barracks Commander. That makes me, not you, the expert in the arena."

Lyon had been looking for the right time to enter the conversation and this was it. "Correct me if I'm wrong - friend," Lyon crossed his arms over his chest. His feet were braced apart as if he were on board a ship. "But if you kill Talon during training," Lyon said bleakly, "you condemn our daughter to certain death."

Mari looked nervously toward the kitchen. She could hear the wood being dumped into the box. Relieved, she turned back to listen to the conversation.

"I find that unacceptable," Lyon finished.

*

Tasut caught the new tone in Lyon's voice. Lyon wasn't a man that anyone should idly dismiss. He was the anonymous Master of the Assassins Guild. That particular title wasn't just handed to any man. To earn it, you had to assassinate every person you were assigned by the

Council of Nine, and never be seen by anyone who lived to tell the tale. Lyon had accomplished that with one exception, he married his last assignment.

Tasut looked at him, his instinct waiting for a wrong move and his mind racing over which moves he would make to kill Lyon on the spot. There were several options.

Lyon's eyes traveled over the solid mass that was Tasut, aware that the situation had grown serious if not precarious. He didn't look worried. "If you kill your son and Brenna dies because of your neglect, you die," promised Lyon with a short bow, hand on heart, "Master's honor."

The promise to kill Tasut was a binding one. Lyon would never rest until Tasut was dead if Brenna died. Tasut understood the significance of the short bow and even admired Lyon the more for making it. His memories of this man qualified the statement to be truth.

"I failed my wife, but I won't fail him," Tasut said, his dark eyes burning with his promise.

The two men stood looking into each other's eyes, assessing the resolve within themselves, and each other, to do whatever it took.

"If the two of you are finished?" Mari stood with her hands on her hips. "Our calling is to train them so both survive what's coming."

Tasut bluntly asked, "What are you doing to prepare your daughter?"

For the first time, Mari looked uncomfortable. "Brenna's only six years old."

"Talon was hunting with a sling at six," Tasut informed her. "He can gather and identify poisons, trap, tan skins, do fourth-level forms, and speak three languages."

Mari shrugged. "Brenna's task is different."

Tasut persisted. "Brenna needs training. The Forest Wife said immediately."

Mari stiffened at this. "She's our child and her training is for us to determine, not the Forest Wife. Unlike Talon," she tried to turn the tables on him, "Brenna has known love and happiness. Training her won't be that difficult."

Tasut noticed that Lyon remained silent during this exchange. He looked back into the cottage at the little girl who had no concept about her future or how important she was. She sat by the kitchen table, shooing flies away from the food. Beautiful or not, unless Mari relented, she would become the world's worst nightmare.

Tasut looked back at the unusually quiet Lyon and then spoke to Mari. His voice was deceptively calm. "As you claim, she is your child. But tell me," he paused and looked directly into her eyes, "has the Forest Wife *ever* been wrong?"

Tasut pulled his very sharp axe out of the chopping block and leaned it against the house. Then he sat on the block of wood to work with the quills and poisons. His eyes wandered to the path leading out of the forest. "The Forest Wife needs your daughter to go to her as soon as possible," Tasut said firmly. "Talon can't do this alone. If he tries, he'll die and that, Marianna Tybar, does concern me."

"He won't have to do it alone," Mari sniffed. "The Sons of Ammon will return."

*

At this point, Lyon looked at the ground at his feet. His long fingered hands were on his narrow hips. He would not disagree with Mari publicly, but he knew better. When he looked at Tasut, he saw the same knowledge there.

They understood that Brenna had to fulfill her own side of the prophecies. It was Brenna's sacrifice that would bring about the end of Sogo, not the Chest of Souls, as many ignorant people assumed. The last time they failed because they had tried to fit the circumstances to their own timetable. The results of that failure were planted firmly in their minds each time they saw Tasut. They could not fail this time. If they did, their children would die and the evil in Sogo would govern the world.

With a solid-sounding thock! An arrow slapped into the log Tasut was sitting on. "They're coming," he calmly announced.

Chapter 6: Explosion

The last mile was the hardest. Talon's heart felt like it would pound through his chest and he wanted to collapse.

Nyk, on the other hand, was excited. "C'mon!" he urged Talon, laughing and dancing on the path ahead of them.

Talon shook his head. Now that he knew where the cottage was and that Tasut was nearby, his legs became like lead. He had slowed to a walk, but visions of Tasut plagued him and lent fuel to exhausted legs. He wanted to weep with relief when he saw their humble cottage. He heard Harcour in the lean-to, snorting and huffing. Talon forgot until that moment that Harcour had broken two of the boards across his stall and kicked a good size hole through the back wall yesterday. He slowed his pace to an unsteady walk and looked ahead, grateful to be home.

Tasut sat on a sawed-off log working with quills. Lyon and his family had returned. This fact did not register with Talon until Nyk gave a loud whoop and made a beeline for Lyon. Nyk jumped right into Lyon's arms and was swung around.

"I won! I told you I would!" Nyk looked back at Talon, flashing a victorious grin as Lyon put him down.

This statement made Talon feel apprehensive. *Was it a race?* He quickly looked at Tasut who was putting his quills away in their pouch. His father stood with his arms crossed over his immense chest and waited. His features were set like carved stone.

"You're back!" Brenna exclaimed with a joyous cry. She started to run toward Talon. Tasut's shovel-sized hand blocked her momentarily while his dark eyes rested on his son. Talon stopped ten feet away from his father. His bloody feet and the scabbing on his chest, shoulders, and back, telling more of the days adventures. He looked like a well-used chew rag.

"You think this," Mari gestured at Talon with derision riding her tone, "is what his mother wanted?" She gazed at the pathetic little boy and became aware of the sensation of heat coming from her daughter. Her expression became one of shock. "Brenna!"

Mari hadn't noticed, in the drama of the moment, that her daughter had been focusing hard on Tasut. She knew the instant Tasut's hair caught on fire, that her daughter was furious at being held back by Tasut's large callused hand. Part of her was horrified at what Brenna had done, and the other part, the stronger part, cheered her daughter on.

It wasn't until his hair instantaneously combusted that Tasut had the tiniest inkling about what the Forest Wife had meant by Brenna's "wild" magic. He thought of nothing beyond putting the flames out. Afterward, he only looked startled instead of frightened. Brenna was halfway to Talon before Mari managed to douse the flames and whisk away the smoky remains Tasut had once called his hair.

"It could have been worse," Mari informed him, concealing her smile

He looked at her as one of his large hands scrubbed over his mostly bald head.

*

Lyon smiled inwardly as he watched his tender-hearted daughter race up to the worn-out little boy and throw her arms around him as if to support his weight, then she released his waist once he stopped weaving and gently held his hand as she blackly glowered Tasut's direction.

Lyon watched Tasut closely for signs of retribution. He remained ready to act if he needed, but he was unable to picture Tasut going after Brenna. After all, Brenna was only a six-year-old girl. Tasut did look at her though, long and hard. Lyon had seen grown men break down in the face of Tasut's displeasure. Yet no fear lurked in his daughter's eyes. In fact, there was raw defiance brimming there.

She had mentioned last night that she didn't like the grumpy giant and furthermore, that he needed "a spanking and sent to bed without a story." He and Mari had shared a smile at the thought. Brenna had a temper like her mother's. Thankfully, it was under-developed at this point. At least, he assumed it was until Talon passed out and landed in a heap at Brenna's feet.

*

When Talon fainted, Mari turned on Tasut like she wanted to skin him alive. "You pushed him too hard and expected too much!" She turned to Nyk who looked slightly worried, "Nyk, go get his bed ready, Lyon, bring him in."

Nyk disappeared into the cottage, Mari following him. Lyon carefully picked up the little boy. He was totally limp. Lyon started toward the door and stopped when he felt a wave of heat surging from behind. He turned his head back to look at Brenna who was glowing as if lit from within.

"Mari!" he called, unable to do more than leap into the doorway of the cottage with Talon in his arms. Hopefully, his wife could stop whatever was coming.

Mari came out of the cottage at a run, looking at their daughter, "Brenna! No!"

Brenna still stood where Talon had dropped, her small arms were stretched out from her sides and her hands were like claws. She was shaking as if a storm whipped through her very soul. Her focus was on Tasut and her eyes bore into him with such intensity, it was a wonder he wasn't consumed. For Tasut's part, he had resumed sitting on the chopping block and returned her stare with one of his own, remaining completely still.

Brenna's eyes lost some of their intensity as she turned her attention away from Tasut and looked at her mother in fear. Her small form continued to shake with the effort of containing the raw energy that threatened to consume her. Mari knew with a sense of dread that it could, and would, kill Brenna if she didn't release it. But where? Mari's heart convulsed as she realized there wasn't a thing she could personally do to help. Her eyes sought a target, one that wouldn't kill their hopes.

Lit with the energy within, Brenna was now nearly too brilliant to look at. She had tears in her eyes and said in a hollow frightened voice, "I can't hold it in!" The shaking grew more pronounced and Brenna's eyes went completely white, the ends of her fingers crackled with unleashed energy.

Mari's eyes rested on the gargantuan tree about thirty feet away and pointed, unable to stop whatever was going to happen. Mari had never seen or felt such a display of raw power. *Father of All have mercy on us!*

Brenna pointed at the tree and screamed, "There!"

The millennia's-old tree, the last of its kind, grew incandescent white with light, contracted, then expanded until it blew apart with such force and sound Tasut was torn off the chopping block. His head slammed into the wall behind him before he dropped to the ground like a pole-axed ox. Mari was unable to shield herself in time to prevent getting knocked off her feet where she had been standing. The moment he saw the tree expanding, Lyon slammed the cottage door shut with his foot, protecting the unconscious Talon before the debris from the tree blew across the yard.

*

Lyon ran to put Talon to bed. Nyk, who had been hiding under the table, followed Lyon back to bedroom and then to the front of the house.

When Lyon opened the door it was so deeply embedded with splinters, it would have to be replaced. His eyes sought his wife, and with relief, he saw she had risen from the ground, and was using her power to shield those who had been outside while it literally rained wood. Some chunks were the size of workhorses. He was alarmed to see that where Tasut had been sitting, a huge splinter stabbed through the stone of the cottage wall.

Brenna ran to her mother, pale with shock, and buried her face in her mother's skirt while the adults stood in a daze. Tasut rubbed the back of his head, wincing as he stared at Brenna and then at where the enormous tree had been. A solitary red leaf, perhaps the only one to survive, hung in the air, floating lazily down to the ground, coming to rest next to a fat caterpillar.

Nyk peeked around Lyon's tall frame. He smiled hugely and whistled into the vast silence, "You'll never have to chop kindling again!"

*

Talon woke up and breathed a sigh of relief. *It was a nightmare!* A sense of peace washed over him until he turned over. His muscles screamed the truth and he bit his lip. *Where's Tasut?* Some of it had to be a dream because he thought he recalled his father's head was on fire and of course, that was ridiculous. He shook off that odd thought as the tantalizing smell of food drifted in.

His stomach roared its fury, tied itself into a knot, and squeezed until he thought he'd throw up. Slowly, painfully, he sat up and swung his legs over the side of the bed. The moment his feet touched the floor, he gasped in pain and looked down. They were raw and swollen. Last thing he remembered was standing in the front yard and Brenna holding his hand.

Though his feet hurt, Talon couldn't deny the unique pleasure that came when he realized that someone felt happy about his return, even if it was just Brenna. Other questions without answers swam to the surface of his mind.

There was nothing to recall beyond Brenna holding his hand, but he felt Nyk must have been okay. He was very grateful he hadn't had dreams about the crabs or, even worse, the Smith.

A pair of large blue eyes peered at him from around the doorjamb, and a smile burst across a pretty little face. *Brenna.* He held the pain of his body close and tried not to cry out as his raw feet touched the floor again.

"Are you hungry?" Brenna asked.

Talon nodded and he swallowed against the nausea. To his surprise, he found he was wearing pants instead of just his underclothes. Lyon had probably dressed him. He felt tears of gratitude come to his eyes for this small service. He rose and hobbled painfully out of his room. As the two of them went down the hallway, Brenna took his hand again, and he was surprised to find that same measure of comfort in her touch. Although he was still slightly uncomfortable, he didn't pull away.

Tasut sat by the fire and looked up at him as he entered the kitchen. Talon immediately released Brenna's hand. He couldn't hide the shock of seeing Tasut, and tried not to stare at the patchy spots of hair on his father's mostly bald head, or the big bruised eye that was swollen to a slit. *What happened?*

"Eat," Tasut nodded toward the table and continued working with the imported fletching on the arrows he had crafted last week. Talon had helped gather the best of the wood for the arrows and watched carefully as Tasut taught him how to prepare the wood. Later, Talon helped to fill molds with liquid hot metal to form the tips. Tasut's tips were conspicuously different than those the peddlers sold. Tasut's had four edges and the peddler's only two. All four edges were barbed with two hooks. 'What's the difference?' he asked Tasut that day.

Tasut had risen from his chair by the door, taken a regular arrow the peddler sold, and one of his own with him, and indicated Talon should follow him to where Harcour was stabled. Once inside the stable, Tasut stabbed a sack of grain with each arrow. The hole left by Tasut's arrow made a bigger hole going in and an even bigger hole when Tasut tore it out. With the object lesson over, Tasut left Talon looking at the bag of grain. Talon didn't want to imagine what the arrows did to people, but he couldn't help himself. He thought about it every time he had to feed Harcour, and that was every day. The lesson was simple enough. He was glad when that grain was used up and they could throw the bag away.

"Come and eat!" Brenna gently pulled him into the warm kitchen and all thoughts of arrows disappeared.

Without preamble, he fell on the food like it was his last meal and then suppressed the unpleasant thought that it might be. Unconsciously, he watched the movements in the room while stuffing food into his mouth, regardless of how hot it was.

Mari was watching him with something like affection, but that couldn't be, she was a great lady and he was just a boy. Lyon smiled a few times as Talon ate, but he smiled a lot anyway. Talon noticed that Tasut rose from fletching to go into his room.

Nyk came in and out of the house seemingly all at a run. "It stopped raining wood!" he reported the first time.

He looked around at the rest of the people in the kitchen, but none of them seemed to think this was an odd statement.

The second time Nyk came in, he looked at the heavily laden table and Mari commanded, "Sit down and eat, Nyk."

"I could smell the food all the way out to the barn!" With his unusual eyes sparkling, he took a seat next to Brenna. "I touched all the horses out there! I even touched the big black one and he almost kicked me!"

Talon thought this highly unlikely, but he was content to listen while he ate. He felt hunger down to his toes and drank several cups of water. Brenna sat hip-to-hip next to him on the longer bench and Nyk was on her other side. At first it made him a little nervous to sit next to her, but soon his hunger brought on the ability to disregard her and all else except eating.

"Sounds like you had quite an adventure this morning," Lyon said as he sat across from Talon and Brenna. Talon swallowed as Lyon smiled and tore a piece of bread from the loaf sitting near Talon's plate. Mari was saying something quietly to Nyk.

Nyk, who had left the table yet again, appeared with a large pan in his hands, and eagerly launched into his explanation of the events that led up to the scene where Talon fainted. It was highly exaggerated and oddly incomplete. Nyk left out the Baker, the Blacksmith, and most importantly, the Feesha that had tried to kill them. Nyk avoided looking at him as he completed the tale, but Talon could feel Lyon's eyes rest on him expectantly.

To Talon's dismay, Tasut returned from his room, bringing a familiar and most unwelcome small glass jar. Talon instantly recognized the special salve that burned like flames when first placed on raw skin. It wouldn't do any good to protest. On the bright side, the following day the wounds would be completely healed. In three days there would be no marks left.

Brenna shocked him when she emitted a little cry of protest as Tasut opened the jar and Talon's eyes grew round as saucers as she angrily pushed Tasut's hand away.

"Don't touch him!" she scolded furiously. While wearing a scowl, stamping her little foot, and putting her hands on her hips, she looked like a miniature Mari for a moment.

"Brenna, it must be done, it will help Talon heal." Lyon's voice, although not loud, cracked the quiet and Brenna looked at her father. She didn't move away as Talon expected, but stood her ground, her fists knotted. Talon noticed Brenna would argue with her mother, but not her

father. He wondered if he would have done the same thing if his mother
had lived. Mari made him feel more uncomfortable than Lyon.

Brenna frowned so fiercely at Tasut that Talon forgot about his raw
back until Tasut smoothed the white paste onto his skin. He couldn't
help sucking in his breath with a gasp, which made Brenna hiss.

"Brenna, enough." Her father's voice was edged with warning.

The first touch of the paste on his skin was fire. It quickly turned to
ice, and thankfully left the area numb. Putting the lid back on the jar,
Tasut moved away. He wiped his hands off at the sink and resumed his
fletching. One day last summer, Talon had been foolish enough to leave
his shirt off while he did his chores. Tasut used the same special salve
to release the deep heat from the burn. However, its application had left
Talon biting his pillow to keep from screaming as his raw skin was
touched by the rough callused hands.

When his back was well, Tasut began teaching him how to pull his
mind away from pain using breathing and meditation.

Talon turned his attention to the table and its fare. There were bowls
and steaming pans of foods he'd never seen, and it all smelled heavenly.
He started with a steaming bowl of rice with shredded chicken in sauce
over the top of it. Between large bites of bread and mouthfuls of rice
and cheese, he sipped a sweet drink laced with mint.

To Talon's surprise, when Nyk had finished eating, he filled the
large pan with water that he brought in earlier and sprinkled something
that looked like salt in it, stirred it with his hand, and sat it beneath the
table near Talon's abused feet. He smiled at Talon who was watching
him, "Put your feet in it, it helps the pain."

Fearing the footbath was going to sear his feet like the salve did his
back, he hesitated but relented at Nyk's smile. To Talon's delight the
pain in his feet receded. For some reason, this made his appetite
increase and he reached for second helpings of meat-filled pastry and
more bread. The salt water in the pan went from clear to pink and then

turned a foamy white, but he was too busy to notice. Brenna, however, smiled at Nyk and watched while he added fresh water to the pan three times. Talon continued to feast. He piled white fried vegetables onto his plate, lathering them with butter and spices. He put corn on top of the pile and ate the whole thing, hardly able to get it into his mouth fast enough. He finished half a loaf of the brown bread and with great discontent, found his stomach had no more room. He looked at the table and then at the delicious foods with longing. With complete seriousness, he sat back for a moment to consider how far his stomach could stretch after it was uncomfortably full.

He became aware of Brenna, who picked at the food on her plate. Now that he had time to notice the Tybar's daughter, it seemed she was prepared to stare at him rather than eat.

"Brenna, eat your greens first," her father gently reminded her as she reached for something that looked sticky and sweet.

Feeling Brenna would probably do what she watched him do, Talon quickly gathered a small handful of leafy stuff and put it on his plate and found the slightly bitter taste an unhappy appendage to the feast he had just enjoyed. He had no desire to make Lyon upset with him. Tasut was a good deal more muscular than Lyon, but there was something about the way Lyon moved that made him wary. Tasut rose from his corner and once again went to his room. Talon hoped he wouldn't come back with more torture in mind.

Brenna pressed her lips together and watched him eat his greens. She plugged her nose and put some in her small mouth. Then she made faces and waved her little hands dramatically as she chewed with eyes shut tight. Finally she swallowed and opened her eyes.

Talon smiled at her and she smiled back at him with wonder in her eyes. He thought she must like the greens a lot more than he did.

Her mother had come behind them, "Brenna, please clean off the table."

Brenna regained her focus and started clearing the table.

"There will be more tonight," Mari promised Talon as he looked regretfully after each plate that was removed. He quickly stuffed one last small pudding puff into his mouth before Brenna took the plate away.

"Let me check your hands," Mari said to him as she returned to the table. "I didn't get a chance to look at them very long."

He swallowed the puff and grit his teeth while he held his hands out, palms up. He was ready to endure what he felt sure would be hellish misery. She lightly touched his right hand and smoothed some cool ointment on it. She repeated the procedure with the left. He felt his hands tingle and to his delight, there was no more pain until Tasut returned from his room.

With his father's return, Talon felt wooden, ashy, and hollowed out. The look in his Father's good eye was such that he felt his stomach knot.

"Kindling," Tasut pointed at the door. Talon was pleasantly surprised, but stayed silent.

"Brenna, Nyk," said Mari with a steady, disapproving look at Tasut, "go with Talon. Stay with him. Tasut, I'll get more salve for your eye." Talon wished he could stay and watch.

Talon's first look at the yard was comical. His gaze took in the blizzard of wood that littered the yard and followed its path straight to the tree stump. *What monster did that?* It had to have taken place after he passed out because he ran past the gigantic tree on his return. It had been a landmark. Enormous didn't adequately describe its size. Its shade had encompassed acres. A half dozen Tasut's could have lay across its width and had room to spare. He had overheard Tasut telling peddlers, who were looking for directions, to stop when they came to "The Tree." He looked at Brenna who shrugged and then at Nyk who wasn't even looking at the tree stump but the large piece of wood sticking out of the stone foundation. This also grabbed Talon's attention.

"What happened?" he asked without taking his eyes off the wood.

Nyk shrugged, "I was in the house. All I heard was a noise that sounded like a catapult blew apart."

"What cat got pulled?" asked Brenna, curiosity lighting her eyes.

Nyk looked at her in disgust, "I didn't say a cat got pulled, I said catapult. It's a big machine that throws rocks. I saw one blow apart just like this tree. It killed eight men."

Wide-eyed, Brenna looked at them and said, "I only did the tree, I promise."

The boys looked at each other and both shrugged. They had no idea what she was talking about.

"We better start gathering the kindling." Talon immediately began the task of picking up the larger pieces of wood, and putting them to the right of the door. Nyk, on the other hand, was trying without success to dislodge the large piece of wood from the stone. He was straining with all his might when Brenna started to giggle. He didn't take that well and glared at her. Talon felt sorry for him and went to help. Both pulled and pulled until they were sweaty. Brenna erupted into giggles every time she returned with a few more pieces of wood.

Finally, Nyk had enough of the giggling Brenna and Talon quietly agreed; it wasn't a laughing matter.

"What's so funny!" the infuriated Nyk demanded.

"You're doing it wrong," she giggled some more and dumped the small load of wood out of her arms next to the door. To Talon, it seemed like a pitifully small pile.

"If you're so smart, you pull it out!" Nyk said hotly.

Brenna smiled and stretched her hand out to touch the embedded wood with her finger and said, "Out."

The wood fell out of the stone to the ground and she turned to get more wood. The boys looked at the wood, each other, and then Brenna.

"Why didn't you do that before?" asked Nyk, who was impressed in spite of his tone. "Can you make it stack itself?" he asked hopefully. Brenna nodded and closed her eyes.

"No," a voice from the doorway called a halt to Brenna's attempt. Brenna's eyes popped open and her mother came outside. "Brenna, come inside and help me with the dishes. Boys, get busy with the kindling." Brenna sulkily went inside and Nyk looked at Talon, looking disappointed.

Talon was sure that Mari didn't want Brenna outside with them anymore because of what had just happened, not because she needed help with dishes.

"Let's get busy," Talon told Nyk. He was glad Brenna hadn't done anything. He wasn't sure how she actually got the wood to come out of stone with one word. The idea made him uncomfortable. He let Nyk gather the kindling closer to the house so he wouldn't have to look at the hole the wood left.

As he gathered the kindling, Talon meditated about the previous day. The Tybars had arrived without announcement just before noon. He had been working in the first of several outbuildings. That particular building was the place where he and his father dried the herbs. They had a separate building where they dried the poisonous plants. Tasut didn't want the different kinds of plants to have a chance to get acquainted and poison someone accidentally.

Talon had taken red cyenne peppers from their garden to hang from long wooden poles to dry. The powder from the peppers was used to cauterize minor wounds, and if taken in moderate amounts, helped a person's circulation. If lightly sprinkled into boots in the winter, it kept your feet warm. No one in his or her right mind would take it plain. Talon heard that mothers in the Village used it to cure their children of foul language or telling lies. Once was usually enough to leave a lasting impression if not blisters.

Talon had heard the Tybars approach after he had hung the last of the peppers, and thinking it a peddler, shrugged it off until he heard more than one voice. Thankfully, he was at the last of the chore. All he had left to do was crush the previously dried peppers into powder. For that chore he wore leather gloves, and needed a special Terisian marble bowl and pestle that Tasut used for this express purpose. The bowl was in the house in a special leather bag. It had been his mother's and he was very careful with it. Another leather bag held the cyenne seeds or the powder, once the peppers were crushed. Talon had crossed the yard to the house, intending to get the bowl, and watched the wagon pull up. That was when he first saw Lyon Tybar.

Chapter 7: Yesterday

To Talon's surprise, yesterday, Lyon had insisted on shaking his hand.

"You've grown, Talon. Last time I saw you, you would've fit in your Father's saddlebags." Lyon had eyes the color of storm clouds and a white smile. Talon instantly liked him.

"This is my wife, Mari," Lyon took the hand of the slender, graceful woman who had climbed down from the wagon. Talon noticed Lyon continued to hold her hand.

He hadn't been around many women and wasn't sure how to greet one. The few women in the Village didn't look anything like Mari. He tried to remember if Tasut had ever greeted a woman in his presence and couldn't call anything to mind. What came to his mind was to put his fist to his chest and bow. He saw peddlers do that to his father. He still didn't know why. When he had asked, Tasut ignored him.

"Such a gallant greeting for one so young," she let her husband's hand go and came over to him like she was floating on air. He had found himself looking into one green eye and one brown, both intense and searching. He remembered thinking what long eyelashes she had and that she smelled lots better than anyone he had ever known.

"You'll be taller than your father, Talon, and every bit as...impressive." Talon had been sure she was going to say something else. "Would you do something for me?"

He really liked her smile. He'd looked at Tasut for permission to do her bidding and received a nearly imperceptible nod. He thought he saw a flash of irritation in her bi-colored eyes, but it was gone so quickly he wasn't sure if he had really seen it at all.

"I would consider it an honor if you would watch over Brenna while Lyon and I speak with Tasut."

Yesterday, he had no idea who Mari was talking about.

Lyon went to the back of the wagon and lifted out a tiny person. At least, she looked tiny to him. He wasn't sure she was real at first. She was quite simply a perfect little person.

Brenna had long thick brown hair with lighter parts in it and huge blue eyes that looked at him with something like awe. Then she smiled and he felt a small part of his heart open and the corner of his lips tug upward. Her father had put her on the ground. To his complete shock, she ran to him and wrapped tiny arms around his waist. The little girl's head was level with his stomach. Then with a big smile she took his hand and wouldn't let go when he tried to gently disengage.

Tasut came to the door and had handed him the Terisian bowl and pestle. There was another leather pouch for the powder and the hide gloves to handle the seeds.

Talon felt a bit cheated, but was smart enough to not let it show. He had hoped to grind the seeds while in the kitchen so he could overhear their conversation. Fortunately, he had a back up plan.

He took Brenna out to the small building that housed the herbs. He'd retrieved the small basket of dried peppers and handed it to Brenna. "Watch out, they're hot." He was relieved that it gave him the chance to free his hand from her grasp.

He closed the door of the outbuilding then motioned Brenna to be quiet and come with him. They wandered over to the back room window and ducked behind two large overgrown flowering bushes that had a small open space in the middle. From there, Talon knew from experience, a person could hear most everything said in the kitchen and not be seen. He was confident Tasut didn't know about the place he had cleared in the middle of the bushes because Talon had done it while Tasut was away on one of his trips. As usual, he'd left Talon alone to do chores, in spite of the fact that the place was new, and Talon was only eight years old. Once his chores were finished he could do whatever he chose with his free time, and he had chosen to make a secret place he could call his own and still obey Tasut's order that he stay close to home.

Once they were concealed in the woody shrub, Talon contented himself with crushing a few red pepper seeds from the herb pouch into a fine powder. He wore the leather gloves to protect his hands from the penetrating, caustic oils. He had tried to crush the seeds once in a regular bowl and ruined the bowl in the process. The oil from the seeds ate right through the wood. He asked his father why the oil didn't burn through the gloves and he didn't answer. Whatever animal skin it had come from must have been specially treated with some sort of flameproof tanning solution. In any case, Tasut went to the cupboard and taken out a plate-sized marble bowl. Terisian Marble was mostly white with two colors of swirling green markings. It was very rare and when Tasut told him it was his mother's, he had taken extra special care of it.

Because of Brenna, he had chosen to leave the cyenne husks in the outbuilding. The cyenne pepper husks were easy to crush, but made a cloud of fine dust. If you worked with the husks, you had to hold your breath or wear your shirt over your nose. Father of All help you if you needed to sneeze.

He had to pay close attention to his work in the confined space they were in. There was a common saying concerning the cyenne seed, 'The seeds are so hot you won't need kindling.' It wasn't much of an exaggeration. Once, Talon had barely touched his tongue to a seed and it immediately blistered. He was miserably hungry for a week, but the pain was so great he couldn't eat.

Tasut had been unsympathetic.

"Don't touch any of this," Talon had cautioned Brenna who just smiled, holding the pepper basket while she watched. He continued to crush the seeds and listened hard.

".... just in time," Lyon's voice carried. "We'll be going to Dyman."

"Few remember me," said Tasut in his gravely voice, "and none remember him."

"Don't be so sure." Mari's voice was faint, but could be heard.

"Who would know? They never knew I married Laysha. Nez wasn't as powerful then. The rest of the Council didn't even blink when I left."

"They were too grateful," Lyon said cynically. "No one made them obey their own rules before."

"You took great risk leaving Cubes to Jarow," Mari said softly. "Are you sure you can trust him?"

Tasut gave his usual grunt, this one sounded like an agreement.

What's Cubes and who's Jarow? And why should Tasut care?

"He could cause complications," she stated coldly.

"What would you have me do to him Mari?" asked Tasut in a tired voice.

"If you trust Jarow, confide in him. Perhaps he'll see someone or something you don't."

"I already send the Sons of Ammon I find to Utak…" the rumble of his father's voice got quiet and he didn't catch the last part.

"What about the boy?" Lyon asked.

Talon's ears had sharpened considerably at these words. Brenna had tugged on his sleeve. It had just become interesting, so he'd ignored her. A peddler once said royalty wanted wives from Utak. *That must be where Mari's from - but what or who are the Sons of Ammon?* In any case, he doubted Lyon would give her up.

"War will come. With or without him," this time Mari was speaking. "The Poolseers are watching the signs, but it doesn't take a Poolseer to know Nez is making alliances. If he finds his way into Utak, all will be lost. Despite legend, you know it isn't completely inaccessible. It is a question of when, not if, someone finds that out."

War? He knew what the word meant of course. The idea was exciting and frightening but he hadn't known Utak wasn't unassailable. *Who is Nez and what are Poolseers?*

Lyon said, "My men told me that he's sending people into Acha. If Nez finds you, he'll take the boy."

"I'll kill him myself before I let Nez take him," Tasut said gruffly.

"Don't be ridiculous…"

Talon hadn't heard the rest of Mari's reply. Brenna had practically tugged his shirt off his shoulder with her persistence. He had looked at her blankly, his mind spinning with the idea that his father would kill him if this Nez person found Talon. *Who is Nez and why would he want me?*

Brenna placed her soft hands over his mouth and motioned him to be quiet. Her face was pale and her blue eyes filled with fear as she pointed to the edge of the wood. He looked, and his brain automatically refused the information his eyes tried to register because his mind emphatically told him it couldn't be real.

A dozen things that he had no name for were crossing the clearing toward the cottage. At first, he thought it was a pack of horses, but when they came out of the dappled light of the Rahazi into the bright sunlight, his mind shuddered away from them.

The only way he could describe what he saw, was to say they were horses. That is, if you cut off a horses head and then cut off its hindquarters, and then stuck those two pieces together and left out the middle. To get it right, you'd have to skin the whole thing so all that was left was pink oozing flesh. To finish it off, there were two hairless legs instead of four fur-covered ones ending in claws instead of hooves.

He felt Brenna's little hand squeeze his arm and his hair stood on end as one reared its head back and it made a deep chest-rattling noise. It bared fangs instead of the square, rounded teeth of an omnivore. To his horror, fire shot out of its shiny black muzzle. Where a normal horse's tail would be, there were red swishing rope-like cords laced with pulsing green veins. Their raw pink skin seemed to bleed as if it had been deeply scratched, probably because there was just a thin membrane holding their insides together. The pink and black horse-like creatures moved forward and stopped as if waiting for something.

Behind those monstrosities were men. At least, he thought they were men until they got closer. There was something wrong about the way they moved.

He thought his heart would come through his chest as the whole group turned toward the cottage and he saw that in the middle of their faces, where a normal person's nose would be, were a half-dozen hard woody knobs. Each knob was a different length and possessed an eye on the end. Each eye turned a different way, which made it look like they had a bunch of wiggling snakes coming out of their faces instead of features. The eyes didn't blink, but steadily dripped green fluid. When the fluid met with anything but the woody knobs, it raised wisps of smoke at its touch. With the appearance of the knobby-eyed men, his mind had hardly registered a faint light about fifteen feet above the ground and moving toward the clearing.

What emerged after the knobby-eyed men was a huge block of pale blue ice formed like a man. The ice creature had no hair, but it did have enormous blue-white eyes that swirled. There was no discernable pupil that he could see. Inside its huge chest was a faint light that appeared bright against the dark of the forest. It stopped at the clearing in front of the house, pointed directly at the bush where Talon and Brenna were hiding, and emitted an inhuman shrieking roar.

He wasn't sure if Brenna screamed or he did. It surprised him that Tasut, Lyon, and Mari were already in the clearing, challenging the monsters.

Tasut had a long slightly curved sword Talon had never seen in one hand, and with his free hand, he grabbed the very sharp axe embedded into the wood block near the door. He was heading directly for the ice-thing and Lyon, holding a modified crossbow, shot three arrows in rapid succession at the horse-creatures.

Mari ran across the clearing and gestured at the approaching knobby-eyed things. There was no denying what Talon saw. A long wood-looking staff appeared in her hands. It didn't seem as hard to believe she was magic as it was to believe in the creatures that were stalking across the yard to do battle.

Brenna, pale and shaking, watched the ensuing battle while her hand had stroked the orange and white fur collar at her neck.

"Mee go help!" Brenna had whispered.

Talon was watching the giant ice-monster, when he caught a white streak out of the corner of his eye and Mee appeared out of nowhere chattering wildly. The Shee ran toward the horse-things. He hadn't known at the time what Mee was.

Later, he would notice the details such as Mee had a large tail compared to her body size, eyes that were more human than animal with dark blue round irises like humans. In fact, her eyes were very similar to Brenna's and looked too large for her small head. Mee's back legs were more cat-like and she had furry white paws that resembled a raccoon's. The proper name for Shees evaded him at the time of the attack. He only remembered that their bite was rumored to be venomous. He wasn't sure how successful Mee was going to be against such odds, but his attention was back on Tasut as his father did his best to kill the ice-monster, his face mask-like and his eyes burning with rage.

Talon had never seen anything so brave and he felt a swell of pride and gush of fear for his father. With one mighty swing with his sword, Tasut severed the left foot of the ice-creature. How he had managed with one stroke, no matter how powerful, Talon couldn't guess.

It teetered, righted itself, and the blue-white eyes found his father, who was already running toward the Rahazi Forest. The ice-monster pursued him, roaring and hopping after him on its remaining foot.

Talon had been sure Tasut lost it or killed it because a short time later, he emerged from the forest to help Lyon kill the flame-belching horse-things.

Lyon was quick on his feet. He avoided their fire, and moved to draw them into Tasut's long sword, which his father used to effectively decapitate them in one stroke; his father making it look as easy as slicing through soft butter.

Harcour, who had been screaming his challenge and kicking the sides of the lean-to with his great hoofs, had escaped from his stall and ran some of the knobby-eyed men down. At one point, Talon watched as Harcour leaped into the air. It was an amazing thing to see the back and front hoofs leave the ground at the same time and flash out simultaneously in a movement that successfully sent the creatures sailing in pieces all over the yard.

Mari had been in the thick of things with a strange purple glow surrounding her. She was whirling the staff so fast he couldn't see it, and Talon watched in wonder as it fatally connected time after time with knobby-eyed men.

Then the giant ice-monster had returned. It burst from the edge of the woods, sending large tree limbs and a shower of leafs over the area. Its missing foot had grown back and the creature stood less than ten feet away from the bush where he and Brenna had remained, frozen in horror, but concealed during the battle. The swirling blue-white eyes fixed on them and Talon would have sworn it smiled and its swirling blue eyes lit up with wicked delight.

At that moment, one of the knobby-eyed men crossed the ice creature's path as it headed for the bush. The ice-creature picked up the knobby-eyed man, opened its cavernous mouth and dropped the knobby-eyed man inside. You could see the man struggling inside the creature's body until it was suddenly crushed between two blocks of ice that slammed together in three quick repetitions. Talon was unable to pull his eyes away from the sight. The knobby-eyed man's remains were gone, leaving the ice pink.

When the ice-creature had picked up the knobby-eyed man, Brenna had let go of Talon's arm and bolted out of the bush heading straight for her mother.

Mari heard her daughter's scream and saw the unavoidable danger. In panic, she yelled, "Lyon!"

Lyon was struggling to avoid being burned by three of the horse-things. When he heard Mari screaming his name, the look on his face became one of such determined fury that if Talon had been one of the creatures Lyon fought, he would have retreated.

Lyon yelled "Tasut!" ducking to avoid being burnt to a crisp and jumping back to avoid being bitten.

Tasut threw his axe left-handed and it embedded itself in the ice-creature's side and resumed his desperate battle with the horse-things, but he had looked directly at Talon who was standing near the bushes in indecision before he threw the axe. 'No one else can save her', his father's eyes said, 'It's up to you.'

Talon forced himself to follow Brenna with some sort of crazy hope they had a chance to make it back before they were seen or attacked.

He had one thing in his possession that he could possibly use against such odds. Taking the small pouch of red pepper powder and the handful of seeds, he dashed between Brenna and the ice-monster that had just brushed his father's axe from its side. It had been unable to grasp the axe handle with its slippery hands.

Brenna froze where she was; Mee was on her shoulder growling at all of the monsters, her tail fur bushed to three times its normal size.

Talon threw the seeds he held in his right glove. The creature, which seemed to take no notice of him, was peppered with the flaming-hot fresh seeds, and instantly huge steaming holes appeared in the ice that formed its body. Its blockish head whipped instantly, angrily back to Talon, the blue-white eyes that swirled had no pupils, but he knew it looked at him. Talon was sure he was going to die.

Its huge mouth opened as if in a huge jaw-cracking yawn, revealing yellowed fangs and wart-like pulsing growths in a cavernous throat. Talon took the pouch of cyenne powder that he still held. Using it like a sling, Talon swung it up and into the creature's mouth just as the warty growths exploded open, throwing small bright yellow snakes through the air.

The red pepper powder had immediate effect. If the creature had been capable of screaming any longer, they would have been deafened. Its jaw remained open and its head blew apart, scattering the yellow snakes, which were now writhing and blackening. He watched in horrified fascination as its massive icy body vaporized into a vast cloud of hissing grey steam.

He looked away in time to see a spinning, knobby-eyed head caper across the clearing toward him. Mee jumped off Brenna's shoulder and hurdled toward the horse-things. Tasut was busy chopping the head off the last knobby-eyed man. Brenna had run to her mother who dropped to her knees to wrap her arms tightly about her small daughter.

Lyon had dispatched two more horse-things and complimented Mee. The Shee had just bitten the last horse-thing by leaping up in the air and latching onto its neck. Its legs stiffened, and its raw pink skin turned purple, black, grey, and then it melted into a bubbly puddle.

Obviously the rumors about the bite of a Shee were true. Talon had made a mental note to steer clear of Mee's teeth.

Harcour had jumped the fence in pursuit of one of the horse-creatures. Knowing Harcour, he had probably taken it personally that they resembled horses at all. Tasut had emitted a loud, piercing whistle and Harcour returned in a huff, snorting his disgust, but looking satisfied with himself.

Everyone looked toward Talon. His first thought was regret for the waste of red pepper. Tasut would be furious. There wouldn't be any more red pepper plants until the following harvest.

His second thought was *I'm going to die.* But the quill Lyon had just thrown passed by him at the same time he heard a hiss. Talon had turned his head in time to see one of the snakes had escaped the pepper and was leaping at him, only to be neatly sliced into two pieces by the quill. It shrieked and he watched its little legs kick twice before it died. *It has legs?*

*

Talon returned to the present, dropping load after load of kindling onto the black spot to cover it. *Is that why Tasut punished me? Because I didn't kill the last snake myself?*

Nyk was grumbling about getting a splinter in his finger, and he watched Nyk go into the house to find Mari and get her to remove it. He somehow doubted that Nyk would be back. *Unless Tasut finds out he hasn't finished.* Tasut didn't like things left undone.

Talon returned to the mind-freeing chore of picking up the kindling. His thoughts drifted back to what happened, after the monsters were dead.

"Go find the horses." Lyon had told him, hitching the mules to one of the dead creatures so it could drag the dead Ybarra to a spot between the huge tree and the barn.

Tasut was already astride Harcour, "I'm going to the Village. If I'm not back in an hour, take Talon with you."

Talon looked at Lyon and then at Tasut, who kicked Harcour to a run.

Talon turned and followed the trail the Tybars' horses left. It wasn't hard. In their panicked flight they had pulled the wagon headlong through the smallest path in the forest, leaving parts of it behind as they ran. He found what was left of the wagon lodged between two large and, thankfully, unmovable trees. The wagon was unsalvageable. There was no sign of the horses.

He knew Brenna had come with him, likely against her mother's orders. Mee was running here and there along the path.

"Horse go there!" Mee pointed the way.

Talon hadn't known Shees could track.

When they found them, the horses stood shaking with fatigue, their heads were down, unable to go farther. Their flanks were lathered and they were blowing hard, too tired to move except to shudder. Without a trace of fear for flying hoofs or blunt pinching teeth, Brenna held their heads. Talon took out his knife from the belt at his waist, and cut their traces. Brenna led them out while Talon watched for injuries. Both animals were bleeding from the scratches but none were deep enough to warrant concern.

"Mamah will want her herbs," Brenna said, using a blanket to hold a few salvageable things while Talon led them away from the wreckage.

"Look! I found my doll!" she held up a soft toy that looked like a smaller version of herself. He wasn't sure what use it served.

"We have to get the horses back," he pulled the reins. "Tasut has some liniment for their scratches."

They only walked a short distance when Brenna asked, "Why did the monsters come here?"

He shrugged, "We've never had monsters before." It was a very good question.

"Do you think they'll come back?" Brenna sounded frightened.

He'd been wondering the same thing. "If they do, we'll kill them," Talon said, sure that the adults were already making plans.

"I want to stay with you," Brenna said, looking forlorn.

"Brenna?" Mari had come into the forest searching for them, her eyes filled with relief at finding them safe. "Did you find the glass jar?"

Brenna nodded and reached into the blanket she had confiscated. Mari breathed a sigh of relief and took it from Brenna and smiled at Talon. "Thank you both for being so brave."

"I wasn't brave at all," Brenna's bottom lip trembled.

"Talon was brave enough for both of you," her mother assured her, looking at Talon as she hugged her daughter close. He smiled for the first time since the attack feeling the glow of pleasure at the approval in Mari's voice.

Once they had piled the rancid remains of the creatures together, Mari unstoppered the glass jar Brenna had picked up from the trail and sprinkled its contents on them.

"Stand back," Mari warned.

A small stream of black, acrid smoke rose from the pile of bodies. Then the gruesome stack of mutilated bodies flamed a bright yellow, imploded, and in the blaze of white-hot fire, the huge pile became ash. Talon jumped back and looked at his father, who had returned from a search of the forest. Tasut ignored him and looked steadily at Mari. Talon thought he saw disapproval in his father's dark eyes.

"I know what I am doing, in spite of the law," Mari said to him with a defensive edge in her voice.

Lyon had shaken his head slightly and looked to the forest edge where the creatures had come from, and back to Tasut.

Tasut motioned for them to come into the cottage. They had all stepped over the broken door. It had been ripped from its hinges, but Talon wasn't sure if monsters or one of the adults had done it such grave damage. Mari re-formed and re-attached it with one gesture after they entered. Tasut gave one last look out at the edge of the forest before he shut the door. Little of significance was said, but many looks were exchanged that made Talon uneasy. Brenna had left her mother and clung to his hand.

Yet, for all his fears, he was excited. His life was going to change. He had known it as clearly as if they had shouted it, and he had been happy that the following day was going to be his birthday.

*

Some birthday he thought, back in reality.

On the bright side, he had two friends now. He wasn't sure if girls qualified as friends, but he liked Brenna. Mari had come out and taken her back into the house, again. He continued to pick up the kindling. A short time later, he heard a yelp from inside the cottage. The door swung open and Nyk burst out of the cottage at a full run. Tasut was on his heels for a short distance and then whistled. Talon recognized the call for Harcour.

The stallion ran from the stables and looked at Tasut, who signaled something Talon didn't understand. Harcour spun the direction Nyk had taken and a short time later, Talon could hear Nyk's screams for help. Nyk returned at a full run, looking behind him at the snorting stallion, when he ran right into Tasut. It was like hitting a wall. Nyk bounced off Tasut and landed on the ground. Tasut made a chopping motion with one hand to halt Harcour. Nyk looked dazed and Talon remembered the feeling of having your air leave your lungs.

Tasut pointed to the barn and with a show of inbred arrogance, the stallion snorted and pranced to the barn, whinnying his victory to his stablemates – the mules.

Tasut reached down and pulled Nyk up by one ankle so he was hanging upside down. He crossed the yard and Nyk's hands went above his head, fearing Tasut would drop him. When Tasut reached Talon, he did just that. Nyk caught himself by his arms and then landed on his rear.

"Kindling." He said firmly to Nyk and then Tasut looked at Talon who had the black spot left by the fire nearly covered with wood. For one moment Talon thought Tasut had nodded his head in approval, but of course, that was impossible. When he deciphered it, the message was very clear: Watch Nyk.

Talon next started covering the area with wood where the huge tree had been. As he worked to stack the wood, he noted that whatever Brenna had done to the massive red-leafed tree had left the stump even with the ground. The surface of the stump looked seared, leaving behind a strangely opaque and unexpectedly shiny wood surface. He felt more comfortable when it was done, though he had never stacked such a large pile.

A half hour later, Nyk had wandered fifty feet from where Talon was working, still holding the only piece of wood he had picked up so far. He had used it to draw in the dirt, kill a few bugs, and to toss in the air. Each time he tossed it, he'd run around the house and try to catch it before it fell.

"Come throw the wood in the air," Nyk said, "I can't get it high enough."

Talon ignored him and continued to work.

"Hey!" Nyk yelled with excitement, "Come look at this!"

Talon, curiosity pricked, decided he would start another pile over where Nyk was and while there, it wouldn't slow him down just to look.

To Talon's disgust, it was a caterpillar that had been neatly sliced in half.

"Do you think Brenna did that when she blew the tree apart?" Nyk's voice was tinged with awe. For Talon, the thought was disturbing.

"Let's start a pile over here," Talon said, walking toward more pieces of wood.

Nyk's eyes were drawn to a leaf a short distance away, its edges looked shiny and hard. Just as his hand reached out, Mee came from no where and grabbed the leaf right from under his hand.

"Did you see that!?" Nyk's eyes followed the Shee.

"Nyk!" This time the voice belonged to Lyon, who stood in the doorway, "Get busy and help Talon. If you do a good job, I'll show you what the sponges are for."

Talon was grateful Lyon had found a way to get his friend to focus. The work was going much faster and they had more than ten stacks of various sizes and widths all over the yard. The biggest was directly over the stump. It didn't look like they had done anything when Mari called them in for a break and took Brenna outside with her.

Lyon sat at the table. In front of him were three piles. One of small pebbles as small as a little fingernail, the second was of slightly larger sponges, and the last pile was a stack of three bowls.

"Each sponge has a small slit. Put a pebble in the center of each and then put an equal amount of sponges in each bowl."

Mari came back into the cottage and handed Lyon a bowl full of what looked like flour. Talon watched as Lyon kept hold of her hand and kissed the palm. He also noticed how Mari's cheeks pinkened and she smiled a rather silly smile when Lyon whispered, "Thank you, love." Brenna scooted closer to him and handed him a vial of liquid and then gave one to Nyk and kept one.

Lyon said, "Take the sponges out. I'll put powder into each of your bowls and I want you to put only one drop of liquid from your vials onto the powder. If you put more, you may start a fire."

They did as they were told. Nyk's turned blue, Brenna's was red, and Talon's green.

"Now put your sponges into the bowl and bring them outside, be careful not to spill anything."

Talon was so amazed by the sight that met him when he went outside, he almost dropped the bowl. All of the wood was stacked in neat piles. He looked quickly at Mari and then looked away when her eyes looked amused.

"I'm going to teach you a game," Lyon smiled and handed them forked sticks with little nets attached. "When the sun touches this species of sponge, it immediately dries."

He took a sponge from each of their bowls, one at a time and showed them how to put the ball into the net, take aim, and fire. "Now, the rules are like those in seek-and-find. All of you will choose a place to hide around the stacks of wood. If you see someone else, throw your sponge at them to mark them. The sponge is dry on the outside and wet on the inside, so the paint will let everyone know who hit who. When you get marked, you have to sit out until a winner is declared."

Chapter 8: Steps

After coaching a few rounds of the game, Lyon went inside, confident the children knew what they were doing.

"Well, did it work?" Mari asked, looking up from a thick book.

"Nyk's hard to hit, he's so fast, but Talon's more accurate, and Brenna was cheating and using Mee until Talon told her not to. Mee threatened to bite them if they hit Brenna."

"What!" Mari rose out of her chair.

"Don't worry, Brenna said no crab if she did."

Mari smiled, "I'm sure that went over well."

"After that, Mee went into the barn to ask Tasut if he would get her some crab."

"That's something his men would pay to see."

"How are you feeling?"

"The sooner we get out of here, the better," she sighed. "I still feel that something is missing...or just out of reach."

"I'm going to go out and get the cart packed," he said, kissing her on the back of the neck.

As Lyon packed Tasut's old cart, sadness marked his features and it wasn't because the wagon had been ruined. He looked west where the sun was setting, and the last of the crimson sky was darkening to a deep blue. The cart was packed and ready for tomorrow's travel back home to Dyman.

It astonished him that only yesterday Talon had somehow killed a full-grown ice-monster, known as a Gantec, before it could kill Brenna. *He is clever, this boy.* Lyon didn't want to go in the house. There were issues he needed to find peace with before he could join the rest.

He felt as if he had been harnessed with rash rope and whichever way you moved, it would raise a stinging welt. His conscience pushed the unwelcome information to the surface that Tasut was right. Talon must become a Champion. Not just any champion, but *better* than any other - ever. He did not relish having to tell his beautiful headstrong wife she was wrong. Yet, hope glimmered in him and he smiled. *There is a way.*

With his good humor restored, he went into the cottage. Mari greeted him with a loving smile. Lyon leaned against a nearby wall to observe the children for a moment. The long day was likely the most fun that Talon had ever had. Nyk was showing Talon how to play a board game called Steps.

There were sixty-four white pieces representing men arranged on blue squares. In the middle of the orange-and-blue checkered board, there were four red squares etched with a single large tree. Each person had control of half the board. With a roll of dice, one of the pieces lived or died.

"For example," Nyk told him as they played, "if I roll an odd number, you would gain control of the dice because you're in charge of odd numbered men. On your turn, you get the option to roll the dice again and hope for another odd number to come up, or you can choose a weapons card," Nyk pointed to the small deck that sat to the side of the board. "And hope that whatever weapon you draw, will beat whatever weapon I draw after you."

"Who decides what weapons win?" Talon asked.

"Let me show you." Nyk turned the top card over, "This is a quill and this," he turned over the next card, "is a Garrec."

Talon looked at the Garrec; it looked like a long thin wire with a small loop attached to either end. It still wasn't clear to him how you could know if the Garrec would lose, if the opponent had the quill.

"The quill is a weapon that you throw, so it's best for distance. The Garrec would lose because you have to get so close to the victim."

In Talon's opinion, the quill was only as good as the man who threw it while the Garrec was only good if the man could catch his prey.

However, the basic rules of the game were understood and they began to play. They had been playing an hour when Brenna came to stand near Talon.

"You missed one," Brenna told him after studying the board for a moment.

Nyk, who was losing, looked annoyed, "You think you can do any better?"

In answer, Brenna took Talon's sixteenth piece and sat it on top of Nyk's twenty-third piece. Talon had missed the move until she placed his piece and then he saw what should have been obvious. "Side down," she said. Nyk's mouth hung open and he surrendered his piece.

"Where'd she learn how to do that?" Nyk's pride was stung.

Brenna smiled and pointed to her father. He smiled at the boys, hugging Brenna to his side.

Twenty minutes later, Mari, after making a hearty snack for everyone, went looking for Brenna who had grown bored with the game. She found her next to the biggest wood stack; the one that covered the place where the enormous red-leafed tree had been.

Brenna was sitting on the ground, her back to her mother, playing with her doll. Her daughter made an enchanting picture in the fading light of day. She listened to Brenna's one-sided conversation.

"Who are you?" Brenna asked; there was a pause.

"That's a pretty name. My name is Brenna, it means hope."

Pause.

"Thank you. My father named me."

Pause.

"Yes, mamah is very powerful, but I'm stronger."

This shocked Mari. It was true, but she didn't know that Brenna was aware of it.

"Do you want me to help you?"

Much shorter pause.

"His name is Talon." Brenna giggled. "I don't know anyone called One or Chosen, but I already chose him. He's mine."

Startled to hear her daughter using these prophetic words, Mari stepped around the wood pile. "Who are you talking to?"

"Vaya." Brenna held up her doll which now had auburn hair and pale blue eyes.

"Come in now," Mari tried to shake the feeling that the doll had been brunette and named Annie.

"Mamah, when I'm seven, will Talon think I'm beautiful then?"

Mari smothered her alarm that her six year old was already thinking about Talon that way. "Boys don't think about beauty the way we do."

"Does he know I'm going to marry him?"

Hiding her astonishment, Mari shook her head. "He won't think of marriage for a long time. He has a lot of work to do."

Brenna looked at the wood stacks, "Will he know tomorrow?"

Mari became serious. Her precocious daughter needed to hear the truth. "It will be many years before he can get married."

Brenna stood up. "Talon needs my help."

It was true, but she wanted to know, "Who told you that?"

"Vaya said so," Brenna showed her mother the doll. "How can I help him?"

"By being his friend." Mari decided that it was time to get Brenna a new doll.

*

Lyon's chance to speak to Mari came later that evening when the children went to sleep. He took her hand and led her out to the largest wood stack. He had to choose the moment carefully because it had to take place while Tasut was riding Harcour around the perimeter of the land.

He looked at the full moon and his eyes scanned the shadows. They paused for a moment, resting on her beautiful features.

"Whatever it is you want to say, just say it," she inserted into the circuit of his thoughts.

His voice was quiet in the silence, "Those monsters didn't just stumble across this place. Tasut knows as well as we do that the Feesha was here long enough to get word back to the Assassins Guild in Sogo. Now, someone, somewhere, knows about this cottage. It doesn't leave Tasut with many options about what to do with Talon."

Mari was puzzled. "Surely even Tasut can see that we're his only choice."

"Not his only choice," he corrected, "but the most logical." Lyon reached out and gently took her hands, watching her eyes soften as he kissed them and loving the fact that he had that effect.

"When Tasut failed last time, he vowed this time would be different, no matter the cost," Lyon gripped her hands and sighed. "Last time, his only interest was getting it all over with so he could take Laysha and their son back to Utak. He knows that he tried to force the circumstances that would bring about the fall of Sogo. He won't make that mistake again. It was a terrible choice to make; I'm not sure I would have been able to do it, even if asked by Father of All.

"For now, He'll do his best to plan for the worst and right now his entire focus is to keep Talon alive long enough to train him to survive once he gets to the Barracks."

"He's doing it wrong," Mari said with heat. "Talon didn't even know how to play Steps and he'll be *living* the game once he goes to Sogo."

"I'll be sending word to Monus so he knows about it. He's one of the best at the game. But more than Steps or being the strongest, I want that boy to be happy. It's selfish of me, but I don't want Talon to simply survive long enough to save Brenna. If she's destined to be his wife, I want him to be someone worth loving."

She smiled at him, eyes sparkling. "You have a plan."

He grimaced and shrugged, "Tasut told us not to interfere, but if Talon is to have a chance at happiness, if our daughter is, then we must."

He outlined his plan and the more he spoke, the more she appreciated the man she married. Not only for his skill, but for the great heart behind that skill.

Chapter 9: Living Legends

The next morning, Tasut and Lyon, naked from the waist up, were on the barren ground in front of the cottage before the sun pierced through the canopy of the Rahazi Forest. They were in the third form, having completed the first two sets of forms before the sun touched the yard.

Today, they had an appreciative audience, though both were unaware that four sets of eyes stared at their display. Mari had watched her husband complete the dance-like forms numerous times. Occasionally she had taken the opportunity to learn from him. Lyon was a tenth-level forms Master, and Tasut a former Guardian of Sogo.

Both were living legends.

Today, Lyon had competition from Tasut and Mari could sense his awareness of that fact. Both men were sweating as they moved into the fourth form. Tasut was breathtakingly flawless, and with his newly shaved head he looked even more intimidating, more like a rock than ever before. In spite of his muscle mass, he wasn't slow.

In the Barracks of Sogo, the men he trained feared him. With good reason. In front of Mari's eyes was fourteen years evidence of the price for that reputation.

He wore a network of scars over his body that mapped the many fights he had fought and won. If that wasn't impressive enough, he wore a specific combination of brands on his right arm that marked him as Guardian of Sogo. Each one personally given by Nez Shavae, Minister of Religion in Sogo.

Many times over the span of years he spent in Sogo, he had been taken by Commander Jarow, Tasut's only ally in the Barracks, to the Forest Wife to be healed of wounds that would kill a normal man. *Since when was Tasut ever normal?* The man was seven feet tall. Lyon looked like a teenager next to him. More often than Mari cared to recall, they had given up hope that Tasut would live. *Thank Father of All, we don't know everything.* With divine help, Tasut had made it. Of course, the man had an abundance of sheer willpower and the best reason to remain alive. Talon.

Mari recognized what the watching children could not fathom. Tasut's deepest scar was inside, where it left a gaping hole seven years ago. Tasut's heart was unable to fulfill a purpose beyond beating, and that was the real tragedy, the hidden truth. Only the Father of All could heal him and make him whole once more. If Tasut lived long enough to succeed. He had sworn to the Forest Wife that he would and there was no reason to doubt.

The Forest Wife had reprimanded him each time he was brought to her for his carelessness and scolded him with a fervor that could have scorched sand. More was required from Tasut than from anyone else and he had given all he had. It was a terrible choice to make, and Mari wasn't sure she could have done it, even if asked by Father of All.

The men ended their practice with eighth form. At its completion, Lyon opened his eyes and touched his fist to Tasut's fist. For one splinter of time, Tasut's eyes smiled, and Lyon laughed the way he used to; carefree, and open. Mari ached for both of them. They had been good friends. For this slice of time, it was the way it had been years ago when they were simply a pair of soldiers serving under General Monus.

I hope they wash up before they come in for breakfast. Mari returned to the kitchen to find Brenna getting the food ready. Mari was amazed at the amount of food that Tasut kept on hand. Yet, considering his size, she should not have been surprised at all. He'd need enormous amounts of food just to maintain his weight. At seven foot, he weighed close to three hundred pounds; most of it bone and muscle.

Talon was grateful that he no longer limped when Nyk followed him into the kitchen for breakfast. They had been outside, taking care of the livestock. Nyk had wisely maintained his distance from Harcour who eyed him with suspicious malevolence. The stallion remembered this boy who had dared touch him and Nyk knew he would not get away with it twice. Harcour snapped his large, square teeth in Nyk's direction several times, as the boys worked around the barn. The large mules that shared the barn with Harcour, and did the menial tasks, were well trained. They had been smart enough to remain in the barn during the monsters' attack two days ago.

Nyk used a curry brush on one of the mules while talking about the plague crabs, Brenna, and the Tybars. Talon noticed that Nyk didn't talk about, or ask about, Tasut.

Perhaps that was understandable because Nyk was drawn to the Tybar family. Talon was of two minds about that. In his mind, Nyk didn't exactly fit in, but then, neither did he. While Nyk talked, Talon worked.

"Do you always do what you're told?" Nyk's mouth was full of eggs, his eyes watching Mari.

Talon hadn't really thought about it before. "Yes."

"Have you always done this many chores?"

"Yes." He felt more secure if he did the chores. That way he knew that they were done the way Tasut wanted. Talon never questioned his father's orders. It was easier and less painful to obey them.

Lyon's family sat at the table with Brenna on her father's lap. Her eyes were glued to Tasut. He sat propped in the corner, looking like a large dusty rock.

Talon still had unanswered questions about his father's shaved head. He fervently hoped Tasut didn't expect him to wear the same style while he studied his father and tried to read a course of action in the well-chiseled features.

He didn't question why Tasut sat in the corner. He already knew from experience that a person could see out every window and door while remaining in the corner's shadow.

Mari finished putting food on the table, and they all bowed their heads to thank Father of All.

Talon readily forgot the rest of the world as the aroma of well-prepared food assaulted his nostrils. It made his stomach angrily demand its share of the feast. There were some un-familiar foods but all of them were works of art to Talon. Some were flaky on the outside and full of warm meat and vegetables floating in creamy sauce on the inside. Others were crunchy and sweet or creamy and cool.

An hour later, he had eaten much more than was good for him, but even after he had stuffed himself, he wanted more. He eyed the table with longing but regretfully pushed himself away from the remains of the meal. He went to the front window to look out at the large pile of kindling that hid the only evidence the tree existed, feeling strangely anxious.

"What are your plans now?" Lyon ventured, directing this question at Tasut.

"I've never seen a coordinated attack between different species," said Tasut, looking out the window at the kindling pile that hid the evidence.

"I'm sure you have a plan in place, but I think you would agree that this attack puts a new light on the situation," Lyon said gravely. Mari came and put her arm on his shoulder. They both knew this must be handled very carefully.

"Plans must change," Tasut agreed as his eyes briefly rested on Talon. "Utak must be told." Tasut's eyes scanned the grounds outside the cottage.

"Stay with Talon," encouraged Mari. "Lyon can tell Utak, and set up the lines of communication. In any case, we leave today."

Her eyes rested on Brenna, who was smiling shyly at Talon, who was oblivious to her adoration. Mari hoped Talon didn't get irritated with their headstrong daughter.

"I'll go to Sogo to see if there's anything more to this that we should know," Tasut spoke from the corner.

Mari turned away, putting the dishes back into the cupboard, to hide her smile. *Perfect.* When she turned back, her face was composed, but she caught Talon's look and her heart went out to him.

Talon had turned away from the window and looked at Tasut, obviously hoping that he wouldn't be left alone this time. She knew that Tasut had never dared take Talon farther than the Village.

"What about Talon?" Lyon asked, his grey eyes looking passively at Tasut's son while Mari prayed for the miracle they sought.

*

Tasut took a long look at his son who stood perfectly still holding his emotions in check. Tasut shook his head slightly. "He can't go to Sogo, he isn't ready." Talon's heart plummeted and he felt his stomach sour with fear.

"Are you leaving him here?" Mari asked incredulously, pinning Tasut with her eyes. Lyon and Mari had spoken of this moment last night. Taking Talon to the city of Dyman with them had to be Tasut's idea or it wouldn't work.

"Take him to Tryk's."

It wasn't what they wanted, but better than having the boy stay in the cottage alone.

Talon felt relief and disbelief in equal measure, but Brenna wasn't so quiet about it. She clapped her hands with delight and ran around the table to Talon and nearly knocked him over as she tightly wrapped her arms around him in a big hug.

Tasut interrupted her joy by pointing to the door while looking at Talon. "The wagon and cart."

Talon managed to pull out of Brenna's grasp and left, feeling lighter and more puzzled than ever. *Who is Tryk? How long will I have to stay? What does he mean, I'm not ready?*

Brenna followed Talon like a shadow. Mee was in tow, having a mock-battle with her large tail. Every now and then, Mee would pounce on a bug and make a quick snack of it. She had fixed a red leaf near one of her ears. Talon was curious when Mee kept one of the bugs she hunted, and Talon looked at Brenna as the Shee sat down and petted it.

"Why does it do that?" Talon asked Brenna, uncomfortable because she was staring again.

Mee, her dark blue eyes blinking at him said, "I not 'it'! I be Mee!"

Talon's eyebrows rose in surprise.

Brenna nodded. "Mee's smart as well as pretty. Mee knows what we say."

Mee nodded, walking like a person so she could carry the bug and pet it. She crooned, "I eat you soon, good bug, wait for time."

Talon looked to Brenna for translation. She smiled at him. She seemed to smile a lot. He didn't mind.

"Mee plays with her food sometimes. If a bug is pretty, she'll keep it for a pet before she eats it. She kept her last pet for two whole days!" Talon assumed, from Brenna's tone, that this was nothing short of a miracle.

They went to the small snug barn for the two black mules that shared the warm enclosure with Harcour. Harcour eyed them with disdain and continued munching his oats. It was obvious to Talon that Tasut had already made his mind up to travel to Sogo prior to the Tybars speaking with him. Tasut didn't give Harcour extra rations of oats unless they were leaving. Harcour knew it as well and was greedily filling himself. He was already saddled.

Mee surprised Talon by jumping up on the gate of Harcour's stall and offering the stallion a bug. "Here. Much good bug," she said, her little arm extended. Harcour's disgusted snort blew Mee off the gate. The Shee landed in the hay and came up with nose twitching and eyes glittering.

"Bug gone!" she hissed at Harcour who looked at her with smug indifference.

"Harcour doesn't eat bugs," Brenna explained to her pet. "Your bug is over there." She pointed to the green beetle that was scrambling madly away from Mee who encouraged it to run so she could catch it.

Brenna turned to stare at Talon. He wasn't sure why she kept looking at him. *Maybe it's just cause she's a little girl.* Nyk didn't look at him the way Brenna did. Just the thought of Nyk looking at him that way made him want to punch Nyk. He doubted Nyk would try to hold his hand either. *If he does, I will punch him!* Lyon was making Nyk help him pack things.

The two black mules had already eaten and looked at Talon expectantly. He pulled them out of their stalls and led them outside to the small cart Lyon had filled the night before, and buckled them in the traces ahead of the cart. His mind was churning. There was no doubt left. His life was changing.

Talon doubled-checked the leather traces as he had been taught. Then he pulled the mules to the front of the house with the cart and its contents bumping along behind them. Brenna was also silent, still studying him. It didn't exactly bother him, but made him wonder why she wanted to be with him. He had nearly gotten her killed when he had failed to act more quickly the other day when the monsters came. *She tried to warn me. I shouldn't have ignored her. I won't do it again.*

To Talon's surprise, Tasut was already astride Harcour. The great stallion was snorting and prancing.

Harcour was evidently feeling the rush of strength and energy from his oats. He had the bit in his teeth, a sure sign of his infamous temper. He came as close to disobedience as Talon had ever witnessed as he turned in a circle and shook his great shaggy mane. Tasut wasn't gentle when he reined him away from the two mares that Lyon brought into view. Harcour snorted and whinnied to them. The mares looked up at him and then pointedly ignored him.

Lyon picked up Brenna and put her in the wagon on the seat, "Don't worry Harcour. These little ladies are suitably impressed; they're just not interested yet."

Talon wasn't sure if Harcour stopped prancing because Tasut had such a firm grip on the reins, or if he understood what Lyon said.

"Get all of your things, Talon," Mari told him. "You won't be coming back."

He hesitated a moment to glance at Tasut who gave a firm nod. It didn't take long. All Talon owned was what he wore, one other set of clothing, and his sling.

When he came out of the cottage he noticed that several full crates, now housing two dozen chickens, the rooster, and three piglets with their enormous mother, were loaded into the back of the wagon, along with a few meager pieces of furniture and crates of the herbs. The poisonous ones had been carefully placed between layers of parchment.

Talon had a suspicion that Mari must have conjured the parchment because he had never seen so much of it in one place. He wished he knew how to read better. There was writing all over the pages.

A strange cow was tied to the back of the cart, with her calf content to follow wherever they were headed.

In surprise, he watched small wisps of smoke curling through the many cracks of their outbuildings and tried to determine whether he felt badly about it. He noticed that the enormous pile of kindling stayed in place.

He did feel badly about the tree Brenna had blasted apart. He had spent a lot of time climbing it. He had even slept in it a few times when Tasut was away. It felt safer. One time he even had a dream about a big man, big as Tasut, walking around the base of the tree while he slept.

"Talon, you drive the wagon, and Nyk, you get the cart," Mari instructed.

Talon looked at her in wonder. He had driven the wagon twice in his life. It was an exciting thing to think about. Climbing aboard, he eagerly took the reins and Nyk looked back from the cart looking excited as well.

"Torch the house," she said to Tasut, handing him a large bag that looked and smelled like it might contain herbal tea leaves. "The rest is taken care of."

Tasut guided Harcour around to the wagon and gave Talon a piercing look. "Obey. Protect her." He pointed at Brenna and then rode Harcour around the corner of their cottage. Soon smoke began pouring out of the door and window as they began their journey.

Brenna sat beside him on the wagon seat and smiled. Lyon and Tasut were speaking with one another in the distance, both astride their horses. He watched Lyon nod and salute Tasut with fist to chest. Tasut nodded and kicked Harcour into a gallop heading the opposite direction. He didn't look back at Talon who watched Tasut until he disappeared into the forest.

Talon found Mari looking at him, her look inscrutable. He didn't have time to interpret the look because smoke was billowing out from the thatched roof of the cottage.

Talon had felt a twinge of shock at Mari's instructions to torch the house, but now with the wagon moving forward, the growing excitement of being out on the road was an effective counter against any sense of homelessness. He noticed as he slapped the reins on the back of the mare, that the roar of the blaze could be heard quite a distance.

*

Once they were out of the Rahazi, the sun warmed the early morning air. Talon had been driving the wagon four solid hours. He honestly felt that the mare could pull the wagon without any guidance. He was accustomed to a variety of chores, actively moving most of every day, and being alert.

His mind was trying to twist itself around the events of the past few days and was still trying to reason things out. Sitting beside him, Brenna had finally stopped asking questions.

It was disturbing that he knew so few answers to simple questions such as "What's your favorite color? Where's your mother? How come Tasut's so grumpy?"

Mee had scampered off the wagon and gone into the woods and come back several times.

"Where does Mee go?" he asked once when Brenna took a breath.

"To eat. Mee loves crab," she watched her striped pet. "Mee likes you," she smiled at him shyly and whispered, "and so do I."

This statement brought a pleasant sensation and some confusion about how to respond. At that moment Mee hopped up on the wagon and sat on Brenna's lap, looking disappointed. Talon was surprised when he felt a soft raccoon-like paw on his arm and he looked down at the Shee as it cocked its head to one side. Its eyes were very human-looking with blue irises surrounded by white with a round black dot in the middle.

"Crab?" Mee's hopeful voice sounded like that of a small child.

Talon looked to Brenna for explanation.

"He doesn't have any crab, Mee." Brenna informed her pet.

Mee sniffed in disappointment and sat herself down between them with arms folded and a pathetic look of longing on her face, "Want crab."

Lyon rode up. "There's a small clearing ahead, let's stop for lunch." He pointed to a break in the trees just off the road. Talon drove the wagon there, pleased the mule was docile. His thoughts went to Tasut and wondered where he was and if Harcour was behaving himself. Harcour had actually bitten Tasut. Once.

Mari unpacked the lunch with Brenna's help while Talon jumped down from the wagon seat and led the mules to a place he could tie them so they wouldn't wander.

Earlier, he watched Lyon ride up and talk to Nyk who had been driving the cart. Nyk had nodded and climbed down from the cart to eat his lunch. He ate quickly and left their company at a run.

After lunch, Talon guessed that Mari would take over driving the cart. Lyon hobbled the mares so they could eat and drink, but not wander far.

Briefly, Talon wondered where Nyk went and then decided it wasn't his business, though he was curious. Not knowing what else to do, he helped put the lunch out on a large blanket Mari had taken from the wagon. She looked up at him and smiled.

"You two go down to the creek over there," she pointed to their left, "and wash up for lunch."

Brenna followed him, Mee scampered ahead peering under small rocks and climbing up a few trees. Talon kneeled by the water and his eyes scanned the foliage around them as he dipped his hands into the ice-cold creek.

"What are you looking for?" Brenna asked as she kneeled by him and mimicked his actions, using her skirt to dry her hands on.

He looked at her and shrugged. Tasut had taught him to be aware of who was around and what was going on at all times. It was more habit than a conscious action and definitely not worth the questions she would ask if he told her.

As if guessing what his answer would have been she informed him, "Mee knows when people are around."

Do girls read minds?

Mee came to Talon's side as he washed his face and hands. "Crab?" she asked pointing to the water.

Talon looked into the water and sure enough, there was a small fresh-water crab hiding in the shallows. He reached in, caught it and handed it to Mee.

Curiously, the little Shee took his offering and looked at him with wide appreciative eyes. Mee looked as if she were smiling.

"Tal good. Mee like." She nipped the crab's legs off with her teeth and without effort, ripped off its top. "More?"

"It's better with melted butter and spices," Talon told her, scanning the moving water for signs of more crab. She ignored his comment and devoured the rest of the crab.

Brenna frowned at Mee and told her pet that, "Mama said to have good manners and not ask for more all the time."

Talon didn't actually mind the task of gathering the crab. It gave him something to do and Mee was more polite and appreciative than some people he had known. After she had eaten what he could find, Mee crawled onto his lap and stretched out.

"She wants you to pet her," Brenna said.

He gently stroked her luxurious fur. He silently wondered if there were more Shees and where he could get one. They were much stronger than they looked and they had the advantage of being able to bite whatever attacked.

After they finished lunch and gathered up everything, Mee chose to sit on his shoulder for the ride. He felt rather proud and Brenna gave him a bright knowing smile and took his hand.

About an hour later on the trail ahead of them, three boys who all looked about his own age, straggled up to the wagon, looking hot and sweaty.

Mari pulled her wagon to a stop, said something to one of the boys and he climbed on and took the reins. Then Mari came back to the wagon Talon was driving. He wasn't sure why it made him nervous to notice that Nyk wasn't with them.

Brenna beamed and stood up as she pointed to the boy in the wagon and enthusiastically said, "Iskar!"

The boy she pointed to was nearly as tall as Talon, but Talon sensed Iskar was older than all the boys. Iskar waved at Brenna.

"Who's that?" he asked aloud.

"Iskar Shyn," Mari said, looking back at the three boys.

Iskar had long straight dark hair pulled back from a wide, friendly face with close-set green eyes.

The shortest of the three was introduced as Mal Kayman, a brown-haired, brown-eyed boy with a silent disposition, olive skin, and surly attitude. He wore a scowl as Iskar jumped down from the wagon seat and tried to lift Mal up to the wagon.

"I can do it myself!" Mal grumbled and roughly pushed Iskar's hand away, even though all Iskar did was try to help.

While the two boys glared at each other, a third boy puffed his way up to the wagon. He was a bit thick through the waist and Mari signaled to him to come over.

"This is Rube Jynn. He'll be driving the other wagon and Iskar will be coming back here to ride in yours."

Talon nodded his hello. Rube didn't have enough air to even say hello, so he just gave an exhausted wave. Rube had chubby cheeks, large blue eyes, and hair so white you could see his pink scalp. There were small thin scars all over his forearms as if he'd been badly scratched at some point by a bad tempered cat. Talon studied the ridged scars. Maybe several bad tempered cats. That, or Rube wasn't smart enough to leave a wild cat alone. Rube went back to the first wagon and exchanged places with Iskar.

In moments, Iskar had climbed up in the wagon Talon drove, picked up Brenna, and put her on his lap where she good-naturedly allowed his tickling. Talon wasn't sure why it bothered him, but he thought Iskar a bit too old to be tickling girls.

Talon looked back at Mal who might know more about what was normal concerning girls. Mal didn't say a word, but watched.

Although Mal's scowl wasn't really directed at anyone, it was an effective deterrent to getting to know him better. Talon wasn't sure he wanted to know Mal better if he was so grumpy, but at least he wasn't tickling Brenna.

Lyon had remained on his horse while they moved forward. Looking up the road, the expectant look on his face changed to one of concern. "Where's Nyk?" he asked aloud about a quarter of an hour later.

"He said he had to go home," Mal answered curtly.

Talon watched Mari and Lyon exchange brief looks. Evidently, this was something unexpected and if their looks meant anything, un-welcome. Tension rose in the air, but Talon wasn't sure anyone other than himself felt it.

Mari immediately got out of the cart ahead of them and untied the mare. Talon pulled the wagon to a stop behind the cart.

"Iskar, you and Rube take turns driving the cart," ordered Lyon.

"There's room for Brenna," he said to Lyon. "Can she come?"

"She'll be riding with her mother for awhile. You can always ask her later."

"Want to ride with me later?" Iskar asked Brenna hopefully.

Brenna smiled, but shook her head no and held her arms out for Talon.

Iskar frowned at Talon and put Brenna on the seat, his eyes unhappy as he lightly jumped out of the wagon. Talon was puzzled why Iskar was angry with him, yet felt a peculiar satisfaction that Brenna wouldn't be riding with Iskar.

Lyon continued, "Mal, come back and drive the wagon, and you," he nodded to Talon, "climb on the back of my horse." Lyon steered his mare over to Talon as Mal took the reins.

Talon climbed on the back of Lyon's mare while her father slung Brenna up behind her mothers saddle.

"Hang on to your mother tightly."

Brenna nodded, looking wistfully at Talon. Mari steered her horse up in front of the cart, and Lyon and Talon behind the wagon.

As the group moved forward, Lyon purposefully held his horse back until he could no longer see the cart, wagon, or anyone in their party. He waited until the cart and wagon went around a bend ahead. Lyon guided their horse off the trail and they both dismounted by a small stream where the mare began to drink.

"Talon, don't tell any of these boys where you're from. If they ask, say I bought you at auction and you ran away from an orphanage in Teris in Korlori."

Lyon looked directly at him. "If you want to stay alive, tell no one of Tasut. He has many enemies. Do you understand?"

Talon did, but he wondered about Brenna.

Lyon continued, "These boys are probably trustworthy, but we can't take the chance they aren't. Often, people aren't what they seem."

In Talon's mind, he reasoned out that Mal was the most capable of doing mischief. He'd already shown he was unhappy to be here. The Tybars obviously knew Nyk and Iskar, and he doubted they would trust their daughter to anyone they suspected. He couldn't think that Rube was capable of duplicity, he didn't seem the type.

He decided he'd just keep watching.

Talon was accustomed to taking orders. 'Keep your mouth shut' was Tasut's personal motto. Somehow, he wasn't surprised to hear his father had enemies.

Talon knelt to take another drink and was pleased to note that Lyon also scanned the countryside as he took a drink from the stream. It was confirmation of something Tasut had said: 'A good soldier is always aware of his surroundings.' Lyon, Talon decided, would make a good soldier.

They re-mounted the mare and Lyon kicked her to a canter. Talon had not ridden a horse before, only mules. It was a wonderful experience; this mare had an easy gait and as they rode along, it didn't feel as if his backbone would erupt from the top of his head.

Lyon guided the mare ahead of the wagons to Mari and Brenna. Talon remained on the back. Brenna smiled at Talon, happiness lighting her blue eyes as they met his. Lyon called a halt to their progress by lifting his right arm into the air.

Soon the boys had joined them, looking curiously up at Lyon. Even the somber Mal looked curious.

No, Talon decided, it was more than curious. Mal was alert. *He knows something or suspects something.* He was definitely going to watch Mal.

"There's something wrong," Lyon addressed their entire party. "I don't know what it is yet, so let's keep our eyes open and mouths shut."

"Is Nyk alright?" Talon was surprised at his own question and more surprised at how much it meant to him.

Lyon shrugged and looked troubled. "I don't know."

Chapter 10: Bad News

In a thicket a few miles outside Sogo's gates, Tasut reined in Harcour. The High Priestess Saro's best spy, a Shee named Bot, tossed the expected parchment down to him from the branch just above.

He opened his saddlebags and threw a crab, the standard payment, on the ground. It was unwise to make a Shee wait for payment; they didn't have the necessary mentality for waiting.

He took a few moments to read the message. At its conclusion, his brown eyes were flat and hard. If he had been on the training fields, whoever saw that look would shake in their boots and brace for the worst. With grim determination, Tasut pushed the letter down inside his day tunic and began forming a plan while he waited. In the faint distance, he heard the familiar stride of Jarow's horse.

Jarow Meade was Training Commander on the second floor of the Barracks. Tasut took several deep breaths to calm his fury as Jarow grimly confirmed the news.

"There is a traitor in the Barracks."

They rode on together toward the largest and most corrupt city in the world: Sogo.

*

"Commanders Tasut and Jarow have returned," called Master Genn with a sonorous tone and smart salute at the giant shadow and a second smaller shadow that passed into the city of Sogo.

The well-seasoned guard at the front gate recognized Tasut and Jarow on sight, and had never missed saluting them. It was a point of pride for him to recognize the powers that be, and Tasut was in a class all by himself. Of course, if it had only been Jarow he would still have saluted, albeit not quite as smartly and without the rush of adrenaline.

Another man will die. Master Genn was unable to forbid the thought. It was an unspoken superstition in the city that upon Tasut's return, at least one man would die. Genn felt that it wasn't because Tasut planned it to be that way, but because men like Tasut carried death with them wherever they went.

Genn watched the two shadows head for the High Priestess Saro's Villa, noting the smart salute Tasut got from the Barracks men stationed outside the Villa gates.

Genn had seen Jarow pass out of those gates on his way to meet Tasut not twenty minutes earlier. With Cubes over, there would be fewer real fighting men to protect the High Priestess from someone trying to gain fame by assassinating her. *As if any sane person would dare.*

"Visitin' High Priestess Saro," his companion, a new recruit, noted with a shake of his head. "There's no accountin' fer taste," snorted the younger guard, "or lack of it in this case. Tho' what she sees in him is a blind man's guess." The recruit stopped to pick his teeth with one filthy fingernail. "Can't says I blame him, Saro's one fine lookin' woman."

"That's High Priestess Saro to you, Private! That's all men like us need to know!" said Genn coldly. He knew they were on shaky ground here. It wasn't a good idea to talk about the High Priestess. Even calling her by her title was cause for discretion. Tasut was her known protector and nobody, not even the Council of Nine, openly challenged Tasut's ownership of anything.

Genn had seen Tasut painfully re-arrange a guard's face for openly admiring one of the High Priestess' handmaidens, a widow by the name of Raen. Jarow had been at Tasut's side when it happened and he followed up the re-arrangement by stepping on the man's fighting hand and breaking it.

Tasut and Jarow were a team, inseparable. Speculation about those two men, or their habits, was a good way to get you killed. Genn kept his own thoughts quiet on what he thought Jarow's true feelings for the widow Raen might be.

'A smart man keeps his eyes open and his mouth shut,' his wife had cautioned him many times. 'The day you forget that rule, I'll be a widow. Sogo isn't a forgiving place.'

He knew it was true. Someday soon, his stint in the militia was over and at that point, they hoped to escape. His wife prayed he could make a living outside of Sogo doing what he loved: carpentry. He just prayed that they'd make it out alive. They were saving a bit, now and again, to help them leave the city. It would be a few more years. *Hope I live that long.*

"I wouldn't leave a woman like her alone like he does, ifn' ya knows what I mean." The Private was lustfully staring toward the lights of the beautiful Villa.

Genn watched the new recruit with disbelief. The High Priestess was often referred to as the "Ice Priestess" for good reason. All of Sogo knew the woman had ice chips flowing in her veins and hoarfrost lodged in her heart.

Apparently, this new man had the kind of mind that never had the novelty of an idea cross its surface. This was both good and bad. The good part made him suitable for one thing: being a number. All the men who served in the Sogoian army had numbers and this idiot simply filled a recruiter's quota. The bad part, in Genn's experienced estimation, was that this recruit would not last long in Sogo where the stupid did not survive.

At a whisper of sound, Genn turned to the shadows at their left and saw the Captain of the Guards approach. Genn saluted crisply, just the way the Captain liked it. The Private didn't even hear their Captain's approach much less salute him. Evidently, he was too busy dreaming about the powerful beautiful woman in the Villa.

Genn felt like kicking his companion and sincerely hoped that nothing threatened them in the night that would require skill from the new recruit. On the other hand, if they had anything happen that would require gross stupidity, the recruit would be perfect.

"Her skin looks real soft…" said the idiot, wistfully looking at the stained-glass windows in the front of the Villa, unaware the Captain had appeared.

"Touch the High Priestess Saro and you die," stated their Captain from the shadows. "There are plenty of fleshpots out there. If you believe in self-preservation, don't try poaching another man's preserves unless you have a death wish, especially when Tasut is that man.

"It's your call, but most people prefer their heads remain attached to their bodies. Commander Tasut is willing to remove any that aren't used." The Captain walked away.

"Whats he mean?"

It's going to be a long night. Genn felt he could leave no wiggle room for this particular recruit and told him, "The High Priestess is off limits to every person in this city, except Tasut."

"I heard them stories. He's just a man like anyone else," he snorted, but swallowed nervously.

"Regular men don't pull your family jewels out your throat," Genn warned, his eyes following the Captain who had headed in the direction of the Villa.

"Thems just rumors," insisted the younger guard with a doubtful whine.

"Are you cracked?" sputtered Genn, rounding on the man, "Tasut was **Guardian**! I was there when he killed them all. I've never seen anything like it," Genn's eyes were shadowed by the horror of it. "It was over in fifteen minutes and there he was, just standing there covered head to toe in blood and guts. He never said a word the whole time, he just killed them and ran off into the streets."

"Everyone has gots a weakness!" the recruit insisted. "And his lives there," he jabbed a skinny finger at the richly appointed Villa.

"If you live long enough, you may get to see the next games. Until then, zip your yap!" Genn barked at the ill-fated recruit, aware that the Captain had returned and been standing in the shadows for the last few minutes.

"He's human as the rest of us. Bet he bleeds if ya hits him," the recruit said sullenly, finally realizing Genn was giving him a promise, not a warning. He just didn't want to accept it. "I thinks them what live in the Barracks ought ta throw him out and run away. It's what I'd do."

"Then you've never been there, soldier. Tasut isn't the only thing that keeps them there."

"What else is there?"

"The hell hounds and the curse." Genn couldn't believe the man had no idea about either one.

"Curse?" the dim lights in the man's small brain seemed to misfire on a regular basis.

"Something unholy is said to walk those halls at night."

The soldier spit on the ground, "It's probably just Tasut all puffed up or that lacky of his, what's his name? Jark or something?"

"Soldier?" their Captain stepped into the dim light afforded by torches to address the new recruit. Both men stood to attention this time.

The Captain stepped in front of the new recruit and Genn knowingly stepped back, certain of what was about to transpire. He had seen Jarow speaking with the Captain in the shadows moments ago, and the Captain had looked at them and nodded. "Tasut told me to deliver this."

The young soldier felt the knife slide into his stomach, ripping up to his throat.

After the recruit dropped to the ground, Genn leaned over and picked the knife out of his younger companion's Adam's apple and wiped it on the dead man's pants and offered it to the Captain.

"Keep it Genn, Tasut said to use it wisely."

Genn nodded. He was positive that Commander Tasut didn't know diddlysquat about what just happened. Nor would he care if he did; sympathy wasn't within the man.

"I'll get a new recruit, Sir."

"Genn," the Captain paused and added with sarcasm, "Do us all a favor and hire someone with a level of mentality greater than that of bug dung. If possible, find a man who prefers to think with something other than his glands."

"No locals then, right." Genn stripped the corpse methodically and offered the few coins to the Captain.

"Keep them, Genn, maybe it will help find a someone with quicker intelligence," the Captain left.

Genn frowned as he drug the corpse off to the side of the road. *Find a smart man for two coppers and a quipa?* Not likely. All intelligent men who were not bound to the unholy city had already left or wanted to leave, not guard its gates. *What does that make me?* He already knew the answer: Desperate.

*

The sun rose on the city of Sogo, lighting the large white Villa sitting just inside the northeast gates. Along the streets, various vendors were pushing their carts to their preferred spaces to set up shop for the day. As usual on the day after Cubes, the streets were still full of refuse and even a body or two that the local militia had not found under the garbage yet. *Not that they care when they do.* Jarow kept the thought to himself and focused on the real problem.

Tasut was displeased. Not that he looked different, but if you knew him as well as Jarow did, you could feel the rock within the man solidify until his dark eyes burned like twin chips of polished obsidian.

Tasut and Jarow left the High Priestess' Villa and continued on foot, leaving their horses in the Villa's stable. Whenever Harcour was housed there, the inhabitants of the city knew Tasut was somewhere in the city itself. Thus it was that Saro, High Priestess of the Unknown God, was virtually untouchable. Tasut was ruthlessly vigilant about her protection. She was one of the few in Sogo who could travel to any spot in the city and return unscathed.

If there was any time that could be called peaceful in the largest city in the world, it was in early morning before the heat of the sun baked the pastel colored buildings until they felt like ovens.

The city had once been named the "most organized" of all cities. The city was laid out in straight lines with wide lanes. If it were not for the stench of heinous crime and debauchery, like the odor of fresh blood slicing into clean air, it would have been beautiful on many levels. In the distance, you could see the spires of tall buildings and the garden roofs of shorter ones.

The two famous men traveled the red stone streets in silence, Jarow a few paces ahead and to Tasut's left. They had developed this defensive method of traveling early on in their professional relationship. In an ambush, their strategy was for Jarow to take whatever came from the left, while Tasut took what came from the right. In this way they could avoid confusion and possibly killing one another. It had worked for seven years.

It amused Jarow that Tasut planned his entrance into the city to coincide with the beginnings of the day. Vendors were notorious gossips and the fact he had returned would be known within the day if not hours. Such notoriety was quite a feat in a city of nearly sixty million. His entrance had to be done with style and Tasut was a master at intimidation. He had the presence of a hundred lightning storms.

In a city as corrupt as Sogo, traitors were common. Even the Barracks, almost the safest place in the city, wasn't foolproof. It was a breeding ground for men that hated Tasut. The men Tasut trained hated and feared him, but they instantly obeyed his every order. He earned their respect through fear.

Jarow had argued with Tasut about his training tactics. Jarow's suggestions had been met with deaf ears and a flat stare; the same stare that bred the very death traps that they tried to avoid.

Every member of the Council of Nine wanted Tasut dead. With money as their partner in crime, they tried to have Tasut assassinated. Assassins had plied their trade in the Barracks, the streets, and once, just outside the High Priestess Saro's Villa.

Jarow had been attacked numerous times but not as often, nor as brutally, as Tasut. Jarow scanned the crowds for possible threats, knowing it was just a matter of time.

Jarow knew the message Tasut received from Bot was at the root of Tasut's current rage. It had informed Tasut that one of the men he had personally chosen as Assistant Commander for the first floor of the Barracks had been spying on them for the Council of Nine.

According to the High Priestess' source, the traitor had offered his services to the Nine for a price that she had feared to name. Tasut had demanded it of her and she had hesitantly supplied the information. Jarow had felt his own mouth drop open at the amount of the bribe. There was only one member of the Nine who had that kind of money. Nez, the Minister of Religion; the man –ironically – that Saro answered to as "High Priestess of the Unknown God."

Tasut was in as foul a mood as Jarow had ever seen, and that didn't bode well for anyone in the Barracks. Jarow maintained silent vigilance and concentrated on the task at hand: getting to the Barracks without getting killed in an ambush.

He tried not to think of the lost opportunity for romance at the Villa. He had hoped to see the attractive handmaiden, Raen, but they had arrived too late and left too early. He had been thinking about her more often than he should. A man in his position had no right to consider marriage. Yet, he did. Often.

About a mile from the Barracks, Tasut braced himself even as he walked forward. Jarow read his Commander well enough to know that an attack was imminent. It came as expected, a street farther down.

A small man erupted from a corner stall with knife in hand, a mad grimace to his face, and desperation in his eyes. *An unregistered assassin* Jarow realized as he instinctively covered Tasut's back. Registered assassins were never clumsy and this man must have been deranged to attempt such a thing in broad daylight on the main thoroughfare to the Barracks.

Without breaking stride, Tasut grabbed the man by the neck, broke it, and dropped the body to the street.

"Clif," Jarow called back to the owner of the stall where the assassin had sprung, "tell Gad."

Gad was the acknowledged Assassins Guild Master and he brooked no sloppy work. Those caught attempting such would be executed publicly for bringing humiliation to the Guild. The city of Sogo valued paid assassins more than jewelers. In this case, with such a high profile target, a desperate attempt was usually a rogue assassin trying to make the kill of a lifetime.

Tasut moved forward and Jarow followed, resolved to carrying out Tasut's plan to deal with the traitor named in the note. He was *never* grateful to see the Barracks and that gut-twisting feeling of walking into a castle of horrors was worse today.

Chapter 11: Barracks

Made of grey granite, the Barracks was an enormous circular building that stood three floors high on the northern edge of the city boundaries. It's northern-most edge was bordered by the Western Desert. It had one purpose: to house men as they trained to fight in Cubes, the real-life version of the game known as Steps.

The grounds surrounding the outside of the Barracks were, of necessity, very plain. There were no trees or grass; just dirt, rock, and holding pens. The pens held animals that were fattened and then butchered to feed the men who lived in the Barracks. If there was anything positive about being in the Barracks, you knew you would eat well until the day you died. For the men who made it to the third floor, where Tasut ruled, that meant eating well for seven years.

Each of the three floors housed three hundred men divided into one hundred-man sections. Each floor also had kitchen and mess hall with a Master Chef and twelve assistants, a large pool-sized bathing area, a room used to teach various subjects relating to surviving in the Barracks, and a large weapons room.

Tucked into each floor's southeast corner were the healing rooms. The healers had as many assistants as could be found. Because the men trained in twelve hour shifts, the healers worked around the clock. They were generally haggard-looking men dressed in grey or white.

A Commander and Assistant Commander served on each of the first two floors. If the Commander was killed, the Assistant was promoted, and a new Assistant would be appointed.

The third floor of the Barracks was Tasut's brutal kingdom. He had no Assistant. His men obeyed orders whether he was there or not because the repercussions on his return would not be worth it. Currently, the third floor was empty because the bloody free-for-all known as Cubes had just concluded. All of the men Tasut had been training were dead; killed during Cubes, except the one who had earned the title of Guardian.

The new Guardian was San. For the next seven years, San would serve the Council of Nine. He would rotate through them as their body-guard every six weeks until Cubes was held again. At that time, San would have to defend his title. Tasut knew from personal experience that San wasn't thinking seven years into the future. As the Guardian, you lived moment-to-moment.

The position of Guardian was sacrosanct until the new games in seven years with one exception: the streets of Sogo. If the Guardian was successfully assassinated during the interim, it meant the post was deserted and would remain that way until Cubes defined a new Guardian. If San was alive, he would be in the next games, but that was seven years from now. In seven years, it would be the beginning of the end of Sogo.

Jarow was the Training Commander on the second floor; his assistant had been killed a few days ago. Dez and Cebo were the Commanders on the first floor. All of their men would be promoted to the second floor and become Jarow's, leaving the first floor temporarily empty.

To fill the cots on the first floor, Jarow would accompany Tasut to the Sogoian slave auction. There, they would choose and take the men they wanted. After the space of a year, if the cots were not full, they would take men from the streets, willing or otherwise. The search for men who looked like they could fight and provide good sport for the citizens of Sogo, began the day after Cubes. It was one of the reasons the streets were now so empty. In spite of their thirst for blood sports, the savage citizens of Sogo did not want to be part of the Barracks.

Tasut and Jarow opened the tall metal doors leading into the Barracks and together entered the enormous foyer. The ceiling was sixty-feet tall. The open area was large enough to fit one thousand men in full battle gear, with room to spare . In the foyer were forty dogs in twenty cages, ten on each side of the doorway.

The cages were purposefully positioned to form a vertical hallway. Anyone who entered the Barracks had to pass between these cages. The largest dog, Deja, was the size of a full-grown bull. She was the dominant hound and the others followed her lead.

When Tasut entered, the gigantic dogs began an uncustomary whimpering and groveling. Jarow had made it his practice not to get close to the cages. He knew the animals were more than just large canines. To call them dogs was like calling a war-horse a foal. Even in the dim light of the foyer, they looked like enormous black and grey shadows with mouths large enough to snap a man in half.

Jarow was certain they understood language, to an uncanny degree, and could act upon it. They recognized Tasut as their master and accepted one other man, Yus, as caretaker. Presently Yus wasn't at his station. Jarow scanned the cages looking for the man's bones. It seemed the logical thing to do, as Yus frequently claimed it would happen to him one day. Jarow had been sure Yus was just griping.

Tasut gave the signal to the dogs for silence by making a chopping motion with his hands and the animals went completely, immediately, unnaturally, silent. As usual, when Tasut was present, the dogs put their enormous heads on their chest-size paws and looked at Tasut with worshipful eyes.

Yus was a grizzened old man with bowed legs. He came out of his quarters with ear-blistering words, "What Vael-brained son of a slaver..."

He broke off as his eyes took in Tasut and Jarow. He bowed so quickly and so deeply, Jarow wondered the man didn't faint. As it was, Yus remained bent at the waist and literally shook in his boots with his eyes firmly glued to the floor. Jarow believed Yus was praying for a miracle as Tasut paused and fixed him with a long look. Technically,

Yus wasn't supposed to leave his post, which was to be in sight and sound of the hounds, except for meals and to relieve himself.

Tasut moved on and Jarow followed. After they passed, Yus fell to his knees in relief. Jarow heard him pick himself off the floor and whisper, "I must find another job." Yus had threatened to quit many times but he remained loyal, if not to the Barracks, then to Tasut.

Whatever doors had once graced the arched doorway leading to the first floor cot area, no longer existed. Tasut had them removed when he had become Guardian. No one dared to find out why. However, Jarow had heard a rumor that it was because Tasut wanted the men on the first floor to think about how hopeless the idea of escape truly was.

Two years ago, Tasut had ordered the Barracks blacksmith, who was stationed just outside the Barracks south wall, to build two ceiling-to-floor cages on site. The cages were made of wrought iron and were placed on either side of the first floor entrance.

Each cage held one of a pair of hideously identical statues. They were carved from black stone veined with gold, and had the heads of a fanged bull-like creature. There was no indication of hair anywhere on their heavily muscled human-like torsos. Each statue had long gold horns above human ears. The thick horns curved inward from the sides of their skulls and stretched three feet out in front of their bullish features. The tips were about a foot apart.

Both had a long gold-colored bull's tail and cloven hoofs. Oddly, both wore strange leather-looking pants that reached just below their knees. Their calves were knotted with muscle and had foot-long barbs on the back that looked razor sharp. To complete the nightmare, it didn't matter where you went in the foyer, their freakish solid-gold eyes watched you from behind the black wrought-iron bars.

Even knowing the effect was intentional, Jarow would have preferred something less menacing. He assumed Tasut put them there for intimidation purposes and remained silent on the subject. Over time, he had grown accustomed to the monsters.

Men, when they first arrived, were tested and then assigned their cots according to proficiency in weaponry, tactics, leadership, and strength. This process was uniform throughout the Barracks.

Men could challenge any man on their floor at any time, on any weapon or skill, to earn a higher numbered cot. The higher the number of your cot, the more proficient you had to be. The goal was to be the best, because the best survived.

Men numbering 1-100 were housed in the first section on each floor. Jarow braced himself. What Tasut planned was going to be extreme and the entire first floor of men were going to bear the brunt of Tasut's wrath.

Men, who looked at each other with an alarmingly concentrated lack of intelligence, noted Tasut's entrance through the first-floor doors. There should have been a Call Master to call the men to order when Commanders entered the room. Whoever he was, he was missing.

Jarow clenched his jaw. He wasn't sure how many of these men would be able to drum up the discipline required for the second floor. He firmed his resolve. They were about to get an intense dose of reality.

Dez, the Training Commander on the first floor, and Cebo, his Assistant, had failed to do their jobs. Dez was notably absent. That did not bode well for his future. Last night, while at the Villa with the High Priestess, Jarow had objected to what Tasut had in mind. Now he was grateful that Tasut had the final word.

Tasut's graphic demonstration would have the positive effect of making these poorly-trained men eager to resume their training. These men, sorry specimens that they were, would be promoted to the second floor in the next few hours and come under Jarow's command.

Frowning, Jarow followed Tasut past the first hundred men. He wasn't impressed by what he saw. Many of the men were sleeping. The men who were awake stared at them as they walked through the doorway into the next section.

Jarow noticed that behind them, men's voices began to buzz. The word was getting around. Tasut had insisted that they did not call the men to order, because it would give Cebo warning and Tasut did not want the man to know he was coming.

In the second section, a few men made startled efforts to stand, but no one saluted them. The anger emanating from Tasut was growing palpable. Trying to stop Tasut would be like ordering lightning not to strike. At this point, it would be best to let it strike and hope you were not the intended target.

Tasut's focus was forward and his eyes ablaze as they reached the doorway of the third section. There was one man in the third section that instantly recognized Jarow and immediately stood at attention. Jarow stopped his advance, keeping his eye on the rest of the men who were present. He did what he had always done since he came to the Barracks: watch Tasut's back.

Chapter 12: Object Lesson

Cebo, the Assistant Commander on this floor, was Valenese by birth, so he was shorter than average. But he was very stocky and the wrestling champion among these men. Currently, he was deeply engrossed in coaching two men on a game of Steps. Barracks rules required Steps be played floor-wide at the same time, with the entire third section coaching the men in the other two sections.

Of the men in third section that bothered to look their way, twenty stood at attention. Jarow made a slicing motion across his neck, signaling silence and was pleased to see they knew what he meant. They froze in place and Jarow could feel the fear coming off them in waves as they watched Tasut's silent approach.

Cebo and the two men playing Steps were laughing raucously. Jarow couldn't understand why they couldn't feel the tension building in the room.

Cebo finally turned, but it was too late to rectify his mistake. Tasut's hand reached out and lifted Cebo by his neck and gave him one hard shake. The two men playing the game scrambled out of the way, knocking the game board and the pieces to the floor.

The laughter was over and you could have heard a pin drop as Tasut slammed Cebo violently against the stone wall, still holding him off the floor. Cebo's face was red and his hands tried to pry his throat out of Tasut's grip. Jarow had seen this before from Tasut. He had been amazed then, and he was amazed now, that Cebo didn't die. Somehow, Tasut managed his chokehold on Cebo without Cebo losing consciousness.

Jarow called attention, wondering again where the first floor's Call Master was. At least the men were no longer lolling about. Every one of them now stood with eyes forward.

"Where is your Training Commander?" Jarow was met with silence. "Your Call Master?"

"The Call Master is in the latrine, Sir!" answered the man who had saluted earlier.

Jarow ground his teeth. "Sir!" Jarow addressed Tasut. "All out the house!" This indicated there was no man present who could assume command.

Tasut met his eyes and nodded. This was Jarow's cue to continue. Jarow turned to the men, "Fall in behind us." Under normal circumstances, he wouldn't have had to say the words 'behind us'. However, he wasn't sure if they would know what 'fall in' meant. It disgusted him to think these men would soon become his responsibility.

Tasut pulled Cebo away from the wall and began walking with him still suspended in the air. They traveled back through section two and then section one. Some men in each section belatedly rose to attention, and some just stood. It was very sloppy and Jarow felt his hair stand on his head in a rush of fury.

Jarow wanted, and should have been able to expect, men who already knew the rules on their floor. He swallowed his bile, pushed the thought away, and continued to follow Tasut.

Not one tremor shook the arm Tasut used to hold Cebo above the floor. Later that evening, a slightly unhinged man from the first floor spoke to Jarow. While relating his version of what had happened, he swore Tasut's eyes glowed red. Jarow did not correct this rumor. The more inflexible and barbaric they thought Tasut was, the better off they'd be.

They had reached the huge foyer and passed by the ugly statues. Tasut (still holding Cebo in the air by his neck) and Jarow stood with their backs to the dog cages and waited for all the first floor men to arrive. Yus was at his station and stood at attention.

Tasut had given the growling dogs the signal to be silent upon his entrance. Jarow watched Tasut drop the purple-faced Cebo to the floor. It appeared that Cebo had grown wiser in the last few minutes and was devoting his full attention to breathing.

After the men had formed a semi-circle four men deep, Jarow announced, "It has come to our attention that Cebo, the Assistant on this floor, has not fulfilled his duties as required by Barracks law.

"Cebo did not teach you to stand at attention when a Commander enters your section. Your failure to do so is punishable by flogging."

Jarow waited for the gasps of horror and protests to subside and continued, "We will not punish you for your ignorance this time. However, I suggest you listen to my instructions because your life depends on them.

"Upon our entrance, every man will stand to attention. If you value your life, you will be aware of exactly who is in your area at all times.

"If you are caught unaware again, you will receive punishment as dictated in our laws. Consider yourself warned." Jarow stood with his hands clasped behind his back, legs apart. "As Barracks Commander, Tasut feels it necessary to make an example of Cebo."

Tasut lifted the traitor again from the floor with one hand. Cebo had just regained the ability to get a full breath from his bruised throat. He clawed desperately at the hand that held him. A quick hard slap on the side of his head by Tasut, and Cebo ceased struggling.

"Contrary to what you may have heard," Jarow continued, "Tasut never throws men or their Commanders, out windows on this floor." Jarow paused for effect, "That privilege is reserved for those on the second floor because it is higher off the ground, and therefore more effective."

There was nervous snickering at this until they understood that Jarow was serious. "For traitors like Cebo, Tasut prefers an object lesson."

Tasut passed by Jarow, still holding Cebo up in the air. Jarow added the final part of his speech, "You will watch Commander Tasut's object lesson, and then return to your cots standing at full attention until a new Assistant is appointed."

In complete silence, the men watched Tasut. They were all amazed Tasut still held Cebo above the ground. They had assumed, until this moment in time, the tales about Tasut's strength and brutal directness were exaggerated.

Dez, who was the current Training Commander on the first floor, had finally joined them. His face was red and he was sweating. To Jarow's mind, Dez appeared to be resolved to his fate, whatever that would be.

Dez stood next to Jarow, reeking of alcohol and women's perfume. It was obvious where he had been. To leave the Barracks, under any circumstances, was forbidden to all the men on the first two floors. Commanders were not exempt unless they were accompanied by Tasut.

Tasut turned away from the men, with Cebo still hanging from his fist, and walked to the cages holding the enormous dogs. Jarow was sure that Cebo had no idea what was going to happen to him. Further, Jarow was confident that the idiot thought he had some sort of bargaining chip he could use to escape with his life or a lighter punishment. Obviously, Cebo did not understand Tasut at all.

When it finally dawned on the traitor what Tasut had in mind, Cebo went ballistic, using every ounce of strength to prevent the inevitable.

Tasut nodded to Yus, who grimly saluted. His thin lips were pressed together and his lantern jaw was set. Yus told Jarow previously that he did not like Cebo. Further, he had predicted correctly, that someday the "cockerel" would come to a bad end.

Yus was a grumbler by nature, so Jarow hadn't really paid much attention to him. Jarow decided that would have to change.

Undoubtedly, Yus had access to many secrets Jarow needed to hear. Yus was very grumpy, but he had been extremely loyal for fourteen years, even before the dogs had arrived.

Tasut held Cebo off the floor and walked very slowly by the twenty cages that lined the walkway. Every dog pressed it's large wet nose against the bars and sniffed the dangling Cebo.

To the men's horror, once a dog had sniffed Cebo, its yellow eyes began to glow. Deja, the huge leader of the pack, began a long, drawn-out, bone-chilling howl. Then she violently pushed against the bars of the cage, snarled, and bared her teeth. The other dogs began to do the same until the entire foyer echoed with the sounds of dogs in a murderous frenzy.

All of this drama was just that – the dogs already knew Cebo's scent. What the men didn't know was that Tasut was also motioning to the dogs the signal for 'hunt'. Jarow was grateful when Tasut used his free hand to make the chopping motion to quiet the dogs. Instead of absolute quiet, there was an occasional rumble from the throats of the dogs. Their glowing eyes were totally focused on Cebo.

Tasut dropped Cebo to the floor again. The turncoat began to hoarsely plead and bargain, "I can tell you names! I have contacts! Don't let them kill me!"

Tasut looked at Cebo, quelling him into silence with one hard stare. Without preamble, Tasut stretched out his long arm, pointed out the open Barracks door, and said, "Run."

Cebo rose from the floor, shaking. In desperation, he looked over at Jarow and Dez, sensing talking to Tasut was unwise, "Have mercy!" he begged.

Jarow ignored the plea and finished the object lesson as he informed Cebo, "The dogs will be released when the sun touches the horizon."

Cebo glanced through the bars of the cages and paled as he faced his growling, yellow-eyed death. Then, with one venomous look at Tasut, he ran out of the Barracks and into the streets of Sogo.

Deja went wild at that point, leaping into the air. Her howls sent the other dogs into frenzy and shot a surge of spine-crumbling fear up the backbones of the men.

"Those who have any knowledge of the traitor's activities are encouraged to come forth. If you do, you shall be granted a one-time amnesty and a chance to prove your worth. If it is discovered, at any time, that you withheld knowledge, you will suffer the same fate."

The somber group filed into whatever section of the first floor they belonged in, and stood at attention next to their cots holding their fist to chest in salute.

Dez, who went white at his Assistant's fate, was standing at attention by the stairs that led to the second floor.

"Go to the second floor," Tasut commanded, "and choose your new Assistant."

Dez flushed of any color, saluted with fist-to-chest, and ran up the stairs.

Jarow nodded to him as a last courtesy, already knowing his fate. Dez, in Jarow's opinion, had been stupid as well as lazy. You did not survive either of those qualities in the Barracks. By Barracks law, Dez was required to ask for a volunteer first. If no one offered, Dez had to fight the man in the highest numbered cot who was considered the best of all the men on the second floor. Jarow had seen him fight and had personally trained the man Dez was going to challenge.

If it had been any other day than today, Dez might have found someone willing to be his Assistant. The idea of becoming a Commander on the first floor might have been seen as a better alternative than spending seven years training and hoping you were good enough to become Guardian. However, today was the day after Cubes.

Jarow knew, without a shadow of doubt, his men would kill Dez the moment he asked one of them to become his Assistant. From the look on Dez's face, he knew it as well.

The first floor's Call Master, who had been found in the kitchens, was now positioned against the doorway leading up to the second floor. There was a scuffle of noise at the edge of the stairs, a yell, and Dez's body rolled down the stone steps and dropped heavily to the final landing. The Call Master checked the body. He quietly confirmed what they all knew. Dez was dead.

On their way out, Tasut stopped suddenly in front of the one man who had immediately stood to attention when he and Jarow had entered. For a moment, Jarow's heart sank.

"Your name?" Tasut demanded.

"Tad, Sir!" The young man remained at attention.

"You are now the Training Commander on this floor. Jarow will train you and you will choose your own Assistant."

Jarow did not let his surprise, or his relief, show. Tad was his brother. Jarow had enough experience to recognize that Tad would never make it to the third floor. Tasut had just saved Tad's life although Tad would not recognize it for a time.

"Yes Sir!" Tad was pale, but he stood his ground, looking straight ahead.

Tasut nodded to Jarow and left the room. The men did not dare move until commanded to do so, and Tasut had not released them from being called to attention.

Jarow silently stood in their presence. He looked calm, though inside, a private storm raged. He knew what Tasut was going to be doing, and he didn't like it.

In his mind, he tried to think who, among his previous men, would survive the next few hours. He reminded himself that it was Tasut's privilege, as their new Commander, to test them.

Jarow was also agitated because he knew that he would do something similar to these men, because of Cebo's treachery.

"Come with me," he ordered Tad. "I'll show you where you'll be staying." The brothers entered a small room on the first floor, passing the landing where Dez's body had fallen. Dez's body had been removed, but not his blood. The stain would remain as a reminder to all the men. The room they entered was a pigsty. If possible, Jarow's opinion of Cebo lowered.

"This is yours," Jarow said with disgust in his voice. "Your Assistant's room is in section one. If you're smart, you'll know what he is doing at all times and co-ordinate your efforts so each of you know what to do with your men," Jarow put his hand on his brother's shoulder.

"You will be coming with me to the second floor until some men arrive for you to train. I will send all unqualified men back down to your floor. At most, you will only be with me for one day. I will give you my training schedule so you will have an idea what to do with your men and your time."

Jarow crossed to the small wooden desk Cebo obviously used as a place to hang his clothes. "Until Tasut returns, you have complete control of these men. Be sure to use the time wisely. If my calculations are correct, half or more of them will be returning to you." Jarow grimaced, "I suggest you wait to choose your Assistant from among the new men to be chosen at auction, and keep Cebo's men in the first section as long as possible. Make them prove their worth to you." Jarow bit the inside of his cheek and made his decision, "If at all possible, choose your Assistant from men who have a mark, like yours, on their arms."

Tad looked down at his arm.

"Commander Meade," Jarow felt the need to refer to his brother by his new title, "tomorrow, the Minister of Religion will be coming to the Barracks to brand the men. You'll be required to be there. Watch for any men who have that same mark, and watch what happens very closely. What you see will amaze you. What you experience will tell you what you need to know about yourself."

Tad looked at him, "I already know about the mark. It looks just like yours. No one on this floor has one like it. I know, because I've looked." Jarow waited, staring at his youngest brother. Tad's eyes widened in understanding and he straightened up, "Yes, Sir!"

Jarow nodded his approval, "Keep looking."

*

Among the men on the first floor, total silence reigned. In the distance, on the Field of Blood where the training took place, they could hear the ring of a bell, then screams or shouts followed by the noise of battle, followed by another bell. This seemed to be repeated endlessly.

Slowly, the sun dropped westward and because of the way the Barracks had been constructed, the room became dark, although there was still light outside. No one had eaten lunch and it looked like there would be no dinner. Several stomachs had growled in disapproval, but no one dared move. They only had the gloomy room they were in, and their fear.

Tad had taken his brother's advice to use the time wisely and straightened out his room. It didn't surprise him to find moldy food, dirt huddled in every corner, and grime crawling over every surface. Satisfied for the moment, he left the room to stand with his men. His first inclination was to light a torch, but a voice in his head told him to let them sweat it out. Besides, Tasut hadn't returned yet to give the orders. Tad was intelligent enough to be afraid of Tasut.

An hour later, torchlight came down the stairs, wrapped in Tasut's fist. His torso was bare and appeared wet in the dim light; Tad hoped it was sweat, but the tang of blood hung in the air.

Jarow, who had returned a few moments before, wore a blank face. However, his lips thinned in disapproval. He knew that Tasut had just finished fighting and likely some of the men were dead. Jarow told himself again that Tasut had the right to assign his new men their cots in the order he felt they deserved. Tasut nodded to Jarow who felt perplexed and relieved.

Jarow addressed the silent, hungry men, "All of you will proceed to the second floor. Follow Commander Meade. I made arrangements with the kitchen for some food in your mess hall."

Tad was the youngest of eight children, and it felt good to be in charge for once. "Fall in, men!" The men did not need urging and each of them now knew what "fall in" meant.

Tasut stood by the door leading up to the second floor, observing the men as they followed Tad. Every man saluted Tasut, as they should. Jarow knew that Tad would have to prove himself to Tasut, but for now, Jarow was grateful that Tasut was willing to give Tad a chance.

"There were seven traitors among your men," Tasut informed him. "The others are burying them. I'm leaving for Acha in the morning with the other men and half the dogs. The Mage will be coming to the city."

Jarow followed the men after saluting Tasut. The Mage was Lyon – short for Master of the Assassins Guild Elect. It was a death sentence for more than Lyon if he was caught.

Jarow was tired and hungry. The meal originally planned had been given to the dogs, which upset the Master Chef, but delighted the yellow-eyed beasts because Tasut hand-fed them.

There was waning sunlight in the mess hall, as well as from the kitchen fires, and many torches rested in iron sconces on the wall. Jarow grabbed a piece of bread and some grapes, and went outside. He ate while he walked the short distance between the Barracks and the Villa; his mind alert as he made his way through the street, the crowd parting to let him pass.

He had guard duty at the front door of the Villa tonight. He reached the door just as the sun was setting. The sun touched the horizon and he realized Tasut would be releasing the dogs. He wasn't at all concerned that he would miss seeing the Barracks hounds ripping Cebo apart.

*

Cebo ran faster than he had ever run in his life, dignity be hanged. He knew that he had little time to make his escape. The only person he could go to for help was the man who had promised him amnesty. Nez, Minister of Religion, head of the Council of Nine and the reason he was in this predicament in the first place.

The dark grey building Nez lived in was austere on the surface but Cebo had seen inside. It resembled a squat palace. Everywhere you looked there was marble, rare antiquities, and gold filigree. The grounds surrounding the building were very plain, but well groomed, with many statues holding eternal poses over the course of an acre. Cebo ran across that acre, sweat pouring from him like rain.

In his panic, he pushed past the guards, down the hall, through the atrium, across the midnight-blue marble floor, and onto the outside balcony where Nez sat on a well-padded hardback chair, looking out over the street.

Nearby was a small glass table containing a goblet and a tall silver flagon of chilled wine. Its mirror-like surface beaded with sweat in the heat rising from the street below. In the center of the table was a large brass hourglass with the sand all at the bottom. The two guards he pushed past were at his heels as he stepped onto the balcony. They grabbed his arms and one pulled his head back holding a dagger at Cebo's throat as he strained to reach Nez.

"Tasut is back!" he gasped, breathless, sweat dripping from him.

"Release him," the Minister did not raise his voice or look at Cebo. He had watched his clumsy arrival and known since last night that Tasut had returned. The guards let Cebo go immediately. He fell to the ground and threw them a triumphant look of 'I told you so.'

"Your point, Cebo?" Nez turned empty eyes toward him.

Stunned at the coolness of his mentor's voice, he stammered, "I have until sundown to get out of Sogo before the dogs are loosed!"

"And?" Nez's expression was one of total boredom, his thin handsome face devoid of emotion. Nez swirled the wine in his glass and smelled it.

"But…" Cebo staggered under this unforeseen reaction, "you promised me amnesty!" he angrily shouted. The guards took a step forward.

"I lied," Nez informed him calmly.

Astounded, Cebo stared at Nez, "But they're going to kill me!" Cebo's voice was hoarse.

"What a remarkable grasp of the obvious," Nez's thin lips curled as he signaled the two guards. "You are absolutely right, for once."

All the implications of that statement made Cebo scream, "You knew this would happen! You knew it! You used me!" Impotent rage filled his entire being. The guards were holding his arms again.

"I'm well aware that thinking is not your strong suit, but do try to understand my position," Nez sighed and drilled his point home. "The dogs will be released in a few moments and I do not wish you to be on my premises. It is politically incorrect to have the Minster of Religion house a traitor. I'm sure you understand." Nez smiled tightly, "It might comfort you to know that the Council has bets on how long you will last."

As Nez poured more wine into the goblet, he added one of his favorite recreational drugs and swirled the liquid around, "I believe I will win. After all, we knew each other so well." Nez sneered. "I give you," he looked westward at the setting sun, "five minutes before the dogs find you, and that's if you run as fast as you did while escaping Lydia's husband." The two smirking guards removed the blubbering Cebo. "Oh," Nez called, "be sure to enjoy what is left of today."

He chuckled to himself and rose from his chair to watch the show. The sun was now barely visible. Within moments, Tasut's hounds would be released.

Nez drank deeply from his goblet, feeling the immediate rush of the drug that enhanced senses. He had timed it to perfection. Just as he could see the first dog cresting the hill, the drug enabled him to see each hair on its massive body, hear its chest-rumbling growl, and feel the animal's power and lust for blood.

He turned to the sound of his returning guards with amusement, "I fear we didn't give Cebo much of a head start. It appears I will be off by a few minutes. Perhaps he is faster than I suspect."

His green eyes turned deep violet with the drug, "You know me, ever the optimist."

Chapter 13: Orders

Three days after his father had set fire to their cottage, Talon was having a good time. The other boys were arm-wrestling and Talon was, as usual, within arms distance of Brenna.

She had insisted that Talon help her groom Mee so the little Shee would like him better. Talon was convinced that Mee already liked him because he hunted crab for her. She even sat on his shoulder a few times during the day while he drove the wagon. He didn't mind brushing her fur at the moment, but he had a sneaking suspicion that Brenna asked because she wanted to sit by him. It was a strange thought.

Talon had learned more about the world than any other time in his life. The company of other boys was an adventure.

Rube was like a talking book, Iskar bragged a lot and said things that Talon suspected had never happened, but which were entertaining, and Mal…well, Mal seldom spoke. He didn't complain about anything except the lack of food. All he knew of Mal was by observation.

He suspected that Mal had some training at one point in his life because he seemed to know, without being directly told, that there was more to this wagon ride than just getting from one place to another.

Mee was comfortably stretched out over his lap, Brenna needlessly instructing on the itchy spots, the tender spots, and on the basic care of Shees. "Mee likes to keep things," Brenna said. "Like that red leaf, but she usually likes jewelry."

Since they had left the cottage, Mee had a red leaf she placed carefully on the ground or wore in her fur either near her ears or on her tail. Talon wasn't sure how she made it stay put. It was a leaf from the tree Brenna had blown apart. In a way, it made him feel more at ease; as if the tree was still part of his life.

Mee's fur was luxuriously soft and it was actually calming to pet her. Mee was totally relaxed, her head hanging with her mouth open while resting on his right leg, and her feet hanging off his left leg. While petting Mee, Talon couldn't understand how the fur could protect Shees from the maggots that erupted from the vomit of the forest crabs but he had seen for himself it was true.

"Be really careful when you brush her tail," Brenna warned. "Mee gets very upset if you pull it, and be sure you never, ever, step on it."

Talon's ears picked up the sound of hoofbeats and he looked over at Mari who had risen from the log where she'd been sitting. To Brenna, Talon quietly said, "Let's milk the cow."

Brenna beamed at him and Mee snorted in unhappy surprise at the interruption of her grooming. In spite of this, the little Shee patted Talon's hand as if he were a particularly clever pet and leaped up onto his shoulder. The cow was by the wagons.

Lyon dismounted, but he wasn't taking the saddle off his horse. Talon felt something serious must have happened to Nyk.

"Mee likes you," Brenna said while taking his hand, "She never sat on a boy's shoulders 'til now. She knows you're going to marry me someday."

Talon felt slightly bewildered by Brenna. She said the most disturbing things out loud, as if her private thoughts were simply part of everyday conversation.

"Should I tell you about Mee?"

Talon looked at Brenna's pet and nodded. Anything else was a better subject than marriage.

"Shees are special, 'cause there aren't many left. A bad man in Sogo wanted them all killed because he was afraid they'd bite him. Mee's the most special of them all, do you know why?"

"Because she's the most beautiful?" it was a wild guess.

Pleased by his words, Mee smoothed Talon's hair while she stood on his shoulder and clucked her tongue as she petted his head.

"Mee is Queen of all the Shees, so she's really important."

A butterfly got Mee's attention and she jumped off Talon's shoulder to pursue it.

"Now she can help you protect me until we get married."

He did his best to push Brenna's casual talk about marriage away from his mind as he thought about the unlikelihood of an animal being a Queen. Just because Mee acted like a Queen, didn't mean she was one.

Brenna's assumption they would get married was disturbing. He wasn't sure if he liked Brenna well enough to marry her. She seemed to get into a lot of trouble for someone so small. Her parents were constantly telling her "no" and "don't".

He would obey his father's orders to protect her, but he wasn't going to get married anytime soon. He was going to go to the Ammonite Islands that Rube told him about, or find treasure with Iskar in Ogdones, or maybe go to Sogo and see the Guardian. He didn't think Brenna would want to do any of those things, and when he thought about it, he didn't really want her to because she could get lost or even hurt.

With a heart-felt sigh, he resigned himself to protecting the hand-grabbing little girl. He made it a point to know of her whereabouts when he first woke and last thing before sleeping. It wasn't difficult since she rarely left his sight. He was positive that life was going to be too boring to be borne; protecting her didn't seem necessary when Brenna had a mother with magic.

He got the milking pail and stool out of the wagon and placed it by the cow. He let Brenna sit on it as he put the pail under the cow's swollen udder.

Mee looked into the bucket and pulled a large grey now-slimy bug out of her mouth and threw it in the bucket, "Nice home for bug."

Brenna scowled at her pet and fetched the bug. Talon was grateful there was a second bucket and he gave Brenna a silent demonstration on milking technique while he listened intently to her parent's conversation.

"He was taken," Lyon's voice was unhappy.

Brenna was now milking the cow with Talon by her side. She giggled as Mee tried to do it, and Mee looked exasperated when nothing came out to quench her thirst. Talon showed Brenna how to squeeze the teats to squirt Mee with milk. Mee promptly pushed the bucket over and lay under the cow's udder, with her mouth open, waiting for more.

"Move, Mee!" Brenna demanded, fetching the overturned pail.

Talon was grateful the cow was placid and very steady in her temperament. He squirted Mee's mouth full of milk while he listened to the Tybars.

"Do you know who?" Mari sounded worried.

"From the tracks, I'd say Wesvalen slavers."

Talon glanced over at them while Brenna fed Mee milk.

"That seems far-fetched," Mari's brows drew downward.

"Not really," Lyon whispered as he gathered more supplies and stuffed them in his saddlebags. "Not with the crab infestation in the Rahazi Forest. Wesvalen slavers' regular route runs right through it. The infestation could be much worse than what we heard. He'll be taken to Sogo unless they find out he can run. Hopefully, I'll intercept them before that happens."

"We can send Mee to alert Tasut," Mari suggested doubtfully.

"Mee doesn't like him," Brenna suddenly spoke. Talon had been unaware that she was eavesdropping as well, and part of him was ashamed he'd been listening.

Her mother turned to them. "It doesn't matter if Mee likes Tasut. She'll do as she's told or no crab."

Mee sat up under the cow, hitting her head on the udder as she looked at Lyon, "Crab?"

"No crab," Lyon rolled his eyes at Mari.

"NO crab?" Mee sounded very offended and looked at Brenna for a possible explanation. When no explanation was offered, Mee ran over to Mari and Lyon, her thirst for milk sidetracked. Talon put the bucket in place and milked in earnest to make up for his eavesdropping.

"I think there's a better way," said Lyon. "I'll follow the tracks, and you take the boys on to Acha. I'll leave now, and with luck, I'll join you sometime before you get home." He placed a quick peck on her lips.

Mari nodded, "Take Mee for protection."

"She isn't adaptable," Lyon flatly refused.

Mee stood on Lyon's foot and held onto his leg, "Take Mee," she pleaded, with one paw on her chest in supplication. "Find crab?"

"And she's easily distracted," added Lyon, gently picking up Mee and depositing her on a nearby rock. "If one person says the word crab, she may as well not be there."

As if making his point, Mee asked, "Crab?"

Talon had listened long enough. "Take me," he offered. Maybe Lyon would allow him to help, although Tasut never did. Lyon's eyebrows rose.

Talon ignored Mee and just looked at Lyon, reading the answer in his eyes: too dangerous. Mee looked at Talon with affection, thinking that he meant to convince Lyon to take her and then back at Lyon. Mee was adept at reading body language as well. She sullenly kicked a pebble near her hind paw and chattered in Shee with her arms crossed. It was a good thing they had no idea what she was saying, but Talon felt he had a good idea because he felt the same way even if he didn't have the words to express it.

"Not this time," Lyon refused. "I have something much more important for you to do, Talon, I'm asking you to protect Brenna."

Lyon turned to his wife, "Mari, take the south road into Acha and leave the boy at Tryk's, as Tasut wanted."

The only satisfaction Talon got from it was the tone in Lyon's voice and the look in Mari's oddly-beautiful eyes. Neither of them looked happy about it. *Who's Tryk?*

Perhaps it was because Talon was more aware of what was going on, but this time as they traveled, things seemed quieter and a spirit of foreboding colored the day. Only Brenna kept up a steady stream of chatter as she sat next to Iskar. Talon wouldn't have cared except Lyon had also told him to protect Brenna.

He couldn't do anything about it because the moment Mari had ridden her mare out of sight, Iskar had picked up Brenna and put her on the wagon seat and climbed up to sit beside her. His orders were to protect her, not force her to sit with him. She was still in sight and his eyes had measured and re-measured the distance to grab her if he needed to.

Part of him was glad she was with Iskar because Brenna talked more than anyone he'd ever known. Still, he had orders. Now he had to devise a plan to earn the trust Lyon had placed in him and to obey his father's orders.

Talon was aware that as they ate breakfast, Mari's odd eyes constantly scanned the horizon. He found his own doing the same and whenever he looked at the other boys, only Mal seemed to be doing it as well. His eyes met Mal's a few times, but only for a moment.

Normally, Talon wouldn't pay so much attention, but Iskar seemed to look for excuses to touch Brenna. He touched her hair- often – smoothing back a stray curl, gently tugging her long braid, even winding one long loose strand around his finger. Then Iskar reached his arm around Brenna, as if to keep her warm. It was a warm day. Iskar acted as if Brenna was his girlfriend. He watched as Brenna pushed Iskar's arm off her shoulders.

The fact Brenna didn't want Iskar's arm there, spurred Talon to act. He calmly handed the reins to Mal, who had been watching the whole thing with Talon. Once he'd jumped off the slower moving cart, he ran to Brenna's side of the wagon. He reached his arms out to her and felt his heart lift as she smiled, jumped into his arms, and wrapped her legs around his waist as he piggy-backed her to the cart.

"Hey!" Iskar's protest fell on deaf ears as Talon sat Brenna on the cart and a smiling Mal climbed into the back as Talon took the reins. Ahead of them, Iskar pulled the wagon to a stop.

At that time, Mari rode up from behind. Talon met her eyes. He thought he saw approval there.

"Why did you stop?" she asked Iskar, who had started to climb down.

"I ..." he floundered, red faced.

"Don't stop until I tell you otherwise," she said sternly. As she passed, Iskar shot Talon an ugly look. Orders were orders he reminded himself in the face of the probability he had just lost a friend. He didn't have many to lose. He did notice that Mari did not have Iskar and himself in the same cart. He stayed with Mal and Iskar with Rube. Brenna remained in his cart.

As the sun dived into a fat grey cloud in the west, they began looking for a place to sleep. Mari had taken them farther from the road. She made a very small fire. It was a subtle but solid fact in Talon's mind that they were still trying to avoid detection.

"Where was Lyon going?" Iskar asked, looking for his own blankets in the wagon and winking at Brenna while ignoring Talon.

"When are we going to eat?" complained Mal. "Did Lyon go to get us some food?"

Talon was silent, wondering how Lyon could catch up to the slavers and what they were doing to Nyk. He wished he could have been there to help Nyk escape. He felt like he owed him after his help in the Rahazi Forest and in the Village. Talon wondered if crabs left anything after they killed someone and whether or not the Blacksmith had a family.

"Who's Tryk?" Rube asked.

"I like Tryk," said Brenna. "Stop that!" she told her Shee as Mee tugged at her dress asking for crab.

"Who is he?" repeated Rube.

"An old man," Brenna said with confidence. "He eats bugs!"

Mee who had been forlornly petting her thick beautiful tail brightened, "Bug?"

"Who is he?" Rube tried again, ignoring the beautiful Mee.

Mari returned from the back of the wagon and handed them all an apple and a large hunk of bread.

"Time to go to sleep," she ordered, leaving their questions unanswered.

Brenna had other ideas.

Chapter 14: Mek

"I want a bedtime story," Brenna insisted as they all helped to get camp ready for the night. "One about a princess or fairies."

The boys groaned except Talon, who had never heard Mari's stories. He wasn't sure if Tasut knew any. *What are fairies?*

"Not another tweaking fairy tale!" grouched Rube throwing himself on his blankets, looking disgusted.

"I don't want to hear any Vaya-love stories either," Iskar threw in, scowling.

Talon wasn't sure what a Vaya love story was, but it sounded worse than fairy tales.

"How about something scary," suggested Mal, licking the apple juice off his fingers and picking every last bread crumb off his tunic.

"I'd rather have something true," said Rube thoughtfully, "something that really happened."

"Yeah, something with lots of fighting and blood and stuff in it," chimed in Iskar.

"Very well," Mari said from the blankets she shared with Brenna. "Tonight I will tell you a legend."

"What's a legend?" asked Brenna as she petted Mee who looked invitingly over at Talon as if asking him to join in the vast pleasure of scratching her itchiest parts.

Talon had retrieved his bedroll out of the wagon and went over to the fire. He put it by Brenna and Mari's blankets and sat down. Orders were still in effect, though he was sorry to lose Iskar's friendship over it. He had to be close enough to do something if the moment ever came. He wasn't sure exactly how to protect her, but he was sure that Lyon believed he could and that gave him heart.

"A legend is a story that has been told for a very long time that is believed to have truth," Mari instructed.

"Does it have food in it?" Mal asked hopefully. Talon, who wasn't very hungry, tossed Mal his apple. Mal nodded at him and took a huge bite out of it.

"I suppose you might say there is some eating going on – after a fashion." Mari looked at the fire as she brushed Brenna's hair.

"What's it called?" asked Iskar doubtfully, he looked like he was hoping for blood and violence.

"It's called the Legend of the Mek," Mari weaved a braid into Brenna's hair as she spoke. Talon heard Brenna give a long suffering sigh. Maybe she had heard it before.

"Many years ago, there was a great city known throughout the world for its enormous wealth and knowledge."

"Where was it?" asked Mal, his interest was piqued, the apple was already half gone.

"Did they have treasure?" asked Iskar, alert now he was sure that the story wouldn't be about fairies.

"Was it Sogo?" asked Rube, trying to anticipate the end before she had begun.

"Have crab?" Mee's nose twitched.

Mari waited until they were quiet. "This city existed long before Sogo, although, in a curious way, Sogo came into being because of what happened in this city," Mari tied colored string to the end of Brenna's long braid to keep it in place for the night.

"It's real?" asked Talon, intrigued by the ring of truth he heard in Mari's tone.

"Yes, but no one dares live there," Mari's eyes looked into the dying embers of the fire, gathering her thoughts as she straightened her blankets. "Everyone get settled and I'll continue."

The boys exchanged glances and hurried to do her bidding. Now that her hair was braided, Brenna had taken her place next to Talon. Mee sprawled over Brenna's lap and with sleepy eyes, watched a small beetle crawling her way. She held out her paw, "Come nice bug."

"Where is this city?" asked Rube as Mari put away the comb and brush.

"East of Sogo, within a day's ride," Mari quickly edited the story in her mind as she went. Much of it wasn't appropriate for children. "Before Sogo became the largest city in the world, there was a Great War. The place we call Wesvalen wasn't the size it is now."

Mal looked at her with interest and so did Iskar, both being Valenese. "The name of the city vanished over the centuries. It is commonly referred to as the Lost City."

It could have been his imagination, but Talon thought Mal stiffened at the name.

"Tell us about the battle," Iskar encouraged, his mind seizing upon the idea with enthusiasm.

In this battle, the Lost City was under attack from two different enemies who had allied to destroy it and plunder its legendary wealth."

"Mamah, why do they call it lost when they know where it is?" puzzled Brenna.

"It isn't lost in the sense we can't find it but because of what happened there," Mari answered.

"This is a good story," Rube said excitedly. "I heard this from my Grandfather..." his voice died off as Mari arched her brow.

She looked at them, "Do I get to finish the story or should I tell one about fairies?"

"Fairies!" yelled Brenna who was fed up with talk of war.

"We'll be quiet," said Iskar with a warning look at the irrepressible Rube.

"Where was I?" Mari seemed bemused.

"Enemies," said Talon soberly.

Mari looked at him and nodded. "These enemies were very powerful and both armies brought terrible weapons to destroy the city. They'd developed a new kind of Trebuchet to sling Baleks into the city and cause massive damage and confusion."

"Sling what?" Brenna looked as puzzled as Talon felt.

"Baleks," answered Mal, "are huge rocks that take a block and tackle to put into a catapult or trebuchet and that's only if you bring enough men to use the block and tackle."

"What's so special about a rock?" Brenna looked disappointed.

"Unfortunately for everyone, the Baleks they had with them were not a natural part of this world," Mari continued, "They looked like rocks but weren't rocks at all. The armies didn't know that when they came to wage war against the Lost City."

"What do you mean not a natural part of this world?" Rube asked.

"What are they if they aren't rocks?" Iskar asked the question that Talon had wanted to ask.

"Eggs," the simplicity and outrageousness of this statement was confusing.

Mal looked skeptical, "Whoever heard of an egg the size of a Balek?"

"Inside each Balek," Mari continued while looking at Mal, "were a hundred creatures called Meks. According to the Legend, the two armies released their Baleks at the same time, using the newer stronger trebuchets. Mek's were released from both Baleks when they hit the inner walls with enough force to crack them open."

"What did they look like?" asked Rube in spite of the threat of a drubbing from Iskar. "Grandfather said no one knows."

Mari looked at the young faces surrounding her. Even Mee had become quiet, the bug she had been playing with dropped from her paws and she looked intently at Mari, unmoving.

"A Poolseer saw them in the pools of Dyman. She watched the hatching and counted them as they came to life," Mari affirmed. "Both armies released their Baleks at the same time and both hit their targets and cracked open. As I mentioned, inside each were one hundred Meks. In her vision, the Poolseer discovered only one of those hundred was female."

"Where did they come from?" asked Mal, his eyes intense in the firelight and his voice quiet in the dark.

Mari continued, "No one is certain, but they are thought to have come from sandpools, and the armies that brought them believed them to be a sign from heaven. Since the time of the Five who defined our land, sandpools are known to move around. All living things that come through the sandpools from other worlds are changed in some way. It's how plague crabs came to be. In their world, they live in water like normal crabs, but when they travel through a sandpool to our world, the pools somehow alter them and they become monsters."

"What happened?" pressed Iskar.

"Once they were released, they," she looked at Brenna and Talon felt she changed what she was about to say, "uh, consumed the population and then, the Legend claims, each other."

"How do they know it was the Meks that killed the people in the city and not the two armies?" challenged Rube.

"Armies keep logs of their history. I have seen a few of those logs and had an opportunity to read them. There are several logs in private libraries that date from the time of the Lost City that tell about hearing the screams of those inside its walls. When the city gates were finally thrown open, some of the citizens escaped to tell what little they knew."

"What did they see?" asked Iskar, the suspense getting to him.

"Nothing," Mari said with a smile.

Talon blinked and looked at the others who also looked confused. He wasn't familiar with stories but it seemed like an abrupt and disappointing way to end one.

"Nothing?" Iskar asked, looking around as an owl hooted. The inky black of night seemed to be pressing in on them.

"The log reports the two armies continued to bombard the city with the usual things and occasionally stopped long enough to demand surrender. They didn't know there was no one left to surrender. If they had been paying attention they would have realized that the screaming and the noises had become non-existent.

"I read one account of a man who ran out the gates earlier in the battle. He was killed for being a liar when he reported to the conquering armies everyone was dead and he alone had escaped from something he couldn't see. Something he said he could only hear. He tried to convince them he had heard strange growls and had the feeling he was being watched but he could never see anything. After they killed him, one other man who managed to escape reported he had been running in a group fleeing the city and the next moment, the others were swallowed by living shadow. He was released because they thought he was insane."

"How can a shadow live?" Rube was skeptical.

"Those men could have just been battle crazed," Iskar said but there was doubt in his voice.

"Do Seers have to tell the truth?" Mal asked bluntly. Talon frowned at him, but Mal ignored him.

Mari brushed the implication she was lying aside, "No. But more often than not, what is seen is not understood until after the fact."

"So, they can be wrong?" Mal pushed.

Mari nodded. "But the Seerbook has a powerful ward placed on it so all Poolseers must record the truth and the sandpools can't lie."

"What happened to the Meks?" asked Rube.

"The last Mek was first reported in the Seerbook at Dyman, but there have been others that have seen it. The sandpool also showed the Poolseer the other things I have told you and showed her that Meks are nocturnal and hunt in shadow."

Brenna had been quiet until then and asked, "Are those the monsters you saw?"

"*You're* the Poolseer," Talon said with awe. The other boys looked at Mari with new interest.

"Yes," she was pleased with his quick mind. She thought Rube would have seen it first.

"What did the last Mek look like?" Mal asked.

Mari thought for a moment, "Do any of you know what a leopard is?"

The boys nodded their heads. Brenna and Mee shook theirs. Mee was currently under Brenna's right arm, shivering. Her eyes were wide like she was afraid to blink.

"It's like a giant cat," Mari said looking at the boys. "Have you heard of the man they call the Guardian?" She looked at Talon who remained silent while the others nodded. "The Mek I saw was as tall as the Guardian when it was full grown. They are very skilled climbers with razor-sharp retractable claws."

Brenna looked at her mother blankly. "Retackable?"

"Retractable," Mari corrected, "like Mee's back paws."

Brenna grabbed the startled Mee from under her arm and turned her upside down and looked at one of the paws. "I don't see claws," she protested.

Mee did not appreciate this kind of treatment. "Stop!" the Shee squealed, "Rot Bren!" 'Rot' was the equivalent of calling someone stupid.

"I'm sorry Mee," Brenna let Mee's back paw go.

"Shees have very sharp back claws," Mari informed their group. "They need them for climbing up to their well-made nests."

Mee smoothed her tail, looking proud at this and began to preen her ruffled fur and fluff her cheeks. She then climbed onto Brenna's shoulder. Talon doubted Mee would have been so easily mollified if anyone else had turned her upside-down to look at her hidden claws.

"So they look like big cats?" Rube prodded, hoping for more description.

Iskar plopped down with his blankets beside Brenna. Mari noticed all the boys were now closer to the fire and most were wrapped in their blankets against the chill in the air.

"Yes and no," she answered. "In our world, they look like an armored leopard that can walk on its hind legs, only it has no fur on its head, no ears, with a tail that's furry on top and reptilian-armored underneath. It's lightning fast. So fast, all you see is a shadow because it travels in shadows and comes out when and where it's dark. They probably would have just eaten each other or small animals if men hadn't been there."

Mee being a small animal like those that Meks might have eaten let out a squeak of terror and escaped falling off Brenna's shoulder only by grabbing and hugging Brenna's head.

"Mee, let go!" Brenna complained. One white paw slid over Brenna's right eye as Mee tried to gain her balance. This proved impossible and she gave up, dropped to Brenna's lap, and frantically burrowed her head under Brenna's armpit.

"No let Mek eat Mee!" the Shee begged.

"Shhh! There isn't any Mek here!" Brenna said sternly, removing her pet from her armpit and putting her on the ground. Mee was having none of it. She clung onto Brenna's arm as Brenna tried to shake her off and finally succeeded.

Mee looked at Brenna in disbelief and giving Brenna a mutinous look, Mee pushed herself under Brenna's long skirts, her tail hanging out. Talon smiled as Brenna looked at him and said apologetically, "Mee isn't very brave."

"So there were two hundred Meks loose in the city?" Iskar asked, thinking about the chaos. It obviously sounded thrilling to him.

Mari nodded and looked up at the star-filled sky. "The large city was empty of people when the armies went in to investigate how much damage their Baleks had done. All that was left was a little blood, bones, and shredded clothes lying all over the city."

"What do you mean a little blood?" asked Iskar. "If you killed a whole city full of people, there would be lots of it."

Mari glanced at Brenna, "No one knows for sure why there was so little blood. The only reason it was even noted in the army logs was because it wasn't natural."

"What happened to the two armies?" Rube wanted to know.

Mari looked at the fire. "They foolishly made the decision to ransack the city, in spite of what they saw. By the following sundown, they had discovered the treasury and were busy looting when there were shouts and men screaming as they died wrapped in shadow. The few men who had been left to guard the front entrance to the city saw the last man disappear before their eyes in a matter of moments, his clothes dropped to the ground where he stood. Deep claw marks ran from the shoulder to the waist on his breastplate." Mari became silent, her look far away.

"What did they do?" asked Iskar.

"They abandoned the city and thereafter called it cursed. However, I found a scroll in the Sogoian library that claims seven years ago, there was a large infestation of plague crabs." Mee immediately poked her head out from under Brenna's skirts, eyes bright and good humor immediately restored.

"Crab?" she whispered in a high voice, wanting to hear more about her favorite food.

Mari nodded. "It was good news that their migration pattern at that time led to the Lost City. Reports claimed there were so many crabs you could have walked from one end of the city to the other on their backs."

Talon, with his memory of the crabs too real, shuddered at the thought of street after street of the strange green and white crabs whose insides housed ravening maggots.

"Mee!" Brenna tried to push the drooling Mee from her side. For the moment, at least, the Shee seemed to have forgotten the Mek in her obsession over crab.

"So what happened then?" Rube drew his blankets around himself and got closer to the fire. His thatch of white hair caught the firelight and made it look orange.

"All that was left were the shells," Mari said tiredly. "I imagine they're still there."

Mee stopped drooling, her voice painfully disappointed, "All crab gone?"

"Why were there so many crabs?" Talon asked.

"Why did they migrate?" Rube queried.

"In answer to Talon's question," Mari answered, "once he took office, the Minister of Religion had offered a bounty for Shee skin. Shees are the only natural enemy to the plague crabs and he had them hunted nearly to extinction." Mari nodded at Mee who had climbed up to sit on Brenna's shoulder. "As far as why the crabs were migrating, we have no answer. No one thought much about how valuable Shees were until the plague crabs threatened the city of Sogo. The migration was very odd. The crabs suddenly turned from their path toward Sogo and went to the Lost City instead."

"Did the Mek eat them?" asked the inquisitive Rube. "Is that why there are so many shells left?"

"According to Legend the last Mek is still there," Mari continued, "so the logical answer would be yes."

"Do they know how to kill it?" asked Mal, who had been very quiet and reflective throughout the story.

Something in Mal's voice made Talon look at him. His dark brown eyes looked black in the night and were haunted.

"All I know is what I learned from the sandpool at Dyman. Assuming the Legend is true, no one would be able to kill it because you can't see it before it kills you. I haven't been to the Lost City. If it's still alive, it would be centuries old."

"Do you think it's still alive?" Mal asked, his brown eyes intent on Mari's face.

Mari looked directly at him and nodded, "I have no reason to think otherwise."

Mal seemed to expect her answer.

Not wanting the children to go to bed with such a dark story alive in their minds, Mari's eyes looked mischievous for a moment. "I did hear one strange thing," Mari looked at Mee whose blue eyes were wide open in the dark. "I heard the Mek's favorite dessert is tail of Shee." She winked at Talon and missed seeing Iskar's hand as he playfully pulled Mee's tail.

Mee shot out from under Brenna's arm like a runaway comet and ran blindly over the coals left from their fire. She climbed the first tree she saw, screaming into the night, "Mek! Mek!"

Rube and Iskar dropped to the ground laughing so hard tears came to their eyes. Talon was puzzled at their reaction to Mee's fright and Mal seemed to come out of a daze, unaware of why the other two boys were rolling on the ground with laughter.

Brenna put her hands on her waist as she stood up. "You two scared her!" she said crossly.

Mee's little voice could be heard saying, "Bad Ru! Bad Is! Rot!" These words were sprinkled among what probably amounted to Shee curses.

Mari looked at the two boys, her serious tone bringing a halt to their laughter. "Shees hold grudges. The only way to gain Mee's forgiveness is heavy bribery for," Mari looked up at the tree where Mee was hissing and then chattering away in a waterfall of her own language, "a year."

"The worst thing you could ever do to Mee," added Brenna looking sadly up at the tree where Mee was smoothing her ruffled tail fur, "is step on her pretty tail. The next baddest thing is pulling it." Brenna turned to the two boys, who had laughed. "And she doesn't like to be laughed at, it hurts her feelings."

The boys, still smiling, looked up at the furious, glittering eyes of Brenna's pet Shee. Rube called up to her, "I'm sorry!" but ruined his apology by starting to laugh again. Iskar echoed the apology, but he was still smiling. Talon could tell that they were more amused by the situation and were vastly insincere in their apologies. He had the uneasy feeling Mee knew it as well. Brenna went to the trunk of the tree and called up, "They were only teasing, Mee. They didn't know better."

Mee blew raspberries at them all, and flatly refused to come down to Brenna who, after a few moments, had uncovered a fat beetle as a peace offering. Mee ran even farther up in the tree. They could hear the words "rot" and "bad".

Talon noticed Mal leaving the lighted area of the camp. He decided to gather more wood for the fire before the coals died while his mind wandered over the Legend of the Mek. *Could it really still be alive?* He looked into the darkness. The trees took on menacing shapes. The story had them all a little out of sorts. *Maybe fairies, whatever they are, would have been better.*

Mal hadn't gone far out into the darkness. Probably the idea of a Mek was as unpleasant for him as it was for Talon. Mal stood with his face toward the stars, simply staring. Talon watched him for awhile then carefully walked up behind him. "Are you alright?"

Mal turned around suddenly, a strange pain in his eyes, "Do you think there's a way to kill a Mek?"

Talon was silent, not knowing how to answer a question that had never occurred to him. Mal shook his head as if it didn't matter and brushed past Talon, not waiting for an answer. Talon thought about it. *How could you kill something you couldn't see?*

Upon returning with the wood, Talon looked over at Mal who had wrapped himself in his blankets and covered his head. He heard Mee's low chattering from the tree. Talon shook his head. Unbelievably, Rube was already fast asleep and snoring. Iskar was trying to get comfortable on rock-hard ground. Mari handed Talon his blankets. "Your bed is between Brenna and Iskar."

So, she had noticed Iskar's interest in Brenna.

"I'll take the next watch," Talon offered, feeling grateful and not sure why he felt that way.

Mari looked at him and reached out her hand and gently touched his cheek, "I would like you to get some sleep tonight. I'll need you tomorrow."

"I'll go check on the animals," he told her.

What he really wanted was to gather a handful or two of rocks for his sling. He didn't go far to get them. Once he had enough, he placed them to the right side of his blankets. *It's always better to be prepared.*

Talon was half in his blankets when he looked over at Mari who sat by the fire, looking out into the night, her mind obviously far away. He knew she had no intention of sleeping. She looked very beautiful in the flicker of the campfire. Brenna was probably going to be as pretty as her mother. He went to sleep with that idea firm in his mind.

The next day Talon woke and from habit rolled from his blanket into first position. He closed thought to all but the forms that Tasut assigned him to practice daily. At final position, he exhaled. When his eyes opened, he found everyone in camp, except Rube who was still asleep, looking at him. Mari's eyebrows were raised and she had a slight smile on her face.

Brenna clapped, "Do it again!"

He self-consciously put his bedding away in the back of the wagon. *Didn't anyone else do forms*? He felt embarrassed that he had been the only one.

Mari had come over to the wagon to get some eggs from the chickens. He kept his eyes on the ground, feeling his cheeks heat.

"You did your set of forms very well. I want you to teach them to the other boys."

Surprised, he looked up. "I'm not very good, but I'll try."

Mari's bi-colored eyes narrowed, "Who told you that you weren't good?"

He remained tight-lipped.

Mari nodded as if she knew the answer. "None of these boys know them. Will you help me?"

He nodded, hoping he could do a good job. He'd never had to teach anyone anything before.

"It's only while we travel," she said. "First form will be more than enough for them – except, perhaps, Mal."

He had subconsciously made notes about the other boys and knew he could spar with any one of them and win. Since he had never sparred with anyone but Tasut and never come even close to winning, it was a singular pleasure to realize that fact. He felt more confident and began to pack the other supplies away into the wagon.

Chapter 15: Wrath of Mee

Mee, Mari noticed with apprehension, appeared to be her normal self. Perhaps a little bit self-satisfied as she meticulously groomed her tail for the day and sat on the wagon seat looking at the group. Her blue eyes were directed at the two boys that Mari knew wouldn't be forgiven without heavy bribery ala crab. The situation was worse than the guilty parties could comprehend. She would have to keep a careful watch on Mee.

Mari was in the process of brushing Brenna's hair when her suspicions were realized. Rube sat up in his blankets and turned toward them with a sleepy smile. Half of his head had been relieved of hair, clear down to his pink scalp.

"Good morning Rube," Mari said as she re-braided Brenna's hair.

Brenna took one look at him and looked at Mee while Mari got the pans to cook their breakfast.

Rube nodded a greeting and then, as was his habit, he ran his hand over his head. Obviously Mee had watched this behavior. She had chosen her revenge well. Rube looked at them, his eyes wide and his hand rubbing over the surface of his now half-bald head. Mee sounded like she was snickering as she smoothed the tufts on the tips of her ears.

Brenna curiously asked her pet, "Did you do that?"

Mee blinked, trying for innocence but failing as her eyes glittered. "Mek did."

Mari knew it wasn't over. Mee would have done something to Iskar as well. For Iskar, it would be more serious since he had pulled Mee's beloved tail. Mari had witnessed one Shee kill another for this offense. Mari made breakfast while keeping watch on the Shee. Normally, Mee would have been off catching breakfast in the form of bugs, yet Mee remained seated on the wagon, her eyes intent on Iskar.

The second part of Mee's revenge took place when Iskar pulled on his boot. The stench did not strike until his bare foot was ankle high in the deposit Mee left inside. Iskar yelled and pulled it off, gagging at the smell while he vigourously scrubbed the offal off onto the ground. He shot a venomous look at Mee and angrily threw his soiled boot at the Shee. Mari's eyes darted to the Shee to see if there was to be any retaliation.

Mee calmly yawned and stood on his boot with blue eyes glittering.

"Mee," said Mari in a warning voice.

Mee sniffed at him and Mari relaxed as the offended Shee dashed off into the woods. She was probably headed for the nearest water to look for crabs. Mari dished up the eggs and ham she had cooked over the open fire. She was eating her own breakfast when the Shee returned.

Rube thought the incident hilarious, including his own half-bald head, until Mee, who had been intently watching him, placed a large, crunchy beetle in his meal when he put his plate down so he could pull his boots on.

He found half of the beetle still wiggling and then lost the first half of his breakfast. He continued to gag off and on for the next few hours.

"I'd look for river crab if I were you," Mari told the afflicted boys as they cleaned up after breakfast. "Her tricks will continue until you make it up to her."

"What'd I do?" asked Rube, rubbing his half-bald head.

"You laughed at her," Brenna informed him as her mother shook out the blankets and they all packed the rest of their personal belongings away.

"How can I clean it out?" asked Iskar who had fetched the offensive boot and held it arms length away with his nose plugged.

Mari's nose wrinkled at the noxious odor. "You can't. The boot will have to be thrown away."

Iskar sent an evil look at the Shee who was the picture of serenity as she petted her tail and made little noises as if to comfort it.

"Mee ate garlic bulbs, stink bugs, which she really doesn't like, and wild onions just to make it worse," Brenna informed Iskar.

"How do you know that?" Talon asked.

"Tryk pulled her tail once. After he cleaned up the mess she made in his shoe, he asked Mee what she ate and she showed him." Brenna giggled, "Tryk had to bury his boots twice because she dug them up the first time, put dead fish in them and put them under his bed. He didn't know she was that mad at him. Now he gives her crab every time she goes to his house. He built a special crab cage just so she can eat some whenever she comes. She loves Tryk!"

Rube had run off to the water edge and found a crab almost immediately. It was fairly large and certainly looked like it would fill up one little Shee. "What do I do now?" he asked Brenna as Mee eyed him with whiskers twitching at the smell of the crab.

"Put it behind your back, tell her you're sorry and then give it to her," she advised. "If she takes it, it's a good thing. If she doesn't you have to try again, but with a bigger one."

Mari carefully watched as Rube took it to the Shee. Looking crestfallen he said, "I'm sorry Mee, I didn't know that I hurt your feelings. I forgot how smart you are. I won't forget again." He laid the crab down on the wagon seat beside her.

Mee accepted his offering and bit off the crabs pincers, ripped off the top shell, and finished it before he could even think about what else to say.

"Will she let me pet her?" Rube asked cautiously.

Mari shook her head. "Maybe later."

"Hey, Shee, look what I brought you!" boasted Iskar, dumping the two large crabs he found before her. Mee looked at them scuttle frantically around looking for water. Mari stepped forward when Mee did what no one had ever seen her do. Mee kicked the crabs off the wagon seat onto the ground and looked directly at Iskar, "Bad! No good!" Inside her throat she made a noise that made Mari step between them.

"Iskar," she warned, "back away and don't go near her again."

He went pale, backed slowly away and tried to ignore the threatening noises Mee made every time he got near her after that.

"I told you Shees hate it when you pull their tail!" Brenna shook her head at Iskar and took his hand as if in commiseration for his misery.

Mari didn't bother scolding Mee for her behavior because there was no reasoning with the offended Queen.

Mal and Talon looked at each other and were grateful they didn't have the wrath of Mee to contend with.

Breakfast was over, everything was packed, and their company was assigned what they would be riding in or on. Talon and Mal were in the first wagon, with Mal driving. Rube was driving the cart with Iskar, a now bare-foot passenger, just behind the wagon. Much to Talon's relief, Mari rode the mare with Brenna sitting behind her.

As they left the camp, Mee came up to the moving wagon Mal was driving. Her little cheeks were puffed out and Talon felt Mal freeze and hold his breath as Mee hopped up on the seat.

"Tal," she said and removed what looked like a large pebble from one cheek and put it on the wagon seat next to him. It looked like a raw nugget of gold. "Mal," she said and placed one for him there as well. She petted both of their arms and said "Good," and then scampered off. They looked at each other and Mal, for the first time, smiled and asked, "Think there's more?"

Talon shook his head, "We have to wipe them off before we touch them." Talon used the edge of his tunic to wipe the Shee slobber from their nuggets as the wagon rolled forward over the hard-packed road. Mari and Brenna rode ahead of them.

It appeared that Mee was never going to forgive Iskar for pulling her tail. Talon noticed that whenever Iskar came near Brenna, she made low gurgling noises and she'd say, "Bad Is!" as her blue eyes glittered. Iskar would freeze for a moment and slowly back away. Talon thought Iskar wise to do this. He was positive that Iskar wouldn't enjoy dissolving into a puddle. He wasn't exactly sure why he felt so good about the situation.

*

Acha turned out to be mostly valley and forest situated between a long rocky mountain range on the west called Lomond and another called the Mamatch Mountains that sat between Acha and Teris.

At least that was the geography Rube was describing to Talon as they walked alongside the wagon.

"The Rahazi ends near the Acha border. A smaller forest, I think they call it Erisha, is where the Achaites get their famous wood for bows. In ancient times, they held Ryke festivals."

"Where'd you get all those scars? Did you have an accident?" Talon had noticed them when Rube had pointed west.

"Something like that," he said, looking at the scars, a slight frown on his face.

Feeling like he had stumbled onto the path of friendship he asked, "What's a Ryke?" Talon looked at the peaks in the far distance, their caps still covered with snow. He was amazed at Rube's vast knowledge of the world. If he had been watching his traveling companion, he would have noticed Rube's sudden nervous behavior.

Rube shrugged, "A bird."

"Do you know who Tryk is?" Talon was speculating that it had to be someone fairly innocuous or Brenna wouldn't have confessed her fondness for the man. *Who is Tryk and why leave me with him?*

Talon looked at Iskar. He liked him although he did have a tendency to tease. Talon had been getting a great deal of ribbing from the other boys because he didn't really know how to tease. Tasut didn't tease or joke.

He was surprised to find he enjoyed teaching the others first form. Even Brenna and Mari had joined in.

Talon enjoyed the scenery. All around them was farmland as far as the eye could see. Sometimes in the distance, you could see a farmer, or a small house and a barn but not much else. *It's better than monsters.* But hour after hour of it became tedious. He was grateful that there were others with him on the trek. He wasn't sure about Mal yet. If he had a favorite 'friend' among the others, it would be Rube. There was just something about him that made you feel he was completely reliable. He looked better now that Mari had evened up the hair cut Mee had given.

Iskar claimed Rube was boring but Talon, hungry for knowledge, soaked it all in and found himself hoping that Rube would be with him at least part of the day so his questions could get answered.

Iskar was a fun, very physical person. He relied on his legs, hands, and actions to get him through whatever it was he wanted to accomplish. Although Iskar pretended it didn't matter, Talon knew it bothered him that Mee was still hostile toward him. Mostly, Talon thought, because it kept him away from Brenna. Iskar tried to make up to Mee every single day, mostly when he thought no one was looking, but Mee would not accept anything that he gave her. Not once.

There were times that Talon thought about Nyk. He hoped Lyon found him and they were on their way back. It seemed years ago that they left the burning cottage. He wondered about Tasut and when he would see him again. And then there was Brenna. He wasn't sure what to think of her. He thought he liked her but at times she was ex-asperating. She asked "why" so much that his ears felt tired. He liked how she trusted him although he was of two minds about that. He gave her rides on his shoulders, and when Iskar challenged all of the boys to races, Talon insisted Brenna take part in them. She smiled her thanks but it wasn't necessary, he knew what it was like to be left out.

Just when it seemed like they were on the road to forever and in no hurry to get there, they finally turned onto a different road. It was a stretch of one's imagination to call a deer path a road, but they followed it as Mari directed and trees began to thicken. About a mile in, there was a small shack.

To Talon, the main part of it looked like an outbuilding of Tasut's. It was a fairly common design in Acha. It looked like a small barn chopped in half lengthwise, with several smaller additions attached to it in a hodge-podge of confusion. Thrusting up from this like brick fingers, were several smoking chimneys.

Mari dismounted from the wagon and told Mal to keep the reins in hand. "I'll be right back," she promised. She walked into the house and within two minutes, Brenna announced, "I'm going to go see Tryk."

Talon's mind brought up Lyon's last words to him: "Talon, you guard Brenna." He felt almost grateful about his responsibility because it meant he could follow her into the haphazard collection of boxes. Talon handed the reins of the wagon to Rube, dismounted, and followed her.

Naturally, there was mutiny among the boys. Rube obediently stayed behind while the rest of the boys followed Talon into the house. Once he entered, Talon ascertained that Brenna was in no danger, at least any danger that Talon could recognize.

Tryk's house was a fascinating cubbyhole kind of dwelling, with odd machines of various sizes and in various stages of disassembly.

The machines lay amidst mountains of parchment scattered on top of and stuffed underneath furniture of all descriptions.

The boys followed Brenna through a maze of such oddities. They were hard pressed to keep their hands to themselves. There was such a curious collection of knobs, levers, and things that begged to be touched, pulled, or merely examined. In fact, Mal pulled Iskar away from something that looked quite intriguing. It was a ball that lifted into the air and changed color.

Voices were ahead of them. One was obviously Mari's and the other had to be Tryk's. They came upon them just as Tryk crawled out from under an enormous wooden…whatever it was. All Talon could see of Tryk upon this first meeting was his bony south end followed by a thin waist, slender shoulders and at last, a fuzzy brown-grey head with a bald spot right on the back. When he turned to face them, Talon grabbed Brenna's hand and pulled her back. Iskar was on his other side, effectively blocking even more of her from the crazy-looking old man. His face was shocking.

Brenna ducked under their arms to run and hug him. Mari simply smiled at the boys, "This is Tryk."

Talon found it hard not to stare at the man called Tryk. His face looked like an old wizened apple with a sizeable scar running from eyebrow to chin diagonally across his face. This disfigurement left one of his eyes permanently blind with its dead iris white and freakish.

Tryk swung Brenna up in the air and returned her hug.

"Where's Lyon?" he asked Mari, holding Brenna with one arm. Talon noted the man was stronger than he looked.

"He went to find someone," Mari said quietly. Talon was sure Mari could have said more. Perhaps she would when she was alone with Tryk.

Talon had been told to guard Brenna, from what he had no idea, but it didn't appear to be from this odd old man who seemed harmless and fascinating. Tryk put Brenna on the ground.

"Where's Mee?" Tryk asked. As if on cue, Mee came scampering in right up to the old man and extended her paws as if she were a small child waiting to be picked up, "Crab?"

Tryk didn't seem offended by her request. Quite the opposite, he was delighted.

"Iskar," Mari said, "I'll get some hooks and you take Mal and Rube fishing. There's a small stream out back. I want you boys to catch some for supper tonight. Talon, you stay here with Brenna." The boy's left and Talon noticed Iskar turned around with a smile and motioned for him to follow but Talon regretfully shook his head. No matter how much he was tempted to go with them he would obey orders to guard Brenna.

"Of course my dear Mee," Tryk was saying as he lifted the beautiful Shee and put her on a long table nearby. "But first you must earn your crab." Mee stood on the table, preening, while Tryk pulled up a three-legged stool that had wheels on each leg so he could glide across the floor.

Mee patted the ugly man on his head with her paws and then sat perfectly still on the table, expectantly looking at Tryk. The old man took an odd metal thing with two prongs that opened and touched it to the sides of Mee's jaw line. He wrote something down on parchment and he had her open her mouth. He cocked the eyebrow on the side of his head where his good eye was and pointed at the table.

Mee crossed her arms and said "Humph!" in her high childish voice. This, Talon had learned, was a sign of stubborn refusal.

"Come now," Tryk said with some exasperation, "spit them out."

Brenna giggled. "I told you he'd see. C'mon Mee, let him have them."

"No crab until you do, pretty one," Tryk threatened as he held a wooden cup in front of her mouth.

This threat would likely make any Shee unhappy but to be crabless for Mee was to be in deepest abject misery. Mee immediately spit out two large gold nuggets and several smaller ones.

Tryk shook his wizened old head. "I wish I knew how she did that."

It seemed to Talon that Tryk was talking to himself.

"The conclusion I've come to is that the poison she produces somehow changes the stones and turns those silly river pebbles into gold," he continued muttering as he checked her tall ears with their tufts. Surprisingly, Mee tolerated this until he seemed satisfied. Of course, this could be due to the fact that Tryk was muttering such things as what an honor it was to examine the most beautiful Shee he had ever seen and other such flattery.

As he put his various instruments away, Mee clasped her raccoon-like paws together as if she were going to pray and in her most pleading way asked, "Crab?"

"Out back," Tryk said with a nod toward what must have been the back way since Mee dashed off that direction. He could hear her cracking the shell from her feast within seconds.

Seeing Talon's curiosity Tryk explained, "I have a small tank in back that I keep well stocked for Mee. She comes over fairly often when she's in Acha." Tryk carefully wiped off the gold nuggets, "Thankfully, her saliva isn't poisonous enough to kill you unless she bites something, but it can make you ill."

Mari returned from the back, smiling and shaking her head as Tryk placed the gold nuggets in a little box near one of the work tables and finished writing notes in a well-worn notebook tied with yellow ribbon.

"She's such a fascinating little creature!" Tryk smiled at Mari. "I suppose you wouldn't consider letting her stay with me for…oh, say a fortnight?" Tryk looked out toward the noise of crabs being eaten.

"We're willing if Mee is. You know that," Mari answered, "but Mee has a mind of her own and knows her own way home. Although I doubt you have enough crab here to suit her."

Tryk, who seemed well aware that Mee was a notorious glutton when it came to crab laughed, "I doubt we have enough crab in the whole of Acha to please that beautiful creature."

"Tryk, we have a favor to ask," Mari's face became serious.

He turned his unprepossessing face toward her with interest. "Somehow I suspected this wouldn't be a social call."

Mari put her arm around Talon's shoulders. "This is Talon. He needs a place to stay while he is in Acha until other arrangements are made."

Tryk focused on Talon, who stood perfectly still. Talon knew Tasut had ordered Lyon to leave him here, but he'd hoped Mari would forget that part of it so he could go on with the others. Somewhere deep inside he felt the pain of being left behind, but he didn't let it show. Brenna, however, became hysterical.

"He's mine!" She grabbed Talon's hand, "I'm not leaving him!" Brenna dropped to the ground and circled Talon's legs with her legs and arms and held on as tight as she could.

Mari looked at Tryk who gave a slight nod but kept his good eye on Talon. She pulled a frantic Brenna from her death grip on Talon's legs. He stood helpless, not knowing what to do or say as Brenna wailed for him. He knew what it was like to feel lonely but he couldn't understand Brenna's complaints, her parents obviously loved and cared for her.

"Talon," Mari said brusquely, "we'll be coming to see you, be prepared."

The tightness around his heart lightened and he took a breath. *Be prepared.* That meant they wouldn't leave him here permanently. A few moments after they disappeared out the door, Brenna ran back in, her grip around his waist so tight that he couldn't breathe for a moment.

"I came back to kiss him goodbye," she told Tryk, who studied her like he had the Shee. Talon looked helplessly at Mari who stood at the doorway, arms folded.

"Kiss?" Mee's voice piped up from under the table with renewed interest. "If kiss, get more crab?"

"You flawed delight!" Tryk laughed, "You ate that whole tank full?"

Mee hung her head with a long-suffering sigh as if the meal had been days instead of moments ago, and nodded.

Tryk shook his head, "I've never met a Shee with such obsession. I wonder if it has anything to do with how she was created?" He looked over at Mari who shrugged. Mee, in the meantime, was waiting for his word on whether kisses would earn her more crab. Talon could hear the regret in his voice as he said, "No my beautiful Mee, no more crab, too much is not good for Shees. You must go home now."

Mee shuffled out the door, head down to the ground, stomach only slightly bulging.

Talon asked, "How come she's not fat?"

Tryk looked at Talon, "Shees have a very fast metabolism. I estimated that she ate four times her weight one day."

Brenna, who had released him, dried her tears and dragged a stool over to Talon and climbed on top of it. She turned his head and puckered her lips, overbalancing the stool so he had to hold her in place. With an angelic smile, she planted a big wet kiss on his cheek.

"That means your mine," she said with a shy smile.

Mari sighed. "That's enough Brenna. Talon, take her back to the wagon."

He blinked in surprise and touched the wet spot her lips left as she dismounted from the stool. Dragging Talon by the hand, Brenna left the room. Mee raced ahead of them saying, "Crab! Home!"

Talon was unsure why Iskar said kisses were supposed to be wonderful. It was wet and Brenna's lips slicker than he had thought. Mari followed them out of the house in a few moments and she mounted her mare.

"Hand her to Rube," Mari instructed Talon as she reined her mare to the front of their small entourage. Brenna held up her arms to him and he lifted her, only to find she wouldn't let go of his neck once he tried to put her on the wagon.

"Brenna!" Mari had enough and Brenna knew it by the tone in her voice. She kissed him again, this time a quick wet kiss on his eyebrow. He quickly put her on the wagon seat.

"Here's your bedroll," Iskar said and chucked it at him. He didn't miss the angry look Iskar gave him or the feeling behind the throw. Mal tossed him his small rucksack of clothing without the malice.

Talon stepped back and watched the wagon and cart roll away. It was hard not to feel left out as he watched them drive into the dusk.

Brenna had moved from the seat to the back of the wagon and waved at him until he couldn't see them anymore. He wondered who would guard her now.

He was surprised that he was sad she was gone, but it wasn't just her, it was all of them. Even Iskar, who would probably like him if it wasn't for Brenna.

Chapter 16: Fara

Brenna sulked all the way home and Mee wasn't much better. Mee sat at the rear of the wagon and looked longingly back at Tryk's far longer than Brenna expected and said things like, "Must have crab. Need crab. Tryk need Mee to eat crab"

The more miles they went, the lonelier Brenna felt.

That night, after the boys were asleep, Brenna asked her mother, "Why can't Talon live here and be with me?"

Her mother paused for a long moment. "Talon is very obedient to his father's wishes."

Any form of the word "Obey" made her feel mutinous and eager at the same time. Brenna settled for giving a loud sigh as she leaned against her mother and watched the water ripple across Belly Band Lake.

An hour later, her father had returned and her parents went into the house. Brenna knew it would be almost impossible to get her mother's attention until they had talked about whatever it was that was keeping her father away.

Rube and Iskar decided to take an early morning swim and Mal fought them both off when they tried to throw him in the water. Her parents came out of the house and everyone had breakfast.

Right after they ate, her father left with a still-dripping Iskar, a sun-burned Rube, and a dry but still unhappy Mal.

Brenna hated to be left behind and her mother knew it. She felt her mother's comforting hands on her shoulders.

"When your father returns from Utak, he'll bring the daughter of a friend," her mother said quietly. "Her name is Fara Chel."

"Does she like me?" Brenna asked anxiously.

Mari smiled, "I'm sure she will."

The moment Fara came, the fair-haired girl took Brenna's hand and Brenna took her to her heart.

Blonde, pert, and pretty, Fara accepted Brenna with a shy smile and Brenna took it from there. Brenna and Fara were inseparable for the entire day Fara stayed with them.

"Tell me more about Talon," Fara said when Mari left them alone. Brenna felt her heart lighten and she told Fara everything.

She was finishing with, "…and his papah is a mean giant that makes Talon do lots of chores and they lived in the woods by this great big tree that I…"

"Brenna?" her mother's sharp voice came from behind them. Fara actually jumped at the sound.

"Why don't you ask Fara some questions about herself instead of talking about your other friends?"

Brenna looked guiltily at Fara, who was staring at the floor, red-cheeked and somehow looking nervous.

"In fact, why don't the two of you come out and we'll make cookies?"

Brenna thought her mother made Fara nervous. She asked her lots of questions, but Fara kind of acted like Mal. Like she had a secret. Brenna thought maybe Fara would tell her the secret, but her mother kept them busy. Then it was time for Fara to go.

"I'll write you!" Fara promised, waving back and looking rather disappointed that she couldn't stay. Both of them had begged her parents, but her mother wouldn't yield.

Brenna's gift, a flower Brenna made for her, was in Fara's other hand and she kept waving to Brenna until the wagon went around the bend.

"Time to leave," her mother said. "Go get packed."

Brenna felt her temper rise. "You promised I could see Talon!"

"Where is it you think we're going?"

On the way to Tryk's Brenna turned to her mother, "How do I write a letter?"

"Tell me what you think about Fara," her mother said.

Brenna smiled, "She's my best friend, after Talon and Iskar."

"What did you two talk about?"

Brenna thought for a moment. "Talon."

"What else?"

Her mother seemed nervous and Brenna wanted to soothe her. "Just Talon. Fara asked me lots of questions about him."

"If you see Fara again, talk about something else."

"But why?"

"Talon is your best friend, right?"

Brenna nodded.

"Talon is very very special and I think it would be best to never mention him."

"Keep him secret?"

Her mother nodded.

Brenna thought about it. She liked the idea of Talon being her very own secret. She'd never had one before. "I don't think Fara would mind if I had a secret, cause she has one."

Her mother stared at her. "How would you know that?"

"Cause she acts kind of like Mal. He has a secret too."

"Do you know what either secret is?"

Brenna shrugged.

"Did someone tell you this?"

"Vaya."

"Who?"

"My doll."

Her mother seemed tense.

"I lost her."

"Your doll?"

Brenna sadly nodded. She almost told her mother that she'd given her doll to Fara, but that was Fara's secret and she had promised to never tell.

She even told Fara that she didn't think Vaya would talk to anyone else, but Fara's face was so full of longing that Brenna had surrendered Vaya. She hoped she could see Fara soon and ask her how Vaya was doing.

"When can I play with her again?" she asked her mother. "I want to talk to her some more."

"So would I. We'll see what happens," her mother said. Her voice sounded odd so Brenna looked at her, but she didn't know what the tone meant, only that it sounded like it always did when her mother wanted to do something to somebody.

Chapter 17: Field of Blood

Comfortably seated in his favorite chair Nez Shavae read the book in front of him. The Book of Benamii.

"If you do not study history," his former teachers told him, "you are doomed to repeat it."

He turned the pages of the dry tome because he had no intention of repeating mistakes; his true intention was to dominate the world from Sogo. His eyes refocused on the book of scripture before him. He was weary of its repeated call to Sogo to repent.

According to Sogoian religion, over which he ruled, the Book of Benamii was blasphemy. The rebellious zealots claimed it was a holy book written by several prophets who in writing claimed they had written it at "Father of All's command".

Nez believed them – to a point.

Years ago, he had confiscated this part of the forbidden book while his men administered justice to its owner. On its last page he read about his own demise: "…and the one eye shall beware the Shee for therein lies his death…"

The tantalizing sentence ended there, the remainder of the book had been tossed on the fire. His continued search to find the other half or, preferably, a whole copy, was fruitless. He'd perhaps been too insistent that anyone found with the book in their possession would be immediately executed and their copy burned in the Temple of Veesh.

Once he read that passage, he had immediately offered a generous bounty on Shees. Their skins were very valuable so he had no problem procuring them from bounty hunters. He had an entire room nearly filled to the rafters with the skins, and another room filled with gloriously silken soft Shee-tails waiting for the right market.

In spite of the warning in the book, he found an almost obsessive interest in the contents of those rooms and he kept returning, time and again, to touch the skin of his enemy as if to reassure himself that Shees were not a threat any more.

It was an unfortunate side effect that the demise of the Shees caused a surge in the plague crabs. Seven years ago, when the plague was moving toward the city of Sogo, the people had insisted he stop the killing of Shees.

To gain favor, he had publicly announced that killing Shees was now forbidden. Those having skins in their possession would be offered a one-time amnesty if they would bring the pelts to his mansion and turn them in. Thereafter, the hunters would be heavily taxed. He won on both counts. The hunters turned in the pelts, which he would sell for a vast profit - someday, and he collected the heavy fines incurred by lawbreakers. Ironically, Shees had made him a very wealthy man, which in turn had cast him into a more firm position of power.

It gave him great satisfaction that there were no more Shees outside the west wall, where in times past there had been hundreds. It appeared that his public announcement rescinding his bounty came too late. Shees would never be able to return to the numbers that they had been and the plague crabs seemed to prefer the quiet of the Rahazi Forest.

Thankfully, the plague had bypassed Sogo in preference of the Lost City. Whatever curse inhabited the ruins of that forsaken city had killed them according to reports. To capitalize on this good fortune, he made the outrageous claim that he was personally responsible for the change the plague crabs made in their destination and the people, grateful for any good news about the monsters, cheered him for it.

Shees had not come out of the Rahazi Forest for many years, but he knew there were a few Shees in the city. The High Priestess Saro had one; a temporary setback for his plan to align himself with her. He was positive that could easily be remedied in the future, when the timing was right.

He had recognized himself in the Book of Benamii as "the one-eyed beast." The definition wasn't very flattering, but accurate. His forefathers had chosen as their flag, a single eye set in the center of three vertical stripes. The left stripe was black and indicated power, the middle was yellow and stood for glory, the right stripe was red and originally symbolized mortality with honor. He had privately changed it to immortality. It was his right, he reasoned, because he was the last of his bloodline, being an only child.

However, he smiled at the thought there was now an alternative. He had finally found a natural enemy other than man to decimate Shees. He had heard for many years that there were odd sounds like people screaming or someone in distress outside the west wall of Sogo. He had sent the militia to investigate only to be told the same thing. They went to the site and found no one, but they had confirmed hearing strange, eerie screams. Nez went to investigate for himself.

Once there, accompanied by two guards, he saw a strange lizard. At first, it was simply a very common looking reptile with the browns and greys of its kind. It had a thin green stripe racing down its back and another edging the flap of skin around its head that flared out. It caught his eye because it was running on its hind legs chasing a rabbit. The lizard sprang at the rabbit, grabbed hold of the fur on its neck and bit hard, nearly severing it. He watched in morbid fascination as the lizard used its jaw like a snake, unhinging and then swallowing the rabbit.

He had returned home later that evening to scry the truth from the private sandpool in his house about the lizards. He discovered the strange lizards had come from a sandpool but were not venomous. He ordered his men to return to that area and trap more of them. In all, they returned with thirty-five of the lizards and they were now out on his grounds. The lizards weren't picky eaters.

All is well he thought, closing the book on the prophecy and placing it under the cushion where he sat. He liked sitting on the holy words the prophet Benamii wrote. He had personally ordered the prophet Benamii killed and felt a small sense of satisfaction each time he used the chair.

He had a great deal to accomplish today; he rang the bell and his nameless servant came in, his eyes staring at the floor.

"Is everything ready?"

"Yes, Minister, the 500 militia you requested are standing outside the gate, waiting for your orders."

"I'll be there shortly." Nez dismissed the man. Today, he was going to the Barracks and test the mettle of the Barracks Commander, one of two enemies still left in Sogo.

*

Jarow stood looking over the exercise yards from North Tye, a short tower that sat at the end of the Field of Blood. He saw Tasut enter the field from the side door reserved for the men on the third floor.

While puzzled as to why Tasut's men were dressed in full battle gear, he felt absurdly grateful that Tasut had interrupted the training exercises. It had been futile to get the men from the first floor into fighting shape and Jarow had lost his temper more than once. Tad, his brother, had given him several looks of puzzlement. Probably because he felt Jarow would have more control over his emotions.

Today, he didn't.

Jarow nodded at Tad who already had the signal flags in hand; they both understood that Tasut's men were allowed to have the field anytime without warning.

Tad waved the signal flags and blew the signal trumpet and the inept men stopped fighting. Jarow signaled 'clear' with his right hand and his men left the field so Tasut's men could have their time. There was one ray of light these days that was more than welcome, and that was the fact Tasut had forbidden the general population to watch their trainings. He wasn't sure if he could tolerate what the incompetence of these men would do to his reputation as a Commander. The least of it would be more attempts on his life on the street.

The very men who were entering the field today in full battle gear had complained about the training Jarow had given them; he was willing to bet they didn't complain within Tasut's hearing. They were as well-trained a group as he'd ever had, and he watched them gather to the field with a measure of pride. He had trained them hard, but Tasut was still harder and they would get no mercy from him. Ever.

Jarow stood with his face to the sun and his thoughts were scrambled. He was glad to watch his former men. He had Tasut's permission to do so whenever he chose because Tasut trusted him.

Today he'd felt a wave of disgust each time he looked down at the field at the clumsy laziness of the new men. He grimaced at the memory. If Cebo hadn't already been dead, Tasut would have eventually killed him anyway because he hadn't fulfilled his responsibility in the Barracks. His men were woefully inept except at the most basic tasks. At least six men didn't even make one mile on their first morning run, and on the second floor they had to run six miles every morning. If they had been properly trained, they would be doing it while carrying weapons and wearing armor.

Earlier, he had tried re-training them on the basic weaponry, whips and blade slings. Their bungling had cost him his temper and one man's left ear that the surgeons were trying to reattach. Jarow wasn't sure he wanted the man back even if they could sew his ear back on. It hadn't worked when it was still attached to his empty head.

Two more of the men were busted back down to section one on the first floor for a total of sixteen men demoted, so far. He knew there would be more if today were any indication of their abilities. The sad story concerning these men had to be told to Tasut.

Tad had done what he could with the men who were willing to work with him during Cebo's stint as Commander. The rest were simply

Cebo's mistakes and most, if not all, would pay with their lives. During the first month of being under Jarow's direction, most began to realize how much Cebo's lay-back attitude would cost. The first man killed had been one of Cebo's cronies. Jarow made every one of the men he was responsible for dig the grave, each taking a turn with the shovel until it was dug. It was a very sobering, life-altering experience for them to see their future in the large graveyard next to the Barracks.

Jarow had been furious two years ago when he saw Tad training out on the Field of Blood. Tad was one of those rare men who actually volunteered to be part of the Barracks. Jarow was grateful to Tasut for choosing Tad to be a trainer rather than die at Cubes. His brother was a good man but not a natural born killing machine. Currently he was doing an excellent job with his new duties.

Jarow escorted the two men he had busted down to the first floor, to Tad's side as Tasut's men came out on the field. He told his brother, "These men will fight to the death for lowest cot on your floor."

Tad nodded, his mouth in a frown as he grimly escorted them from the field. They were not worthy of the second floor and never would be. *Tasut isn't the only one with death in his wake.*

Jarow's prime goal was to send Tasut the best of his men, fully trained and competent in all weaponry and survival skills. If asked for men to replace those lost on the third floor, he wanted to send men skilled enough to have a chance to survive. The men he had inherited from the first floor had no chance at survival on Tasut's floor. Cebo had made sure of that. This depressing fact would mean possible confrontation for Jarow with Tasut. If Tasut decided he wanted more men to fill his cots, Jarow would have to tell him they weren't ready and would die anyway.

As he slowly walked down the stairs of North Tye, Tasut looked at him and Jarow stopped as he read those familiar eyes. The message was clear – stay. Tasut continued up the tower steps and he followed. Jarow looked at the fifty men, Tasut's best, who walked out onto the field. Jarow recognized all of them. Gradually, he realized Tasut's jaw was tighter than normal. He had just returned the previous evening from Acha. Perhaps he had received bad news from General Han about the Ammonites.

Tasut had no Assistant Commander. However, he had chosen a loud-mouthed man Jarow had never liked by the name of Vek to act as Call Master. Vek blew the signal horn and Jarow remained quiet, watching Tasut signal Vek to blow a command on the curled horn that called the men to a half-circle battle formation. In addition to full battle gear, the men wore the belts and pouches that indicated they would be using quills and swords.

"Nez will be coming to the field today," Tasut said quietly.

Jarow hid his shock. No one got into the Barracks without Tasut's permission.

"He's ordered me, again, to train the militia," Tasut reached behind him and retrieved a white Umpah ball.

Jarow felt fury building. They both knew Nez's goal was to have spies within the walls of the Barracks and find a way to eliminate Tasut.

Before he could voice his protests, the warning bell sounded and Tasut's fifty men stopped their warm up practice and took position in the middle of the field. Jarow realized that Tasut was going to give Nez another object lesson. He wondered what the repercussions would be as the men retrieved armed quills from their pouches and unsheathed their swords.

The double doors leading from the first floor to the training field opened to reveal Nez, dressed in his ministerial robes. Jarow quickly calculated the ranks of men who followed. There were 500.

Jarow felt himself tense as if for battle, and he watched the Minister waiting at the side of the field for Tasut. He was in for disappointment.

Tasut would never go to him, under any circumstances. It didn't take Nez long to arrive at that conclusion.

Jarow knew what was coming and it was all about timing. Nez crossed the field and the moment his foot touched the bottom stair of the tower, Tasut looked at his men. Their eyes were fastened to the white Umpah ball in Tasut's hand.

He looked at Nez and dropped the ball. "I will train any man left standing." It was all the warning Nez got. The moment the ball dropped, the Call Master stabbed a silver flag into the ground.

With a deafening, hair-raising battle cry, the fifty men attacked the unprepared militia. Nez spun around to his men and yelled at them to attack, but they had little or no practical experience. Some of the men dropped their weapons and fled into the Barracks. Jarow now understood why Tasut had spoken to Tad earlier. Jarow overheard Tad pledge to follow orders or die trying.

As the butchery commenced, Nez furiously ran up the steps of the tower and demanded Tasut stop the bloodbath. Tasut pointedly ignored him and watched the slaughter. It didn't last long. Afterward, Tasut's men resumed formation at the side of the field that lay covered by hundreds of dead militia.

Tad was pale as he came out the double-doors of the first floor. He was followed by his men, who carried the corpses of those who had run from the Field of Blood. Their bodies were dropped in a pile near the edge of the field. Nez was white with fury and with his fists clenched, Nez glared at Tasut.

Tasut just looked at him until the Minister turned and made his way back through the Barracks, stepping over any bodies in his way.

Tasut signaled Vek, and the men gathered the dead and took them to the empty wagons outside the Barracks. All the men in the Barracks were mustered to lend a hand in getting rid of the bodies, confiscating their weapons, and any money. Money and anything of value would be gathered over the course of the next seven years and put into a treasury that the Guardian would receive upon winning Cubes.

Tasut looked at Jarow as the men began their gruesome task. "Nez just threw away 500 men."

Jarow snarled, "He was looking to place another spy." There was no need for Tasut to answer.

Tasut signaled Vek, who left the field after planting a gold flag. There were three flags used on the Field of Blood; bronze meant practice, silver meant kill or be killed, gold was for mop-up.

Jarow left the Field of Blood and headed for the second floor, his eyes scanning for trouble while his mind dredged up the past. It was a love-hate relationship he had with Tasut. He watched the cold brutality, accepting it because there was a far different goal than simply appeasing Sogo's thirst for carnage. Jarow recognized that there was a reason, if not an excuse, for Tasut becoming what he was – and wasn't.

True to an unholy tradition, once again men had died upon Tasut's latest return. Jarow had never known it to be otherwise since the day that Tasut became Guardian.

Only Jarow knew the truth. The men Tasut killed on purpose were either traitors, who were uncovered by Jarow's and Tasut's own inner network of Barracks spies, or they were inept and likely to get even more men killed in training. It was a novel idea in such a city, to kill in order to save. The general population thought Tasut was some sort of soulless monster who reveled in gore and required blood sacrifice. *They don't know him. I'm not sure I know him anymore.*

Jarow had been living on faith for a long time. He would never betray Tasut even though there were times he wanted to kill him. If it were not for the woman he loved, he would have left Sogo long ago. But she was here, bound to duty just as he was. She wasn't even aware of the depth of his love. *For now.*

Jarow's thoughts returned to Tasut who honestly didn't care what the men thought of him. Tasut was very simple in his approach to training. The first law he would lay down with his men was the fact that he demanded complete and absolute obedience, period. Jarow had told himself time and again that Father of All willing, Tasut would regain what he had lost and they could become true friends again.

As it was, they had an understanding. They would do it Tasut's way. In Jarow's opinion, Tasut's way wasn't always the best way. Jarow headed up the flight of stairs to his own men.

The Barracks, now that Tasut had returned, became quieter, more orderly, and observations more keen. Jarow's men were constantly on the alert after Cebo's disgrace and the pointed object lesson. Every one of them saluted anyone that walked through their doors, including their cook who appeared gratified they recognized his power over their lives. Even Tasut almost smiled at that when Jarow had shared it with him. *There is hope.*

Jarow frowned in thought. He wondered if Nez had been trying to exact revenge for the time that Tasut and Jarow went to a Council meeting prior to Cubes, to let them know things were changing in the Barracks.

Tasut opened the Council chamber doors unannounced, took three steps into the room and said to them, "You will not enter the Barracks unescorted under any circumstances. If you choose to do so, I will not hold any Barracks men responsible for what will happen." He turned and left the room, leaving the stunned members staring after him as Jarow shut the door.

Evidently, Nez had not listened well enough or he had done just what Tasut said: throw away 500 men to see what Tasut was up to.

Jarow loathed the Minister of Religion and detested the stench of burnt flesh that polluted the Barracks every branding day. He had been pleased that the men heeded his warning that Nez liked to inflict pain, and if they reacted too strongly he would make them suffer. Whenever the branding was taking place, Jarow liked to run 'kill Nez' scenarios through his mind. Each time Nez branded another man, he expanded the scenario in his mind until all of the Nine were dead at least ten different ways before the branding ended.

Jarow was aware Nez did not consider him a threat. Jarow was simply a person to be noted, but not noticed, as was the Temple Guardsman, or even the handmaidens of Saro, the High Priestess of the Unknown God. Actually, Jarow preferred it that way. It left him free to do what needed to be done.

Tasut however, was another matter. If there was one man that Nez feared or grudgingly respected, it was Tasut. It was an open secret that on the third floor, they no longer practiced, they used real weaponry. Jostling for cot position was a permanent part of their lives and deadly traps were used in their training. It was always a tremendous shock for the men who promoted to the third floor after Cubes; despite all of Jarow's warnings.

The biggest and most unpleasant blow for the men, was that each one of them would have to spar with Tasut for ten seconds and try to stay in one piece. Jarow had watched their initiation to Tasut's command with a mixture of pride and frustration. Jarow tried hard to prepare the men for Tasut. Few could wrap their mind around the idea they would be fighting a living legend and that Tasut didn't care if they survived or not. In a city the size of Sogo, holding roughly sixty million people, there were always replacements available.

Tasut was personally involved in every aspect of the training on third floor. But even Jarow felt Tasut had a brutal regimen. Tasut wasn't interested in second-rate men. Jarow estimated that Tasut had killed at least twenty of the men he had sent upstairs. *What a waste.*

With resolve, he opened the outside doors leading to the second floor. When he reached the mess hall, his men went silent and stood to attention as he had instructed them. He had to get his point across to them about their own choices and accountability.

He stood quietly for a moment. He would eventually choose an Assistant Commander for this floor. No one came immediately to mind, although he did take note of those without blood splatters staining their tunics. Men without stains had not taken part in the militia's demise. Suspects.

He marshaled his thoughts and spoke, "Under my command, you've had the opportunity to run six miles a day before you break your fast." Jarow paused to let that sink in, "On third floor, that continues, but you will have less time to do it since you will train four hours at a time three times a day."

Jarow ignored the stifled groans. He had saved the worst for last, "Each of you has been gifted with the rare opportunity to see our Barracks Commander. Everything you do under my command is to prepare you to meet the expectations he has for the **lowest** numbered cot on the third floor.

"If you think my training is too hard, you won't survive his. I arranged for you to see one session of his first section's weaponry training. I hope it gives you the motivation you need to survive because Tasut won't bust you down a floor when you fail his lowest expectations."

As he expected, some of the men looked cheered by this information. Jarow noted who they were, and then paused for effect, "He kills you." The silence was deafening.

"You've had a year on this floor just to catch up on what Cebo failed to teach. Today is your one-year anniversary. I won't waste more time on protocol; you know it or you don't. Those of you who have faulty memories, will be busted. For now, be warned that open-hand combat will be full contact from this point on and to that purpose you'll train with Tenth Level Sensei's to perfect your forms. You need to complete eight levels in the next six years to barely meet Tasut's lowest expectations.

"From now on, you'll have one break for your mid-day meal. Don't miss it. After you eat, you'll spend time with a rock pile and chopping wood for the kitchens. Until we get more men, the first section on this floor will have all the duties you had when you were on the first floor, including mucking the stalls."

He saw a few of them get a belligerent look and he marked them mentally. Traitors were notorious in Sogo. However, the Field of Blood leveled things out in short order.

"I'll choose an Assistant Commander from among you to keep an accurate record of all that is accomplished on this floor. I'll be recording your performance myself until I find my Assistant."

Outside they heard a horrific scream come from the field followed by a short blast of a horn, which signified that the medics were needed. Jarow ignored it as a common occurrence until his neck prickled and he felt Tasut's presence. He quickly turned with fist to chest. His men mimicked the action, several going pale.

Tasut was drenched with sweat, blood, and worse. He looked at the men and quietly said, "Training field." They saluted and left, looking relieved.

After the men left, Tasut nodded toward the stairs that led to the third floor. As Jarow followed Tasut, he had the distinct feeling it wasn't good news as they walked across the colorful mosaic tiles and the various hand-woven carpets that bespoke of the entitlements of living on the third floor. The cots had thin mattresses and large ornately carved chests sitting at the foot of each cot. There was a chest for their armor and clothing separate from their weapons.

Dinner on the third floor was an elaborate dining experience. There was a talented chef with six assistants. The third floor had the best cooks. The one entitlement the men in the Barracks looked forward to when they were on the third floor, was the longed for day each month they would be allowed to wander around Sogo doing as they pleased as long as they traveled in pairs and were back by dusk.

Tasut's own quarters lay beyond the third section and up a flight of stone stairs. There was a thick metal door that led into what the men called the "Cave". It was austere compared to what his men had. Tasut didn't want luxuries.

Tasut closed the door and leaned against it. He gave Jarow a long look and his eyes grew cold, "Eder was the one who tried to kill Saro last week and, last night he tried to kill her handmaiden, the widow Raen."

Rage exploded through Jarow. Eder had been one of the more trusted men promoted to the third floor. In fact, Eder had been among those that slaughtered Nez's militia. It was hard to believe that he would be foolish enough to attempt to murder Saro. Tasut had been raging about it for a week. Now his target was Raen, the High Priestess's handmaiden and that made it personal. Jarow tamped his fury down. His own face reflected the stone of Tasut's. "The horn?" he guessed, remembering the horn signaling there had been an injury on the field requiring the medics. Tasut nodded, studying the one man he trusted implicitly.

"Where is Eder now?" Jarow asked grimly.

"The infirmary."

Tasut had given him all the information he needed. Jarow was stiff as he saluted. Most people already believed that Jarow was death's messenger. Today it would be true. It couldn't be soon enough for Jarow since the attempted assassination had happened on his watch. *I'm becoming Tasut.* At the moment, it didn't bother him.

Chapter 18: Cave

Two days later, Tasut reached the room everyone referred to as 'the cave', closed the heavy metal door behind him, and lay down on his cot. He was exhausted. The men on the third floor were scattered from the mess hall to the infirmary. The lucky ones were dead.

None of them dared come to the cave to see how he lived, but he had heard the rumors and they naturally suspected he had traps set that would kill them. He didn't. However, if anyone had dared to violate his one source of semi-peace, he would take it personally and kill them. Anyone stupid enough to brave a look into his room was stupid enough to be a spy.

Tasut was well aware his reputation had grown out of proportion to the number of men he had actually killed. Most people's opinions had stopped meaning anything a long time ago.

He had one window in the room and tonight there was a full moon. He began meditation, a prelude to prayer. It was during this time he evaluated the day.

Training went badly. He had taken time to watch Jarow's men on the Field of Blood. They were like glittering jewels of incompetence and when they finished, he silently swore at the dead Cebo in eight languages. If possible, he would've resurrected the man and killed him with his own two hands. When Jarow first refused to send him more men, he had suspected Jarow had been holding back.

He should have known that Jarow would be absolutely correct in his assessment. Even after a year, the men were so incredibly inept it was a wonder they knew what end of the sword to hold. In the end, they'd pay with their lives. Likely, hopefully, before Cubes.

In all the years he had served in his position as trainer there had never been a more useless group of men. Cubes would be a disaster if these men were the best that could be found. If Cubes was a disappointment, he could be fired and he was not going to allow that to happen. He would save his son, no matter the price. He had promised on all that remained holy that he would.

In six years, he must have men equal to the task of entertaining the blood thirsty Sogoians and their corrupt leaders. After speaking to Jarow, he had agreed to maintain the number of men he had for at least two more years and wait for Jarow's group to show more promise.

There was another, albeit welcome, complication. Sons of Ammon would be arriving at the Barracks in seven years. Neither he or Jarow knew the how, only that it *would* happen. Those men deserved the very best training.

In only thirteen years, whoever the Guardian was at that time, would fight Talon and Talon would win.

Tasut wouldn't allow one man to be weak in spite of Jarow's protests. This was about more than any one person, even if that one person was his son.

He was aware of the talk in the Barracks. It was said that he could not be the Barracks Commander forever and that he had already 'slipped a cog or two' in his strength. Under normal circumstances, they would be right to think so, but Tasut had never fit into a category labeled normal.

Still, he couldn't afford that kind of rumor. He used the men who repeated the rumors as his sparring partners and they soon changed their minds about his hypothetical weaknesses. He made it a point to spar with them in front of the other men. He knew he was the kind of man that they loved to hate. Their bitterness became his ally and their hatred became their weakness.

Jarow had committed himself to spend the next thirteen years in Sogo as Tasut's only ally. Jarow thought he would maintain his position as Training Commander on the second floor. Tasut didn't bother to tell him he'd be promoted to be Tasut's Assistant, the first man to be assigned that position since Tasut had taken over the third floor. His promotion would take place in eight to ten year's time. If Jarow's brother, Tad, proved to be as trustworthy as Jarow, Tad would take Jarow's position on the second floor, and one of the Sons of Ammon would become the final Training Commander on the first floor.

Jarow would be attending the Sogoian slave auctions when he couldn't be there. Jarow knew what to look for after all these years. If it could be arranged, they would go to every slave auction for the next dozen or more years. They were committed to find every last Son of Ammon. Father of All would arrange events for some to show up at auction. All Tasut had to do was take the opportunity to gather them and stay on course.

He sat up and looked around his room. There was a small table and chair, a mirror, cot, and a plain chest for his clothing. In the cave there were no rugs or wall hangings, nothing unnecessary to the naked eye except the mirror. Tasut could have cared less what he looked like, but shaving in the Barracks was imperative. It kept the clean disciplined look he wanted in his men and demanded of himself.

He avoided looking into his own eyes when he shaved because they reminded him of his greatest loss. If eyes were truly the windows of the soul, he didn't have one. His dark brown eyes looked dead and would continue to be that way until prophecy healed them.

Anger was the one emotion left to him that still spoke from his eyes, but for the most part they looked inhumanly cold --- like observant, assessing blocks of obsidian.

He did not look into his eyes if he could avoid it. Somewhere deep in those orbs existed the man he had been before. He turned the mirror face down after he shaved.

He thought about Brenna and how she had burned his hair off his head. He had noted the hastily concealed surprise of the men when they first saw him upon his return. She didn't know she'd done him a favor.

Being bald meant less time at the mirror and the new, more intimidating look gave him a new edge.

The men raised from the second floor were in excellent fighting trim but their hair was too long. That would be corrected on the morrow. He leaned against the wall looking out at the darkening sky. He had been trying to avoid thinking about the inevitable coming of night.

He had chosen this room because it held the light longest of all those on the third floor. Of all the time available in any given day, Tasut resented night the most. It consumed time better spent preparing for what was to come. He would rather use these dark hours to train, to do anything else but dream. He wasn't master in that realm and it made him feel more vulnerable than if he were naked.

He opened his large plain trunk and pulled out the thick cloth mat. He reached above his cot to the rack that held the metal training balls, called Umpahs, and lay down on the floor.

He began his nightly ritual by balancing one of the eight-pound balls on the ankle area of his two feet. He raised his legs slowly, ever so slowly, and held the position until his muscles began to complain, and then he lowered his legs inch by inch until they also began to shake. He held two other Umpahs in either hand, raised them an inch above the ground with his arms outstretched above his head, and began his meditation. Twenty minutes later he put the Umpahs back on their rack above his bed, beads of sweat dripping from his brow as he assumed final position.

There was only one power that Tasut believed in anymore, and regardless of what anyone thought, it wasn't himself.

He recognized at an early age that he had no power beyond what Father of All gave him and that was what kept him sane while holding the most barbaric profession in Sogo. That and the knowledge there was an end in sight, a goal to achieve that would free him of the unfeeling world in which he existed.

Final position after his night exercise was for prayer and prayer alone. It was his only relief in a full day of sweat and blood. He focused his every thought on listening for the guidance he sought, and at the end repeated what he had as a child. *Thy will be done.*

Jarow would be on guard, listening this night for what might come to pass. They traded off nights because there was no alternative. Jarow was the only man he could trust. If possible, Tasut would never sleep and he would allow Jarow the pleasure of the company of the woman of his choice. As it stood, whoever wanted Tasut would have to go through Jarow first. He had fewer problems sleeping when Jarow was there. His problem was dreaming. He had one that recurred with disturbing regularity.

He fought sleep, but knew he needed it to stay alive and continue forward. In a perverse way he wanted the dream because he could see his wife, briefly, and touch her for an instant. He always knew when he was dreaming because he had the luxury of emotions in dreams. He could remember emotions, even if he no longer felt anything but anger in the waking world. He drifted downward, falling and jerking back awake, and then falling again, this time into the dream he knew awaited him.

Once more, he was in the Poolseer cave in Dyman with several other people. He ignored the others and focused on his wife. He held her hand, reveling in the softness that had been his too briefly.

In the dream he looked at her beautiful oval face and read the fear lurking in her eyes behind the resolve that brought them to the cave. His entire body was rigid with displeasure at what was going to happen.

The fact it had to happen didn't mean he had to like it.

He had even threatened some of the others with retribution if anything went wrong but it was in vain. His temper accomplished nothing. The Father of All commanded him and that alone stayed his hand. If it had not been for that one consuming fact, he would have taken Laysha and their son, and left the others to find another willing sacrifice.

Laysha had offered herself in spite of his objection. His offer to replace her as sacrifice was refused. He kept telling himself that it was something that had to happen, something he agreed to because only he had the strength to make it right. They had a chance to destroy Sogo and they had to take it.

In the dream, he could feel his arms close around his wife, locking them in position.

He told himself to wake up before she began to jerk in his arms, before he could hear her endless screaming, but it wasn't meant to be. He was locked in the dream. His eyes brimmed with tears and he nearly lost his grip on her thrashing form.

Tasut yelled at them to stop, that she was dying, that he could feel Laysha dying. Her final screams echoed around the cavern. At that moment, the last he remembered in the cave, she went limp in his arms and all they had been together died as she jerked one more time and his heart was no longer whole.

Her act of sacrifice had robbed him of his humanity and his love. In the dream, his face was wet with tears at her agony. Afterward, he felt nothing. He found she was no longer within his heart and mind as she had been. He was half of nothing. That barrenness was all he had from that day until now.

In the end, things were not in place and he had failed his wife. In spite of reassurances by those who had witnessed that he had done everything humanly possible, he'd failed.

He swore each morning he lived to see the sun rise that he wouldn't fail their son. That helped him keep going.

His dream always repeated itself in the same manner. From the sacrifice it took him to the Field of Blood. Talon was fighting, and there was someone coming up behind him.

Tasut could never see the face of the man who stalked his son. All he knew was that Talon was going to die, and he could do nothing to stop it, although he was ready to die trying.

*

Jarow used the wooden dowel near the door to touch Tasut, to wake him from the nightmare that possessed him. Jarow had not been there when Tasut's wife made her choice, but General Monus had been and Jarow could recall the unconcealed horror in Monus's voice whenever he spoke of it after all these years. There was no doubt in Jarow's mind that Tasut suffered. It was the only thing that made him human, this nightmare. It was a blessing and a curse.

Tasut was a different kind of man at one time. Jarow couldn't remember a time when he didn't have to hold that idea to himself, like a child does a favorite toy, because there were times he really and truly hated Tasut. Not for what he was, but what he did.

If it weren't for the woman he loved, Jarow would walk away from it all and leave Sogo and be done with all the blood, the training, and the bleak thought that he was just a butcher looking for the next package of meat for Tasut to grind.

Chapter 19: Tryks

It was nearly a year since Talon had seen his father and Talon gladly stayed at Tryk's. He enjoyed regular visits from the Tybar's while at Tryk's and appreciated the food Mari brought.

The inventor was undeniably, utterly brilliant in his odd way. He didn't care that Talon was young, he eagerly showed him his newest inventions and bitterly complained, for the length of Talon's meals, about the Sogoian government not listening to him about an invention he had created years before that they had stolen and perverted.

"They have no idea what they did!" he exclaimed, the wizened face becoming fiercer. "I used to stand in those chambers every year to tell them that they cheated me!"

This seemed a waste of time to Talon, but politely he asked, "What did they take?" as he stuffed his mouth full of bread slathered with jam.

"I suppose it won't hurt to tell you," Tryk snatched an apple for himself and tore a chunk out of it like it had personally offended him. "When I was younger than you, I came across some ancient texts in the city of Sogo. Sogo was already in the early stages of the cesspool it is now. The texts helped me create something that would have changed life for all of us.

"I made a device that would allow people to design their own homes." He paused, "I combined that knowledge with something I learned while watching turtles." Tryk shook his head to clear it, "It was very difficult to perfect this instrument while living in the city of Sogo but I finally had the prototype ready."

"The what?"

"A prototype is a working model, usually the first one, of whatever invention you make," the one-eyed Tryk explained. "I had it nearly perfected, but needed more money to finish it so I made the biggest mistake of my life." The flyaway hair on his head bobbed as he shook his head.

"What happened?" Talon peeled a boiled egg and waited for the genius to finish his thoughts.

"Boiled-idiot that I am, I invited the Council of Nine to see my invention. They confiscated it and claimed it was dangerous. Furthermore, they took the land it sat on."

"Did they destroy it?" Talon knew how much Tryk loved his rooms full of stuff.

"I wish with all my heart they had," mourned Tryk. His voice was full of loathing as he plopped down on a stool with a crack in the middle that bit your rear when you stood up.

"They ordered me thrown out of the city and confiscated all of the texts they could find; thank All that my sister had most of them!" a slight smile twisted Tryk's homely features. "I fought them but they were too strong." He pointed to the diagonal scar. "They gave me this after they threw me and my wife out into the street."

"Didn't anyone do anything to help!?" Talon was outraged.

Tryk looked at him curiously, "Yes."

Talon recalled something Tryk had said about when he got his scar. "It was Tasut."

Tryk grimly nodded. "No one dared challenge him, not even then, before he became what he is."

"I hate him," Talon said, looking directly at Tryk to see if he was shocked. He half expected Tryk to defend his father. After all, Tasut had saved Tryk's life.

He was surprised when Tryk said darkly, "I hated him too."

Talon was surprised at the words. Within him warred a curious mixture of wanting to defend Tasut, and at the same time, ask more questions.

"Don't misunderstand me boy," said Tryk as he twisted some sort of wheel with a knob on it. "I appreciate the fact that I'm able to continue my research. It's my life and will be til the day I die."

"Then why do you hate him?"

"Because he saved me instead of my wife."

Talon wasn't sure what to say so he asked, "What did they do with your invention?"

Tryk winced as his finger caught in a moving part of one of his inventions, "They perverted it like everything else they do. They took something beautiful in concept and changed the purpose it was intended for. It would have brought prosperity for all."

"What was it?"

"I called it Hymshi. It means home in Valenese."

"You said they confiscated it," Talon wanted to go find the Hymshi and give it to Tryk. "Do they still have it?"

Tryk gave a bitter bark. "Oh yes, they certainly do, and they use it, the dung-eating Pursha's!"

"What for?"

Tryk stopped what he was doing and looked at him out of his good eye for a long moment, his face a mask of sorrow and regret, "Cubes."

Talon decided to change the subject. It seemed to make Tryk angry. "I think I'll go to bed."

Tryk didn't answer. He appeared to be brooding about the loss of his invention.

During the year Tasut had been gone, the conglomeration of organized chaos known as Tryk's house was never comforting in the dark. There were no windows in most of the rooms and Tryk wasn't the type to fuss over such things as fixing a meal. Talon grew hungry on a fairly regular basis.

Talon had just resigned himself to going to bed without supper when Tryk growled, "No use trying to get more done," and he squinted at

Talon. "I'll have to wait until morning." He seemed personally affronted that the sun went down without his permission.

He looked at Talon steadily, the white eye seemed to glisten, "Did I ever tell you that I know Tasut?"

Talon was stunned. Of all the things for the man to say to him, after a year of knowing him, this wasn't what he expected. He had known Tryk must have, or he wouldn't be staying with the inventor. He also knew Tryk must be trustworthy for the same reason.

"Are you hungry?" Tryk wiped his hands on an already dirty cloth.

Talon smiled and nodded with relief.

"Good, let's get something to eat."

After they had dined on meat, baked tubers, and bread, the conversation continued.

"You're much like your father when he was younger, at least, in sheer size."

Talon looked at Tryk expectantly. *At last! I hope he knows my mother.* Most people told him things about Tasut he already knew, which wasn't much.

"He's a hard man," Tryk fingered his scar and rubbed his face. A habit he had formed, Talon observed, whenever he was tired.

Am I hard? In silence, Talon cleaned up his plate and washed the few dishes they had dirtied. He didn't want to discuss Tasut with a stranger. He liked Tryk but there were some things that Talon just didn't discuss openly with others. Tasut was one of those things.

"Did you know my mother?"

Tryk nodded as he swallowed his food, "Laysha Keepay was one of the most beautiful women I've ever seen, and the one woman who was more than a match for Tasut."

Talon nearly stopped breathing and looked at Tryk who looked at the fire while sipping on his fresh-pressed grape juice.

"What happened to her?"

199 | *Chest of Souls*

Tryk studied him. "If Tasut didn't tell you, I won't."

Talon bit back disappointment while Tryk drank his own glass of juice. "I'd like to keep my brain inside my skull. Your father wouldn't leave it there if he knew I told you anything he didn't want me to." Tryk nodded at him and rocked in his broken chair.

"Why doesn't he tell me?" Talon felt a bit stubborn even though he could understand Tryk's refusal to cross Tasut.

"I've never understood Tasut's motivation," confessed Tryk. "I'm a man of mind, not unescorted muscle." He paused, "I'll tell you one thing about yourself, you look like her."

Great, I can finally ask questions about her and he tells me something I already know. Talon felt ungrateful and more than a little irritated. Not with Tryk, but the rules Tasut put into place.

"I'm going to take a calculated risk and tell you one more thing about her that may do some good some day," Tryk continued, his one good eye reading Talon like a book. "Laysha had that giant father of yours wrapped so tightly around her finger it's a wonder his spine didn't snap."

Talon found he couldn't picture Tasut being wrapped around anything.

"Believe it or not, in the end, what happened to her was something beyond their power to control."

Tryk pulled a circular object out of his pocket and threw it to Talon who caught it. It was a metal ball. "There was little that Laysha could ask that Tasut wouldn't do for her.

"Face this fact boy: you didn't know him. I'd bet my Slasher skin boots you still don't know him. All you know is what he has allowed you to know. It's not giving anything away to say you have a very intimidating father."

Tryk sat forward on his chair with his elbows on his knees as he looked into Talon's eyes, "Few men are foolish enough to stand in his way if he wants something done." Tryk sat back and studied Talon's face for a moment, as if curious to how his young mind worked. "You appear to be an intelligent boy. My guess is you've given this a lot of thought. What do you think happened to her?"

Talon shrugged, disheartened, "Whatever it was, I think my father was involved."

Tryk wasn't surprised that Tasut had chosen to keep Talon in the dark. *And I can't tell him. Tasut would kill me, if the Forest Wife didn't first.*

*

Two weeks later, Talon had the startling thought that he missed Tasut's cooking. The trade, however, was worth it; he had reason to smile whenever the Tybars came for a visit.

Brenna had entered Tryk's five minutes ago.

"Brenna Tybar!" Mari's voice came from outside Tryk's hovel. "You need to knock before you enter someone's house!"

Talon had known Brenna was coming from the time he arose, but he didn't know how he knew it. Feeling restless while waiting, he had chopped wood for Tryk, fished for breakfast, and found two more crabs for Mee. Then he went out to the fork in the road and waited for her, and when she saw him she had started running, calling his name. When he saw her, he felt the tightness that pinched inside disappear as if it had never been.

Together, they went into Tryk's place.

Tryk said to Brenna as he fiddled with some string and a curved bit of hook, "Your mother told me about the attack last year at Tasut's place. She said the creatures gave you nightmares."

"What were they?" Talon asked eagerly. He hadn't mentioned the monsters to Tryk. He didn't know if he had the right, so he kept his opinions and questions to himself.

"Abominations!" Mari spat from behind them, her eyes flashed at her daughter who stood near Talon. For one moment, he was more afraid of Mari than of Tasut.

He didn't ask Tryk for more information but had a feeling Brenna would. She didn't disappoint him.

"I thought the Gantecs were all dead," she said.

It was times like this that Talon realized how ignorant he was of the world, its customs, and everything else except work. It was rather nice to be thanked for whatever he accomplished during any given day. When he had chopped wood for Tryk, the man had taken time to admire the large stack.

"So did I," Tryk said shortly. "It is against all that is sacred to create one. According to old Sogoian law, those guilty were to be…killed."

Talon noticed the pause. He got the idea that there was more to it than just a simple killing for those who created them. *How does one create something like that on purpose?* "What are they anyway?" this question came out on its own volition.

Tryk answered, "The biggest, which I believe you killed," Tryk nodded to Talon, "was a Gantec. It's a creature made of living ice. The snakes in its mouth are Neps. The horse-things are called Ybarras. You probably knew that since you own a pair of gloves made from their hide."

Talon hadn't known that. He tried to figure how the pale pink bloody skin of a living Ybarra could be tanned into pale brown leather.

Tryk climbed under whatever it was he was working on now. His voice was muffled, but Talon could hear him say "And the many-eyed men are Urches, who were once human."

"What do the Neps do?" Talon remembered the yellow snake that had nearly bitten him.

"Those they bite become Gantecs." Mari's mouth twisted in distaste as she unpacked a large basket of food. Talon's mouth began to water.

"Originally, they were created to make an invincible army," Tryk crawled out from under his creation and frowned. "However, like most evil things they twisted into what they are now."

Talon tried to imagine an entire army of Gantecs. *Thank Father of All that Lyon was quick with the quill or I would've been one.* It was a sobering thought.

He shook the image out of his head as Brenna took his hand and smiled up at him. He had grown accustomed to her hand-grabbing and knew it was pointless to try and avoid it. Now and then, he even took her hand, which made her be quiet and wear a smile.

That Gantec wasn't ancient," Mari spoke softly, her eyes troubled. "It was new to this world. According to the Forest Wife, they don't come this far south. I think the Council is messing with more than just our laws," Mari finished.

Talon was going to ask who the Forest Wife was when Tryk slammed his open palm on the table.

"Nez!" Tryk spat the name of his hated enemy and looked at Mari with his good eye.

"I agree, Nez is the only one that has that kind of power and would make that kind of choice," Mari said with disgust.

"What is it that you wanted to ask me about?" inquired Tryk, bringing them all back to the present.

"Brenna, tell Tryk what you were thinking when you set Tasut's hair on fire."

Talon's eyebrows rose in surprise. *She did that?* He recalled his reaction to Tasut without hair. It made him look even more dangerous. It had probably all grown back by now.

"I was mad at him because he wouldn't let me go help Talon!" Brenna explained with a trace of defiance.

"I mean the moment you made his hair catch on fire," her mother clarified.

Her big blue eyes looked away from her mother. "Fire."

"Why fire?" Tryk asked, his attention riveted on Brenna.

Brenna shrugged, "I was mad, but I didn't want his skin burned because I remembered how bad it hurt when I touched a hot pan."

"How did you make the fire do what you said?" inquired Tryk.

She gave a little shrug. "I just told it to sit on his hair."

Mari exchanged looks with Tryk, still astonished at the simplicity of what Brenna had done. The feat was one that only seventh year Mages learned. It was a very strict discipline to manipulate the elements and have such tight control.

"Tell him about the tree," her mother directed.

"What tree?" asked the ever-curious Tryk.

"The huge tree at Tasut's," Mari explained. "Brenna blew it apart."

Tryk's uni-brow slid up into his non-existent hairline.

"I didn't know where to put all the heat," Brenna's chin quivered.

Talon put his arm on her shoulder to reassure her, and changed the subject hoping they would answer, "Where's Lyon?"

"He should be back soon," Mari said evasively. "I wouldn't have come so early but Brenna started to walk here without me." She cast a hard look at her daughter who hid behind Talon again.

"I would ask where Mee is," laughed Tryk, "but I can hear the feast from here."

"Where are the other boys?" Talon liked Brenna but he craved the company of other boys.

"Iskar and Rube are in Utak helping with the planting. They'll stay until after harvest," Mari smiled at him.

This information silenced him. According to what he had gleaned from eavesdropping over several conversations, Utak was enclosed in a large bowl-shaped valley by mountains. It had deep, pristine lakes with legendary abilities. To do what, he hadn't heard.

Near one of these lakes was the center of the city. There were supposed to be incredible buildings there, unlike any in the world. What made them different, Talon couldn't understand.

He had been hiding in the center of the large lilac bush listening to the conversation and it was dark. He was supposed to be in bed. Visitors, however, were rare and even if it meant punishment he found himself unable to overcome his curiosity. There was something peculiar about the people, but Talon couldn't remember what it was. "After all," the peddler had said expansively, "the royal houses would pay much to get into that valley. Everyone knows the most beautiful women are there." Tasut had just grunted his usual non-committal grunt.

The peddler then said, "Nez claims he will marry a woman from Utak." The reason the conversation stuck in Talon's mind was Tasut's reaction to this statement.

"He'll never get past the Guardian!" It was said in such a way that the hairs on Talon's arms rose in warning. The peddler was instantly humbled.

"Right...right! The Guardian is the only thing that men can rely on in our times."

Nez? Guardian? Tasut obviously knows the Guardian. What is it? Obviously, whatever this Guardian was, it was powerful enough to keep men from entering the valley, plus it sounded like Nez was afraid of it. *Maybe it's a monster.*

The peddler wasn't finished though, "There's no such thing as impossible. You of all men, know this. It's what you died for."

Died? It hadn't made sense at the time and it still didn't. The talk went on to other things but Talon had not forgotten the words. He knew that Tasut had been to Utak. Since Tasut wasn't the kind given to telling tales, Talon knew his father had ridden to Utak once a month, sometimes more often, no matter where they had lived.

Talon was intelligent enough to realize that this wasn't a normal course of events. It was said by more than one peddler to be a mark of power if one could get to Utak. *What kind of power does Tasut have?*

Utak, it was said, was 'great *and* terrible.' How it could be both was a mystery.

Peddlers, at least the ones that Talon had been able to meet, liked to brag as a general rule, but not one had ever claimed to have been there and back again.

How does Tasut get there? Is he friends with the Guardian?

He was almost sure it must be a monster for all the peddlers to act fearful of the name. To keep everyone away from an entire valley, it had to have some sort of magic. *The Guardian must be very powerful.*

*

After being gone for a year, Tasut returned in time for Talon's tenth birthday. He was staying at the Tybars.

It was inevitable, Lyon supposed, that Tasut would want to see his son on his birthday, but it would have been so much better if he hadn't. Mari was still slamming things around in the kitchen and murmuring things under her breath he was grateful he couldn't hear.

Tasut had ridden up like a Utakian ice storm was at his heels, called for Talon, who jumped up from the game he had been playing with Brenna as if he had been slapped.

At Tasut's jerk of the head, Talon followed his father over to the shores of Belly Band Lake. Tasut picked up his son and threw him in saying, "Swim."

The man hadn't stopped to see if Talon would be able to make it to shore. He hadn't even wished him well for his special day. Brenna was so shocked she'd looked at her father to see if it was some sort of adult joke that she didn't quite understand.

Mari was more vociferous and demanded that Tasut jump in to rescue his son on penalty of dealing with her if he didn't. In spite of the threat from Mari, Tasut climbed back on Harcour and left.

Brenna didn't wait to see the outcome of the adult's debate. She could see Talon going down for the second time and with a scream of "I'll save you!" she jumped in. She didn't know how to swim either, which meant Lyon went in after both of them, followed by Mari who was so angry her eyes turned deep purple and he feared Belly Band Lake would dry up with the heat coming from her.

As it was, he and Mari managed over the course of the summer to give the two children swimming lessons.

Better, Talon had learned to smile and revealed a sense of humor! Lyon tried to tell Mari it all ended well and that they had the added advantage of having Talon stay with them.

He was positive that this wouldn't be the last they would see of Tasut. If he came at no other time in a year, he was sure to show up on Talon's birthday.

Lyon was proud of the boy! Instead of crying and insisting on being taken out to dry, Talon had put all of his concentration on learning how to swim and Brenna, seeing that it wasn't an activity meant to punish, learned right beside him.

The summer passed pleasantly and they went swimming almost every day that Lyon and Mari were home.

When they were away on business, Talon and Brenna went to stay at Tryk's place with Mee leading the way, singing praises about crab.

Chapter 20: Tybars

Mari was too fond of bathing. Talon's opinion was firm on that point. Bathing once a month or so was fine with him, but she insisted on a quick wash of the face twice a day and his hands had never seen so much soap! With Tasut, his bar of soap lasted close to a year. Of course, this soap was softer and smelled better. Other than this fetish she had for cleanliness, he spent the most delightful time of his whole life so far at the Tybars.

"Talon, your father has ordered you to continue running and help with any farming," Lyon's mouth had a peculiar twist to it as he read a parchment delivered by Tryk. For a moment, Talon saw fire in the grey eyes of a man who looked like he had just been given vinegar to drink, but it quickly disappeared.

"I guess you're in luck, I'm not a farmer, and have no intention of becoming one. I'll teach you something I'm good at. What do you know about silver or jewels?"

Talon shrugged, "Nothing."

"The best place to start," Lyon smiled.

Later that same day, Mari led him to the small library in the cottage and his education began. It was much harder than it looked.

"I'm not sure Tasut wants me to read much," he confessed, hoping he didn't hurt her feelings.

One of her eyebrows went up like the back of a cat and her lips made a funny kind of expression, then she said, "Your mother would want you to, and Tasut doesn't have to know."

This was a novel thought for Talon. He had never hidden anything from Tasut in his life. If he discovered you lied, it was sure to be a memorable and most likely painful experience. It had never been worth lying.

Talon decided that if Tasut asked him directly he would tell him the truth. *He probably won't care anyway.* The thought gave him a little pain but he tucked it away with all the rest bestowed by his sire.

If anyone knew where Tasut lived in Sogo or what he was doing, they hadn't told him. When he thought about his past life, it seemed more like a dream at times, yet somewhere inside of him he knew it would only be a matter of time when Tasut returned. This thought filled him with apprehension and a touch of despair. How could he go back to what he had been doing?

If Tasut ever bothered to ask Talon how or what he liked about his stay at the Tybars, he would have answered: 'Lyon, because he talks to me.' He answered almost every question Talon asked.

Lyon not only taught Talon something of the art of setting precious stones and silver or gold into chains, but he was willing to give Talon reasons and direction. The closest Talon came to farming was Mari's garden and she was fussy about it so Talon seldom did more than pull weeds.

"Talon," Mari said from the kitchen, "you can finish reading that tomorrow."

He looked up from the primer. He had been slightly resentful of her attempt to teach him to read better and write until Mari mentioned that the stories she told; the legends and folk tales, all came from books.

He now knew what fairies were and decided that the other boys were right, he'd rather hear about heroes and war. He looked over at Brenna as he reluctantly closed the book. She was supposed to be reading, but, as usual, she had been watching him and when she saw him look her way, her smile lit up and it made her eyes shine. Maybe, once in awhile, it would be okay to hear about fairies.

Three months later, Talon's eyes popped open in the heart of the night. At first, he wasn't sure what woke him. Then he realized it was quiet. Impossibly so. He turned his head and looked out at the constellation known as the Three Sisters. Above them sat a crescent-moon encircled by a ring. Superstition labeled such a sight an omen.

Talon wasn't exactly sure what an omen was, but the ring looked harmless and it was pretty enough to make you want to keep looking. Most of the time there was a slight fog that swirled and eddied around the base of the largest trees in this part of the world, but this night it was so clear outside that the very stars looked crisp and closer than they could ever be in reality.

Something felt different and he wasn't sure what it was. A feeling of anticipation coated him. Instead of dread, he was excited to the point that he sat up in bed and looked out the small window as if whatever it was would appear on the moon-lit path behind the house.

That's when he saw a small white figure in the distance, headed down the road. Something about it... *Brenna!* He didn't stop to consider, ask, or tell. He simply reacted.

Out the window, his bare feet hit the ground at a dead run. Pelting along the path, he hoped that whatever it was she was up to wouldn't get her killed. Talon didn't dare call her name in case someone else was nearby.

Brenna was still a good distance ahead and he pushed himself harder. If he hadn't been watching at the precise moment he did, he wouldn't have seen her go over the rise in the road. He intended to reach the rise before she took a different turn. He forced himself to go faster to reach the small pinnacle of the hill, a little surprised that he reached it so easily. He was grateful for the hours of running, chopping, and more hours of forms than he had ever considered doing.

I'm ready. It was an odd thought and he didn't pause in his stride to consider what he really meant. He just obeyed the rhythm of his feet as they moved: Save her, save her, save her...

He caught a glimpse of white as it peeked through the trees. She headed down what was probably a deer path. He almost laughed in relief as he realized that he was gaining on her. So far, he hadn't seen anyone or anything else on the path. Part of him knew he should be upset with her, but he wasn't. In fact, he felt a sense of direction pulling at him, as if he was the needle of a compass. He reached the pathway she had taken and was now within sight of where he thought she was headed.

An ancient Temple, now in ruins, sat at the foot of a canyon wall, silent and dark. It was coal-black until Brenna went in. Then it lit up as if by a thousand thousand candles, then the entire building glowed.

He came to a staggering halt and pushed into the brush near the ruins. His breathing slowed, but his heart still pounded in his eardrums.

He couldn't take too long to make a decision about what to do. Whoever was in there could hurt her.

Talon chinned himself up to a side window and peered in. Gratefully, it was an empty room. He hauled himself up and into the building, thankful his chores had given him the ability to do it quickly.

Placing his feet quietly on the marble floor of the room, Talon quickly and quietly ran to the doorway. He heard voices coming from deeper inside the building, where the light was blazing the brightest. He cautiously made his way to the double-doors where the light bled profusely from beneath them, lighting most of the halls and building.

He tried thinking of another way to do it but could see no alternative. He had to go in, knowing he would be temporarily blinded by the light. He took a deep breath and reached his hand out to push the doors open, crouching to avoid possible arrows.

The doors opened, revealing Brenna's smiling face. She literally glowed from the inside out, like a lantern in the dark.

"C'mon, we've been waiting!" Brenna reached down and took his hand, pulling him with her into the light.

"This is Talon," she said to a brighter light.

In the light was a man, but to call Him such was blasphemy because it was Father of All. Talon wasn't sure how he knew it, but he knew down to his toenails that it was true.

His God looked human only in that he had arms, legs, and the appearance of mankind. The exact way he differed from humans was too hard to describe. The only thing that came to Talon's mind was that somehow, Father of All was lit from inside, but there weren't enough candles in the whole world to make the kind of light that radiated from Him.

Father of All smiled and nodded to Talon who sank to his knees. Brenna knelt beside Talon and took his hand. They both stared at Him.

"My children." Father of All spoke with gentleness and to Talon's surprise, His eyes revealed humor.

There was so much to Him - his voice went inside you and through you and was part of you. There wasn't one fraction of Talon that did not hear every word. It was if every hair on his head heard the voice, lifting from his scalp in a field of goose bumps, eager to obey.

"The citizens of Sogo have been given a season to cease their wickedness. They have murdered the prophets I have sent, even my servant Benamii. My children in Sogo commit all manner of evil against me. I will not be mocked. The city of Sogo must needs be destroyed and all that live within its walls."

As He spoke of Sogo, there was inhuman grief and godly anger in His eyes. "My son Talon, know that I am well pleased with thee. I have but two tasks for thee now.

"First, I command thee to remain pure, for I delight in purity of heart, mind, and body.

"Your second task is to keep my daughter Brenna safe that she might fulfill the task laid before her in the Great Council.

"Continue thy training with all thy might, that thou shalt be sufficient to the task given thee before the foundations of this world were built."

Talon didn't remember a Great Council, but he felt the words ring true.

"There will be other companions that will join thee to prepare for the fall of Sogo."

Companions? As in friends? He nodded his agreement, remaining on his knees.

If he had been commanded to fly, he would have because he knew that Father did not give commands that could not be fulfilled. Tasut had said it was so. Tasut, with all his faults, did not lie.

Father of All addressed Brenna, "My daughter, thou must also remain pure for in this shalt thou be made safe."

He gently smiled, "Thou must learn to obey even as my son Talon hath done."

Brenna shyly smiled and nodded.

"It is well. I leave my blessings with thee that my purpose shall be fulfilled through ye, my children."

Father of All was gone.

The Temple, however, still glowed where he had been sitting, as if His power had infused the very stone.

There were two small stones left on the steps where His feet had been. Brenna gathered them and gave Talon one.

He rose from his knees and took her hand. "We need to get back before your parents wake up."

Talon noticed as they walked back to the house that he felt different somehow. He felt greater connection and responsibility for Brenna. Talon surmised that it was different to have a God tell you to protect someone.

He would have done it anyway, because Lyon and Tasut had told him, but now it didn't feel so much like a chore.

Brenna's small hand in his was soft and he sensed her happiness. For once, it wasn't uncomfortable. She smiled up at him and looked perfectly happy, content to leave her hand in his forever.

She looked delighted as she asked, "How do you obey?"

Chapter 21: Memory of a Mark

Two weeks later, Mari and Lyon were astonished at the number of rocks Brenna collected.

"Just leave them outside, dear," Mari told their daughter as she sorted the pile. "We'll have to go to Dyman."

"I can't," she insisted. "I have to choose one for Talon. It has to be extra special. I'm not sure the one I have is the best."

"What is it supposed to look like?" Mari hoped to make a rock appear that fit the description.

"I don't know, I haven't seen anything better yet."

"Why do you want to give Talon a rock?"

"'Cause he's going to give me one."

"Did he tell you he was going to do this?"

"No."

"Then why do you think he will?"

"All said so."

Mari looked at Lyon, who smiled and said, "You've been trumped, my love."

"When did All say this?"

"When papah came home. You were sleeping and He called me, so I went."

Her parents looked at each other and back at her.

"Where?" Lyon asked, his forehead creased.

"To the Temple."

"When?" Mari shoved the panic down.

"Don't worry, Talon went with me. I think the tigers were busy."

"Tigers?"

"Well, they weren't tigers all the time, sometimes they were men," she admitted.

Mari relaxed, "Imagination is a wonderful thing, which reminds me, we have to get her a new doll."

"I don't want a doll, mamah, I want a rock."

"Talk to your father, he's the one who knows rocks."

Brenna looked at her father, "What kind of rocks do you have?"

"Come with me and I'll show you," he said, leading her to his jewelry case. "There are amethyst, rubies, emeralds…"

After several minutes of studying them, Brenna heaved a great sigh. "I guess I'll give him the one I have. Thanks, Papah."

Lyon put his work away and went to Mari. "She is the first girl I know that didn't choose a gem."

"That's because there are many gems and only one Talon."

He thought about it for a minute and decided she was right.

Talon was currently waiting for Lyon to come and teach him another set of forms.

"Be right back," he placed a quick kiss on her neck and left.

Two hours later, Lyon was watching the two children out the window.

"Did you see how quickly he picked up the advanced forms?" He was in awe over the level of precision in such a young boy.

Mari snorted in disbelief, "What I noticed was the depth of concern that he got it right the first time."

"Tasut doesn't suffer fools gladly." Lyon acknowledged in a neutral voice.

"I can't understand why the Forest Wife doesn't do something about that man," she frowned.

"That isn't our affair, Mari," Lyon watched his daughter concentrate on the precise movements that Talon made as he finished his night forms and prepared for meditation, legs crossed, hands on knees and face turned upward as if to greet Father of All. "We don't have to agree with his methods."

"Methods?! That stone-fisted wonder threw his son into the water and took off like the Five creators were after him! We should break something of his next time he comes."

"How will that help Talon?"

"It would make me feel a lot better," his wife murmured, ripping a brush through her hair.

"That's not really true," he frowned. Lyon was disgusted as well but he let go of things easier than Mari.

"You're right, Talon *is* brilliant at forms," Mari said softly, laying her brush down and putting her hands over Lyons where they rested on her shoulders. "In fact, Talon's very good at whatever he does."

"It's more than that, Mari. You need to give Tasut some credit for teaching Talon to follow through. Whatever that boy begins, gets finished." Lyon's grey eyes looked into her bi-colored ones and her brow arched in response.

"That doesn't change the fact Talon flinches when he makes a mistake."

"No it doesn't, but we know the reason even if we aren't accepting excuses for Tasut's brutality."

"Well," Mari announced, "he's ours for the moment!" She picked up her brush again as Lyon moved away.

He hid his smile. Mari was fierce in her love. She was a woman of passion and during their years together, he had gained a healthy respect for her unrelenting ability to champion causes whether they were lost or not. He would hate to have her for an enemy.

Lyon watched his beautiful wife brush her waist-length hair. It seems he never tired of it. It was long, silky, and the perfect frame for her beautiful face. She hummed softly as she counted the strokes.

The Council of Nine had been right and wrong about her. Right about the fact she was dangerous and wrong to order her death.

"Remember the night we met?" Lyon lay back on their bed as he watched her through his lashes. He was eternally grateful that he had failed to fulfill his assignment to assassinate her eight years ago and he was even more grateful that she had ordered him to marry her. In hindsight, he could see divine intervention from the first time he read the instructions. Up until that day, he had never questioned orders.

"You mean, after you followed me around for three days?" she loved to rub it in, the fact that she knew he was following.

"I couldn't get enough of looking at you," he smiled.

"And here I thought all this time, you were just trying to figure things out," she smiled in pleasure.

"The assignment rubbed me the wrong way," he candidly admitted. Something about her and the situation had given him pause. He had noted she was very beautiful, obviously Utakian with their customary willowy form and gracefulness, but with Marianna, there was something more. This 'something more' was what put him off balance and delayed him fulfilling the mission.

"Admit that it made you nervous when I looked at you in the market," she gave him a sly grin.

"I was merely admiring your beauty while planning a quick and merciful death," he said while suppressing a shudder.

In his minds eye he saw the market bathed in morning light. The stalls were pale yellow as they sat like wood monuments waiting to be worshipped. He had been watching her from the other side of the marketplace. To his complete astonishment, she had looked directly at him with those bi-colored eyes.

Somehow, it was as if she knew what he was thinking or planning, and she was amused! Her eyes, one green, one brown, had sparkled and her mouth bowed into a beautiful smile. She had shaken her head slightly as if to say 'silly boy' while he was still reeling, stricken with the idea that his mark had seen him. He had never before experienced the disconcerting feeling of being seen by his mark.

"What made you hesitate?" she gave him a saucy smile, enjoying the game.

"Gut instinct." Back then he wasn't sure what made him hesitate. He had seen beautiful before in all its varieties and had still not failed taking out his mark. With the other great beauties, he had merely completed the task and moved onto his next assignment.

"Then there was the handwriting on the orders. It looked like Delf's." Assignments for all registered assassins in Sogo came in black leather pouches that were left in their rooms, unopened, on their beds at the Guild. Mort, an ancient moth-eaten looking Shee who worked for crab or fish eggs, delivered them. Mort wasn't as particular as Mee about hygiene, nor was he attached to any one of the assassins emotionally like Mee was to Brenna. However, Mort was a fanatic about delivering the mail and therefore useful.

Mari rolled her eyes, "Delf has fried his brains too often to think a solid sentence, much less compose a note. You told me the written orders said I was to be killed because I withheld valuable ancient artifacts, right?"

He nodded.

"I seriously doubt Delf can spell the word artifacts, much less have the brains to suspect that I found sandpools. Your insight was just trying to tell you the truth."

Lyon rose from their bed. "My sight told me a lot about you..." he took the brush from her hand and began to kiss her on the neck.

"You never looked like any of the Poolseers I'd ever seen. Most importantly, you didn't act like a thief."

She stood to face him, comfortable in the circle of his arms.

He continued, "Then there was that mansion you rented. It was large and spacious, indicating you had wealth, influence, or both. Yet, you didn't act the part. My employer's note claimed you were a Poolseer, but I knew the list of seers by heart and your name was missing."

"Is that when you wondered how I escaped registration? Or was it later?"

It was a fair question. Pool scrying was a rare talent and all those with that talent were supposed to be registered by law, willing or not.

"Actually, it was the first question I had."

"One of many dilemmas?" she teased, kissing the corners of his mouth.

"Their mistake was making it too easy, Mari," he confessed, a crease in his brow let her know the facts still rubbed him wrong.

"I remember it was Full Moon Festival," she traced his jaw line with a fingertip and then kissed him on the chin.

"That was another thing that made me crazy," Lyon crossed the room to prop their bedroom window open. "Nez always gave a deadline whenever he ordered death. Delf was sloppy as his handwriting. The note just had all the earmarks of Nez attached, only without Nez's signature."

"Did you start to wonder if you were being set up?"

He nodded, "Everyone knows about Nez ability to use magic. It's the only way someone could get into my room at the Guild."

Lyon was the Master of the Sogoian Assassins Guild – the person who gave out the assignments. Personally. A fact that the Council of Nine did not know and never would.

Unknowns were the invisible assassins that all heads of state feared because no one knew who they were, other than the Nine and the Guild Master. They were sent to take out whoever the Nine thought politically incorrect, inept, or dangerous. Lyon was the best, like his father before him.

Lyon crawled out the window. It was an open secret that Nez had a not-so-secret passion for becoming ruler of Sogo. *He can have it, cesspool that it is. Good business for the Guild though, you never run out of scum that needs to be eliminated.*

"Tell me more," she whispered in his ear as he reached in and pulled her out into the night air.

"Don't you ever get tired of hearing the story?"

She smiled, "Well, it was the most earth-shaking thing that had happened to me up to that point."

He sighed, "You already know about the coffin and the witness."

Lyon was supposed to meet the man in the garden just long enough to verify the death and then Lyon would put the body in the coffin and drive off. These details were just odd enough to attract both his attention and suspicion.

"I went in early and searched all the rooms while you were still at market. That's when I came across the letters that told me you were a Magi as well as a Poolseer."

All his inner warning signals had gone off at that piece of information. Magi were even more valuable to the population than the Poolseers. "I couldn't understand why they would kill a national treasure so I hoped to find something incriminating to justify what I was ordered to do. If I found one reason, I was committed to doing the job."

"It became even more mysterious when I found letters you were writing to a friend in the library. I was even more confused and impressed when I read them."

"You were surprised that I could read and write?" her voice was amused.

He nodded, unembarrassed. The women in Sogo were devious but generally uneducated. The letter's subject matter revealed a sense of humor as she described the festivities, and an acute business sense when she noted that the open market could use more variety, especially flowers.

"Of all the rooms you might have chosen in that mansion, you preferred the library; I figured it was because it was the one room with a fireplace."

"Why did you wait so long to do something interesting?" she asked as they walked down a flagstone path to their small garden.

"You intrigued me," he took her hand and kissed it. "A barefoot woman who reads the history of the Five while she hums Ammon's March is irresistible."

He had watched her from the shadows the first two evenings as she sat and read before the fire, wearing a pale blue wrap. It amused him that her feet were bare. He was charmed that she hummed a fighting song as she read.

"When did you decide to kill me?"

"The third day," he was uncomfortable with the thought and pulled her into his arms and tried to forget how he had spent the day searching, hiding, guessing, and still had nothing to go on. Thus it was, he had decided to go on faith that whoever wanted her dead knew what they were talking about. He would kill her.

He'd moved quietly down to the lowest level of the house. She sat near the fire once more, looking absolutely breathtaking in an emerald gown with sedate ruffles at the neckline. He had already decided he would break her neck instead of obeying the direction to slit her throat. It seemed more merciful and less messy. There were shadows aplenty in the room to hide in. She had drawn the curtains and the fire had died down somewhat. One candle flickered nearby as she perused a book called Legends of Kham, which he planned to take as part of his fee. It was a very valuable book.

"But my instinct rebelled," he whispered against her hair. "I couldn't do it."

In the dancing yellow light, she'd looked carved from fine ivory. Her bare feet were tucked under her to keep them warm. Her right hand was near her ankle, the other holding the book. He was positioned in the shadows behind her, still reluctant to make the kill. Then something happened that completely threw him off.

"That's not the way I remember it," she said with wry amusement.

"Then let's re-write history," he said, holding her closer as they slow-danced over the grassy turf.

"Our history has a happy ending," she reminded him, twirling under his arm and he stopped the dance, keeping her locked in his embrace.

"I was shocked when you asked if I was going to kill you or stare you to death, " he admitted.

That night, the dagger he had up his sleeve had slid to his hand, at the ready.

She'd given a little wave with her hand and closed the book, "Lyon Tybar, no one has ever been able to get this far before. You are the best."

It had really annoyed him at the time that he had felt flattered and that her unusual eyes held him in place. She was amused, but cautious. The hand resting on her foot had slid under the hem of her gown and he thought he saw it bunch, like it was making a fist.

"I still remember what you said," and Mari quoted, " 'Tell me, Marianna Ryn, what does the Council of Nine want with a Poolseer and Mage?'"

He smiled, "I couldn't resist turning the tables on you. What I remember most is how beautiful you looked."

Mari smiled, "I remember that night even better than you do."

"The point is, love, we're dancing together now," he brought the dance to an end by giving her a kiss that made her grateful he was hers and more than grateful that he didn't know the truth about that night.

Chapter 22: Eyes

To this day, their ninth anniversary, Lyon still did not know Mari was Hi-Sha of Eyes, leader of a secret organization of women. They were dedicated to protecting Brenna at any cost.

In point of fact, Mari did remember that night better than Lyon. Her two sisters, both Eyes, were in the house that night and he had been standing in the crosshairs of poisonous darts. They had watched and listened to the proceedings, waiting for her signal. She gave it to them – the wave of her hand indicated they should leave.

In the early morning light, Mari looked at her sleeping husband, wishing she could tell him the whole truth and knowing she wouldn't. *Not yet.*

Lyon slowly smiled and spoke, his smoky grey eyes slowly opening, "I knew after you told me your story, my life would never be the same."

"Neither was mine," she confessed as she layed her head on his chest. "Especially when you mentioned my burial and transport into Utak."

He gave her a squeeze. "If you remember, you said no."

She rose up to her elbow and frostily said, "The terms weren't exactly romantic."

"Remind me what it was you wanted," his eyes were full of laughter.

"You," her cheeks looked faintly pink even now, but her bi-colored eyes were as serious now as they were then. "Do you remember your reaction?"

"If fairies had appeared and stuffed my nose with magic dust, I doubt you could have stunned me anymore than you did," his voice smiled.

"That goes double for what you said after I told you that you had to marry me and we'd have a daughter."

He chuckled. "I remember saying, "Just as soon as we bury you."" He was silent for a moment, "Right after that, I fell in love with you."

She laughed at the absurdity of his statement in light of the situation, and he couldn't help but smile back.

The day they were married, they had arranged a very public, very spectacular death for him. He was 'killed in action' while leaping from the roof of a famous brothel.

Only one person in Sogo knew that he wasn't dead, and that was the official Master of the Guild. In exchange for his silence, he was paid well and currently had the prestige of the title.

"Do you ever regret giving it up?" Mari asked.

He shook his head, "I know at the funeral they said I was faithful in following the honored tradition of my father and grandfather, but you know I never wanted to be an Assassin.

"I thought for a long time that it was the only way to fit in my family. You never met my father, but he was greatly admired for what he did. I used the excuse that I had to have a life beyond the Guild when I became what I wanted to be. Which reminds me," he smiled and reached beneath his pillow. He pulled out a slender silver case with the initial M inscribed. "I didn't forget what today is. Happy Anniversary."

She sat up to open it and he gently laid his hand on hers, the warmth of it giving her goosebumps.

"I've never loved anyone but you, Mari. I've never wanted anyone the same way – or even seen anyone the same way. I can trust you and that means more to me than any treasure, any kind of excitement my former life offered."

Tears of guilt sprang to her eyes as she looked at the gift, hoping he would think they were tears of joy, "It's beautiful." The bracelet was a mix of gold and silver, with diamond and emerald clusters.

He nodded, looking concerned, "Loni gave me your father's old watch and two broken necklaces which were your mothers," he sighed. "I couldn't fix them without changing the entire design so I melted them down. I wasn't sure if you would approve, but Loni told me the idea was a good one."

Mari nodded, touched that her sister had surrendered the pieces. She felt a tear trickle down her cheek.

Lyon was a jeweler at heart and officially a gold and silversmith by trade. He was the best and far more than she deserved. She wanted to tell him and it was on the tip of her tongue, but she couldn't.

The tears came faster as he put the bracelet on her wrist and kissed the palm of her hand; which led his lips to the inside of her elbow and then her neck.

It was an enjoyable morning.

*

Lyon looked at his sleeping wife, her hand was palm up, her beautiful face calm and untroubled.

His heart swelled in one of those rare moments where he was at peace with the world, still in love with his passionate wife and twice amazed she returned that love.

He could not possibly love anyone the same way he loved Mari. He had believed he couldn't hold any more love in his heart because it was so full of what he felt for the willowy beauty that had been at his side for nine years.

Then Brenna had come into their life to make their joy complete.

He had helped deliver his daughter, growing pale at times, gritting his teeth often. What could be worth that kind of pain?

Then Mari held Brenna and the glow that filled her took his breath away. He had gently kissed Mari's forehead and the Forest Wife, who had finally arrived, shooed him out with, "Wait in the garden."

It was a glorious day, the best that had ever been. The back door had opened and his smile disappeared at the look on the Forest Wife's face.

"She's stubborn," the Forest Wife said, handing Brenna to him, clean and wrapped tightly in a fleecy white blanket. Brenna's extraordinary blue eyes peered up at him and a never-forgotten smile crossed her perfect features before she promptly fell asleep.

"She smiled at me," he said out loud, his heart pounding with the fervent need to let the world know he was a father and that his daughter was the most perfect child ever born.

The Forest Wife broke into his thoughts. "Your daughter *is* very special."

He hadn't taken his eyes off his beautiful daughter as his smile broadened. Then she said the words that rearranged their lifes.

"She is the One."

His heart shuddered and he glanced at her. "What! How can you possibly know that?" As soon as the words left his lips, he recognized his own ignorance.

Ever practical, the Forest Wife said, "Keep her hidden. I suggest moving often, but you must never take her to the Islands."

He was about to ask why when she flummoxed him with, "She will be your only child." She let that settle a bit and then added, "Mari didn't know she was pregnant when she summoned the Chest of Souls. The amount of power that had flowed through her made her sterile. In fact, I'm amazed your child survived."

Lyon felt concern for his wife, who had always wanted a large family. "Does she know?"

One curt nod, and the Forest Wife opened an airdoor to the other side of time. "Your child must learn obedience; it is the first law anyone with power must learn."

The airdoor closed. With a heavy heart, he looked into his daughter's beautiful face, smoothing her coal-black hair away from her eyes. "I will always protect you," he promised, holding his daughter closer, his eyes automatically going out to the wood beyond, then back to the house. "Let's go talk to your mother."

Propped up in bed, Mari was staring out the window.

"Did you know?" was his first question.

Mari shook her head, "I'm s-sorry, Lyon." Then she began to cry and for the first of many times, he told her, "It doesn't matter, Mari. Raising her is going to take all we have. We wouldn't be able to care for any other children. They'd become targets."

Mari dried her tears, reached for, and held their only child, "What do you want to name her?"

He shrugged, "You did all the hard work, you chose."

"Brenna."

He blinked. It wasn't a family name, but it was fitting - Brenna was the Utakian word for hope.

Still wrapped in that early memory, Lyon rose from their bed and left to tend to the animals. He should have done it earlier, but had purposefully delayed it so he could spend time with Mari on their anniversary. Brenna was with Tryk and Talon, her favorite place to be.

Lyon had held Brenna for most of three straight days after she was born. He had marveled at the miracle that Father of All had given them. He had memorized her face, rocked her, and sang to her.

Mari had been amused. She was positive the novelty of it would wear off, but it never had. Brenna was the apple of his eye and Mari the caretaker of his heart.

The night of that third day, while he was rocking her, he was trying to recall what he had read in the Book of Benamii. In truth, he hadn't been a spiritual man. He had been raised all over the world and seen too much injustice to believe in a supreme being.

Mari had begun the process of helping him understand. Brenna was polishing his education of faith in something greater.

"You have given me a cause to fight for," he whispered to his sleeping daughter. "With your mother at my side, you will be raised to believe."

He thought he'd finished with learning more about faith. He had read the Book of Benamii without really reading it in a personal way. It was personal now.

The shadow of doubt did not mar the conviction in his soul. His family was to be a large part of it. The destruction of Sogo was coming and their daughter was going to be at the center of the maelstrom that took it down.

It was frightening at times, but exhilarating. There wasn't a better time to be alive and there was no one more qualified than Mari and himself to protect the One.

It was time to move again. Brenna would not be happy because it meant more distance between herself and Talon.

He frowned. If he had been given his choice, he would have chosen to take Talon with them. However, he knew Tasut wouldn't allow it, no matter how much Mari thought otherwise. Logically, it made sense to keep them together for now, but Tasut wasn't ruled by human emotion or logic.

Lyon thought about where they could move. They owned several small cottages that dotted the country of Acha under various names. One thing was certain; before they moved again, they would have to see Tahloni and, heaven help him, Haddy. Mari would insist and she would be right. Ryn Orphanage was as safe as anywhere else in the world; perhaps safer.

It might be time to head north to Jahjah, or maybe as far north as Quivah. There had been some excellent ore found in that vicinity and he could use some good quality material to work with. It wouldn't take that long to smelt enough to make several valuable pieces.

Mari had him making hundreds of dual-leaf brooches in his spare time as graduation gifts for the girls who had been trained in the orphanages and were now seeking their way out in the world.

Mari always received the very best he made, but many of the women of Sogo wore his work without knowing it.

Lyon had first learned the trade from a man called Flynn who had a little shop in the eastern part of Sogo.

Flynn was very talented, but a thief at heart. He had been patient with Lyon, who had been working for the Guild at the time. In exchange for his teaching, Lyon kept him off the hit lists and had also crafted one dozen necklaces, each of different stones in as many settings.

His final piece had been an emerald and diamond necklace, a fanciful piece that Lyon had wanted to give to Mari. He had sacrificed it out of gratitude and given it to Flynn, who had been speechless.

Lyon knew the value of bribery and felt he had just purchased a lifetimes worth of blind, deaf, and dumbness for Flynn.

It had been worth the price of that necklace. Lyon was invisible anytime he came to the shop. Flynn never spoke to him unless Lyon spoke first and never demanded more work.

What made their arrangement more solid, was the fact Lyon knew Flynn was courting a woman without morals; a woman who had kept company with some of the Nine.

Flynn coaxed secrets from her by gifting her with the unsaleable jewelry as gifts. In turn, he gave the information to Lyon.

It was a win-win situation. Flynn didn't dare slither out from the cracks of his own deception, not without Lyon's permission.

Chapter 23: Persuasion

Tahloni Ryn, lovingly referred to as Loni, arrived in the small settlement of Chanz, the Tybar's newest residence. She came amidst a rainsquall that bubbled down from the Ammonite Islands and ferociously slapped into the far corners of Acha. Lyon smiled when he saw her, and waved from the barn where he and Talon were grooming the animals.

Mari hurried her dripping sister into the hallway and then into the kitchen.

Lyon and Talon returned to the house a short time later to find Brenna eating cookie dough, sitting on the braided rug near the kitchen table. The red ceramic bowl, most commonly used to mix batter, was sitting in the folds of Brenna's skirt.

"Where's your mother?" Lyon asked, taking a look at the hook on the wall where Mari kept her outdoor cloak. It was gone.

"She gave me the bowl and left you a note," Brenna said with a sticky smile. "Talon, come have some, its really good. Aunt Loni made it, she makes the bestest cookies!" With a look at her preoccupied father who stood by the kitchen table reading the note, she took a large handful of the dough and put it behind her back.

Lyon finally seemed to notice what Brenna was doing and took the bowl and spoon away from his daughter and picked up the note from the kitchen table. From behind her back, Brenna brought out a large fistful of dough and tried to give it to Talon. He smiled and shook his head while he watched Lyon begin to move pots and pans around.

"Obey," Talon said to her. She looked regretfully at the dough in her hand and solemnly walked over to the table and put it back in the bowl. Talon noted she licked the remaining dough off her hands.

"Did she say where they were going?" her father asked looking slightly confused. The note had merely said, "Gone with Loni, Love, Mari."

"Aunt Loni said to tell you she needed mamah's help at the orphanage." Brenna continued to lick her fingers.

Lyon nodded absently. Mari's older sister ran the Ryn House orphanage and he trusted Tahloni completely.

Their younger sister, Hadasha, however, was another story. Hadasha or Haddy (a nickname she hated) was very pretty and she flaunted it. Hopefully, his wonderful wife wouldn't have a reason to take Haddy to task. He knew this was mostly wishful thinking because Mari, as much as he loved her, wasn't as kind or patient as Loni. Mari wouldn't put up with Haddy's selfishness. He was glad to miss the fireworks between the Ryn sisters. He happily spent the morning making cookies with his bubbling-happy daughter and the boy who had become the son he would never have.

"I have to go to the village and get some supplies," Lyon said. "You two stay here and…"

Brenna frowned, "Please, can we go?"

He looked at her, noting that Talon looked eager as well. "Very well, but I think we'll need to take a few precautions. Brenna, you have to wear that big scarf over your head; the gray one. Don't use your gifts if you can help it and Talon must be with you every moment."

Brenna's smile grew wider and she hurried to get the scarf from the bedroom. While she was gone, Lyon whispered, "I trust you to keep her out of trouble."

Talon nodded, but his excitement dimmed a little with the prospect of keeping his eyes on Brenna.

Once they arrived outside the small city, Lyon stopped the mules and pulled off the blanket that covered them. Lyon lifted Brenna out of the wagon, gave her a kiss on her forehead, and set her on the ground.

Talon jumped down and took Brenna's hand. As usual, she smiled up at him.

Talon saw that Lyon had stopped in an alley where the buildings had no windows on the sides.

"When you see me leave the supply store," he looked at Talon, "I'll be heading back here to wait for you. You may make it before me. If you do, stay out of sight."

Lyon looked Brenna right in the eyes, "Alright little lady, promise me that you'll do whatever Talon tells you to."

Brenna eagerly nodded and Lyon tied her scarf on just a bit tighter. "Keep your hair covered and Mee…"

Mee, who was wrapped around Brenna's neck and pretending to be a collar, blinked at Lyon.

"…you're to stay with them. If you are especially good, I'll get you a crab."

Mee instantly went back to being a collar. Talon heard her muffled "Kay."

To Talon he said, "Stay on the main street."

Chanz was a small city and Talon thought it fascinating. Although a bit intimidated, he still enjoyed walking up and down the street, even if he did have to hold Brenna's hand.

"Oh, look!" Brenna said as they passed a shop window.

He paused and looked at what she pointed to. It was another doll. He looked at a Steps game board next to it. The colors were the same, but not as grand as the one that Lyon had.

"It's nice, isn't it?" Brenna said. She'd been watching him look a the game board.

"Where are you going?" he asked as Brenna pulled his hand.

"I want a closer look, but you have to do the talking."

When Brenna entered the shop, the storekeeper glanced up and then looked again – at Brenna, who tugged on Talon's shirt. He leaned down to listen as she whispered, "Tell him I want to look at the doll and the game board."

Talon straightened up, his stomach in knots. He wasn't sure if this was the right thing to do. Lyon had told him to keep her out of trouble, but just looking couldn't hurt. Without him saying a word, the shopkeeper eagerly came over and smiled at Brenna, ignoring Talon.

"What would you like to see?"

Brenna pointed to the doll in the window.

It was just the beginning. Just before Brenna left she whispered, "Thank you" to the man. The shopkeeper's eyes became vacant and he started humming tunelessly, staring at nothing.

"We can't just take all this," Talon protested. In the large basket the storekeeper gave them, there was the doll, the Steps game, a new scarf, and a large variety of sweets.

Brenna looked at him in surprise. "He just gave it all to us. Mamah said it's rude to refuse gifts."

What Brenna said was true. The storekeeper had insisted they take every single item as his gift for "such a winsome smile". He hadn't meant Talon's because Talon was scowling.

"I don't think he knew what he was doing," Talon insisted.

Brenna looked guilty and Talon knew he'd struck a chord.

"We have to put it all back," he said, starting with the doll.

"But we could give it to the orphans!" Brenna lamented.

"You can't steal from people and give what you take to others, it's wrong," Talon insisted.

Brenna looked shocked. "I don't steal!"

"Did you pay for it?" he asked. Brenna shook her head.

Talon put everything back while Brenna sulked. Then he tapped the bemused storekeeper on the shoulder. "Thanks for letting us see the toys."

The man blinked as if waking up from a nap. "Certainly. Anything, uh…anything else I can do for you young man?"

Talon shook his head and pulled Brenna out of the shop.

"Are you mad at me?" Brenna asked a short time later.

"No," he said. "But how did you do it? What did you do to that man?"

"I don't know," she sounded like she was telling the truth.

"Does it happen all the time?"

Brenna thought about it. "Only when I really want something."

"I thought you had a doll." He was a bit disgusted.

"I did, but I gave her to a friend and I thought if I gave her a different one, she'd let me have mine back."

His heart softened a bit. "What about the game?"

"I thought you wanted it."

He had, but not if it meant stealing.

"The scarf?"

"Mamah has a dress just that color and she said when she had time, she'd get a scarf to match."

"The sweets?"

"I wanted to get something for all the Ryn House orphans."

He was feeling better about her motivation now. All she wanted to do was give to others, even the doll. Still, it was wrong and he knew that Lyon and Mari wouldn't want her to do it. "That was nice of you to think about everyone, but you can't do it that way anymore, Brenna."

"He has lots of…"

He shook his head to stop her, "That storekeeper has to pay for everything before he can sell it, so it would have been stealing from him."

She was silent and he half expected her to pull her hand away, but she didn't.

"Will you tell papah?"

"I won't lie to him," Talon said.

"I'll tell him," she said. "That way you won't get in trouble."

He wasn't so sure about that. What had seemed a great adventure had soured. "Let's go wait for the wagon."

Brenna told her father what had happened on the way home. It didn't go the way Talon had thought. Instead of anger, Lyon became very quiet. The trip was made in silence.

"I'm disappointed in you, Brenna," Lyon finally said as they arrived back at the house. She burst into tears and the moment he put her on the ground, Brenna ran for the house. Talon was surprised that he felt sorry for her, but he was worried about his own punishment and braced himself.

"Thank you Talon."

In shock, Talon looked at Lyon.

"You showed great integrity and more self control than many men I've known."

Talon's face flamed under the compliment. "All I did was tell her to put it back." He jumped down from the wagon seat to help Lyon unpack the supplies.

"Exactly."

As they worked to unload the wagon, Talon asked the question that had been bothering him. "What did she do to that man?"

"Brenna is very persuasive."

"But it's more than that, isn't it?"

Lyon nodded. "When she was three, we took her to town with us to get supplies for the orphanage. Without excepton, every person Brenna looked at wanted to give her something, even if it was just a hello. All she did was smile.

"I wasn't sure, at the time, what was happening. But when a complete stranger gave me a pure-bred horse I'd shown to Brenna, I knew I was experiencing a different kind of phenomenon.

"I tested my theory by calling the merchants and storekeepers over to my wagon and letting Brenna smile at them. Before we left, the wagon was full and the orphans got badly needed supplies. I slipped the money into the merchants pockets before they left the wagon."

"We knew we had to keep a sharp eye on Brenna. Mari was able to control the amount of damage her smiles can do to the weak willed, but when she speaks, no one has a chance."

"Even you?" Talon asked.

"Once you know what she does, it won't work. Of course, the stronger your will, the less effective her persuasion would be."

"Why didn't it work on me?"

Lyon smiled. "You are your father's son. He has a will of iron."

Talon couldn't argue with that.

Chapter 24: Sisters

Chun Ta was looking out the dirty second floor window of the brothel for the thousandth time that day. The sun was setting, melting in a pool of crimson and gold. It would have been beautiful if not for her present circumstance. The clients would be showing up and she and her sister Wysh would have to be on guard.

Thank goodness for Tiz. Although she was of two minds about their Shee. He was all they had inherited from their dead mother. He favored her sister Wysh, probably because she was so quiet and babied him at every opportunity. Yet, he could be fierce if the situation warranted. He had already saved them twice from clients who had wandered into the wrong rooms.

Her thoughts returned to the present as she heard women's quiet voices on the other side of the painted paper wall. She longed to return to their former room that had real walls and a lock on the door, but she had tried to run away with Wysh once and for the last three years, they had been prisoners on the second floor in the corner room.

In two weeks, I will be one of them. Her heart sank with a sense of desperation and despair. She had been doing everything humanly possible she could think of to get her and Wysh out of this miserable hole. She had been fighting this desperate battle ever since their cousins had sold them to pay for their brother Yun's upkeep. She did extra laundry, cooked extra meals, and fasted twice a week to save what money she would have spent on food and still she could not get them out from under the roof of the brothel.

Today she was watching for their little brother as she did every day. After the fire that had made Chun, Wysh, and Yun, orphans, their cousin, who had no sons, took Yun. She held her breath as she caught sight of him. As usual, he came with the cousins near sundown to the open market. The ramshackle stalls lay just outside and to the right of the window where she stood looking out. He was a handsome, sturdy boy with black hair and slanted brown eyes. He was nearly six years old.

For three years she had been praying twice daily for a sign that one day they would escape and she could hug Yun again. She had nearly missed seeing him the first time he had come to the square with their cousins.

On that day, Chun had looked through her tears and been unable to breathe for the pain in her soul. Yun had looked right up at her; his sad little face streaked with tears. He was three years old when she and Wysh had been sold. One of their cousins roughly jerked him and slapped his sweet cherub-like face and Chun had hidden away, crumpled to the floor and cried. Her heart ached with such pain she thought she would die and that pain solidified into anger and determination. One day, she had vowed, that cousin would pay for what he had done to them.

Chun grew melancholy at the memory and rubbed her sleeve on the window so she could see his now six-year-old face better.

Tonight might be their last chance to see each other again before she became someone he would not want to know. The next time he saw her, she would be someone their cousins would never recognize in public. No decent man would. It bothered her, this separation of who she really was and what she would become if circumstances did not change. Her twice-daily prayers had become one solid prayer lasting all day, every day.

She had never felt anything so deeply, wanted anything so much as their freedom and it was for this miracle she continued to hope. She still had a chance to believe and as long as she did, she would.

Tiz, her sister's tiger-striped Shee was once more preening himself, using the cracked mirror braced against the bare bedroom wall. Wysh sat in the darkest corner on a broken rocker, pale and silent. Chun could feel the fear emanating from Wysh like the fingers of winter touching her soul. She didn't know how to reassure her blind sister that all would be well. She felt it would destroy her soul if she became what they all said she would be. A harlot. Condemned to being a plaything for perverse men. It would be worse for Wysh. The owner of the brothel had already put the word on the streets that in two years time, there would be a blind girl for use.

It had been Wysh who had heard not only her own fate, but Chun's as well. Wysh refused to eat or drink until Chun promised her they would escape before that could happen, even if it meant killing Wysh herself. It was a rash promise. Chun had given it in desperation to save her sister's life by getting her to eat again. She had such determination and hope for the impossible, that she could not *would not* entertain the idea that she would have to kill Wysh. She felt ill every time Wysh brought it up. That unpleasant conversation always ended with, "You promised."

Chun felt large salty tears slide down her face, and she impatiently brushed them away. She had always been able to think of a way out before, but time was nearly gone. If she remained here, there was no way she would be able to take care of her family. She closed her eyes to pray. *Help me find a way!* She refused to give up hope. Just the other night she had a dream that left her with hope of escape and a reunion with Yun.

As she watched Yun glance up at her from the street below, a tall woman wearing a non-descript grey cloak with its cowl covering her head crossed the street. Two other women in similar garb followed her. *Could it be?* Hope flamed within her and she held her breath. *My dream! That woman was in my dream! My prayer is answered!*

"Tiz!" she said trying to keep her excitement out of her voice. "You know what to do. The soda tablet is in my top drawer. If any of the men show up, be sure to put on your best performance. I'll be right back,"

Chun promised. "There's something I need to see." Chun made her way quietly down from the top floor to the landing where she could watch what happened. She hid under the red velvet curtains that went from ceiling to floor and framed the only window on the second story. A window with bars. She brushed the heavy curtain aside, listening intently for possible detection.

Her dark green eyes adjusted to the light from the many candles below in time to realize the three women wearing cloaks had entered through the side door. Every occupant of the brothel knew that it was forbidden to enter through the doorway leading to the alley. No client had ever come through the door that she knew about. Hope swelled again and she felt tears come to her eyes.

*

Mari whispered a word and the rusty lock gave up. She quietly entered the side door. Her two sisters, looking like grey shadows, slid in behind her. Now they were in, Loni would make the first strike.

Mari watched her oldest sister quietly melt into the hallway and cautiously make her way up the stairs, her pale-green eyes glittering in the waning light that peeked weakly through the dirty red-clad window.

Loni's job was simple and it was the one she insisted performing each time they made one of these raids. She would kill the owner. She despised all brothel owner's with a purple-eyed passion.

Haddy's job was also simple: watch the door they had just come through. It was the only job Mari trusted her with. She wasn't happy about it, but curbed her tongue for now. Loni had practically begged Mari to let Haddy come. Mari had said no at first, but finally gave in to Loni who so seldom asked for anything.

However, being the person she was, Mari could not resist warning her younger sister before they left the Ryn House, "One mistake, Haddy, and you will *never* come again." On this job, Haddy was out to prove

that she could follow orders as well as or better than Loni did, to satisfy
Mari.

*

There's no satisfying Mari. Haddy thought as she stood by the door,
sincerely hoping the festival on the other side of town was still going on
when she returned. She didn't dare tell Loni that the only reason she had
wanted to come was curiosity. She had no desire to help tramps or save
anyone that lived in a brothel. *If they aren't smart enough to escape,
they get what they deserve.*

*

Mari crept to the front door to pull the red-tasseled shade, lock the
garish purple door, and flip the sign from open to closed. If all went
well for the Ryn sisters this night, it would never open again.

She looked up as Loni returned. Her sister was slightly out of breath
but her green eyes showed satisfaction. Mari knew the first part of
Loni's job was done. The man running this brothel was dead.

Loni nodded at Mari. The two of them had planned this over a year
ago and it was finally coming to fruition. Mari's full lips pulled into a
tight, determined line as she pushed the deep cowl back from her face
and she shot a quick glance up the stairs at a young girl she had noticed
earlier, just after they arrived. *Good, she's still safe.*

*

Chun pushed herself back into the shadows as far as she could. The
woman knew where she was and had done nothing to her. Chun had the
glorious feeling none of these women would hurt them. The woman
who had seen her reached inside her cloak, and was reading a scroll she
had pulled from under its folds. Now that her features were not hidden
in the shadow of the cowl, she was one of the most beautiful women
Chun had ever seen.

She glanced over at the tallest woman of the three who had come in
the side door. She had also pushed back her cowl and stood at the

bottom of the other set of stairs. Chun was surprised to see that she was much older than the first woman and very plain. However, in the plain woman's eyes were equal amounts of determination and good humor. She actually winked at Chun who had to return the smile. Chun turned her head to the third woman who was younger. Whoever she was, she was angry and sullen. She had tossed her cowl back as if to say 'get on with it' and Chun got the impression that she was bored and impatient. She was beautiful as well, but you didn't notice it right away. Chun supposed it was because she wore such a resentful expression. She stood at the bottom of the staircase closest to Chun, yet she didn't spare Chun a glance.

The most beautiful of the three women nodded at the tallest one who reached up and rang the bell rope. The ringing of the bell falsely signaled the women who lived above stairs that the night's clients had arrived.

Chun quickly hid herself behind a large, ornate, and rather ugly vase full of peacock feathers on the eastside of the landing. From this vantage point, she could see the back of the head of the woman who issued the orders. Bedroom doors opened and closed. She could feel the air and smell the perfume of the tenants as they sauntered by. Chun wished she could see their expressions when they got to the bottom of the staircase to find three women and no customers waiting.

The woman that had locked the front door waited for all the harlots to come down. When they did, their expressions were comical as they exchanged looks with one another. They started asking questions, but none of them were answered until they all settled.

"Who are you?" demanded Pash, the oldest woman in the group at twenty-three years of age, according to the scroll Mari read. Mari had created the scroll years ago with magic and under the Forest Wife's tutelage. It never failed to impress her by what magically appeared on the scroll concerning the people in the house. She could take it into any dwelling and it would give her the names of everyone in the house, a physical description of them, and often some little tidbit about each person. Usually the tidbit was something they preferred to keep secret. It even listed Mari as "Tall, beautiful woman of the house of Ryn. Utakian born, Achaite by choice, one brown eye, one green. Wife of Lyon Tybar and Hi-Sha of Eyes..." there was more, but she didn't read it.

Pash's dark blue eyes gave each of the Ryn sisters a sweep, remaining on Mari. Pash was a slender blonde with a firm jaw and disposition. According to the scroll, Pash was also a widow who had been tricked into the brothel and kept prisoner. She had killed one of the clients and was normally given kitchen duty.

"I am here to offer all of you an opportunity to be free of this place," Mari said with an arch of her brow at Pash.

"Where's Yang?" asked one of the redheads. Mari noted her name on the scroll as Tyn.

"Dead," Mari looked up from the scroll to see several heavily painted mouths open and remain in that position. It never failed to amaze her that the women in the brothels actually felt a loss when the man or woman who had enslaved them died. She returned to the scroll and spoke, "I have a list of the names of those who live here. Those who wish to stay, stand to the left. Those who want their freedom and a chance to learn a new trade, to the right."

From between the banisters, Chun had watched the names of every woman, including hers, appear on the blank parchment the woman held in her hands. She had no way of knowing Mari was magic, she only knew that she had her miracle and could arrange for the three women to take Wysh away. She gathered her courage, as she had so often before, determined that she would ask them.

Chun listened as the thirty-name list was read. Mari knew each before they acknowledged themselves. The final name, Zaya Kahlani, had just been uttered when the beautiful woman suddenly turned around and looked straight into Chun's eyes, "Chun Ta, are you coming?"

Chun's surprise went so deep that she felt confused. Something between awe and fear climbed into her heart and nested there as those bi-colored eyes stared into her own. The ladies standing below in the parlor all turned. Their eyes showed various degrees of bewilderment or suspicion, none of them had befriended her, but few were cruel. Most just ignored her and Wysh. She slowly walked down the stairs and toward her only hope. She stood before the women and struggled for courage.

"Madam?" she said to Mari in a soft tear-filled voice. "If it is not possible that you could take me, would you please, I beg you most humbly, take my sister Wysh when you leave?"

The tallest woman left her position and put her arm around young Chun Ta's thin shoulders, "All who desire to come with us are welcome."

Chun tore her eyes away from the scroll reader and looked up into pale green eyes, "So that means my brother who was taken from us can come too?"

Loni exchanged a glance with Mari, "Is he here?"

Mari shook her head.

"He's outside," Chun explained.

"We'll talk of it in a moment, dear," Loni said as she put a work-roughed hand on her shoulder.

"Let's begin where we have a path," Mari's heart had been touched by the pretty little girl. "Where is your sister?"

Chun, whose tears were now dry, felt excitement that she had not felt in a very long time. She pointed up the stairs and said, "Third door on the left."

Mari turned to Loni, "I'll get her sister and you do what needs to be done here. You," she ordered Haddy, "begin gathering the things we will take."

Haddy whistled out the side door, and five wagons began rolling towards the brothel. Each had an experienced driver who had once been part of a brothel or under other extreme circumstances.

Next, Haddy went into the kitchen and began opening cupboards and drawers. The wagon drivers began searching all nooks and crannies for items they could empty into waiting wooden crates that they brought in. They would take everything that would either fetch a price at the second-hand merchants, or be used to outfit another orphanage.

This brothel, Haddy noted, was well stocked with food. She found herself eager to go up the stairs into the rooms and make her own claim on things that the former occupants didn't want. Many of them wouldn't wear the dresses they had been given, but Haddy liked many of their things because she was clever with a needle and could make alterations.

The drivers from the wagons entered the door. Haddy set them to work and went back out into the parlor and up the stairs to hurry the women in their selections. Perhaps there would be some that would only take what they wore and nothing else, hating the life they had led and unwilling to be reminded. Those were the kind that usually made it good outside the brothel and had been forced into it through circumstances beyond their control.

As she passed by the women on the bottom floor, she could hear Loni was busy trying to talk some of the more belligerent women into wearing something more respectable.

What Haddy wanted to say was 'Let honor hang! They don't have any honor! Let's just take what and who we can and leave.' She held her tongue. Barely. She wanted to get to the festival. Even from here she could faintly hear the music.

Loni looked at the painted faces. Most of the women were suspicious and some were angry. "There are two choices ladies, one is to stay in Dyman and be homeless…"

"Who died and left you queen!" Pash demanded with some heat.

Loni ignored the outburst but Haddy walked right up to Pash and got about an inch from her face, "Don't talk to her that way slut!"

"Don't tell me what to do!" growled Pash.

Loni saw Pash was afraid that what they had in mind could be worse than what she had suffered, but patience and understanding were not Haddy's strong points. Loni saw Haddy's dark green eyes flash and she knew that she would be unable to stop her younger sister's mouth.

"I hope you do stay so I can burn this whore house down around your ears!"

Pash did what no one had ever done to Haddy. She slapped her across the face as hard as she could. Haddy's knives came out. Pash backed up, her pale face went completely white and the other women went quiet and moved quickly away. They had seen cat fights before.

Mari returned at that point, Loni was sure that she had heard the cruel remarks Haddy made and Pash's response because Mari gestured and the two women found themselves upside down in the air. Pash's skirt went over her head to reveal a rather old-fashioned pair of pantaloons. Haddy looked annoyed but also grateful she wore pants under her skirt, "We have a time frame. The Festival won't last forever. The wagons are ready." Mari looked down at Loni, "Let me know if you find out where the safe is."

"Try the last bedroom on the right," Loni said. Then she tried again to talk to the other women in the room, ignoring the two red-faced women hanging in the air knowing that after catching a glimpse of Mari's abilities, most of them would now listen.

"We are not telling you what to do. In fact, we are giving you a choice. I doubt one of you chose this profession. I'm not judging you,"

Loni said as some faces grew harder at her words, "but let's face facts. In your present occupation, once your looks are gone, so are you."

It was cruel and blunt but it was also true and they knew it. She had their attention. "If you stay the same course, what options have you? The pox? Stoning?" It was a fairly common practice for the former inmates of brothels who were too old to work anymore to find just such an end. Far too often they would be stoned to death, or thrown on a pile of well-oiled straw and burned to death, by former clients who wanted to silence them.

"Why are you doing this?" asked a suspicious voice from somewhere near the fireplace. Loni thought the name of the girl was Zaya. The girl was young. She was of medium height with an oval shaped face and soft brown eyes. Her hair had an artful unkept look, so the ash brown hair was layered and feathered around her face and hung into her eyes. *She would be very attractive, if her hair wasn't always in her eyes.*

"Does it matter?" asked Haddy furiously, trying to bat her skirts out of her face, her body rigid with embarrassment. "We're giving you a chance to be anything but tramps."

Loni regretted pushing Mari to bring Haddy with them.

"You mentioned two choices," Zaya said, afraid to hope. "What's the other?"

Loni nodded, "To leave here...."

"And go where?" Zaya interupted, managing to sound hopeful *and* depressed.

"What does it matter who we work for when all we know is one job?" Pash snorted as she hung in the air next to Haddy. She had managed to push her skirts back up and then knot them so they couldn't fall over her head again.

"You can and will be taught different trades." Loni emphasized, "Any of you that are willing to work hard are welcome to come and learn."

"Why should we believe you?" Pash asked with the bitterness of someone unable to trust.

"We don't care what you believe!" Haddy yelled, taking a swing at the woman hanging in the air next to her and only succeeding in making her skirt tangle worse. "In about fifteen minutes we're going to burn this place down!"

Loni ignored her younger sister, "I don't lie, but I believe you already know that Pash. The rest you will have to take on faith."

*

Mari had followed Chun up the stairs and opened the door. To her surprise, inside the sparsely furnished room, standing on the arm of a battered chair, was a thin scraggly-looking Shee. He was striped like a tiger, his bulgy dark eyes were crossed, his open mouth was foaming, and his rather odd bumpy head was shaking furiously back and forth while he growled.

He shook his head too hard and promptly fell off the arm of the chair, landing on his head on the wooden floor with a loud, "Ow! Grrr! Grrr!" His raccoon-like paw had obviously sustained damage during the fall because he was shaking it with every Ow! And his other hand was rubbing at the bumps on his head where it had slammed against the hard wooden floor. If it had not been for the solemn presence of the little blind girl, thin and trembling, Mari would've laughed out loud.

"It's alright Tiz! She's a great lady, and is taking you and Wysh to a safe place," Chun explained as she reached for her sister.

Tiz picked himself up off the floor, crossed his arms, and said in no uncertain terms with white foam still sliding down his chin, "No. I stay Wysh. Want be safe. I much big!" Tiz threatened while puffing out his chest.

Mari was grateful she had experience with Shees. She knew that Tiz meant strong when he was saying he was big. However, with one bent ear, foam leaking from his mouth, and too scrawny for any respectable Shee, he looked more comical than formidable.

"You will come with us," Mari informed Chun, "and you," Mari looked at the scraggly Shee, "will get to have a friend."

"Good one?" Tiz asked Chun. Mari knew he was asking if she were a threat that he needed to bite or scare her away.

Chun nodded, happiness filling her heart as much as her eyes.

Tiz looked at Mari, "What be fren?" he asked curiously while wiping soda foam from his mouth and tenderly rubbing his head and un-bending his poor ear.

"All of you come with me," Mari gently helped Wysh to her feet, Chun on the other side, feeling alarm at how thin Wysh was. Together, they led her down the stairs where the women were gathering. Mari gestured again and Haddy and Pash were released from their awkward positions in the air and gently placed on the wood floorboards.

A rather hard woman with dead-looking eyes said, "You can't take her. The blind doxie has been promised to Delf, the Minister of Trade."

Chun felt Mari stiffened.

"Take her to a chair," Mari said to her, the edges of her voice going frosty. Chun avoided going near the woman who had just spoken as she led Wysh to a chair.

Mari turned to face the woman. "If he's interested, the Minister is welcome to talk to me himself," Mari's voice was like ice. "I would welcome the chance to show him exactly what I think of him." She looked at the woman who fell silent. A sudden smile crept up the corners of Mari's mouth. "Then again, perhaps we'll let Tiz handle him."

Mari stepped sideways. Tiz had been sitting on the floor behind Mari's skirts. The women gasped when they saw him.

If he was anything like Mee, Tiz likely thought they were taken back by his very handsome features. However, it appeared that he was excited by the idea of having an enemy to fight. He started to growl with his claws extended, but the effect was ruined when he coughed, hissed, and coughed again. He hissed once more, and then stopped and looked puzzled, "Who? Where?" He couldn't see any enemies, just the same women who had worked at the brothel that he had seen before. Of course, they had never seen him.

His verbosity elicited a few colorful metaphors from the women who were obviously unaware Shees were capable of speech. Without a doubt, some would think she had put a spell on the venomous animal. Chun stood by Loni, weeping tears of joy, covering her face and sobbing. Wysh worriedly stroked the back of her sister's hand and snapped her fingers. Tiz immediately went to her and sat on her lap, looking confused.

"You saved us, just like you promised," Wysh said softly to Chun.

Wysh could not see the icy resolve that formed in Mari's eyes or her dark look at the co-habitants of the unhappy dwelling. "I strongly suggest you gather whatever you wish to keep," Mari told the rest of the women. "You have ten minutes."

This was the only time the Ryn sisters could remember that each and every woman in the brothel decided that a change was exactly to their liking. Mari felt it was because of the Ta sisters' open gratitude that day. Whatever the reasons the former inhabitants chose to end their slavery, she was grateful.

Outside of the brothel the wagons waited for the women. With the help of the drivers, every last wagon overflowed with goods. When all the women met one last time in the parlor, Mari noted which of them had washed their faces and changed clothes into something less revealing.

The two who had changed the most were Pash and Zaya. Both had come down without makeup, had re-combed their hair to suit travel, and wore the most modest of immodest dresses with shawls to cover what the dress didn't.

Mari and Loni had gained enough experience after several brothel raids to know if the women released would remain silent or truthful. Over time, they had devised a fairly accurate way to assess who should be assigned to go where. Thus they waited in the parlor.

The thirty prostitutes and the two girls sat, lounged, or stood looking at Mari as she began to speak, "Those who sent us wish to conduct a test to determine where you will be sent. First, I will have you turn your backs toward me and then I will blow a whistle. If you hear a bird, sit down, if you hear nothing go upstairs, and if you hear any other sound, go to the kitchen."

Mari blew on the whistle and heard Wysh say very quietly, "That was beautiful." Tiz didn't agree. He hopped off Wysh's lap and onto Chun's shoulder and violently plugged his ears with his paws.

The sound wasn't that of a bird. To the twenty-one women that claimed they heard a bird and were now sitting, Mari said, "Pack your clothes and prepare for life in Wesvalen." Experience had educated them that, in general, the women who lied about the sound would be those who returned to the same occupation. Wesvalen, already corrupted by Sogo, would not be worse off for the arrival of twenty-one more corrupt individuals.

Twelve other women went upstairs. They had truthfully claimed they had heard nothing. Their honesty had earned them a place in Utak to be trained in honorable professions.

Those who went to the kitchen were Zaya, Pash, and Chun who led Wysh, and was followed by Tiz who kept himself busy poking his paw into cobwebby corners for bugs. These four women had heard a bell, the correct sound. They would be eventually sent to train in Utak as Eyes.

Most would serve in Phoenix House orphanage first, as a proving ground, but eventually, they would all serve Mari and be stationed all over the world.

She saw the concern Loni had for the Ta sisters. She would be able to reassure her older sister that she had no reason to fear; Mari knew exactly what to do with Chun and Wysh, because she knew the girls would be happy no matter where they went, as long as they were together.

Chapter 25: Honor

Haddy was in the kitchen of the brothel. She preferred to keep an eye on Pash whom she didn't trust, but rather liked. Part of the reason she liked her was because she knew exactly where she stood with Pash. Currently it was somewhere between hatred and violence.

She felt edgy and wanted to goad the older woman into a rage just to see what she would do. Haddy absently stroked one of her hidden knives. She looked at the blind girl with pity, *I'll bet she got burned* and then looked at the blind girl's pretty sister, Chun. *She moves like a dancer.*

Chun, who had been looking out the kitchen window, gasped in surprise when she saw that Haddy had entered the room, and then shyly looked up at her, "Will we go to get my brother soon?"

Haddy asked, "Where is he?" as she felt a flash of irritation at the girl's request followed by a desire to get out of the place. *I can't believe I gave up a party for this!*

Chun pointed out the door and Haddy peered out into the streets. There were a few people wandering around who had not gone to the festival. Among them she saw a little boy, six or seven years old, looking up into one of the windows of the brothel. *He sure is starting young.*

"He's looking for me," Chun whispered.

Haddy felt a small pang of guilt, quickly squelched, for thinking the boy was looking for trouble or excitement. "I'll go get him."

"No! I'll get him. That man," she pointed to a rather chunky man with long moustaches and a drunken leer, "is my cousin. He is an evil man," Chun confessed, her pale cheeks growing pink with shame. "He will hurt you if you try to take Yun. He likes to hurt beautiful things."

Haddy was pleased Chun recognized her beauty, "Then you better stay here." Haddy winked saucily as she went out the door. "You can watch me if you want."

Haddy knew she was doing the wrong thing. She shrugged the guilt off and approached the cousin first. He was a pleasant enough looking man, but his eyes were hard and greedy. She knew exactly how to reach him.

"I need a slave, how much for the boy?" Haddy asked with snotty arrogance.

The man's drunken face was alight with greed, "He is not for sale." The man looked at her with open interest, "Are you?"

You couldn't afford me, you son-of-a-slaver. "To pay for your lack of respect you will accept what is in this purse. I'm taking the boy." Haddy tossed him a bag of coins just as Chun opened the door and motioned for her brother to come into the kitchen. Yun ran without looking back.

The man, coin bag held against his chest, went after him. He failed to notice that Haddy stuck out her foot. He landed hard and skidded through a pile of fresh horse manure.

When he got up, Haddy was gone and so was the boy. Enraged, he went to the door where the kitchen was and pounded on it, screaming for Yun until the door flew open.

The last thing he saw in this life was a pair of fiery, snapping green eyes. He fell back down the steps of the brothel, a dagger in his throat. From inside the kitchen, Chun, Wysh and Yun were all hugging and weeping. Haddy didn't want their thanks. Taking out their cousin was a lot more fun than dealing with harlots.

Zaya smirked at her "I'd take ten to one that your pretty friend upstairs skins you alive for not waiting. Personally, I'd strip you and prance you through the streets naked if it were me, but then you'd probably enjoy that too."

Pash joined in the conversation. "Dead bodies may not be a big deal where you're from, but Dyman is small enough to make it hard to hide that kind of idiocy.

"If I were you, I'd find a way to hide the body. The wagons are still in front of the body for now, but the women will come down soon to add more to what's left to the load. Take my word for it when I say that most of them would scream like the wenches they are if they saw it."

Haddy grimaced. As much as she hated it, Pash and Zaya were right. *Besides I left my dagger and the coins.* She went out and pulled the dead body into the kitchen and stuffed it behind the pantry door. Haddy retrieved her dagger and the money. *After all, he isn't going to need it.*

Eventually, eight wagons rolled away from the brothel in the dark, each heaped with people and goods. The Ryn sisters wore their hooded capes and rode in one of three wagons headed to Ryn House, a mere four miles away.

Mistress Genn was in charge of three other wagons that were headed to Wesvalen with the women who had lied about the whistle. Mistress Shu, matron of Phoenix House was in charge of the last two wagons which were headed to Utak with the women who were honest and would be apprenticed to a trade.

Mari had set the brothel on fire before she got into the wagon. By design, it would be a slow burn until it was far too late to save the building. They had planned this to coincide with the festival, so that most people were away from the seedier part of town. By the next morning, all that was left would be smoking embers.

"Do you smell that?" asked Haddy.

"It's the fire," Mari's voice was like ice.

"It reminds me of papah."

Loni looked puzzled, "Why?"

"I don't remember him very well, but I always think of him when there's a fire."

"Probably because he used to hold you on his lap in front of the fire and sing you to sleep," Loni smiled and looked up at the stars.

Haddy sounded wistful when she asked, "Was he a good man, really?"

"Yes."

Haddy's tone grew stubborn. "No, I mean it. Was he really good or we only thought he was good but he was bad, or what?"

Loni thought about it, "Papah always did what he thought was right."

"That bothers me," Haddy sniffed. "Why can't we just say it the way it was?"

"What do you mean?" Mari had entered the conversation.

"Like right now, why can't you just say that papah was a stonecutter or that he beat his wife, or whatever the truth is?"

"Because it isn't that simple," Mari disagreed.

"It should be," Haddy grouched.

"Who said life is simple?" Loni was feeling a bit disgruntled about questioning their father's character.

"I don't know anything about him – other than he cut wood. I don't know why he did it, or where he went or anything the least bit personal."

Loni looked at her, "Personal?"

Haddy shrugged uncomfortably. "I just want to know more about him, something I don't already know."

"Well, we lived in Utak."

Haddy seemed shocked.

Loni nodded. "I know I don't look the part, but I was born there. We moved around a lot. The reason we moved back to Utak was to keep me safe."

Haddy looked like she wanted to say something but didn't know how.

"What?" Loni asked.

"Why would he have to keep *you* safe?"

"He became a hunted man."

Haddy looked skeptical. "I thought he was a wood carver."

"He was."

Mari entered the conversation. "He was also an assassin."

"You *lied* all this time?"

Mari rolled her eyes. "We just didn't tell you the whole truth, there's a difference."

"Then what really happened, I mean, after Mari's mother died giving birth?" Haddy demanded.

"Mari's mother didn't die in childbirth, she died to save me."

Haddy blinked. "How?"

"An assassin got in during the Utakian festival. We were in the marketplace setting up the flowers that Tyresha wanted to sell. I was in the back of the wagon, taking care of Mari and helping with the flowers. Papah always said the man that threw the quill was aiming for him and he probably was. In any case, Tyresha saw the assassin throw the quill and I got in the way.

"It all happened very fast. I heard her scream no, I turned around in time to see her get hit in the back of the neck and all I could do was catch her." Loni swallowed against the tightness in her throat. "I knew quills were sometimes poisonous so I tried to pull it out, but she was already gone."

"Why didn't you heal her?" Haddy asked Mari.

"I'm not omnipotent. Mamah was dead before Loni caught her." Mari cleared her throat.

"The quill sliced my fingers." Loni rubbed the two tallest fingers of her right hand. "I was told papah killed the man."

"Another lie," Mari said in a tight voice.

Both of her sisters looked at her. "That's the official story, but the truth is, I was the one that saw the assassin first. He was acting strangely and I was young enough to be ignored. If I had said something, it never would have happened."

"You don't know that Mari." Loni shook her head.

"Anyway, I wasn't sure how I did what I did, but it was the first time I used my power and I didn't have control. I only meant to make him stop so papah could catch him."

Loni paled.

"What did you do to him?"

"It doesn't matter," Loni whispered, putting her arm around Mari.

There was silence for a few minutes then Haddy said, "But if Tyresha died in Utak, how did she get buried here? Didn't she start to…well, stink?"

"I kept her frozen until we came to the spot where papah said he would like to build. Then we buried her in the place she is now."

Loni finished the story. "Three years later, papah met your mother and after she was gone, we were happy here, the four of us."

"You're wrong, Loni," Haddy said in a solemn voice," I've never been happy there."

They made the rest of the trip in silence.

By the time they arrived at the Ryn House, Loni could see that Mari was angry. It didn't take a seer to see that she was riding the edge of her infamous temper. Haddy on the other hand, was oblivious to anything but herself.

How could she be so insensitive? Loni sighed inwardly. Her weak arm ached with the strain of the day's activities. In hindsight, it was worth it. Armed with the satisfaction that three orphaned siblings were rescued, and women were set free from bondage, she pushed herself to smile and make conversation.

Pash and Zaya, in the wagons behind them, would continue on the road tomorrow with Mari to begin their training.

Loni looked at the familiar paths leading to her home. Loni could see two palomino mares in the pasture. Evidently, Lyon and Brenna had come to pick up Mari. Brenna would be in bed by now, but it was a good thing Lyon was there to help.

She tiredly climbed down from the wagon, not waiting for Lyon's help. He was busy kissing Mari and ignoring Haddy. He would put away the wagons and take care of the horses.

There were presently twenty-eight children of various ages and needs staying at Ryn House. Most often these children were saved from street life or worse, and Loni loved them all. She checked in with the older girls who had been left in charge and once assured all was well, she entered the kitchen thinking of the first things to do on her list tomorrow.

She stumbled over something and looked down to find Mee looking up sheepishly from her newest mess. Mee had opened a sack of flour and had been happily, until that moment, bathing in the freshly sifted powder. Loni shut her eyes for a minute to gather strength. Then she heaved a great sigh and recalled that Brenna had been doing something similar last time she had visited, only Brenna had used her mother's scented powders. Mee had evidently been entranced by Brenna's actions enough to copy them.

Mari, who had followed Loni in, wasn't so patient with the Shee. "Clean it up Mee, now!"

Instead of obeying, Mee sought escape and shot toward the back door in a cloud of flour.

Mari nodded and the Shee, frozen in mid-stride, came floating back into the kitchen, her blue eyes wild. Mari unfroze the Shee, with the exception of her tail. Mee looked back at her stiff tail in panic and Mari arched her brow, "Once your mess is clean, your tail will be free. Not one minute before."

"Why not let the little rat have her tail free?" yawned Haddy entering the kitchen. "What'd she ever do to *you*?" Her intent was to point out the fact that Mee made a habit of annoying Haddy as often as possible.

Loni braced herself for the inevitable. "Remember to set the ward first, Mari."

Haddy looked very surprised to find herself on the floor. Her long thick hair was wrapped in Mari's fist and she was staring into one blazing green eye and one cold brown one. The shock overcame the pain for the moment.

Mari's fist pulled upward and Haddy felt her own blood begin to boil.

"What were you thinking!" Mari let Haddy's hair go and moved away, but her glare was enough to burn through steel. It wasn't over.

Loni felt she could see the thoughts spinning in Haddy's mind. Loni had known this moment was coming and while she hated to choose sides, she knew Mari was right. She was grateful the orphans were upstairs sleeping. Considering the temper Mari was in, Loni felt it best to intervene, "Hadasha!" Loni said with some fervor of her own, "There are rules to be observed during a mission. You should have informed us you were going to get the boy."

Haddy directed her venom at Mari who was still blazing with anger. "I saw an opportunity and I took it, Mari! What was I supposed to do? Let the stone-fisted cousin take Chun's brother so we had to waste even more time getting him? I already missed out on the festival tonight, wasn't that punishment enough?"

Loni wanted to roll her eyes. She knew Mari's reaction to such an idiotic statement wouldn't be to gloss it over. She wasn't surprised when Mari blew the back door off its hinges, but she was startled and even a little frightened for Haddy when the staff appeared in Mari's hand. The staff had one purpose - to kill.

Loni moved herself between them and looked incredulously at Mari, who had never threatened Hadasha in this way before. She had seen what Mari could do with the staff and grew cold just thinking about it.

"Mari, put it away," Loni's quiet, firm tone left no room for discussion. The staff disappeared, but Mari still radiated volcanic anger. In fact, she shook with it.

"You nearly surrendered all Loni and I have worked for these past eight years!" Mari's back was ramrod straight as she shot verbal arrows, "Our lives, the children who live here, and the Eyes were on the line tonight. The Ryn House was nearly compromised. If **one** of those women had chosen differently, we would no longer be able to stay here."

Hadasha went white and Loni felt the same shock. She hadn't considered the whole picture, but she knew Mari was right. If even one woman had decided to stay in Dyman, the Ryn House would be rendered useless. Loni, as its matron, would have been compromised, because she could have been identified as more than a helpless old spinster who helped orphans.

The backbreaking effort of just getting the orphanage up and running played through her mind. Flashing before her eyes was the absolute secrecy of their training, the plotting, the long hours, buckets of tears, and crushing pain when missions had not gone well. The thought of losing all they had gained was more than she thought she could bear. She felt physically ill as it all came home to nest in her stomach and she sat down.

Mari's countenance changed from fire to ice and she pinned Haddy with her eyes. Loni felt the first stirring of real fear lance into her heart.

"Haddy, if you ever do something like this again, you will not live to regret it, sister or not, Hi-Sha's honor," Mari touched her forehead and chin. Then she coldly looked at Loni who could not bridge the impossible gap for the two of them.

Mari's words were final in a way Haddy would not realize. Loni was also magically bound by the covenants made as an Eye. She put a hand on her churning stomach and looked at her two sisters. They were so much alike and so very different. Both had terrible tempers and both were unwilling to bend.

Loni looked over at Mee who broke the tension of the moment by looking hopefully at Mari. "Done." Mee pointed to a large bump in the rug. The bump was obviously the flour's new residence.

Mari nodded at Mee and with a gesture, unfroze Mee's tail. Mee quickly gathered her luxurious tail into her arms and gave it a loving squeeze and patted it fondly, "I find bug for you. You be much nice then." Mee glanced up at Mari and raced from the room.

"I'll stay the night," Mari gestured and the back door was returned to its proper place without a scratch. Without looking at either of her sisters, Mari strode out of the room and up the stairs to the room kept specifically for her.

Haddy looked at Loni, not daring to move until Mari left. For many moments she had felt like a mouse in the talons of an owl, "How else should I have done it?"

Loni's smile was gone, "You tell me, now that you've seen the consequences."

"I don't know! If I did, I wouldn't be asking," said Haddy irritably. "I save a little boy and what does Mari do but act like a cross-eyed Harpy!"

"Haddy!" Loni interrupted, "learn to control your impulses! Please don't cross Mari again. She won't let you have another mission if you can't follow simple orders."

There was a pause. "Do you think she's serious?" Haddy bit her lip and looked into the clear green eyes that she had trusted since they were orphaned.

"You know her well enough to answer that question," Loni said quietly. "You made the covenants as an Eye, what do you conclude?"

Haddy swallowed and looked down at the floor. Mari would kill her and Loni could not stop her from doing it.

Chapter 26: Saro

High Priestess Saro had a problem and her name was Yemet. A problem she was about to rectify. Yemet, at this point, held sway with the Council. The High Priestess Saro had other plans and they did not include a self-indulgent murderess.

In the marble halls of the Council Chambers, she and Yemet sat on opposite sides of the long solid oak table on either side of Nez Shavae, the Minister of Religion. Saro felt Nez both wise and foolish to put the women on opposite sides of the table. Wise because he knew they had great enmity between them, and foolish because he wanted to observe them at their worst.

Saro looked at her current adversary as she would a bug that needed smashing. In her opinion, Yemet even looked like a pale grey bug, if bugs could look inherently cruel. Her eyes were glassy grey, the pupils dilated with whatever current drug of choice she'd used before coming. Her hair was ash-blonde and her skin, because of her addictions, had a grey cast to it. She was a thin, reedy woman with a nasal voice who enjoyed disemboweling those sacrificed to Veesh, the god of Sogo. Yemet was known to joyously bathe in the blood of sacrifices and arrogantly claim it was the will of Veesh.

Yemet, in reality, was no more than a puppet of Nez and Saro knew it. She planned to use that information to lock things into place for the future.

Saro was the newcomer in this room. She had only held the position for nine months. Since the ruins of the old Temple had taken so long to re-build this was her first official meeting. At the core of everything she did or said in this room was the raw fact she despised every one of the Nine. She would use any or all of them if the opportunity presented itself; preferably, as fertilizer.

She should thank Yemet. She was, ultimately, the reason Saro had become High Priestess. Saro looked around the table. She had made it her business to know about those who held the reins of power in Sogo. Tasut and Jarow had tutored her well during their brief visits and she had never been more grateful than she was here and now - sitting in the stuffy chambers with the most powerful people in Sogo.

Sitting to her left was Dana Cline, Headmistress of Cells (population control), and the only woman on the Council.

"She is the weakest of the Nine," Tasut explained.

Jarow added, "Her greed for jewelry and coin is legendary."

Saro mentally filed away their observations about Dana and quietly disagreed. Dana, in Saro's eyes, was more dangerous to her plans than any of the men on the council, with the exception of Nez.

Dana's skin was black as her heart and her wide set brown eyes looked slightly bulbous as if she had been squeezed too tight at one point in her life. Not that there was much to squeeze; she was built like a stick. Her thin frame was draped in brightly colored silks, cut low to reveal her jewelry, the true passion of her life. She wore her hair nearly shaved off to control the curl, making her prominent cheekbones stand out from her too-thin face. Rumor had Dana and Nez romantically involved, but if so, they were better actors than Saro gave them credit.

To Dana's left was Grutlek Komane, Speaker for the Nine. According to Saro's sense of smell, he was in need of a bath. The first thing you noticed about Grutlek was the large, hairy, black mole on the side of his nose. His face seemed to be a genetic cross between a human and an orange ape, complete with a long face, sagging jowls, and square brown teeth. His physique was like a huge, rumpled square. He may have been strong in his youth, but his dissolute lifestyle had caught up with him and drubbed him hard. His thinning orange hair was brushed forward from the crown of his head and cut straight across just above the eyebrows in front. His clothing was wrinkled and stained. He was sweating as if he had run six miles and had wet stains under the arms of his camel-brown robes of office. She doubted if he ever had the robes washed.

To Grutlek's left were the depraved brothers Scive and Raze Fellstein, who were dual heads of Sogoian security. They looked enough alike to be twins – both resembled pale-faced blue-eyed slugs; their oily black hair slick with slime.

"Scive is the eldest of the two," Tasut frowned as he coached her. "He's under the illusion he runs internal security affairs. Raze isn't quite as blind. He knows they're figureheads, but he hates his brother enough to let Scive make an idiot of himself at the cost of his own reputation. The only person they hate more than each other is Nez, who controls them."

This, Saro thought, was sure to go in her favor at some point.

At the end of the ornate table was Corizor, the slender, apologetic link to the Assassin's Guild. His right arm and leg were *reported* to be useless. He used a cane to move around. Tasut's face was bleak as he told her, "Many people underestimate Cor because he's easy to overlook."

Tasut was right. Cor had a plain face, brown hair, eyes, and tan skin. His very mediocrity in the looks department had given him the ability to blend in without calling attention to his actions.

Jarow, normally silent during these lessons from Tasut, spoke, "There are rumors that Cor trained Lyon Tybar and then ordered him to be killed. It's a twisted lie. Nez ordered Lyon's death."

Nez, naturally, sat at the head of the table on Saro's right.

She supposed he was a handsome man if you liked your men cold and lethal. He seemed partial to the colors brown and black, was clean-shaven, and had rather pale skin; as if he didn't get enough sunlight. His eyes were ashy green and deeply set beneath thin sparse brows. Tall and well built, his dark hair was turning white at the temples and made him look very distinguished. He wore an uncommon amount of jewelry for a man. His long slender fingers wore several rings, sometimes two on one finger. He had a deceptively pleasant smile and had been the picture of courtesy and charm, even gentle with her. She wasn't deceived.

On sulky Yemet's side of the table was Xavier Delisandro, the grey-haired General of the Sogoian army who was built like a brick, slightly deaf, and had been wounded in his last battle – by Tasut. There were two things Tasut despised: cowardice and greed.

"I requested he be stripped of his position and executed for deserting his men in battle," Tasut's face became more stone-like. "The Delisandro's are one of the wealthiest families in the known world. They bought him a position on the Council."

General Delisandro was a curiously aloof man and spoke only when spoken to. He seldom offered opinions. Saro had decided to watch him closely rather than gut him at the first opportunity as Tasut desired her to do.

Weke Hupha was also on the other side of the table, unconsciously dry-washing his hands. He had sandy-colored hair, bulgy hazel eyes and was short and bow-legged.

"He's not much to look at, but he's vain. He commissions a private tailor to make his clothing so he never appears in the same outfit twice. He owns a large part of the Black Market."

Startled, she said, "I thought he was Minister of Justice."

"He is," Tasut assured her. "He also mindlessly writes Sogoian laws as Nez dictates them."

On the other end of the Council table was the shiny pate of Delf Shiraz. Saro noted he looked more skeletal than human.

Tasut's voice had been disgusted as he divulged the nastiness owned by the Minister of Trade and Education. "Delf is an addict in many ways. Drugs, women, and child slavery. It's an open secret in Sogo that he buys children at every auction when there are some available. He owns brothels in four of the five countries."

The drugs explained the man's vacant look and sour smell. She was grateful she sat as far away from him as she did, Grutlek was quite enough for one nose to ignore. She had tried not to smile, when she heard from Delf's own lips that one of his brothels had been visited by an arsonist. She hoped with all her heart they would all be burned down, and that he would be in one of them when it did. When he spoke, his eyes darted around the room as if looking for possible enemies. Before the meeting began, he cornered her to say, "High Priestess Saro, a moment of your time."

She paused to listen in case there was something important he wanted to say.

"We have many important matters to discuss."

This was untrue. She had nothing to do with Trade or Education. Hers was purely an ecclesiastical calling.

"I'm sure we will find we have much in common outside of this room. If you will come to my place at 9 p.m. this evening?"

Realizing the man just wanted to get her alone she used her best and most effective defense. "I'll check with Tasut first and get back to you."

He grew pale and broke into a cold sweat. "Never mind, High Priestess, I wouldn't want to disturb him."

Of course he didn't. The Nine avoided Tasut if they could help it. Saro pushed away the ideas swimming in her head. She knew her turn to speak was coming and she was ready. She had mentally prepared herself before she arrived at the chambers, knowing what would be lost to her if she failed.

Yemet did not recognize death was in the room with her. It was for this one thing she had come to the meeting, not Nez's private request.

Nez repulsed her to a degree he would no doubt find astonishing. It was difficult not to cringe away from him, and more difficult to keep her expression guarded when he touched her. She would do what must be done in order to make her plan work.

Tasut was her guarantee of safety and she kept that fact firmly in mind. Saro needed a position of power to stay in Sogo, and today she would have it. She felt Nez would approve her current plan because he was attempting to lure her from Tasut and curry her favor.

She lowered her eyes as if in humble contemplation and nearly laughed at the thought. Did the cretin really believe Tasut would turn his back on any kind of infidelity?

Saro pretended to listen to Grutlek as he laboriously read everything from the parchment in front of him as if he were afraid the words would change if he took his eyes off the page. She ignored his sonorous voice as she mentally rehearsed her part.

First, she would not stand when it came time to speak as all the others had. It was a subtle stab at her refusal to obey custom. She was here to change things.

Second, she would speak quietly, forcing them to listen to her voice. And they would listen. Her voice was a selling point. She had been personally trained by her mother, a professional singer. All those hated lessons had now come to be a vital part of her role in Sogo.

Tasut had repeatedly warned her, "Don't make it personal."

However, Tasut wasn't here and that was good. He would be tempted to interfere. Today, Yemet would die, and Saro would have her first taste of revenge. At this point, she couldn't care less what Tasut thought.

"What says the High Priestess Saro?" Grutlek finally inquired as he rubbed his nose and winced as he pulled the hairs growing out of it.

The moment had finally come. It was time to draw her first line in the sand.

She calmly looked directly at Nez, waiting for his eyes to meet hers before she spoke just above a whisper, "I request sacrifices on behalf of the Unknown God." She turned her head to meet the eyes of every one of the Nine as she spoke, ignoring Yemet's snort of derision. "He hungers to give Sogo all she deserves." Saro continued and this time she looked directly at Yemet, "His Temple would be in use even now, but I have been met with hostility from one who should have been my mentor." She kept her eyes on Yemet and dammed up the river of hate that flowed out of her. Yemet was first to look away.

Now it was time to lay the bait. Saro stood, gathering every eye. While strategy was important, presentation was critical in this chamber.

She had chosen her gown carefully. It was sumptuously rich; a deep burgundy silk with gold shot through it and had a v-neckline to expose a magnificent ruby necklace. The necklace was a gift from an anxious jeweler who wished to avoid being sacrificed. Master Flynn was a true artisan. The rubies, thirteen in all, caught the light. Dana's eyes had fastened themselves to the necklace with open longing. It was critical that Saro pause and give Dana time to properly covet.

"I do not wish to take away sacrifices due to Yemet, so I wish to make a suggestion," Saro said.

"Which is?" Nez asked. He seemed to be enjoying the tension between herself and Yemet very much. She reminded herself that his time was coming.

Saro pulled small cymbals from the pocket of her gown, put them on her fingers, clanged them lightly together, and put them away. Immediately, two of Tasut's men, dressed in battle gear, stepped into the room and stood on either side of her chair.

"I propose taking these two men with me and systematically find each and every child within Sogo to use as sacrifices to the Unknown God," she said with calmness that belied her racing heart. Revenge was within her grasp.

"If their parents refuse?" asked Dana, while her eyes caressed the blood-red gems at Saro's throat.

"Then they shall join their offspring in the sacrificial ritual." Her eyes glittered at Yemet whose mouth opened in protest. Saro held the floor and Yemet had to wait. Nez watched the two of them with cold humor. Saro continued, "I also lay claim to any and all strangers arriving into the city and all slaves who are useless or disobedient. Yemet may have the rich and powerful who wish to buy their way to Veesh, and I will take those Yemet has called unclean. We begin today."

"Does Tasut know of this?" Nez asked quietly as his thin fingers caressed the velvet of his robe.

"Does it matter?" she asked him with a direct look, her heavily made-up eyes taking note that he was amused, even delighted.

"That is not fair!" spat Yemet, jumping to her feet. "Most of my sacrifices are children!"

Saro sat and smiled, hiding her hate-filled delight beneath hooded eyes. If nothing else, Yemet was predictable, which made her an easy target as well as a fool.

*

Nez quelled Yemet's outburst with one cold look, "It is not for you to decide, Yemet. Sacrifice falls under my jurisdiction." He looked at her thin frame, up and down, with distaste. Drugs had all but destroyed her once-attractive form and now ate her mind, made her hair dull, and left her eyes glassy.

He looked at the High Priestess Saro, who sat regally erect; like a block of beautifully carved ice. *No wonder Tasut has chosen her. She is as heartless and emotion-free as he is.*

Nez was determined to take her away from Tasut. However, he still hadn't found a chink in the armor of their relationship. It was understood by all of Sogo that she was Tasut's. Nez was confident. *In the end, she will be mine.* His eyes shifted to Delf who looked upon the High

Priestess with open lust. Delf had the same chance of attracting Saro as a bleeding Pursha. "Continue, High Priestess Saro."

*

Saro recognized the moment was ripe. It was time to curry favors and give Nez a chance to admire her ability to play politics in Sogo. "I also beg a small indulgence from this Council. I seek to reward the Mistress of Cells with a token of my appreciation for her efforts."

In fact, Dana had done nothing except send a fruit basket, which Saro had thrown away, fearing poison.

Saro removed the ruby necklace and rose from her place at the table to deliver the gift to Dana. The Mistress of Cells had no idea the necklace was suffused with magic that would cause her to become forgetful. Saro tried not to gloat as she placed it on the table in front of Dana with a small nod.

Dana beamed at the necklace, which she immediately put around her thin black neck. She was so excited, her voice shook as she told the others, "I vote to grant High Priestess Saro the right to kill... uh, to gather sacrifices from among the population of Sogo."

The necklace held the kind of organic magic that Nez could not detect. Yemet was looking daggers at Dana, whose long bony fingers were caressing the blood-red stones at her neck, thereby activating the hex. Saro was a bit amazed that the dark eyes went blank so quickly.

"Sheer Bribery!" screamed Yemet, her thin face growing red with the effort, her bony chest heaving with indignation.

"That is the second time you have spoken out of turn, Yemet. I will not ask you again to respect the rules of the floor," Nez said quietly. His tone was bland, but the Council members knew it was a death threat.

Yemet fell back into her chair, now trembling with fear as well as rage. She bit her lip in effort to remain alive. Her predecessor had made the same mistake in this very chamber.

Nez informed them, "And I hereby grant to the High Priestess Saro, all privileges and powers due to her as a High Priestess to the Unknown God."

"I desire the High Priestess Saro prove her right to hold her office," Xavier Delisandro challenged.

Thankfully, she had expected this.

"Yes, grant us a vision!" Yemet demanded, near hysteria.

"Prove your power," Cor said quietly, looking bored.

Nez leaned forward with interest, and the other men looked nervous as Saro gracefully made her way to Yemet, speaking as she walked, "I have had a vision for several nights that concerns Yemet. The Unknown God is not pleased with her work. I prophesy that within three days of this chamber meeting, she will be struck down with a plague. The Unknown God has spoken." She stopped when she reached Yemet's chair.

"You lie!" hissed Yemet. She was once more on her feet and this time, she faced Saro.

Saro placed one long fingernail under Yemet's chin, tipping it upward. She could read the fear in Yemet's drugged eyes.

"You're a fake!" spat Yemet as Saro's fingernail dug into the skin under Yemet's chin.

Saro coldly looked into her eyes. "You will soon provide proof that what I say is true." Her long painted fingernail sliced a short furrow into the thin tight skin of Yemet's neck.

With a cry of pain, Yemet grabbed at her neck, eyes widening in horror. Saro did not bother to look at the woman as she calmly returned to her seat.

Yemet turned to the Council, her hand still pressed against the bleeding gouge there. "She's a false Priestess!"

"If you are alive in three days, you may voice your complaints then," Grutlek said, pounding his gavel on the table. "We shall meet at that time to discuss the matter. If Yemet does not come to that meeting, her accusations against High Priestess Saro will be claimed false." One more tap of the gavel signaled the meeting was adjourned.

"And if her words are false?" asked Delf. His eyes roved over every part of Saro as if afraid that Yemet would not die.

"Then Saro will be given to Yemet for sacrifice," Nez said from his end of the table. Saro looked at him with ice in her eyes but no facial expression beyond that.

"The Unknown God has spoken," she reaffirmed her stand on the issue. *One down.* Saro felt Nez's eyes upon her and she turned her head to give him a brittle stare.

He smiled at her, leaning forward to whisper, "I will see you in three days."

Her eyes remained cold, "I will not be here in three days, Minister." She rose gracefully from her chair, "I will not waste my time waiting for a corpse." She left the room, Tasut's men following.

Nez turned to Yemet who was weeping, "You look unwell, Yemet, perhaps you should go see a physician." He left his former lover alone in the chamber, sobbing uncontrollably, holding her neck.

*

Nez was well aware of the fact that he was asleep. He was sure of it because Benamii, the self-proclaimed prophet, was alive and stood before him once again.

The pathetic 'holy' man was accused of heresy and being a traitor to the government. The Prophet had foolishly refused to give them the information that would lead the Sogoian army to the land of Utak.

Benamii's criminal records recorded charges of disturbing the peace, evading capture, espionage, blasphemy, and murder. Some of the charges, in particular those of evading capture and disturbing the peace, were true.

Sogoian courts were open to the public and anyone could offer evidence. Throughout the reading of the charges, the entire court was hushed, eager for more sport.

Benamii, the Prophet of a God called "Father of All," had patiently endured the brutal interrogation. Afterward, he stood alone in the center of the marble square.

The weight of chains nearly sent his dried-up old frame to its knees. He looked like a bag of bones ready to topple at a mere breeze. Nez sincerely wished he would. So far the decrepit prophet had not offered the crowd more than a groan. He wasn't giving the crowd the titillation they craved.

Nez adored Sogoians. They were as depraved and corrupt as he was, though on a smaller level. It made his office that much easier to bear, since he had no intention of being religious in any moral sense of the word. His own gods were power, affluence, and money.

"How do you answer these charges?" demanded Nez, effectively cultivating a calm demeanor that he felt would be a credit to his office, but not smack of self-righteousness. In Sogo, the Minister of Religion had to be on guard against flagrant righteousness.

He watched the so-called Prophet struggle for every breath, willing Benamii to die and end the boredom. He wished the prophet's God would strike him dead, at least that would be unexpected, even astonishing. The crowd was thirsty for more.

Benamii remained silent with his eyes downcast. The back of his head was matted with old blood and spots of new blood stained his ragged tunic. Then the old Prophet looked up. Inexplicably, Nez felt his heart freeze as the shaking man appeared to grow stronger, and his hoarse voice penetrated to every corner of the building.

"The Father of All has spoken and none here can alter His will. By blood and horror shall the city of Sogo be destroyed, along with all of its inhabitants, from the eldest to the youngest down to the last unhallowed stone. Repent, Sogo, or be destroyed from the face of the land."

The crowd gasped and then laughed scornfully at his audacity. This wasn't what they had expected nor wanted.

"And this shall be the sign," the prophet raised his voice and the crowd hushed. "The daughter of light shall power the Chest of Souls and the Three Sisters shall fall."

Nez quickly jotted the information down in his notes. The ignorant old peasant had possessed the gall to tell them not once, but many times to repent!

Nez wanted to wake before the crazy old man finished. It had shaken him back then and it still shook him.

Though old and barely breathing, Benamii had held himself erect and the shaking stopped. His soft brown eyes were set in a nest of wrinkles, but they seemed to burn into Nez's. "I further prophesy, Nez Shavae, in the name of Father of All, that maggots shall fall from thy lips instead of words. He who will not be seen shall take thy sight and consume thy flesh."

Nez had forced the bile that rose in his throat to remain in his stomach where it roiled as if alive. He looked away from the blazing whiteness of Benamii's countenance, fear coursing through his veins at the finality of the words, his soul burning with the truth. Outwardly he retained his icy calm.

"Kill him," he ordered without emotion, wishing for a weapon to do it himself. He had been too merciful granting this public exhibition. Next time it would be different.

The sword was swift and the Prophet's remains unceremoniously taken away. The crowd only half-heartedly cheered. His death had happened too quickly and left them feeling empty, somehow unsatisfied and disturbed.

Deep inside, even in the dream, Nez was dazed. He felt the truth of the old man's words and did not want to believe.

In the morning, he reassured himself that the last of the prophets lay dead and it was he, Nez, who had made it come to pass. In hindsight, he wished he had waited a mere six weeks. It would have been so entertaining to execute the Prophet during Cubes.

Chapter 27: Growing pains

It had been two years since Talon had lived with his father. During that time, he had seen his father twice. Both times on his birthday. His first year had been spent at Tryk's with a few days each week spent with Lyon's family. The second year had been the reverse.

Now, just as he was getting ready to leave with the Tybars for a place called Swen beyond the Gerton mountains, Tasut had returned without notice and Talon was resigned to the fact he would be leaving with his father the next day. He would have been taken away the moment Tasut returned, but Mari insisted, with ice in her voice, that Talon be given a farewell dinner. Lyon added his desire to speak with Tasut – alone.

Talon was sure that it was Lyon's request, not Mari's, that altered Tasut's resolve to leave immediately. While the men went out of earshot to talk, Talon packed his things and then helped get the meal on the table.

Mari wasn't in a good mood. From the time Tasut had appeared at their front door, she had been riding the edge of anger. When he caught her looking at him, he thought he saw tears in her eyes.

He remembered a peddler saying he'd rather wrestle ten Bleeding Pursha's than make one woman mad. Talon had never seen a Pursha, but he doubted ten would be a match for Mari today.

He didn't feel like eating anything. For some reason, it kept sticking in his throat. Brenna was so quiet he wondered if she might be ill. When he glanced at her, he realized she was ignoring her food and sat next to him in stony silence.

If looks alone could destroy Tasut, Brenna's eyes would have obliterated his father. He wanted to warn her that giving Tasut dark looks wasn't the safest thing to do, but he could hardly say it in front of his sire. Seeking to defuse her temper so it wouldn't get her into more trouble, he managed to sneak his hand under the table and squeeze one of her little hands in reassurance.

The effect was astonishing. She instantly stopped looking at Tasut and turned her eyes on Talon with open adoration. It made him uncomfortable enough that he missed getting the food in his mouth twice, but it was better than worrying that Tasut would do something to her.

Mari packed up most of the food she prepared and gave it to them to take to the new cottage. She had hugged Talon fiercely to her and promised, "We'll be in touch."

His eyes stung, but he stuffed emotion away as Lyon had shaken his hand, ruffled his hair, and wished him "Good life" and "We'll visit soon."

Brenna was another matter.

She stood at the doorway staring at him as if her heart would break. Large tears rolled down her cheeks and then the sobbing began. She threw one final glare of pure hatred at Tasut and ran into the house.

Mari's eyes were flinty and hard as she looked at Tasut and said, "She's afraid she won't see Talon again."

Oddly, these words made Talon feel a bit better, but he didn't dare smile. Talon went behind the house to the barn to get the mules and hook them up to a cart Lyon had loaded with supplies.

He could hear Brenna crying as if her heart had been torn out and he nursed a growing resentment toward his father as he climbed onto the cart to drive it.

As soon as Tasut mounted Harcour, they headed away for wherever 'home' was now, knowing that he had just left his true home.

Tasut started out at a slow pace. Talon looked back at the Tybar's cottage.

Brenna had not come out to wave goodbye, but her parents did. Lyon had his arm around Mari's shoulders. Talon felt so choked up, his vision blurred with tears as he gave a feeble wave of his hand.

It was just as well that Tasut didn't speak. Talon had nothing to say to his father while his mind was back with the Tybars.

They arrived at the new cottage by late afternoon. It was closer to the city of Diego than the Tybars' but outside of the city itself. Once again, the place Tasut had chosen was buried to all people unless you knew what you were looking for.

The new place was slightly larger than their cottage in the Rahazi Forest. Naturally, once they arrived, Tasut left Talon with a command to do the chores. He was grateful for something to do and even more grateful the remainder of the day was uneventful. He contemplated the journey he had taken and tried not to look too far into the future because it seemed so bleak. He had become accustomed to Brenna's endless chatter, Mari's singing, and Lyon's whistling. Most of all, he missed conversation.

As Tasut had instructed before he left, Talon prepared for bed by completeing open-hand exercises, meditation, and getting the house ready for an attack. Tasut usually handled the arming of the house, but Talon had been taught to do it for whenever he was alone, like now. Now that he knew Tasut had enemies, he was more careful setting the weapons.

He wondered where Tasut went as he placed weapons near the front and the bedroom doors. Then Talon checked all the bolts on the doors. How Tasut would get in, he never asked. It was just another unanswered question. It was very quiet in the house, the silence nearly deafening. He wished very much for the laughter and happiness that were part of the Tybar's world.

The noise, when it came, was quiet. Like whispers. He slid off his bed and immediately held his breath, melting into the shadows of the hall where he extinguished the only candle and picked up one of the quills laying on top of the hall table. His eyes opened and with quill in hand, he quickly focused on the noise. Turning, he threw the quill and there was a scream in the dark. He felt a sense of panic. *It couldn't be!*

He re-lit the candle with shaking hands. "What are you doing here?" he whispered fiercely.

Brenna was crouched on the floor with the quill buried into the wall behind her. Mee was chattering madly and pointing at Brenna, "Bren be bad! Bad!"

Brenna stood up and looked at him wide eyed. She looked at the quill and her gaze narrowed, "You nearly killed Mee!"

"You shouldn't have come here, Brenna!" Talon yelled at her, his eyes looking for signs of his father. "I have to take you home before Tasut finds out!"

"You don't want me?" Her large eyes spilled the tears that appeared at his cross words. Mee climbed right up Brenna's leg onto her shoulder and stroked Brenna's hair, glaring at Talon as if it was in some way his fault.

"Want me bite Tal?" she offered, her blue eyes glittering at him.

"No," Brenna sniffed and turned away. "Let's just go home."

He felt the bite of guilt. "Brenna, Tasut would…I can't…" he was torn between feelings and duties.

There was the sound of horses racing toward the cottage. Talon knew the sound of Harcour's heavy stride and it wasn't present in the hoof-beats outside. It had to be her parents.

Brenna also heard them and moved over to him. With trusting eyes she took his hand. He wished it didn't feel so nice to have company. It had been a big mistake for her to come. Talon steeled himself for what he knew was certain to happen.

The door opened to reveal a scowling Tasut, who was followed by a white-faced Mari, and then a stern Lyon. Talon felt a wave of gladness mixed with some trepidation for Brenna's sake. Lyon looked as cross as Talon had ever seen him. Mari was like a thundercloud, complete with lightning. She fairly crackled as she came into the house, her eyes landing on Brenna with real anger in their depths.

To Talon's complete shock, Brenna immediately dropped to the floor and clung to both his legs shouting, "I don't want to go!" at the top of her lungs. Mari pried her away, dragging her out the door. He wondered if their partings would always be accompanied by a tantrum.

Mee chattered at Brenna, flicking her bushy tail with irritation. But Brenna wasn't in the mood to be reasoned with and broke away from her mother and ran back, throwing her arms around Talon's waist this time. Automatically, his hands steadied the determined girl, but Talon immediately dropped his hold at Mari's approach.

Once again Brenna was pried away from him. She directed a mutinous pout at her mother, and then a silent plea for help at him. Remembering what Lyon said about her power of persuastion, he shook his head firmly. Still, he followed them outside while Tasut stayed in the house. When she got Brenna to the wagon, Mari handed her to Lyon this time. He lifted her up and sat her on the wagon seat with a firmness that must have hurt.

To Talon's growing dismay, the moment Lyon went around the horses to get to the wagon seat, Brenna jumped into the bed of the wagon and hopped out the back. She ran to him again, in her eyes were equal shares of desperation and determination.

This time she launched into his arms and locked her arms and legs around him. Shocked to his core at her actions, he tried pulling her arms from around his neck. Her head burrowed into his shoulder and she began to sob. "Don't throw me away."

Surprised, he immediately stopped and just held her.

Mari motioned for him to bring her. He hesitantly took her to her parents.

"Tell her to come with us," Mari's tone was crisp as she ordered Talon. He was grateful that she had stopped trying to pull Brenna from his neck.

Talon looked helplessly into wet eyes the color of the sky after dusk, eyes that locked into his with wordless pleading. The small chin quivered as he gently placed her on the ground near the wagon.

Mee was waiting on the wagon seat grooming her ear tufts and making rude noises. He thought he heard her say, "You *Rot* Bren!"

"Go with your parents," he dutifully told her, but as the words left his mouth he felt a strange bristling anger. She wanted to stay with *him*. A voice seemed to tell him, with some amusement, what he needed to say to her. "I'll come to visit you." He was shocked to hear his own voice saying such a thing.

Amazingly, she brushed away the tears, "Promise?"

He curtly nodded and with sinking heart, wondered how he would ever keep such a promise. He reached into his pocket and pulled out one of the oval-shaped nearly flat stones that Father of All had left behind for them. He had polished it all last winter until it gleamed and caught the colors of the rainbow. He gave it to her, "Now I'll have to, won't I?"

Her face brightened. "I'll keep it forever!"

Lyon sent Talon a commiserating look, picked up Brenna, and sat her by her mother on the wagon. She sat still this time, grasping the stone tightly in her small hand. Mee sat on her shoulder, looked directly at Talon, and nodded. In hindsight, Mee couldn't have nodded, but he was sure all the same that the Shee had been pleased by his gift to Brenna. He watched until they disappeared.

Tasut didn't say a word the entire miserable evening. Talon sat looking at the fire, his mind occupied with Brenna's family. He thought of his promise and how to keep it without incurring the wrath of Tasut.

*

From the corner where he sat, Tasut observed that Talon was no longer the same little boy who went off with Lyon's family. Talon would be twelve years old in two days, and was six feet tall. *The training must continue.* In one respect, Tasut was pleased at the spectacle that had just passed. The Tybar's daughter was strong-willed. This was welcome because she would have to be to withstand what was coming.

On the other hand, he was uneasy with some of the things that he sensed in Talon. He had watched his son soften toward the girl, even in the face of her disobedience. *There is no time for that. He must be the Guardian in all but name before I take him to Sogo.*

*

Two days later, Talon discovered that chopping wood was the hardest thing he had ever done. Lyon had worked with Talon chopping already gathered logs and it had been hard, but for whatever reason, easier. Perhaps it had been because Lyon talked while they worked, answered Talon's questions, and Mari would come with a basket of food and Brenna would stay afterward, stacking the kindling and try to get Mee to help. Just remembering brought a smile to his lips.

It was different with Tasut. Naturally, Tasut made it look easy when he had shown Talon how. Chopping trees down that Tasut marked with black-feathered arrows, hauling them by mule to the house, then unhitching the mules just to repeat it all was exhausting. Then he had to strip the logs of their limbs.

That was just the beginning.

He still had to complete all the other chores first and in the order Tasut insisted upon.

"Why?" he dared ask. He was already too tired to care if it earned him extra chores.

Tasut had given him a long assessing look, "You must be ready to live in Sogo." Tasut had gone out to the barn.

Stunned, he had gone back to his chores. His mind rang with the news. For the first time Talon could remember, Tasut had given information about the future.

His mind chewed on this information as he continued to chop. Sogo was the largest city in the world. Lyon had called it cursed. Mari had remained silent, but her silence was cold and evidence enough of what she thought of it.

His mind re-oriented when the blisters on his hands popped and became raw. When he finished work, he went into the house to wash up for the meal.

"Show me your hands," his father said

He silently showed his father the abused hands. He should have known better.

With a grunt, Tasut went to his room and returned with a foul-smelling concoction. He stuck Talon's hands into it without warning him first that it would be like sticking them into forge fire. He had bitten off the scream and shut his eyes to stop the tears as his whole body went rigid with pain. He prayed that Tasut would let him die in peace.

"For chopping, use the hide gloves in the barn. After today, chop once every four days for a month until the trees I marked are cut. Haul and strip them on the days you aren't chopping. Always start at the front and work your way back into the forest.

"After a month, chop every third day until you have them all hauled and stripped, then every other day until you have them ready for us to saw."

The only thing that made Talon's 12th birthday bearable was the sound of familiar hoofbeats that didn't belong to Harcour.

With a grin, he ran out the door of the house in time to see Lyon. Talon beamed, though his heart fell a small notch. He had hoped Mari and Brenna would be there as well. Lyon wore non-descript brown clothes and boots and was leading two beautiful charcoal-colored mares with white manes and tales. On the back of his own horse, was a bedroll and large tightly woven basket. *He must be traveling.* Tasut stood in the doorway behind Talon.

Lyon reached into his saddlebags and threw a package to Talon, "Happy Birthday!" then he addressed Tasut, "These two are ready. Do you want them in the barn or the pasture?"

Talon knew Lyon dreamed of a "perfect" breed of horse. This was yet another attempt to raise the perfect breed by crossing Harcour with Lyon's purebred Nahways. Talon was puzzled. *Why would anyone want a pretty horse that bites?*

"The pasture," Tasut answered.

"What about thieves?" Talon asked, concerned that Lyon's beautiful Nahways would be stolen. He watched Lyon dismount and Talon swung open the gate to the pasture.

"We'll let Harcour worry about them," Lyon laughed as he removed the halters and lead ropes from the mares.

Talon wasn't sure that Tasut wanted a mild-mannered horse. He watched his father cross the yard and enter the barn where he addressed the huge stallion as he opened the stall where he was kept, "Watch over those mares."

Harcour didn't need to be asked twice. He snorted and lit out after the two mares. He didn't bother with the gate, he leaped over the pasture fence and thundered after them, nostrils flaring.

"We were about to eat," Tasut said, "join us."

Lyon looked at Talon, who was sure that Lyon was going to say he couldn't. To his delight, Lyon agreed, tied his gelding to the post near the barn so it could graze, and came in with the large basket. It was full of Talon's favorite foods.

"I have news of Nyk," Lyon said to Tasut. Talon forgot about the still unopened package as Lyon continued. "There are reports of an unbelievably fast runner capturing large purses in northern Wesvalen. According to my people, the runner is 'Hauzian and wears blue."

Tasut continued to eat, but Talon could tell that he was listening intently.

"I'm heading to Wannapair, hoping to make the race circuit in time to see if it's Nyk. My gut tells me it is, but I have to confirm it."

Tasut shook his head. "It won't be in Wannapair. The next race is being held in Fistbown." Tasut washed his food down with water.

Lyon stiffened and looked dismayed. "The usual source?"

Tasut gave a brief nod. "Wannapair and Port City races were cancelled because of a plague."

"What's after Fistbown?"

"Coppertown, then Kenkut and Granger."

"The finals?"

For some reason, Lyon looked very hopeful, even excited.

"Owdawak."

Lyon's smile was tight, his eyes had a feral gleam, "Perfect. I can help him escape there."

"Are you sure you should?"

Lyon looked at Tasut, suspicion and wariness creeping into his features.

"Sogo is close," Tasut said. "Things may be happening this way for a reason."

"Let's go outside to talk," Lyon said, "I have other news."

Talon knew this was to exclude him from more information and he tried not to feel hurt, but Nyk was his friend and he wanted to know how Lyon was going to get him away from the bad men who had taken him. He felt guilty that he hadn't thought about Nyk for a very long time.

Talon took his package to his room to open it later, after he did the dishes. *They're still outside, I can open it now.* With excitement renewed, Talon opened the wrapping to find a hand sewn pouch, a knife from Lyon, and a new shirt from Mari. Talon put on the new shirt and looked at the knife for a long moment, delaying his dish duties. With a smile, he opened the small pouch. At the bottom he found a small note: Dear Talon, I made this. It's Ybarra hide. I miss you. Happy Birthday, All My Love, Brenna."

He put the pouch under his pillow, put the note in his pants pocket, and hurried to get the dishes done.

Lyon came in. "You opened them!"

Talon straightened up from the dishes and smiled, "Thank you and thank…them." He swallowed past the sudden lump in his throat. He wondered where Tasut was.

"Your welcome," Lyon smiled, but it didn't reach his eyes.

Talon felt like he was trying very hard to be pleasant.

Lyon winked at Talon and said in a conspiratorial voice, "Your father has given his permission for you to come visit as soon as you have the wood gathered for the winter. I'm sure we'll be seeing you sooner rather than later. I'll be stopping by now and again to see how the mares are doing."

Talon felt the tightness in his chest loosen and joy burst through. He only managed to nod. For some reason, the lump just got tighter.

Chapter 28: Chores

In three months, Talon finally had calluses hard and thick enough to withstand the constant strain of chopping wood. His goal was simple: finish and he could go to the Tybars.

Lyon did come through and each time he did, he helped Talon, frowning when Talon told him Tasut had gone back to Sogo for awhile. There was a letter for Lyon that Tasut left. When Lyon read it, his face darkened.

"The race circuit changed again," he swore and handed the note to Talon. It said: Circuit finals held in Cob City.

"You won't be able to get Nyk?" Talon's hope of seeing Nyk died.

"Cob City is quite a bit farther than Owdawak, but I may be able to get there in time if I take the Misty River to the branch of the Washakie. Even then, it'll be a gamble."

Talon waited for the answer to his question.

"I'm beginning to think Tasut's right; there's more to this. For now, I'm staying here and helping you get the wood in. Otherwise," he ruefully smiled, "Mari will skin me alive and Brenna will run away just to see you again."

Talon tried not to think only of himself, but he couldn't quite quench the fierce gladness that rose within him knowing Lyon was staying.

"Do you really think Nyk is alive?" Talon asked as they worked.

Lyon nodded, "Absolutely. The slavers that caught him aren't going to ruin their best money maker, so they'll keep him fed and take care of him physically."

That made Talon feel a bit better about Nyk's predicament.

"What about my other friends?" Talon didn't know what else to call Rube, Mal, and Iskar.

"They're still in Utak. Iskar's having a bit of struggle."

Talon wished he could help Iskar, though he doubted Iskar would want him to. "What do you mean?"

"Let's just say that Iskar will never be a farmer."

Talon felt he knew what that was about. Farming was hard work.

With Lyon's help, the work went smoothly and Talon learned easier ways of doing it. Tasut had still not returned a week later and the first snowflakes fell.

Several times during the wee hours of night, strangers had come to the cottage and given Lyon messages. Talon wasn't sure if he was supposed to know about these men, so he never asked Lyon what the messages were about.

One evening, Lyon's hand was over Talon's mouth and he nodded to the window, climbed through and waited for Talon, who pulled on his pants and followed. With a strange sense of deja-vu filling his head, he imitated Lyon who soundlessly ran into the forest and kept going in deeper until Talon couldn't tell where they were.

Lyon stopped in front of a huge pile of wood, "Stay here," he ordered, pushing Talon into the pile.

To Talon's surprise, what he thought was a wood pile was a hut of sorts. Inside was dry, warm, and already had Lyon's and Talon's gear.

It seemed a very long time before Lyon made it back. When he did, there was a faint smell of wood smoke.

"I hope you weren't attached to your house."

"Does Tasut know?" Talon's eyebrows rose in surprise that Lyon would feel okay about burning the house down.

"He's the one that warned me," Lyon confessed. "We have to move you. Actually, I'm supposed to take you to Tryk's first, but considering what just happened, I'm taking you with me for awhile. I already sent a message to Tryk so he'll be aware of where he has to move."

"What happened?"

"I can't answer that right now," Lyon said and grabbing their packs, they fled. "I can tell you that your father was the target, not you, not yet."

Not *yet?* As long as he got to be with Lyon, he felt safe. Somehow, it would all work out.

*

Tasut returned the following spring and Talon followed him to a new house. This one near a Village by the name of Beej. It took them two weeks just to reach it.

Two weeks later, they moved again. A week after that, Talon was left in Lyon's company because his father had been called back to Sogo. It was somewhat disappointing for Talon to be settled in with Tryk in his latest abode rather than go on with Lyon.

His father returned a month later and they moved yet again. Now that Lyon had informed Talon why they moved so often, Talon found the frequent moves easier to bear. The best news was they were once more in southern Acha.

It was early summer and once again Talon dreaded his birthday. He hoped Tasut had forgotten it in the web of life and duties. He wasn't really surprised when his father pulled him out of bed and shoved him out the door with another word, "Dyman."

He wanted to object but it would be useless. He was grateful he had learned how to pace himself and to get as much out of every breath that he could.

It was a bit of a shock fifteen minutes later to see a trio of familiar faces on the road ahead of him. Rube, whose face lit with excitement, Iskar, who whooped and jumped in the air, and Mal, who seemed to measure his acquired height with a degree of surprise, quickly masked.

"You're huge!" was Rube's greeting as Talon slowed and they caught his pace and continued running.

"What are you doing here?" Talon felt the experience was surreal.

"Lyon said he wanted us to run with you today," Iskar said, looking glum.

"Do you run everyday?" puffed Rube, who had slimmed quite a bit.

Talon shrugged. "I don't mind."

Mal seemed to have no trouble running with him and while Mal wasn't the person he would have preferred to run with, at least he had company. He was sure that Lyon knew how much he had wanted to see his friends. Even Mal.

"We'll have to find food and water along the way," he said after the first mile.

"Is it always this cold here?" grumbled Iskar as they ran along the frosted path.

Talon was surprised that he was surprised. It had been so long since he had noticed anything like the weather, the comment felt out of place. Yet, there was steam coming out of their mouths and until Iskar complained, Talon hadn't really thought about the cold. It was one of those things that he had accepted as part of things he no power to change.

Mal pointed out, "You'll warm up soon enough."

"Lyon said not to hold you back," Rube panted. "If you need to go faster, he said to tell you to leave us behind."

Talon considered it. He didn't like leaving his friends, but he knew Tasut would be waiting and he'd ask why it took so long. For some reason, Talon didn't want Tasut to know about the others. He felt it was a gift from Lyon and he didn't want Tasut to forbid him from going to the Tybars.

Iskar dropped out first, though Talon felt that this was sheer laziness. He had listened to Iskar's breathing and it seemed fine.

Rube was next; he had played out a few miles later and once Rube had disappeared behind them, Mal silently handed Talon a letter and turned, running back toward Rube.

Puzzled, Talon looked at the letter, slowed to a walk, and knelt next to the nearby stream. He kept looking around as he drank. When he had his fill, he kept moving to prevent his muscles from knotting. When he quickly undid the note, a second note fell out addressed to Tasut. He read the first one. If you have this note, then you are alone. Do not go to Dyman, return at once to your father. His life is at stake.

Talon did not stop to question the note, he began running as fast as he could toward home. Toward his father, whose life was in peril according to the note.

He did not see any of his friends on the road, which worried him a bit, but he had no time to find out what happened. Perhaps Tasut would know.

He ran full out until his lungs burned, his legs burned, and his body screamed at him to stop. He pushed forward, falling twice. When the cottage came into sight, he spurred himself onward, sprinting toward the house, note in hand.

He flung open the door only to find Tasut standing in the middle of the kitchen wearing a scowl and Talon's heart sank as he handed the note to his father.

His father didn't bother reading it, he threw it onto the fire and turned on Talon.

"Why are you back?"

Talon felt confused by the question, the action, and the entire scene. "The note said you were in danger."

"Who gave it to you?"

"M…" Talon closed his mouth. He wasn't going to betray his friends. Yet, why had Mal given him the note? Who was it from? He realized too late that these questions should have been asked earlier, when Mal was still there to answer.

"This time, it was a training exercise," his father said, his dark eyes hard and somehow disappointed. "Next time, you will know if it is from me."

Tasut took him to the table where he had a piece of parchment ready. He made a small tear in the upper right hand corner, quickly folded the parchment, and tied the twine around it. "There will always be two distinct knots on the twine and a slight tear on the right-hand corner. When all three are present, it means you can trust the person carrying the note. If any one of the three are missing, it will be from enemies and you will need to run or fight; perhaps both."

"It was in your handwriting," Talon protested, feeling defensive.

"Handwriting can be forged."

"Where am I supposed to run if it's someone I can't trust?" Talon didn't like the dark thoughts that were coming.

"I doubt they'll give you the chance," Tasut said. "But Tryk has offered to teach you geography while I'm gone to Sogo this time. He has maps; remind him you need to see them."

Tryk was often so preoccupied, he forgot to get completely dressed.

"You're leaving?" Talon had already studied the maps Tasut was refering to.

Tasut nodded, gathering up his usual supplies as he went. "If I'm not back in two weeks, go to Tryk's and stay there. If I'm not back in two months, go to Lyon's."

Talon swallowed. *Two months?*

"He won't be there, Mari will."

"Where is he?"

"He wanted to see if he could find the 'Hauzian boy."

"Nyk," Talon said flatly.

Tasut looked at him strangely. "There's a package on your bed."

He ran to his room, ignoring the flare of anger his stomach produced. On his bed he found a few gifts. Lyon had sent a book on battle strategy with a note that said Mal was studying the same book. Mari sent more clothing and a pair of boots. Brenna sent a note with a surprise drawing of a map of where they lived. It was less than five miles south.

That close and Tasut had never told him. *Did I really expect him to?*

Because of this new information, he grew accustomed to long runs once a week to Dyman and short runs to the Tybars and back on three other days.

He was at the Tybar's when Lyon returned from Wesvalen empty handed and frustrated, "I saw him! He was there for the first race and then those sons of slavers cut and ran for it."

"Was Nyk well?" Mari asked, slipping more eggs onto Talon's plate.

Lyon nodded, "Faster than ever. It didn't even look like they chained him."

"Isn't that a good thing?" Talon asked.

Lyon shook his head, "It's actually very bad. It means he could escape, but didn't. The only thing I can think of is that they have some other kind of hold on him."

*

Talon's birthday was a plague on the calendar. He hated it even as he accepted the ritual.

This time, his father rode in on a new Harcour, a magnificent piece of horseflesh twenty-one hands high at the shoulder. He was the five-year-old product of a previous Harcour and Lyon's first Nahway mares. He was dark silver-grey with black mane and tail, a finely arched neck and knotted muscle rippled beneath his hide. There the beauty ended. Unfortunately, this stallion, like his predecessor, was possessed of a demonic temper. Perhaps just possessed was a better description. He had tried to not only bite, but kick anyone but Tasut.

"He'll be fully trained when I return," Tasut assured Talon as they took care of the animals.

"Does that mean he won't bite?"

His father didn't answer.

To Talon, it looked like Lyon's plan to breed a better disposition was doomed once again. Tasut looked near collapse he was so tired.

Tasut ignored him, "You've hit your growth spurt. I'll leave a special tea for you to drink daily to help your mind remain clear as your body stretches. This year, it's time you learned to think. Instead of just keeping your mind busy, Lyon and Tryk can open your mind to new thoughts."

He felt slight alarm as Tasut swayed.

"I'm going to bed. Leave me alone until I wake. If I don't wake after two days, get Mari, she'll know what to do."

Talon cautiously followed his father, who collapsed onto his bed fully clothed. An anomaly. Once he pulled off his fathers boots, he couldn't leave him alone. It was disconcerting to have his father sleep like the dead hour after hour. His father felt feverish and his features were pale.

One long day stretched to two. He would have to get Mari. He ran there and back, not waiting for Mari to gather her things and come in the wagon.

Lyon came with Mari and she hissed, looking at Talon. "How long?"

"Two days."

"What was the big brute thinking?" she scowled.

"What's the matter?" Talon asked, his alarm growing in measure with Lyon's bleak look.

"He's exhausted and he has an infection, probably from a cut."

"Can you help him?"

Mari nodded, "Yes, but I'll need you to keep Brenna occupied while Lyon helps me. She's outside."

Talon nodded, sure it wasn't the whole story. It was even more suspicious when Tasut came out of the cottage moments later, looking like he'd had a week of rest. *Mari must have used her magic. It's the only explanation.*

Talon had grown accustomed to the hardness that lived in his father's eyes. He was always sensitive to his father's presence if Tasut was near. But this year there was something new in that look that made Talon uneasy. It was more assessing and seemed to weigh Talon and find him wanting in some category Tasut alone envisioned.

"I'm leaving for Sogo and I won't be back until next year," Tasut said when Talon came in to eat. "Continue the chores in addition to whatever Lyon and Tryk are willing to teach."

Lyon taught him how to hunt with more than a sling, and Tryk showed him how to decipher maps. When he was at the cottage, Mee delivered small gifts from Brenna.

It meant extra work when Mee delivered something because crabs were fairly scarce where they lived. Nonetheless, she insisted on payment and he didn't really mind. Mee spent a few days with him each visit and it took the sting off his loneliness.

Chapter 29: Amethyst Child

The people in Dyman were unaware they were under an enchantment. Mari had used her power in such a way that the people knew there was an orphanage and that Loni ran it, but had difficulty recalling where it was and no one in the city remembered there were three sisters.

Loni had so much to do the day she met her daughter that it was a small miracle she was able to think about, much less act upon, a little voice screaming for its mother. Before she could locate the source of such lamenting, she happened upon a few women standing in a semi-circle in front of the richest mercantile in Dyman. In the group were some of the socially powerful women of the city. Loni smiled at them as she silently passed by, wishing for invisibility.

"Mistress Ryn?" called the storekeeper's wife, Silva Ortuse, the President of the Helping Hands Society. Loni turned back to them and waved, but it was no use. Mrs. Ortuse wasn't to be detoured from her quarry and her sycophants followed in her rather large wake.

The crowd parted as if for royalty, as well they might, Mrs. Ortuse considered herself an authority on everyone and everything that happened in Dyman. Get on her bad side and your reputation was subject to the worst kinds of half-truths. Loni knew Mrs. Ortuse would have been aghast, if she had been informed about what she didn't know.

"I was just heading back home, Mrs. Ortuse, to give my children their lunch," Loni informed her, silently praying that the woman would pick up on the hint that she was busy. She didn't want to exchange words that, no matter how innocent, would later be dissected and reviewed by gossips.

The newest member of their Helping Hands society, Mrs. Strait, looked timidly at Loni and asked, "How many children do you have?"

"Thirty-six," Loni said and then frowned. "Sorry. Not sure why I said that, there's only thirty-five."

The woman's eyes grew huge and she looked at their leader, who didn't seem to think this a strange number.

"They aren't really hers, dear," Mrs. Ortuse smugly provided the explanation. "Mistress Ryn and her sister…oh, what was her name?"

Loni remained silent, rummaging through her basket of produce looking for something to appease the still-screaming child, that is, if she could still find the source of all that grief once the "Helping Hands" left.

"In any case, her sister is a beautiful girl if there ever was one. A bit of a hot head to be sure, but with a face like that, men will put up with any number of bad habits." Mrs. Ortuse looked at Loni's plain features, the fine reddish-brown hair pulled back in an unfashionable bun, and flushed, "The Ryn sisters run an orphanage."

"I didn't know we had an orphanage in Dyman!" Mrs. Strait said looking troubled. "Where is it?"

Mrs. Ortuse's eyes became slightly vacant, "Its – well, its…hmmm," she laughed with embarrassment, "my age is catching up with me. I don't exactly recall…" She seemed to come out of the daze and as if to make up for the lapse in concentration she added, "But I know they do a fine job of it, and don't you doubt it!"

This seemed to make the new member of their Society relax. Loni's stomach growled at her delay. She had been up since 4:00 a.m. with one of the orphans. Her injured arm was aching abominably. Yet, still pulling at her was the return of a child's high-pitched wail. It had grown weaker, but there was something in it that spoke of such suffering that she felt compelled to discover the source.

"Excuse me ladies," she interrupted their diatribe on the ills of raising children today, "I think I'm needed."

"She is a complete saint," she overheard Mrs. Ortuse say as she was leaving. "Now that sister of hers…." Loni didn't wait to hear the rest.

It wasn't uncommon in the area she traveled to hear the caterwauling of little children begging their parents to take care of them. A plague had scoured the area recently, leaving behind an abundance of orphans.

Mrs. Ortuse told Loni she heard the plague had been brought by the High Priestess of Veesh. Seeing her oozing sores and red bumpy skin, no one had let her in and she had died alone on the streets. Unfortunately, she had already infected every person she had contact with. In turn, those infected carried it with them. Several plague orphans had already made their way to the Ryn House doorstep. Thankfully, all of them had relatives to claim them, so far.

Blood is thicker than reason. Sometimes Loni feared for those who had to go with their relatives. She steeled her heart against the tug of intuition as distant relatives came to claim them. She had to release the children to questionable custody at times and it haunted her. *If I find out one of them is in danger...* Well, finding out would mean travel, research, and absence from her duties. *I'd just have to find another way.*

Her pale-green eyes canvassed the nearby streets and her ears were cued to pick up the wails she heard earlier. Silence greeted her. Hopefully, the child's parent had been found. Momentarily satisfied, with purchases in hand, she was nearly thrown to the street as two small arms and a thin body slammed into her knees and a child's voice jaggedly sobbed, "M-mama!"

Not being the most graceful of women, it was nothing less than miraculous she was able to keep from crushing whoever had just latched onto her legs like a vise. Awkwardly, she looked down to find a small, very dirty child.

This stray, a dirt clod in non-descript rags, was hugging Loni's knees with all the strength that her two scrawny little arms possessed. Buried in Loni's freshly cleaned and pressed skirt was the crusty face of a small green-eyed waif. Loni looked up and around to see where the child's mother could possibly be. She was met with downcast eyes and no one to claim the shivering little girl.

As caretaker of thirty-five orphans of various ages and sizes, she was accustomed to all levels of dirt, confessions, and emotional outbursts. She could recognize true need and her generous heart opened. *There is always room for love.* One more wasn't going to hurt.

That was not to say she took every child in. In the past, there had been people who bribed children to pretend to be orphans. The insidious goal was to track down the location of the orphanage and take the children to Sogo to be sold. It had not succeeded so far with any orphanage under her care.

The most heinous of those seeking children was Delf, the Minister of Trade, whose minions remained in the dark about the enchantment.

As for the Minister, he was on the Ryn sisters list of those to remove from society. She would do this herself, if possible, as a service to mankind, but especially children. *When I have time.*

In the meantime, reality was a dirty little girl who believed Loni was her mother. A title Loni desired with all of her heart. The opportunity had been cruelly dashed beyond hope or resurrection when she was sixteen.

A practical woman, she wasn't afraid of truth. She knew herself to be a plain self-employed woman, with no husband, no children of her own, and no prospects for either in her future. Her life and all her love were spent on the children of the Ryn and Phoenix orphanages, two sisters, Hadasha and Marianna and her brother in law, Lyon.

Loni led the tiny girl to a small bench on the common, near a vendor she knew as Yanni. The bones in the little girl's hand felt as if they were no more than shadows. When Loni sat, the child crawled immediately onto her lap, her words causing Loni's kind heart to ache.

"I know you told m-me not to s-steal but," she stopped with a hiccup, "I was hungry."

Loni took mental note to discover later if the girl's hair was blonde or brunette, because it was so dirty she couldn't tell.

"I'm glad all your red bumps are gone," the child continued, her crossed eyes wet with tears.

"What's your name?" Loni softly asked the orphan.

She hadn't counted on the reaction her words brought as the green eyes filled with pain. Incredulous tears filled them and spilled onto dirty cheeks, "You forgot me?" she whispered. "It's m-me, Wynna!"

It is meant to be. She told herself even as she hugged the child to her, "Of course it is, dearest."

"The red bumps made you forget again," the child said sadly, dashing the tears away.

One day, she will have to face the truth. But right now, we'll let the healing begin. She smoothed Wynna's stringy sweaty hair, "I'm sorry you felt you had to steal, it's wrong."

"Are you mad at me? Are you going to stop calling me Wyn?"

"I'm terribly disappointed that you stole something. However, Wyn," Loni took her newest daughter by the chin and lifted it, so their green eyes met. "It's never too late to set things right and I know you will never do it again." She wouldn't have to because Loni was now her mother.

Wyn solemnly nodded and Loni took Wyn off her lap and put her on the ground, "Now, who did you take the food from?"

Wyn looked around and pointed where Master Yanni sold fruit and bread. Loni breathed a silent sigh of relief. Master Yanni was a kind-hearted man and one of her favorite people in Dyman. In truth, he was the one who knew most of what went on in Dyman, at least, the important things. The things she needed to know.

For his part, Yanni knew the homely face of Mistress Ryn very well. She was one of his favorite customers and she was well known by the entire town for her kind and generous heart. He had a feeling that the little one would somehow come to orbit around Mistress Ryn.

"I'm so sorry, Master Yanni, my daughter has stolen some of your food. She will apologize and never do it again."

The waif painfully stuttered her apology, her thin pale face miserable and crossed eyes full of tears as Loni handed her the money for the food she had stolen and she handed it to him

"She be one of yourn now?" he asked as she handed the orphan an apple that was paid for.

Loni's eyes narrowed. She had no intention of explaining herself. "Any objections?"

"Meant no offense," his hands came up as a peace offering, "the plague don't ya know." He said in a low voice "both 'er folks is gone. I was thinkin' 'bout takin' her home to the missus, but didn't want ta risk it."

Loni appreciated this information. It meant her heart had been right. Her lips curved into a great smile, transforming her plain face, "Thank you for helping my daughter."

From the look in Yanni's eye, he wasn't only aware the little waif had stolen, but had turned his back so she could do it. He had a soft heart for the plight of homeless children. He had been one at some point in his distant past.

"Wyn, dear, please hold onto my skirt."

"B-but the f-fire could come again! I h-hate fire!"

Loni then understood that the girl's parents, whoever they were, would remain anonymous. Those who died of the plague, and all they owned, were locked inside their houses and burned.

Her heart swelled with compassion, "Wyn, dear, there is no fire here." She balanced her purchases to fit comfortably in her arms and they walked to the small wagon and Wyn climbed up and sat right next to her until they reached home.

"Hadasha!" Loni called from the front porch. She sat the purchases down. She took the grubby hand of the sleepy Wyn. She tried not to think how much her weak arm ached. Haddy should have been watching closely enough to show up and relieve Loni of the bundles she carried from the market. *Where is she?*

When she entered the parlor, a clerk from the Mercantile was sitting on the couch and Hadasha, who was a very talented gymnast, was showing him her back-bend into vertical splits, all this taking place while wearing skirts!

"Hadasha Ryn!" Loni gasped, deeply shocked at the leggy display.

Haddy, startled, slammed down into the splits sooner than she anticipated. The young man flushed and stood up so quickly that he knocked over a vase of flowers and caught the vase, minus the flowers, before it hit the ground. Loni pointed at the door. He immediately left, nearly catching his heel with the heavy door as Loni shut it behind him.

Haddy had the grace to look embarrassed. *More at being caught, than because what she was doing was inappropriate.* Loni pulled Wyn toward Haddy, "There's food on the porch; I could have used your help."

Haddy looked at the dirty little girl, "Who's that?"

"Please, just get the food and take it to the kitchen while I get Wyn cleaned up."

"You brought *another* one home?" Haddy complained, stretching and lazily strutting to the front door.

Loni arched her brow and was gratified to see Hadasha pick up the pace.

"Where is everyone?" Loni surveyed the empty kitchen as Hadasha came in, carrying the baskets of food. The usual hub of life at the Ryn House orphanage was silent, not a good sign, and the tables were barren.

"You didn't take time to fix lunch?" Loni said with real bite in her voice, "Haddy, some of them are too young to go without food."

Haddy shrugged and put the baskets of food on the table.

Loni took a deep breath and shrilly whistled. Wyn clapped her hands over her ears and stared at Loni in fear and amazement. A scrambling sound and running footsteps came from all corners of the house and yard. Wyn grabbed Loni's skirt with one grubby hand and wiped her nose on the already starchy sleeve of her own raggedy clothes.

Haddy wrinkled her nose at the sight, "You're too paranoid Loni. You know Pash and Zaya won't let them starve."

Pash and Zaya had returned from their training with Mari at Hourglass Lake. They were assigned to Ryn House two weeks ago to take some of the stress away from Loni and they had done a wonderful job. Possibly too wonderful, if Haddy's current attitude was any indication of their abilities.

Loni's eyebrow rose further, "Pash and Zaya are running the errand I told you about before I left, but that's not the point. I left a responsible woman named Hadasha in charge. I'm not sure exactly what happened to her, but I'm sure you have many creative explanations as to where she went and why she left you in charge."

Loni put an apron over her clothes and with Wyn still hanging onto her skirts, got a knife from the drawer and handed it to Haddy. "It was highly irresponsible of her. I certainly expected better than this," both of Loni's eyebrows were touching her hairline and Haddy's full lips pouted.

"You will take her place fixing the meal for these children," she informed Haddy, "while I take care of my daughter."

Ignoring Haddy's surprised look, she took Wyn's hand and headed down the hall to her own room where the large copper bath sat. The cleaning took two hip-baths and two hair washings before Loni was satisfied. She toweled off Wyn and helped her change into a fresh set of clothes. With a deep breath and her back straight, she adjusted Wyn's blouse.

"Let me see," she turned the little girl to face her, "when was your birthday?"

"Y-you're silly," she laughed. Wyn was a pretty girl once the dirt had been scrubbed away.

Loni's smile and good nature had returned and she said cheerfully, "How many candles would you like on your cake this time?"

"T-ten."

Ten! Wyn looked half that age. Her heart ached for the little girl. "I wonder what they've cooked up in the kitchen. Shall we see?"

Wyn smiled and nodded her head vigorously. Loni chuckled and opened the door to go down the hall, "From the smells I would say we have bread, stew, and apple pie."

Loni enjoyed the moment when Haddy looked up and something like shock lit her eyes when she saw the pretty little girl that had been hidden under layers of filth and woes. Loni's brow arched and Haddy's mouth closed.

"I see my youngest sister has returned at last, where have you been all morning?"

Haddy shook her head and snorted in her most un-ladylike fashion startling Wyn, who looked at Haddy and stuttered, "H-h-horse?" as if she were guessing the sound from a game she had played, perhaps with her mother.

Haddy's countenance darkened and Loni laughed, "Very good Wyn."

Wyn smiled, "C-Can you do m-more?"

"Hadasha's very busy right now, but she'll be telling everyone a bedtime story later. I'm sure she wants you to feel welcome on your first night here and will do a good job."

Loni didn't see Haddy stick her tongue out and cross her eyes at her newly claimed daughter.

*

Haddy stood in front of the freshly washed children who were all ready for bed. Their bright faces full of anticipation.

She glanced at Chun, who was leading her blind sister, Wysh, to a clear spot on the floor. Their brother Yun was already waiting for them. Haddy hated story time and had tried everything she could think of to get out of it, but Loni offered the only option she hated more: bathing the little monsters.

If I have to tell them a story, I'm going to make it a good one, not one of those idiotic fairy tales where everything is squeaky clean and everyone's so happy la-te-dah. Lies.

"Listen up!" she snapped at them and then, with effort, moderated her tone. "No questions, no talking, and if you need to go, go now, I'm not stopping. I'm. Not. Loni.

"Now, Once upon a time, the Amethyst child was walking through the forest-"

"Whats am-me-thist mean?" asked one of the boys.

Haddy glared at him and he fell silent, "Purple. Now, the Amethyst child had long dark hair and eyes the color of gold. She was very beautiful and a joy to be around…until she decided she wanted your blood."

All the children's eyes went wide with terror, some gasped. One of the youngest hid her face in her brother's side and didn't look at Haddy again.

Haddy grinned, enjoying the reaction. "The Amethyst child had no blood of her own, so she stole it from all who crossed her path. She wouldn't bother hiding, she *wanted* to be found.

"She didn't have friends, but the Amethyst child had a crippled warrior who was always by her side to do her bidding. If she couldn't find someone, the warrior would. He had fought in so many battles he'd lost the use of one arm and had to drag his bad leg behind him like this, scraaatch-thump, scraaatch-thump."

Haddy made staggering-stiff movements as she crossed the wooden floor, holding one of her arms tightly to her. The children who were closest pulled away.

"The warrior was completely loyal to his master because she had promised him he would have eternal youth and live forever as long as he would help her get the blood she craved. She kept her word."

"Would she drink children's blood!?" the blind girl gulped.

Haddy snorted, "No… she used children to keep herself young, sucking their years away, turning their eyes purple and leaving them an empty husk. It would have been *better* if she'd killed them.

"One day the Amethyst child was walking through the woods with her warrior and they could hear men's blood singing in their veins and horse hooves clomping along the path. The creaking of rattling wagons made the Amethyst child smile. She was hungry…"

"What did she do?" Chun's eyes were wide with terror and she was hugging a shivering Wysh. Yun buried his face in Chun's lap.

Haddy's grin was wicked. "What she always did when she got hungry. Her skin would change from pink and rosy, to a burning purple.

"She told her faithful crippled warrior to go and lure the men her way. She was thirsty…" Haddy looked over her captivated audience with pleasure. "When the warrior returned, he reported there was a large caravan."

Two children from Catsfour, a city known for child slavery, held their necks where there had once been collars, their eyes wide with fear.

"There were three carts of prisoners, one each for the men, the women, and the children. This made the Amethyst child angry. Her parents had been captured and taken from her by slavers when she was small.

"Her golden eyes burned with hatred and purple tears ran down her face. When she looked up, the very forest that was around her burst into flame! She ordered the warrior to draw his sword.

"With the Amethyst child's skin aglow with purple fire and the crippled warrior at her side, they burst through the burning trees!

"The crippled warrior went to work, his wicked blade singing through the air. The Amethyst child watched hungrily until someone got close enough and then she'd turn and consume them where they stood, leaving a beating heart to feed to her warrior, to whom she had pledged eternal youth."

Haddy saw the sun had gone down and quickly finished the story, "After they were finished, only the wagons, prisoners, and two out of ten horses were left. The Amethyst child was still hungry, but in memory of her parents, had the warrior free the prisoners.

"They all grouped together, terrified of what they'd seen the child and her warrior do. All, but one child and that child was… a Cannibal!"

Here there were more gasps and one child fled the room, running as fast as his fat little legs could carry him. Haddy was enjoying herself so much, she didn't pay attention to who it was, nor did she care.

"Yes, the Cannibal was a black-hearted, sharp-toothed devils child from forbidden Cancor Island. When the Cannibal child saw the glowing Amethyst child, the wretch fell down on its face to worship her and didn't dare move.

"The child stretched out her hand and pulled the Cannibal to its feet with her power. She looked at the prisoners who feared her and stated that she would spare their lives, this time, and would take the brave Cannibal instead.

"The crippled warrior picked up the small Cannibal, who began to scream, and walked off into the burning woods because he liked his food cooked. The Amethyst child with a bloody smile, said, 'Any children who won't go to bed when you tell them to, will disappear in the middle of the night. My warrior will stuff them in a sack and bring them to me so I can steal their youth! And like the Cannibal child, you will never see them again.'

"With that, the child turned and walked into the forest, commanding the fire she had unleashed to disappear. The Cannibal, the crippled warrior, and the Amethyst child were never seen again. The End."

Haddy's smile faltered. The room was silent, eyes were wide in pale frightened faces, and some children looked ready to cry. Wysh and Yun had white-knuckled grips on Chun's arms. Wyn's large green eyes were peeking out at her from under the large Loni's covered rocking chair.

Eli, one of the children who'd been left on their door step when he was younger, was biting off the cuff of his shirt, staining his mouth with red dye. It was the first hint Haddy had that perhaps she had gone overboard. Eli only chewed his sleeves when he was terrified.

Which he is, constantly. Haddy rolled her green eyes, "Story's over. Now get to bed. If I were you, I'd be asleep when Loni comes in."

In one bound, every child was on their feet and scrambling up the stairs to their rooms. Chun had Yun on her back and was leading her blind sister up the stairs, looking like she'd like to run, but refusing to give in to her fear. *Good for her; she might make a decent maid some day.*

When the orphans had disappeared, Haddy sat back on the rocker and silently laughed, until she felt a hand clamp down on her shoulder. She shot forward, tucked to a forward-roll and leapt to her feet, swallowing a startled scream.

Her knives flashed in her hands and she took aim. She had half a mind to skin the brown-eyed elfish-faced woman in front of her, "Zaya! I'll gut you the next time you do that!"

Zaya's dark eyes held a challenge, she cracked her knuckles as she spoke, "Never make promises you can't keep. That was quite a bedtime story. Smart Haddy, real smart."

"That's right, I am smart," Haddy felt cross and her cheeks were burning with anger at being caught off guard.

"We'll see how far smart goes when they wake up screaming tonight," Zaya's eyes narrowed, "because you're going to be the one tending to their every whimper."

Haddy yawned. "I'm going to bed and I'm staying there. I don't care if they scream."

"Did Loni know you were going to tell them that story?" Pash asked from the doorway, holding a small infant in her arms while Eli chewed on her skirt. Half his cuff was missing, the red dye was still staining his frightened face. If it weren't for the terror in his eyes, the dye on his mouth would have cast him as the Amythest Child's blood-thirsty warrior.

"What are you doing out of bed!?" Haddy snapped at Eli, who stopped chewing the skirt and jumped behind Pash.

Pash's blue eyes went flat, within three heartbeats she had given the baby to Zaya and growled at Haddy, "He has nightmares about ships from the last time you told stories! He thought the purple child was here because he heard your scream and hid under my bed!"

"I never told a story about ships," she snarled. "You know I hate the water! Besides, how's that my problem? It's Zaya's fault for sneaking up on me."

"Stop blaming everyone else for your mistakes!" Pash's blue eyes flashed.

"If we hear one scream in the night, you better be the one tending to it – if Loni sets one foot out of her bed, we'll let her know what story you told!" Zaya threatened.

Scowling, Haddy stomped up the stairs, knowing that Zaya and Pash wouldn't follow. It was difficult not to turn around and see if they were going to throw something after her. Pretending indifference made her sweat. She brushed aside the twinge of guilt, it all but disappeared once she had reached her own bedroom door. *I'm not going to baby-sit tonight!*

Chapter 30: Complicated

"If Tasut is in Sogo, doesn't that mean he's in danger?" Talon frowned and looked at Tryk. He had spent much of the last two winters with the inventor. The rest of the time had been spent with the Tybars.

Tryk debated the wisdom of answering, but decided to tell Talon the truth. "Listen closely and don't ask questions until I'm finished."

Tryk leaned back against his chair, his hands still rubbing the cloth over the small metal ball. "In centuries past, Sogo was the center for learning among the civilized world." Tryk rubbed his scar, a clear indication of his mood. "Sogo's government was a great republic and the citizens were fortunate to live there. The library was unrivaled in size and content. The greatest minds of the age came to teach and study. Enormous scientific progress was made, ancient artifacts were gathered from every country, and put into the museums."

To Talon, he looked regretful, as if he wished he had been born in those days.

"The most talented artists filled the streets and walls with such exquisite beauty their craftsmanship is still talked about in history books. They made it sound like the pictures that were painted were so life-like they could talk. People spoke of the greater good for all, and meant it. Inside the walls of Sogo, there was no war for the space of two centuries."

Talon was puzzled. "You said it was a Republic? I thought it was a Democracy." Talon had been reading some of those books. The historical ones seemed boring although the parts about battles were interesting.

"I said it **was** a Republic!" Tryk corrected as he held the metal ball he had been polishing up to his good eye, frowned and went back to polishing it. "People got lazy about who they elected. It's an unfortunate side-effect of freedom. Most people do better under adversity than prosperity," he said with a shake of his head.

"In any event, the people voted those into office who promised them the easiest life, wanting something for nothing, thinking only of themselves." Tryk's look was distant and he said, "The more prosperous the citizens were, the more selfish and prideful they became. In the end, the entire government collapsed because those in control gave the people everything. This had the downside of breeding a lazy, contemptible society who only wished to be pampered and spoiled. They wanted no struggles in their life so when their government failed, the hard times came and they had no backbone, no strength, and no idea of what direction to turn.

"Their weak-mindedness gave rise to the Council of Nine; at that time they were no more than the stronger land barons. They took power into their hands and made it look like they had accomplished what the government couldn't. In truth, a dictatorship followed the fall of Sogo's government. In spite of everything the Nine claim, that is the form of government that exists in Sogo."

"Wait," Talon shook his head in frustration, "how can Sogo have a dictator when it's run by the Nine?"

"That's what the average citizen thinks, because that is what those who are in power want them to think, and Sogoians are too lazy to care. Its called apathy. As long as no one is rocking their boat, they're willing to continue their way of life.

"Sogo is run by Nez Shavae. The Council members are nothing more than his toadies who supported him in getting that office through murder and every dark deed you could name. Nez is responsible for the murder of the Prophet Benamii. He rules by fear. It is the greatest of all thieves. Fear kills a mans heart, weakens his mind, and crushes his soul. That is why this is the time of tooth and claw it speaks about in the Book of Benamii."

Talon felt an alarm go off inside of him at the name Nez. His mind recalled the conversation he overheard on the day the creatures had attacked his home in the forest. Tasut had announced, "I will kill him myself before I let Nez take him." *Nez is on the Council of Nine?* Talon digested this with some discomfort. "Isn't anyone going to do anything about it?"

Tryk nodded, "Yes, thank the Father of All!" Tryk handed Talon the metal ball, attempting to close Talon's hand around it and taking it back. "Do you believe in Prophecy?" Tryk asked.

Talon shrugged. "Tasut said it's true."

Tryk snorted. "That isn't reason to believe, young man! You need to know for yourself."

"How do I find out?"

Tryk stood, put the silver ball into his pocket and returned with a small, leather-bound book labeled "Book of Benamii" and handed it to Talon who read the title.

Surprised, Talon looked at Tryk "This is forbidden."

Tryk laughed, a coarse raspy sound. "By whom?"

"I guess by the Council." Talon frowned.

"So, the Council of Nine already says what books we're allowed to read in Acha. With that in mind, what do you think?" Tryk was intrigued.

"It's a bad law."

"You don't know the half of it," Tryk muttered. "Read that book and we'll talk about it the next time you come to visit."

"What about Tasut?"

"After what I told you about Sogo, what are your conclusions?" Tryk stated with exasperation.

Tasut is in danger but he isn't the only one. Talon didn't know how to voice his conclusion but Tryk seemed to read his answer in his face and gave a satisfied nod of the head, and crawled under yet another invention.

Talon opened the book and began to read. He never heard Tryk go to bed.

*

Talon had returned a week ago to the Tybar's cottage near Belly Band Lake. Since his return, he'd had the opportunity to meet more people under the guise of being Lyon's slave. Lyon took him as far north as Hahman and east to Acha's capital city, Fletching, where he saw the enormous Cessue Dam and Donner Falls that spilled over into Teris.

Currently, Lyon was waiting for a peddler while they chopped wood. Talon's awakened curiosity came to the forefront. It was a question that had burned in Talon for a long time and he finally had courage and trust enough to ask it.

"Why doesn't Tasut take me to Sogo with him?"

Lyon was quiet, his face a perfect mask as he answered, "It has to do with who he is and what he does. It would be safer for everyone if you never mentioned your father by name unless you absolutely know we are alone."

Talon looked around. "We are alone. Will you tell me why?"

"It's complicated…" Lyon paused, seemed to struggle and then said grimly, "and extremely dangerous."

Unsurprised, Talon nodded.

"Your father understands the danger and doesn't want you involved for as long as possible."

There were underlying tones in Lyon's voice that Talon tried to interpret. *"…as long as possible…"* seemed to stand out. Talon carefully said, "Tasut told me I have to learn to take care of myself."

"And to protect Brenna," Lyon added with a strange intensity that Talon didn't understand.

He had never explained to anyone that even on those occasions when he was off with Lyon, Brenna would come to his mind. It was odd, like a warm blanket was wrapped around him when he thought of her and then the front part of his head tingled. Inside his heart, he felt the reason was because of that special night that they had shared a divine visit. Another secret that he kept. Somehow, that visit had planted an awareness of her within him.

"Here he comes," Lyon said, pointing to the peddler. "Why don't you go finish with the mares?"

Talon hurried to the barn to curry the beautiful even-tempered mares that Lyon rode. Talon had chopped enough wood to last the Tybar's through two winters, but he and Lyon were still chopping every day. He peeked out of the barn, aware that Lyon was agitated with the man who had come because Lyon was pacing, a real clue that something was wrong.

The man looked like a peddler, but Talon had his suspicions that the man wasn't one. Every peddler, other than those that visited Lyon and Tasut, was purposefully loud, alerting everyone that he was ready to do business.

He didn't grudge Lyon his secrets; he had his own. He wished he could tell Lyon everything, like how he could have pointed right to Brenna, no matter where she was, and told anyone who wanted to know how she was feeling and therefore, Lyon didn't need to worry. Right now, Brenna was happy. Most of the time, she was and it helped him deal with his father's expectations.

Tasut said to listen to the voice inside and it would tell him the truth about what to do and believe. Talon found it confusing at times. His inner voice told him the Tybars were more than they appeared to be, but not what.

After the peddler left, Lyon had looked at Talon in an assessing way. He seemed to come to a decision and asked, "What do you know of the Assassin's Guild?"

Talon looked carefully at the brush he was using to groom the two mares. "It's a Guild for assassins?"

Lyon laughed. "Good guess."

The result was an education in how the Guild worked in Sogo.

"There are four stages of skill within the Guild, but only three are recognized publicly," Lyon informed him.

"Why?"

Lyon nodded as if he expected this response, "Sogo has complicated laws."

"That's why everyone knows about it, but only talk about three?"

Lyon brushed the other mare slowly. "Yes. What I'm about to tell you are details the general public is unaware of. The first stage of training is called Acolyte. I'll tell you more while we do forms." He hung up the brush and motioned for Talon to do the same. They went outside and Talon followed Lyon to the area where they did open-hand exercises.

"Do you see that group of plants?" Lyon pointed to the small plot of land next to the house. Talon had recognized them as poisonous and simply stayed away. "An Acolyte studies poisons and their antidotes, grows, and sells them. If he fails to find the correct antidote, he dies for his ignorance."

Death seemed a harsh sentence for getting one wrong, yet Talon was familiar with Tasut's kind of logic and this seemed similar.

"The Acolytes are also sparring partners for those studying advanced forms. They are allowed to defend, but not kill," Lyon motioned for Talon to stand in the training circle. "In Sogo, if an Acolyte accidentally kills someone, their name is added to a list the Guild uses to train the second group: assassins."

Lyon had taken seventh position and Talon had assumed the defense against that position.

"Assassins actually kill people. First they watch and follow the person they call their mark and make detailed observations about their life, habits, friends, etc. Then they report to the Guild and are given permission to make the kill, which is called a hit, or move onto another assignment. Assassins can only kill with permission."

Seeking to divert Lyon, Talon asked, "Who was that peddler?"

The diversion didn't work and Talon found himself pinned. Lyon released him. "As you've no doubt guessed, he isn't a peddler. He came to tell me there is at least one Feesha in the area."

Talon's mind flashed back to Nyk running through the Rahazi Forest, himself following. Nyk had told him the man chasing them was a Feesha. Talon miscalculated Lyon's next move and found himself on the ground, motes swimming in his eyes as he struggled with the idea of a Feesha being close. *Why is a Feesha here?*

"Feesha are the third group," continued Lyon. "They are also known to Sogoians as the damned."

Lyon offered his hand, and as he pulled up Talon, he was caught off guard as Talon used the leverage to pull him off balance, and found himself on the ground. He laughed and Talon joined him.

"Why?" Talon gave nothing away about what he planned against Lyon's attack. He took no direct stance to give any clue, but had calculated many defenses in his mind. None of them worked.

When Lyon came at him, it looked like he would attack head-on, but launched himself from a rock jutting out of the ground, flipped over Talon's head, touching Talon's shoulder as he flew by. Talon smiled, knowing Lyon would now teach him that move.

"Feesha usually take out common marks," Lyon pulled a sawhorse from the area they used for chopping wood.

"Common?"

"People that any citizen of Sogo can pay to eliminate without giving reasons." Lyon showed Talon how to use his hands to launch off the sawhorse and then helped Talon attempt it.

The first time was unsuccessful and Talon winced as he got off the ground and dusted his clothes off.

"More speed, Talon, and be sure to arch your back more at the height of the flip."

He tried it again and failed. "They can kill anybody?" the idea offended him even as he shook his head to clear it when he landed wrong again. Lyon reset the sawhorse Talon was to launch himself over, remaining in place to spot Talon. It was difficult but after several more tries, Talon did it.

Lyon nodded his approval, "The last group, the one that people fear to discuss, is called the Unknown. They must master all other stages of training. Laws of Sogo protect them as national treasures. In essence, they are the private assassins for the Council of Nine and are generally feared."

"Generally?" Talon thought everyone would fear the Unknown. He prepared to do the flip again. He wanted to perfect it.

"There are a few brave souls who have no reason to fear them." Lyon nodded and Talon ran, executing a perfect flip. Lyon clapped him on the back and smiled.

"Like the Council of Nine?" Talon guessed.

Lyon shook his head, "The Nine are among those that have the greatest fear of them. They are always trying to bribe the Guild Master so they won't be hit. Those bribes keep the Guild producing the best assassins."

"Guild Master?" Talon felt this was very complicated and wondered if assassins liked it that way to confuse everyone. *Aren't they just glorified murderers?*

"The position of Guild Master goes to a man who has gained the most respect among the other assassins. He stays at the Guild and makes assignments when orders come in. He's considered the most powerful person in Sogo after the Nine."

"Why would you need a Guild Master?" It seemed a terrible profession in Talon's opinion.

"I was always told it helps keep the level of corruption under control. For instance, Sogoian law requires all assassins to be registered.

"Those that are not on the books and who attempt or even complete an assassination, are hunted by the Guild and killed."

Talon focused, final forms were coming up and he wanted to be ready. Lyon put the sawhorse away. The conclusion that Talon reached made his heart pound. Brenna told him Lyon lived and worked in Sogo before he was a jeweler.

Yet, here, far from Sogo, numerous people came at odd hours of the day and night to bring information. Most looked dangerous, but not as dangerous as Lyon or Tasut.

The final piece of the puzzle snapped into place when he remembered his father respected Lyon and Talon knew Tasut didn't respect anyone that hadn't earned it.

"You're the Guild Master," Talon said with surprise. Then he frowned, "But that can't be right. The Master has to stay with the Guild and deliver assignments to the others."

Lyon's face became a mask.

For the first time, Talon noticed the change. "Lyon?"

"I'm training you and telling you these things because you must understand the players to win the game. Ultimately, you are their mark, Talon. You are alive because they haven't found you - yet."

Even as Talon absorbed this information, he was surprised that he wasn't afraid. It wasn't like the last time, when Nyk and he ran blindly into a nearly fatal meeting with a herd of plague crabs.

"What do I need to do?" Talon asked.

"Not die." Lyon wasn't joking.

It sounded good to Talon.

Chapter 31: Orders

The Forest Wife wasn't happy. She'd come into her cottage from the garden with brows down and mouth pinched. Her favorite tree, one that shaded some of her most valuable herbs and poisons, was slowly dying and she couldn't figure out why.

She had spoken to it, watered it, fertilized it, and still it died inch by inch. *It has to have a worm or some other creepy-crawly thing.* She'd simply have to ask Luv to watch it and see if the Shee could see anything out of the ordinary. This was easier said than done. After a quick look around the cottage, Luv was nowhere to be seen. The Forest Wife looked out the window at her garden.

"Bastian?" she called, "I could use some of your expertise here."

There was the sound of a book slamming shut from the other room where her son Bastian, who also served as her assistant, had been studying. "Shall I grow legs and come to you or was that a hypothetical assignment?" he replied.

She smiled for the first time that day. Bastian was her solace in this odd place and time. He was her salvation while she was so far away from her husband and the other members of her family. She rose and went to his side.

From birth, ten-year-old Bastian had been crippled. His days were spent in a wheeled-chair in whatever room he chose. He preferred the library. The mystery was the fact he was a Son of Ammon and therefore destined to help destroy Sogo. He was one of a distinct group of men that she had temporary stewardship over. She didn't know how it was going to happen, but she had no doubts that it would; otherwise, Father of All would not have given him the distinct mark all of them would wear.

"I thought you were going to Sogo," he said.

"I am," she smiled at him and lovingly smoothed his wavy chestnut-brown hair. Bastian was going to be very handsome. He was already kind. Her heart often ached for him. He seldom had anyone his age to visit in this place that was out of time, and so far from where they longed to be.

"If you have a moment" he began, his large wistful brown eyes catching her immediate attention, "could you go to Tryk's and get some books for me? Last time he came, he forgot to bring any."

"More books?" her gaze took in the room, books from ceiling to floor and stacked on every available surface. Bastian had read them all. He had a brilliant mind. Despite what Tasut said, the heartless wretch, this boy was someday going to prove to be as valuable as the Chosen himself!

"I need two in particular. One on antidotes and the other on legendary creatures and myths."

She nodded and felt a stab of uneasiness, remembering the garden. "While you're reading, if you come across anything on tree diseases, let me know." She felt his forehead for signs of fever. He didn't pull away, evidence of how badly he wanted more books. He didn't look ill, but his skin looked moist like he had been sweating.

Satisfied he was well, she put two fingers in her mouth and blew a shrill peeping whistle. Luv came bounding in the window, her fur flying every which way from a vigorous chase with a hopeful male who had been leaving Luv many objects on the windowsill to indicate his interest.

"Watch him Luv," she ordered and walked out the door.

Luv stood with arms crossed and made the "Humph!" sound that Shees made when they were at their most peeved.

Bastian looked at his mother, "Luv wants to go with you to Sogo." He didn't say he wanted to go as well, though she saw it in his eyes. He knew he couldn't. Not yet.

"Absolutely not!" she looked at her Shee, who turned her back, a sign of serious rejection. "Luv, last time you broke your promise to behave." Luv had been unable to resist the enormous variety of crabs that were available in the open marketplace of Sogo. She had jumped from the wagon onto the vendors stall and began ripping and devouring his wares.

Visions of the people screaming and trampling one another to escape the mad Shee would have been comical, if it hadn't drawn so much unwanted attention. Shees were extremely rare and just to see one was considered a mark of prestige. To own one was to be invited into higher circles of society outside of Sogo.

Luv had returned with a large fat snow crab twice her size, carrying it over her head and walking on her hind feet, acting as if she owned the street.

Tasut had not been happy.

The Forest Wife informed her, "I will buy you a crab. In fact, I will buy three, a pair to put out into the special pool so they can produce larger species, and one for your very own."

Luv grabbed her thick tail and wrapped her face in it, hiding her laugh. The Forest Wife was relieved. When Shees hid their laugh behind their tails, it meant they were no longer angry. Angry Shees were deadly. Their poison had no known antidote.

"Yum!" Luv hugged her tail with delight, "I good. You get big big crab."

"I promise," the Forest Wife gave her adorable pet a pat on the head and left their world through the closet that led to Tryk's.

*

Luv watched her pet leave and nodded with satisfaction. She began to groom herself, ignoring the handsome male Shee outside the window who was currently courting her. She had no desire to accept his gifts, him, or any of the others who had come to court her.

Luv looked at Bastian who had dropped heavily to the floor and began to do his exercises, something he did every time his mother left.

"I'm ready, Luv," Bastian panted. She climbed onto his back to give added weight. Whenever he pushed his arms straight, it had the bonus of letting her see the male Shee who was busy gathering gifts for her begin a fight with another male over the right to be her mate.

*

The Sogoian slave auction was in full force when the Forest Wife arrived. Her handsome companion, Jarow Meade, had arrived late – looking as if he had just eaten something that disagreed with him.

"They think we're lovers," Jarow apologetically informed her as he climbed into the wagon, shooting a very short glance at the Villa.

She nodded her understanding and also glanced at the Villa. "Good, it will detract from the truth." She wanted to put the good man at ease.

For Jarow, it wasn't good news. His heart was already taken and he didn't want the object of his affections to think the rumors were true. She knew he wasn't comfortable sitting with her in this wagon where the woman he wanted to marry could see him and perhaps wrongfully judge him.

That wasn't the only reason the rumors were unwelcome. To attract any attention to her was like painting a target on all they were trying to do. It really wasn't Jarow's fault, she reminded herself. It was Tasut's. She believed in placing the blame where it belonged and she was going to lay it on the thick, wide shoulders of the giant Barracks Commander.

Naturally, all would be forgiven if Tasut made the slave purchases by the time they arrived and all she'd have left to do was wait for him to load the ragbag of human misery into the large wagon.

The wagon so large and heavy it took four draft horses to pull its weight. Jarow drove through the crowd with some irritation. It was such a popular event that people and carts clogged the major thorough-fares. It was always a risk to come into Sogo with Nez present and the danger grew expotentially the closer she was in proximity to him because he could feel her power. She always managed to avoid being found, but that didn't mean he wouldn't search for the source of the power he'd feel emanating from her. With so many people moving in and out of the way, the effect would be confusing. She liked the idea of making him sweat.

Jarow pulled the team to a halt and gave her the reins. Riddled with impatience, he cleared the way of people. Most moved out of the way once they saw the blue and black livery he wore, but some had to see his expression and it didn't go well for those who dawdled in front of the Training Commander. She watched him take a man and throw him out of the way. His show of temper was unusual. Most of the time, Jarow was unfailingly polite. This, she felt, was also Tasut's fault. Jarow walked in front of the wagon with sword drawn and continued to burn whatever demons were plaguing him by getting physical with those who thwarted his desire to get the wagon to the auction.

Once the wagon came to the loading area she spoke. "Jarow?"

The Commander turned to her and she handed him the carefully wrapped package she had kept beneath her robes. "Give this to the widow, Raen. It must be tonight."

She noted that his eyes brightened, but he remained silent and stuffed the package into his tunic. She looked up and Tasut, head and shoulders above everyone else, nodded to the slaves he had chosen. Sometimes, when Tasut attended the auction, there was nothing left for anyone else to purchase. This made many who wanted to come to auction, wait until Tasut was finished. Nez was one of these and was therefore, absent. She was grateful that she wouldn't have to try and avoid him, though she didn't let her guard down.

It was a law in Sogo that the Barracks Commander had first choice of all auctioned and could choose any of those sold.

Her interest perked as she noticed the High Priestess Saro at Tasut's side. Jarow had escorted her from the Temple earlier on Tasut's orders and she was the reason Jarow had been late.

Saro was wearing a beautiful deep green velvet dress. Covering her arms was a transparent green and gold wrap. It was modest, which the Forest Wife approved, but the dress was far too fine to be considered daywear. In the High Priestess' silky dark hair, sat a simple gold-and-silver-weave ceremonial crown. Her mass of soft deep brown hair cascaded through the back of the crown and down her slender back. Her eyelids were striped with the vibrant green, gold, and yellows that matched the stunning gown. It was both artful and dramatic. She was not a woman who did things by mistake, therefore the gown had a purpose. As Jarow said, Saro was beautiful – and cold.

The Forest Wife watched as Saro said something to Tasut and he gave a brief nod of his head. She turned on her heel and glided to the long narrow platform, where the remaining people to be sold were lined up. The Forest Wife watched the surrounding population watch the High Priestess. Sogoians loved beauty and danger and looked spellbound by the thrill of being so close to such a lethal combination. The crowd quieted as Saro adjusted her shawl.

"I demand the divine right, as High Priestess, to choose those the Unknown God wishes for sacrifice," Saro addressed Delf, Minister of Trade and Education. He nodded his head, though his expression was disappointed. He would undoubtedly delight in watching her sacrifice those left, disgusting parasite that he was.

The Forest Wife knew enough about the perverted Minister to know he would have sold the children for a fair price at the brothels he owned. She hid her smile as Saro, with an imperious tilt of her head, declared, "All children that come to auction are mine by the Minister of Religion's decree."

Delf's smile was pasted on and the look in his eyes declared what his lips never would. Anyone who was watching could see the lust there and that he heartily wished Tasut would leave the area, or at least, Saro's side.

Delf was not going to get his wish. The Forest Wife watched Tasut follow Saro, his huge arms folded menacingly over his enormous, well-muscled chest. For Delf to allow Saro to stake her claim on the remaining souls up for auction without making any objection, brought to light that he was currying Saro's favor. The Forest Wife knew that to Delf, Saro presented the ultimate challenge.

Delf hated Tasut and likely spent time assuring himself the luscious High Priestess would be his, if Tasut were gone. Jarow always told her whenever there were attempts on Tasut's life and there had been hundreds over the years. Mari had informed her that Delf had assigned over a dozen on his own. The other Council members were of like mind.

There was a loud scream, and the Forest Wife looked up to see a man fly up over the crowd, and land on the spikes of the fence surrounding the auction compound. A quick look let her know that the now-dead man had been too free with his eyes or hands concerning the High Priestess. Her eyes flickered over the comely Saro, whose cold face remained impassive, looking untouched by the drama.

She felt Tasut's eyes upon her and he gave a nearly imperceptible nod.

Jarow left her to order his men to escort the group of souls the High Priestess Saro had just demanded, down the streets of Sogo. Jarow took the lead, just ahead of Saro. Two of his men, one on either side of the High Priestess, kept their eyes to themselves and their swords drawn.

The haughty look the Priestess wore as she walked after Jarow was daunting. It was doubtful any Sogoian would dare approach her, she had presence enough to quelch any rebellion with a look. Her long robes flowed behind her. The Forest Wife turned her attention back to Delf, who watched Saro with hot eyes. To his horror, when he finally looked away, he met Tasut's measuring gaze and he backed away, looking like he was watching his life flash before his eyes.

Tasut ignored him and gave orders to those he bought for training, "Follow the wagon to the Barracks."

The High Priestess was out of sight. Her sources told her that the souls Saro had demanded would be taken to the Temple of the Unknown God. There they would take part in purification rituals that seemed shrouded in mystery, but she knew they were merely washed, clothed, and fed. Once they had passed through the ritual, they would have the dubious honor of becoming sacrifices.

She looked at the group of miserable men known throughout the city as the sanitation crews, who were debating how to remove the man's body that Tasut had thrown onto the spikes. By now, Nez had been informed that there was no reason to attend auction. If he stepped outside his door at all, he would be able to sense her power and it would draw him to her. She had to avoid that at all costs.

She needed to speak with Tasut before she returned home. She hid her impatience, and waited while the men who were marked as Sons of Ammon, and therefore chosen by Tasut, were unshackled, and started to follow the wagons headed for the Barracks. Her wagon filled with unsold women, children, and those who were too ill to work. There were four large wagons ahead of her and she would check every occupant.

Tasut would have two of his men walk in front of her wagon, escorting it to the Barracks. The other wagon carried wounded men and between the two wagons, ran those who were destined for the training the Barracks would offer. Tasut would follow the Forest Wife's wagon atop his enormous stallion, flanked by fifty of his men – on foot. Tasut had been attacked many times while in procession after auction, but fewer times while he was riding.   Harcour, she noticed, looked testy at the moment. She calmly looked at the stallion. This Harcour was familiar with her. She had turned him into a mare one day when he was feeling his oats and she'd never had trouble with him since. As expected, he lost his desire to bite anyone he could reach and began to behave in a way more becoming to a fully trained warhorse. She turned her attention back to her team of four sturdy workhorses.

Once at the Barracks, her wagon would separate from the others and she would take whomever she wanted from the group. There were four wagons in front of her holding twenty teenage boys and thirty men. Her wagon had twenty-seven more. She remembered the looks on the boys faces as they were loaded. Likely none of them were older than sixteen and all of them looked frightened. She couldn't put their fears to rest yet, and they would not believe she had just done them the greatest of favors. They would not have to be killed in training for Cubes or die fighting the odds of becoming Guardian. The time was coming when Father of All would put people and things into position to crush Sogo.

Once the wagons were emptied and the newly bought men were in the foyer, Jarow and Tasut would personally separate the Sons of Ammon from the others. Her duty was to gather them, return with them to Utak if they were younger than 20 and take them to the other side of time if they were older. All of them would be trained for the last battle that would defeat Sogo.

Once the recruits were separated, Tasut came to her side, his dark brown eyes angry as usual. "Don't come here again."

"I shouldn't have to," she frowned at his tone of voice. She hadn't been there when Tasut had earned his title of Guardian, but she had heard of it. In spite of this, he didn't scare or intimidate her. He *did* frustrate her.

"Does Raen know what to do?" he asked.

"Yes. I made the firesand myself. The rest is up to her."

He nodded.

"There's only one jeweler who can do the job – Master Flynn. He won't need to wear gloves to handle it. Don't let anyone else touch it. Remind Raen to wear the gloves I sent her anytime she handles the crown. Tell her to ignore it if the jewel flashes."

Finished with the conversation, she turned to the gathered men, Tasut by her side.

He gave those gathered a choice: "Go with this woman or die."

Supressing her sigh at his blunt words, she turned and pinched at the air in front of her and a door appeared in the air, "Follow me."

Chapter 32: Kissing man

Wynna Ryn never remembered what her last name was before she came to the orphanage, nor did she remember her birth mother. Life for Wyn began at the orphanage with Loni, the woman who was her mother in her heart and mind from that time forward.

For the first six months of her time at Ryn House, she was in sight of her adopted mother if not clinging to her apron or skirt. Loni never told her how inconvenient it was, nor did she push her away.

Wyn had a few faults. She was absurdly shy, could not stay away from puddles of water, and she was a cookie thief.

On this day, banished from the kitchen by a strong admonition from her mother to 'leave the cookies alone dear,' she had removed herself from temptation's power and wandered out to the yard. She didn't feel like playing, which was the chore her mother had set for her. She wasn't exactly sure what playing entailed when Brenna wasn't there because the other orphans ignored her except Eli who was usually busy running or hiding from things that frightened him.

With a heart felt sigh, she looked into the woods just beyond the yard.

The woods were strictly off limits to the orphans. However, if she gathered some nuts from the giant tree that was just on the edge of the forest, she could take them to her mother to use for cookies!

With this marvelous plan in mind, she opened the side gate and made her way into the forest. Keeping the direction of the walnut tree firmly fixed in her mind, she continued with her strategy. She imagined her mother's delight when she returned laden with the treasures that would make the cookies taste so good. She was sure her mother would let her eat some of those that were already baked that morning while she waited patiently for more to be made. The warm sugary invitation of those cookies made her mouth water.

She heard voices and stopped to listen. One of them sounded like Aunt Haddy and the other was a stranger. The voices didn't matter though because she found the walnut tree! To her disgust, the squirrels and probably Mee had cleaned up everything that might have fallen on the ground. There was no other choice. She'd have to climb. She found a low enough branch and crawled up the tree.

She had just started picking nuts when the voices got closer and she looked down to see Aunt Haddy kissing a tall bearded man. Wyn covered her mouth with her hand, praying her aunt wouldn't see her; she had a bad temper. She watched her aunt whisper something to the man and he smiled. It wasn't a very nice smile, but her Aunt couldn't see it because her eyes were closed while she whispered. The man hugged her and kissed her some more and then Aunt Haddy ran out of the forest, heading the direction of the orphanage. The man stood there, looking after her for a moment. The bad smile was back, and then he turned and went the other way. Wyn was glad he was gone and hoped he wouldn't return. She didn't like the looks he gave her aunt.

For a moment, her dreams of cookies looked like they would have to be delayed for want of a basket to put the nuts in. After some thought she took off her dress and made a sack out of it by tying the hem and sleeves.

She wasn't sure how long it was before she heard more voices, but she looked down and two men stood under the tree. One of them was the tall man that kissed Aunt Haddy. The other man was tall, bald, and skinny. He also smelled really bad. Wyn could catch a whiff of his body odor now and then.

"Does she suspect?" the stinky man asked.

"You hired me, Minister. You know what I am," the kissing man said in a mean voice.

"I know you're expensive, Feesha, and I pay for results - not insubordination. No information, no money, remember that."

"I'll remember - as well as you remember the name of the grave you were just looking at. Anyone you know?"

The man named Minister stiffly walked away and the bad smile came back to the kissing man. Wyn didn't like him and wished she could see well enough to throw a walnut at his head. Her crossed eyes made a direct hit improbable if not impossible.

The stinky man had called this man a fish, but she couldn't understand why. They weren't worth a walnut, anyway she decided. She needed every nut for the cookies her mother would bake. She was glad he walked away, slithering like a snake in the shadows. When she knew he wasn't coming back, she knotted her dress altogether and dropped it, full of nuts, to the ground and climbed down after it, her thin face full of anticipation.

*

Loni looked up in surprise as Wyn, wearing only a thin slip and carrying a bulging dress, came into the house, "Where have you been?"

Wyn smiled, smelling the warm cookies, "L-look!" with that word, she turned her dress over and emptied the contents onto Loni's freshly scrubbed counter. Out poured a bushel worth of unripe nuts, some beetles, and leaves. Loni did her best not to let Wyn see her exasperation.

"Where did you get these?"

"I-in the f-forest," Wyn stuttered, "for cookies!"

"The forest is off limits," Loni said sternly.

Wyn looked at her mother. Her face drained of color, she blinked away tears, and kept her eyes on the floor.

It was difficult to chastise her daughter. Wyn looked so adorable and her heart was in the right place. She had even worked to provide nuts for the cookies she so desperately wanted. Loni tried to ignore the mess the nuts had scattered over the kitchen counter.

Wyn whispered, "I w-was just t-trying to get n-nuts!"

Loni steeled her heart. If it had been any other orphan, she would do the same thing. "You disobeyed the rules. Please go to your room, I'll be up shortly."

Wyn fled the room, her sobs beginning before she was out of Loni's sight. Loni heard the bedroom door open and the sound of Wyn jumping up on the bed; likely to bury her face in the pillow. Loni winced, hearing the heart-wrenching sobs.

Loni, in the meantime, threw away the unusable nuts and cleaned the counter while coming to grips with the feeling that she had slapped a well-meaning, but clumsy puppy.

Is this what Mari feels?

Loni had raised many children over the 18 years she had taken in orphans, but none of them affected her like Wyn. Somehow the child had found the deepest and most tender places in her heart. The truth was, Wyn wasn't like the other children. The petite girl was the daughter of her heart and she loved her so fiercely, she was afraid of the power it gave Wyn over her. She sent a silent prayer heavenward that she would be strong enough to guide the poor child, who had just lately been able to go for a few hours without holding onto her skirts. She asked Zaya to watch the cookies that were ready to come out of the oven.

Rules are rules. Loni firmed her resolve and went down the hallway and into the room next to her own. She found Wyn had moved from the bed to sit in a corner rocking with her skinny knees against her chest, her green eyes rimmed with red and her hair messy. Loni sat on the bed and opened her arms. Wyn launched herself at her mother and the crying began all over again. Her storm of weeping left her with a stuffed nose. Loni dried Wyn's eyes and gave her a handkerchief.

"I'm s-s-sorry," Wyn whimpered softly, blowing her nose. Loni knew that when she was upset, her stuttering became even more pronounced so she held her tongue for now.

"D-Did Aunt H-Haddy tell on me?"

A warning bell went off in Loni's head. "Hadasha was in the forest?"

Wyn nodded and hiccoughed, "She was k-kissing somebody!"

"Was it someone you know?" Loni tried hard to keep her emotions tucked away.

Wyn shook her head, "N-no b-but I d-didn't like either m-man."

Loni became very still and her heart dropped. She swallowed, "There was more than one man?"

Wyn nodded. "But she only k-kissed one. She d-didn't see the stinky man."

Loni tried to keep her fear at bay. Haddy kissing men was hardly ground-shaking news, but the fact there were two men made her worry. She would simply have to ask Haddy herself.

"Wyn, get a clean dress on and go to the kitchen and help Zaya with whatever she needs. I'll be in shortly to help you frost the cookies." Wyn joyfully bounced off the bed, good humor and tender heart restored with the assurance of her mother's love.

She debated for only a moment before deciding which Eye to send after Haddy, who was supposed to be upstairs teaching dance to a group of the older girls.

Loni went across the hall to the nursery and found Pash rocking the tiniest baby, a week-old-infant, to sleep. Pash had changed a great deal. She was a great source of comfort to Loni who often expressed her thanks to the reformed prostitute. Her story was a sad one.

It was a surprise to Loni when Mari had confessed, "Loni, I want you to keep Pash here as long as possible. She needs this kind of work first. She can still train with you and Zaya, but her true passion is children."

Loni was always wary of anyone who would be taking care of the youngest children, but she really did need the help. Over the course of the following weeks, she blessed her sister for the pair of Eyes she had sent.

Apparently, Pash had been a widow and forced out of her home by her husband's family. With no where to go she became desperate and finally found someone who knew where she could get work. It was a trick and she found herself in a brothel.

"The rest," as Pash said in a raw voice, "is history."

Like Loni, she had never had children. Now she had six under the age of five in the nursery that kept her mind off the past and gave her hope for the future.

"If there's one Eye that I would recommend become a permanent part of the orphanages, it's Pash," Mari had said.

Pash had just said the other night, "My soul was saved by this work."

Loni agreed and continued to work with Zaya, knowing the youngest of the charges was secure with Pash. Zaya, on the other hand, still needed to hoe a few weedy rows in the garden of morality.

She addressed Pash, "Will you please find my sister and ask her to come to my office?"

*

An hour later, Haddy left Loni's office. With her face burning hotter than the fire of vengeance inside her heart, Haddy made her plans. Loni's explanation of how Haddy had been duped royally didn't set well.

Loni still didn't know that Haddy was going to see the "kissing" man again, once more. The little tattletale, Wyn, hadn't heard everything. *Thank goodness.*

Wearing leather gloves, she procured the rash rope she had purchased over a year ago when she thought she would be going on more of the brothel raids with her sisters. Her idea was very simple and direct. Kill him. The moment he came into sight, she was going to take advantage of his ignorance and proceed to teach him a lesson he could take into the eternities. If all went well, she would dispatch him to a fiery lake of bad memories where he would eternally burn.

It was early evening when she waited for him. This time she paid attention to the details. He came from the south, the direction of Sogo. She looked down at the ground to hide her distaste. Mentally she had prepared herself as she imagined Mari did. She was ice outside, volcano inside. She had told him to meet her within sight of the orphanage, although she never called it that publicly, obeying the rule to keep the Ryn House's location hidden. What she had planned would be dangerous but necessary. The children would be safe, Loni none the wiser and Mari completely ignorant…the way Haddy preferred it.

The autumn sunset filtered sideways through the trees and the air was getting crisp, making it absolutely perfect weather for what she had in mind.

"Hadasha?" he called into the twilight. If he had been someone she loved, it would have been very romantic. But she wasn't in love and never had been. *Why did I ever think his voice pleasant?* She turned with a bright smile pasted on her face, secretly thinking of what was to come. *Traitor! You used me!* her pride shrieked, but what she did was lower her voice seductively and said, "You came."

"Did you doubt?" he opened his arms and she ran toward him as if eager to feel his embrace. A good five feet from him, she leaped into the air, one leg kicking upward, catching him under the chin. She saw the surprise in his eyes just before her foot hit. He fell like a shooting star, covering some distance before he lost consciousness. She smiled and after putting on her Ybarra-hide gloves, she tied him up with the rash rope and thought about what to do with the body.

Listening closely, she heard Loni call in the distance, "Dinner!" and the faint metallic ringing of the bell.

Perfect. A hour later, Haddy patted the last bit of sand down with the shovel, praying it was deep enough until she could move the body.

Burying him in the backyard sandbox had not been in the plans, but it was getting late, she was hungry, and his body had been too close to the orphanage to leave it lying on the forest floor. The deciding factor was when she had tried to dig into the hard-packed dirt of the forest floor and decided it would take too much time and effort to bury it deep enough before Loni came looking for her.

That's why she had dug the hole first and then dragged the body a hundred or so feet into the yard, listening intently for children. The hole was shallow but she had no choice. She planted the kissing man a mere three feet down in the soft sand Mari had imported from the Eastern Desert.

She told herself it was dark and the children would be enjoying the stories Loni told after dinner. It was already close to bedtime and no one would be coming out to the yard – especially to dig in the sand pile.

She had a twinge of uneasiness she easily dispelled. She promised herself that she would arise early and take care of business. She smiled. At least it was over now and the betrayer was buried along with any emotions she had felt for him. She felt slightly sick whenever she thought of what might have happened if…she immediately closed her mind to that thought. She tossed her head, wiping away the sweat and taking the shovel to the barn… *ifs are common and I'm not… no matter what anyone else says. What's a few kisses? There's a lot of men in the world. Better men.* She smiled as her brother-in-laws face came to her mind.

She leaned the shovel against the wall, impatient because she was still feeling jumpy. Her mistake was very serious.

According to Loni, the 'stinky' man was none other than Delf Shiraz, one of the Nine! and he had been looking for more inmates for his multiple brothels and the children of Ryn house were his targets.

Not while I breathe! She patted herself mentally on the back as she dusted off the sand from her hands and skirt At least the kissing man was no more. She tidied her hair and frowned. If it hadn't been for Wyn… *The little sneak!* Loni, with arms folded, took her role too seriously. *Wyn is way over-mothered.* Wyn was a tattletale and Haddy couldn't fathom why Loni loved the cross-eyed spineless orphan as much as Brenna, who was beautiful, well-mannered, and listened with rapture to Haddy's advice.

As she went into the house, she found Wyn alone in the kitchen eating cookies and milk.

"G-good night W-Wyn," Haddy mocked the child's stutter and went up to bed, never seeing Loni's shadow in the hall.

She had barely closed her eyes when there was a knock at her bedroom door. Loni entered without waiting for an answer and when Haddy opened her eyes, Loni's eyes were fierce.

"Was mocking your niece amusing?" Loni's voice was iced with patience, but Haddy could tell by the fact she kept her arms folded that Loni wasn't as calm as she sounded.

"She's not really my niece and I'm trying to sleep," Haddy moaned, closing her eyes.

"She is my daughter, Haddy."

It sounded like Loni wanted to throttle her.

"Did you know you made her cry?"

I made her cry? Haddy ignored the memory of Wyn's shocked white face. But when she felt Loni step next to her bed, she automatically opened her eyes. Loni was the most patient of her sisters, but once riled it meant serious trouble. The look Loni gave her was the same one she wore when they raided the brothel. Disappointment, determination, and deep-seated anger.

Haddy felt a twinge of guilt and shut her eyes again. "I was only teasing her!" *She better get used to it!*

"I'm going to say this once, Hadasha Ryn!" Loni's voice was hard as ice. "I never want to hear you say anything unkind to any of the children again. If you do, you will have to deal with me."

Better than dealing with Mari – any day.

"Understood?"

Haddy nodded and Loni left the room.

Sleep did not come easy to Haddy that night. She was haunted by a dream of Loni's ghost moaning at her that she had betrayed them all, and Wyn had a knife in her hand, a leaf in her hair and threatened to kill her. She spent a good deal of time in that dream running, but from what she wasn't exactly sure.

Sleep didn't come easily to Wyn either. She was consumed with self-loathing. She had decided long ago to stay out of Haddy's way and she had tried her best, but it wasn't always possible. It was obvious her beautiful Aunt wanted nothing to do with her, although Wyn wasn't sure why. On the other hand, Aunt Mari was very kind to her and Wyn really liked playing with Brenna, who was so popular with everyone. Somehow, she had made a mistake by telling her mother about Aunt Haddy kissing that bad man. She vowed she would never do it again.

*

Mari was stunned at the report that came in from Utak. Haddy, it appeared, had taken things into her own hands while she had made a short visit to Phoenix House last month. Without direction and apparently without thought, Haddy had made a hit along the way without directive. Knowing her younger sister as she did, Haddy probably assumed that being M'Sha (third in line of authority for the Eyes) gave her the right to make such a decision.

Mari felt a swell of anger. Seven months of careful planning, an entire year of watching, and two more years of undercover work were gone. Worse, the original target had disappeared. One of the men responsible for kidnapping and selling children to the city of Catsfour, a city built on the blood and sweat of children was nowhere to be found.

She blamed herself for not even considering Haddy as part of the equation. She sat for a good hour just staring out at her husband doing his morning forms, trying to rein in her temper.

Mari was grateful that Brenna was at the Ryn House visiting with her Aunts and having a wonderful time. Going to the Ryn House gave Brenna a chance to be around other children, and gave her parents time alone.

Until now, it had been blissful.

Mari was notorious for being the sister with a temper, but she worked very hard to keep it under control. Right now she wanted to throw things, scream, rant, and rave. Most of all, she wanted to get to Haddy. A confrontation was inevitable. She needed to get to Ryn House today. She hoped there was a logical explanation, something that would countermand her promise to kill her sister.

Lyon knew she was out of sorts, but had no idea why and she couldn't tell him. Her best acting surrounded the position she held as Hi-Sha for the Eyes. Lyon would be the first to know if she ever decided to tell anyone outside the organization, but she didn't want him to interfere with her well-laid plans and it was inevitable that he would demand she risk less and delegate more. Mari couldn't do that, yet. There was too much at stake.

While he finished his forms, she packed.

"I'm sorry Lyon," she apologized for her mood as he came in the back door. "I think I'll go wish Loni Happy Birthday a bit early and pick up Brenna. I'll probably stay overnight so don't worry about seeing us before noon tomorrow."

"Give Loni my best, see you tomorrow," he kissed her tenderly and waved at her as she left.

He had plans of his own and wondered how to accomplish what needed to be done. When she had suggested a trip to Dyman and an overnight stay at the Ryn House, he felt relieved. Mari worried about him too much.

Chapter 33: Birthday

"You can leave Wyn for a few hours, Brenna! It won't take long," Haddy promised her beautiful niece the morning of Loni's birthday. She tried rubbing a little guilt in. "Don't you want to surprise Loni? You know she's been looking at that shawl the whole summer!"

The Village was four miles away.

Brenna looked doubtful, but Haddy knew her niece well enough to know the reluctance could be worked around. "We'll get you back in plenty of time to wrap the present! We can even buy a little gift for Wyn to give to her mother."

The bribe worked. Mari was coming to visit for Loni's birthday and it wouldn't be good for Brenna to be missing when Mari arrived later tonight.

Once on the road, Haddy became nearly giddy with excitement. The clerk in the store was a handsome man and some new material had arrived all the way from Teris.

"I think we should go back to the orphanage," Brenna said, looking apprehensively at Haddy.

Haddy stared at Brenna and pointed at the store, "We're nearly there! It shouldn't take long at all."

Brenna looked unhappy and Haddy thought she heard her say, "I should've brought Mee. Aunt Loni told me to not go anywhere without her."

Haddy rolled her eyes. Her niece was a breathtakingly beautiful little girl, and normally they got along very well, but that obnoxious pet – and Wyn, who was Brenna's shadow, were more than Haddy could stand.

"I'm with you so there's nothing to be afraid of!" she said a bit crossly.

They hurried down the road and into the shop. Haddy was preoccupied with thoughts of the handsome clerk and Brenna was too naive to care about the group of men who watched them from the corner and who slid into the shadows of the narrow alley across the street from the shop.

Haddy had picked over the dresses, shawls, jewelry, and shoes while Brenna grew more uneasy about the situation. She overheard her mother say that Aunt Haddy was irresponsible. She didn't understand the rest of whatever it was that Aunt Haddy kept doing to make her mother so angry. She only knew that her mother had a temper and Brenna had a sinking feeling that trouble would come from this.

She had pulled on Haddy's skirt twice to no avail. All Haddy would say was "In a minute…" and go back to smiling and saying stupid things to the clerk that made no sense. Even worse, the man was acting just as bad as Haddy was. He had a strange look in his eyes. It reminded her of the time Iskar hit Mal over the head with a pole he was cutting to fish with, and Mal's eyes sort of crossed. This man was older than Mal and Iskar but Brenna didn't think he was as smart. He was tall and had a nice smile, but they could have bought an entire store of shawls by now and gone back to wrap them and make the cake. They were missing the fun part of Aunt Loni's birthday and it wasn't fair! *I could leave and she wouldn't even notice.*

Brenna was looking at the doorway with longing when she saw a movement out the corner of her eye, "Mee!" she whispered with a quick glance at her volatile aunt.

Mee was standing in front of the store mirror, a pair of ladies lacy red bloomers pulled over her head. She currently had one leg hole caught under her arm and the other twisted around her tail. Brenna carefully moved over to her pet, trying not to giggle. "You need to put those back before Aunt Haddy sees you," she whispered.

Mee turned around and snorted "Humph!" in Haddy's general direction, but she began to remove the bloomers. Once removed, instead of putting them back, she immediately crammed the bloomers into her cheek pouches. With a wave at Brenna, Mee scampered out the door, startling two people who were walking by. Most people would avoid Shees, believing them to be so poisonous, a mere touch would kill them. Brenna stood at the door watching her pet stop to tease one man by growling and jumping at him while waving her small arms. It was a handy trick she learned from Tiz.

In truth, no one who knew anything about Shees would be very afraid when Tiz did it, but Mee looked quite insane when she preformed. Maybe it was because Mee was different from other Shees and she delighted in high drama.

Brenna thought she should probably tell Haddy that Mee had stolen red underwear, but Haddy would just shush her again. Brenna knew she'd have to tell Aunt Loni so there wouldn't be any trouble. Brenna watched Mee unpack her cheeks in the near-by tree, feeling relieved that her pet had followed them to the store. She looked once more at Aunt Haddy and mutinously decided to run home before it was too late to redeem herself in Aunt Loni's eyes. *I'm hungry and I'm missing all the fun!* She waited until Haddy's back was turned and ran out the door.

Unfortunately, one of the waiting group of men caught her around her waist as she raced past the alley way.

"Mee!" she squealed struggling against her captors for all she was worth. She bit one of them and it made him release her mouth long enough for her to scream.

Haddy heard the scream and at first she was annoyed at the interruption, assuming it was someone other than Brenna. However, when she turned, she caught a glimpse of Brenna struggling for breath in the arms of a filthy man who had his big paw of a hand over her mouth.

Haddy instantly left the clerk, the store, and herself, as Haddy, behind. For the moment, she was M'Sha of Eyes, personally tutored by Mari and Loni, but with a few talents of her own. In her mind, the men restraining her niece were already dead.

"Here comes t'other one!" said one of the foul men with a long hungry look at Haddy.

Specially made daggers were shaken from Haddy's sleeves and slid into her hands. About six feet from the man who had just leered at her, she launched in perfect fourth form, tucked into a ball before she hit the ground, rolled out of it, and buried the knife she held in her right hand into the knee of the man holding Brenna. He let her niece go and screamed loud enough to wake the dead. He bent forward to grab his injured knee. This action put his head close to Haddy's, just the way she intended. Her second razor-sharp knife slid across his jugular and he fell, dead as a stone, as she sprang away.

"Run!" she yelled at Brenna who struggled to her feet and began to run in the direction of the orphanage. Haddy turned to the second man, ducked under his swinging fist, and made a deep slash across his midsection. His intestines boiled out between his fingers as he squealed like the pig he was. She flipped through the air, landing in front of the third man, dropped to her stomach and slashed across his Achilles' tendons, effectively disabling his escape so she could cut his throat. It was a relief not to hear his screams any longer. She looked around. *There were two other men.*

*

The clerk watched in astonishment as the beautiful woman he was currently in love with killed three men in less time than it took to smile. Shaking, he quickly shut the shop door, locked it, and put the "closed" sign in the window. Obviously, she wasn't who he thought she was and he didn't want to know the truth.

*

Brenna's legs took her up the street, pumping faster than they ever had, Mee running beside her on the ground. Mee's tail bottle-bristled and her blue eyes glittered as she encouraged Brenna to "Run more hard!" Brenna didn't think she could run faster, until she heard heavy footsteps behind them and the frightening sound lent fuel to her flight. The bad men's legs were longer than hers and she knew she wasn't going to be able to outrun them.

That's when something happened to her for the first time in her life. She nearly stumbled in shock when she heard Mee's voice in her mind: 'I bite bad, you run hard!' With the words was the image of Mee biting the men. Brenna kept running and Mee turned back toward their pursuers.

Brenna was yanked to the ground by her hair. She didn't see which man Mee bit first, but she heard his scream and heard Mee's voice in her head: 'I come save my Bren'.

The man pulling Brenna's hair had let go as Mee's teeth sank into his leg. A very satisfied feeling colored Mee's mind as Brenna saw Haddy run toward them.

Haddy lightly jumped over the bodies of the would-be kidnappers. Their flesh was bubbling off their bones. Haddy pulled her into her arms and Brenna was shocked to find that her aunt was crying. Not understanding this reaction she asked, "Did you forget to buy Aunt Loni's shawl and Wyn's gift?"

Haddy nodded, and looked at Mee, who folded her arms and glared at Haddy.

"You stay here with Mee and I'll run and get them."

Brenna didn't want to wait for her aunt. Mee ran back to the tree and when she returned her cheeks were puffed out again. Brenna wasn't sure if it was the red underwear, or bugs…maybe both. She looked down the deserted street. There was no sign of her aunt. Her mother was right. Aunt Haddy was trouble. She sniffed and brushed a tear away. Aunt Haddy liked silly stupid men. Brenna's lip trembled so she bit it. She wished Talon was there, he wasn't stupid or silly. Giving up on her aunt, she slowly walked toward the orphanage, Mee at her side.

A short time later, considering how long it had taken so far, her headstrong aunt joined them, breathlessly handing the package to Brenna.

"It can be from both you and Wyn," her aunt pasted on a false smile, her eyes still flashing.

Things had probably not gone well with the clerk.

*

"Where have you been?" asked Loni.

Her beloved aunt's smile lit a warm fire in Brenna's heart. Loni was sitting in the birthday chair in the time-honored tradition of Ryn House for anyone celebrating their special day.

"We got you a surprise!" exclaimed Brenna, happily handing Aunt Loni the package. "It's from me and Aunt Haddy – and Wyn!" she added generously, smiling at her cousin. Wyn was standing near Loni's chair.

Brenna heard a tap on the window and saw Mee standing on the sill. She opened the window and Mee slipped in, looking daggers at Haddy, who let the front door close on Brenna's pet.

Mee reached into her cheek pouches and proudly produced the pair of lacy red bloomers from the inside of her cheek. She handed the now-slimy ill-gotten gain to Loni with a "Hap Day! Put on. Show all."

Loni carefully pinched the soggy material and patted Mee's head, "Thank you, Mee, perhaps later."

Mee nodded and scampered off in search of something to eat.

Loni looked at Haddy, her face a careful blank as she wrapped the startlingly red birthday bloomers in discarded brown paper and put them in the pocket of her apron, "I wasn't aware that you took Brenna to town."

Haddy looked at the floor, her pretty face coloring. Loni's eyes didn't leave Haddy's face. "Go to your room, Brenna, I'll be up shortly."

Brenna's mouth opened and she stared at Haddy, her heart sinking. Hot resentment washed over her as she ran up to her room. She flung herself onto her bed, feeling the grate of injustice. *Aunt Haddy did it, not me!*

There was a knock at her door a few moments later; she wiped her eyes and opened it. Wyn looked up at her, then back down at the floor, knowing how much Brenna hated others to see her cry.

"Aunt Haddy's in lots of trouble," Wyn said quietly.

"Good!" Brenna snapped, still awash with resentment. Then she frowned and went back to her bed. She bit her lip to keep from crying. She knew how much tears bothered Wyn.

"I brought you some cake," Wyn smiled, still not quite meeting Brenna's eyes.

Brenna, bad mood over, smiled back and the two girls shared the booty as Brenna told Wyn what Haddy had done.

*

"You will come with me," Loni said, her voice oddly neutral.

The women went outside together. Haddy's mind ran through the defenses that she felt she could use, but her conscience stung enough to make her mistake very clear. It was the family's number one rule: Never endanger the children – especially Brenna.

Haddy had to run to keep up with Loni, a fact she grudgingly noted. They didn't stop until they reached the small clearing where their father was buried. Haddy knew whatever Loni had going on in her mind was extremely serious to come here.

Most of the time Loni was very mellow; in truth, rather slow and boring. A dear, but boring just the same. But this time felt different. The distance from the house was her first indication. What she hadn't expected was to see tears coursing down Loni's face when she turned around.

"What now Haddy? The clerk was irresistible? A new dress? More material? Shoes? Which of these things made it right to take Brenna into Dyman?" Loni's plain face was red, her eyes bleeding large tears that she dashed impatiently away.

"Nothing happened," Haddy inserted before Loni could continue. "I took care of them."

"You were attacked?" Loni's face went from red to ashen in moments. Haddy felt alarmed.

"Dear Father of All," Loni whispered, looking half crazed, "what have you done?"

"I didn't do anything!" Haddy spat defensively, watching her sister pace. She explained the situation (as she saw it) to her sister, expecting Loni's usual mercy when she finished with "...and Brenna took off while I was...shopping."

Loni stopped pacing and stared as if in disbelief, demanding, "So it's Brenna's fault that you were flirting with the clerk and not watching her?"

Haddy had not seen this side of Loni before, and was at a loss as how to answer the questions. "What was I supposed to do? She ran out the door - probably chasing that stupid Shee of hers!"

"Be grateful that Mee was with her, you foolish girl!" Loni's eyes had become brittle pale green agates and she paced again. "Mee saved her life and yours as well."

"We were never in danger," she insisted, tired of the drama.

"That isn't the point, is it Haddy?" Loni stopped pacing and wrapped her arms around herself, looking like the joy of the day had vanished. "If Mari had been here..." she shuddered, "as it is, she hasn't arrived yet. She already wants to speak to you about what you did in Acha after you visited Phoenix house."

"I see no reason to bring Mari into it. I took care of it." Haddy was impatient with the conversation. *Why doesn't she understand?* Usually, Loni was on her side.

"Are you trying to convince me or yourself!?" Loni asked sharply. "Do you think this is a child's game where each side can get another chance to do it over?" Loni was exasperated and bitterly disappointed.

Haddy had the gall to look surprised, "What are you talking about? We just went shopping!"

Loni just looked at her, incredulity crossing her features. "Didn't you ever listen in class?"

"Only when it was interesting!" Haddy snapped, trying to think which class Loni might be referring to.

Loni took a breath, looked at the ground for a moment and then back up; composed once more. She sighed as if so weary she would fall to the ground and she looked like she had one of her headaches, "I have fought for you Haddy. I've tried to soften what enmity exists between you and Mari. I keep telling myself it's because you're young and too beautiful for your own good."

Haddy felt a rush of pleasure for Loni's recognition of her beauty and tried not to look so pleased. It was no use rubbing it in, after all, everyone knew she was the beautiful sister. *Who could be too beautiful?*

Loni shook her head, "But now I have to question my own loyalties. I love you both, but you've caused needless worry and concern for Mari.

"Worse, I have, in effect, betrayed her by not telling her the complete truth about your minor deceptions and worst of all…" Loni put her face in her hands for a moment and took a breath. She dropped her hands and looked back at Haddy, "I have betrayed you by not being harder." Her face scrunched tighter with the tears she was forbidding to come, looking even more unattractive from Haddy's point of view.

"You know Mari hates me, I can't help that," Haddy felt hurt and wished her voice didn't sound so whiney.

"You're wrong," Loni seemed to grow cold and distant, "Mari loves you more than you know."

"No she doesn't!" Haddy lashed out, "Mari never even comes here except to drop Brenna off, take time to tell me all my faults, criticize me to the world, and then go with Lyon back to wherever they live. She never stays to visit or even ask about us except to tell us what to do, and I'm sick of it!"

"You don't know what you're talking about." Loni looked out toward the forest, "You have no idea what she sacrificed for us, for the orphanages."

"Then tell me so we both know," Haddy sounded hopeful.

For a moment, Loni was tempted to tell her all of it. She was an educator and it was painful to keep back information. If there was one thing that she and Mari had agreed on, however, it was Haddy's inability to keep her mouth shut.

"I've been bonded to a pledge and can't tell you." This was true, after a fashion, she had given her word and that was just as effectual.

"Then what about Brenna's destiny?" Haddy pushed.

Loni turned and looked steadily at Haddy, "I can't trust you with that information."

"Yes you can," her youngest sister insisted. "But you and Mari always think I'm too young. I'm not stupid you know."

Loni shook her head, "If you want to know more, ask Mari. That's if you could stand in the same room with her for five minutes before you start coveting what it is she has that you want." Loni took the opportunity to drive home another sore point that threatened to drive a wedge even deeper within the family.

"And what, pray tell, is that?" Haddy scoffed, disappointed at being left out yet again.

"Lyon."

Haddy felt shock to her toes. *She knows!*

"He isn't who you think he is," Loni whispered. *You have no idea who you are playing with.* "If he were my husband, I would have slapped you until you went blind the way you ogle him and try to get him alone."

"I …he…we never …" stammered Haddy; the heat of embarrassment infusing her cheeks.

"Do you honestly think Mari doesn't know? Or worse, that Lyon doesn't?" Loni rolled her eyes, "Why do you think Mari comes alone most of the time?" Loni wanted to scream at Haddy, but she kept her voice steady "Do you honestly think Mari became Hi-Sha out of sheer physical beauty?"

"She got to be Hi-Sha because she's so bossy!" Haddy snapped.

"You ought to be ashamed of yourself! You've coveted Lyon from the first time you saw him!"

"I did not!" Haddy could taste the lie.

Loni pursed her lips and folded her arms, "Do you remember what you said the night they met?

Haddy's face was red with anger and denial. "All I remember is how stupid she made him look!"

Loni wasn't backing down this time, "Then allow me to correct your memory. You said 'If Mari doesn't want him, I do,' and that has never changed."

Haddy looked at the ground, squirming inside, wishing for a way to hide. *He should be mine.*

"Haddy," Loni began tiredly, "Take my word for it - Lyon loves Mari and he would never leave her for you. It will save all of us a lot of heartache if you'd get him out of your system and take all that wasted effort and put it to use where it will be appreciated."

Haddy bit her lip to keep back a reply. *She can't be right.*

Loni took her sister by the shoulders, "I won't tell Mari this one last time about you taking Brenna to town, but you have to promise me you'll never endanger us like that again."

Haddy rolled her eyes. "Fine." *But you're wrong about Lyon.*

Loni gave her a small smile, "Let's get back to the house and hope Mari hasn't arrived yet."

"I thought she was coming tomorrow," Haddy felt icicles of something very much like fear slide into her stomach.

"Oh, that's right; odd, I thought…well, never mind," Loni looked confused for a moment. "I'd like to talk to Brenna first."

They began walking back to the house, Loni walking next to her this time.

"Another thing, stop telling the children the story of the Amethyst child and the crippled warrior, it's giving the children nightmares. Eli ate the cuff off his shirt and Wyn's slept under her bed for three nights in a row."

"What am I supposed to do when they ask for it? You know it's one of their favorites."

Loni gave her a hard look. "You're the grown up, aren't you? It's your job to protect them from nightmares."

Haddy nodded her head, but her mind went to the sandbox.

Chapter 34: Celebrate

Delf, Minister of Sogoian trade, smiled; content to let the drugs bleed into his system slowly, drawing the experience out so he could tolerate being in the Council meeting.

The drug he inhaled made his mind work faster. It would not pay to be foggy. He wanted to enjoy watching the High Priestess as she wrested more and more control away from Nez. It was his secret delight to help her in any way he could. Withholding the information he had gathered while he was in Acha was part of that.

He had hoped to meet with her to discuss this important matter, but she continued to refuse his invitations. She likely suspected he had an ulterior motive. *Smart woman.*

His motive was simple. He would offer the information about the grave near the orphanage as a show of trust. Then he would spice up the offer with some of the orphans the Feesha would gather from the orphanage as proof of commitment to her and any or all causes she named. It would cost him, but it was a price he was willing to pay for her alliance on the Council.

He called for his coach and pulled on his robes of office. He put his family ring on his finger, a red and yellow eyed crow's head stared up at him. Ugly, but it made his point: he was just as important as the rest of them. More so, if you counted the amount of revenue his drug trafficking brought into Sogo. He had hired his own board of specialists to manage everything else. The drugs brought in seven times what the rest did.

That's why it perturbed him that Nez thought he was an idiot. He climbed into his carriage and his surroundings began to change to a pale lavender color. Nez always looked better with lavender skin.

As he watched the world pass by his coach window, it pleased him that he knew something Nez didn't: the final resting place of Jac Ryn.

Nez had asked about the former assassin who seemed to have disappeared, just like the men Nez had sent to kill him. Delf had sold a lot of information to Jac over the years, so that made two things that Nez didn't know.

He had actually liked Jac, who was clever and had a flawless record at the Guild. He had been the best, at least, until Lyon Tybar had come on the scene shortly after Jac disappeared. If someone could figure out a way to get into the cursed land of Utak, Jac would have.

Jac had been a threat in some way to Nez and that was the crux of Delf's problem. He didn't know why and now Jac was dead. Could it have been because Jac was the most likely to succeed in killing Nez or was it something else? He imagined Nez would give a great deal to know his former enemy was dead. Delf, however, was banking on the idea that the High Priestess would give even more to know about the orphans that lived near Jac Ryn's grave. It seemed her desire to destroy all children. He could help with that.

*

Mari walked into the bustling, laughter-laden world of the orphanage. Pash nodded toward the nursery door and Mari quietly opened it. She leaned against the doorway and watched Loni rock one of the babies to sleep while Wyn rocked a cradle. Her kind face was shining with love as she and Wyn sang together,

> *Dearest Angel, dearest love, think of me from above*
> *I can't teach you all I know before to sleep I must go*
> *Love look up there is no sky, see the room where I lie*
> *It has no ceiling, but two floors, use my window like a door*
> *Where 'ere you sup or when you sleep,*
> *You hold my heart, love always keeps*
> *Dream on my sweet, I love you so,*
> *Remember this, always know*

Where you can find me, where else to go

It was a nonsensical song, one that their father sang to get Haddy to sleep. He sang it almost every night; Haddy had been a difficult child. *Some things never change.*

Loni gently laid her bundle in a crib and nodded at Wyn; they both tip-toed out of the nursery and then greeted her with smiles and hugs. Wyn left to find Brenna and Mari gave Loni her birthday present. Mari had chosen a new dress and shoes for Loni, who so seldom bought anything for herself. They were wrapped in paper Loni had taught her to make many years ago from discarded cloth and various plants. Mari felt happy for the first time that day when Loni carefully opened the package and her face lit up, tears coming to her eyes. She insisted she would try them on immediately.

Mari felt ashamed that she hadn't thought to give Loni more over the years. She had Lyon to make beautiful things for her, and Haddy had Loni making things for her. Few people made anything for Loni except, she noted looking at the many drawings on the wall, the children of Ryn House.

Mari wandered out to the yard, nodding at Pash and Zaya in the kitchen where the birthday cake was getting its last touches. A piece was already missing.

Zaya was still a bit on the defiant side, but Pash, who had taken to training like it was her duty to rid the world of evil single-handedly, smiled at her and it seemed to be genuine. Loni had previously told her that Pash was found in tears, by Wyn, the day after she had come to Ryn House. The dear little girl invited her to join everyone downstairs.

Pash had a particularly tender heart for the infants that were on the first floor. Zaya preferred the kitchen and had been an immense help with meals, and surprisingly patient with the children.

Mari fixed the smile on her face, giving out hugs and kisses while overtly looking for Haddy. She headed out the back door to keep an eye on the large number of children, making a mental note it was time again to make arrangements for apprenticeships, several of the orphans were old enough. However, she would leave those who were already helping with the younger children and they in turn would become good matron's. She would need a lot of them in the future.

She noticed Chun and her blind sister Wysh were sitting on a blanket with their brother Yun, giggling and laughing, and it made her heart fill with gratitude. By now, Chun would have been forced into carnal bondage in the brothel. Wysh would have suffered the same fate. Yun would have become whatever his cousins had in mind for him.

She felt a rush of love for Loni fill her heart and her eyes brimmed with the tenderness. So few would recognize her sister's true worth. Mari's heart had often ached with the idea that anyone could be cruel to her older sister but they had been. Her eyes narrowed, even Haddy had said cruel things to her over the years. Haddy was noticeably absent and that left her feeling uneasy.

*

Loni pinched her cheeks and took some deep cleansing breaths. She loved her new dress. It was well made and had shoes to match. Loni wondered if Mari had the Forest Wife make it, it was so very perfect. The new shawl, which Brenna and Haddy had given her, was a perfect accessory. It was times like these that her heart swelled with happiness and yet ached with loneliness.

"Aunt Loni, how come you don't look like mamah?" asked a voice from behind her.

Loni hadn't heard Brenna come in. When she turned to look, she saw that Brenna had Wyn with her. It was obvious that Wyn had found another puddle of water; this time, a muddy one.

She smiled at her niece and Wyn. It wasn't the first time anyone had asked her "why?" about her looks. children were painfully observant about such things. One of her first social lessons as a little girl in Utakian schools was the undeniable fact that she was unattractive. In her mind came an unbidden and unwelcome memory.

"Where are you from?" the question had come from one of the boys in her school.

"Utak," was the answer she had given.

Back then she had not known the whole truth. Jac, her Utakian father, had married an Ammonite woman. Loni's mother left them shortly after giving birth. Later she understood the other children's confusion. Pure-blooded Utakian girls, like Mari, were beautiful. Something Loni would never be.

Loni returned to the present, sidestepping Brenna's question, "Please knock dear."

"I did, but you didn't answer and we wanted to see how you liked your shawl."

"I just want to be with y-you," Wyn's thin face grew pink.

Loni stood up and twirled around, a smile lighting her face. "It's beautiful."

"So how come you don't look like mamah?" Brenna persisted.

"Can you keep a secret?" Loni whispered, motioning to a spot beside her on the bed. The girls obediently hopped up and sat on either side of her. Loni's hands went to the back of her neck and her fingers unhooked the golden clasp of the necklace she wore. It had been her birth mother's, and the only thing her father had to give her because it was all the woman left behind. He had given it to Loni on her sixteenth birthday along with the story of who her mother was, and why Loni looked so very different from her beautiful sisters.

"D-Did Aunt M-Mari take all the b-beauty so there wasn't anything left?" Wyn asked, looking up at her with open concern in her crossed green eyes.

Loni laughed, "No, actually, we all have different mothers. Mari's mother was Utakian, Hadasha's mother was part Valenese, and my mother was…an Ammonite Princess."

Brenna smiled and said to Wyn, "I told you she had a good secret."

Loni carefully placed the necklace on her lap. Brenna had never seen her Aunt without it; most the time it remained under the prim collar of her dress. Loni caressed the necklace as she spoke, pointing things out to them. "Papah was out chopping wood in the forest near the north coast of Teris and he found her washed up on shore. He said she was beautiful in a different way. A warrior. A woman who would be Queen someday."

"Talon chops lots of wood," Brenna said. "Papah said it makes him very strong. Was your Papah strong?"

Loni smiled, "Yes. Before he died, he gave me the necklace. See this?" Loni touched the pink seashell on the right side of a beaten-gold half-sun, the girls nodded. "This tells you the person who owned this necklace was from a royal family. And this," Loni touched the shell on the left side of the half-sun, "tells you which royal house it is. The half-sun rising is upside down, symbolizing service to others from a position of power. The seven gold beads are how many generations this necklace had been in my family before it came to me. Each stands for some great service members of the family did."

"What did they do?"

Loni said wistfully, "I always thought that someday I'd go to the Islands and ask."

"What about the colors?" Wyn asked as she touched the sun's smooth surface. Loni loved listening to Wyn's clear voice. She didn't stutter at all when calm.

Loni smiled, repeating what her papah said. "The sun is made of a shell called abalone and one side the natives cover with gold. They used abalone because the Ammonites understand there are many kinds of people in this world, with many gifts or colors, to bless others. The gold symbolizes the better part of our soul that needs to be polished and the points of the half-sun are facing downward, because Father of All sends his richest blessings to his children from on high, and we are to be sharp enough, like a point, to receive them. The links in the chain, that hold the necklace together, symbolize service and eternal love. My papa told me all of these things because I didn't remember my mother. She left when I was a baby. In fact, it was within a month of my birth she returned to her Islands, at least, that's what my papa thought."

"What did your papa look like?" Wyn asked, her small hands touching various parts of the necklace.

Loni was surprised that the question hurt. Out of habit she brushed it aside, "He was very, very handsome. In fact, he was Lyon's…friend."

"Did they play together when they were little?" Wyn asked.

Loni had to think of an answer. "In a manner of speaking."

"Did they have lots of fun?" Wyn pressed a little.

"You'd have to ask your Uncle."

She was grateful when Brenna interrupted. "Aunt Loni, how can you tell if someone is pretty or not?"

"What do you mean?" Loni put the necklace back on and lifted the neckline of her new dress to let it settle it in place.

"Like Aunt Haddy. She's really pretty, but she gets into lots of trouble and then she doesn't look so pretty anymore."

From the mouths of babes. "Everyone makes mistakes Brenna, even pretty people."

Brenna thought for a moment, "I heard mamah say pretty needs brains to last, but I don't know what it means."

"Physical beauty doesn't last. People get old and wrinkled. If all you think you are is pretty, you won't have very many friends."

Brenna looked worried, "Does that mean Talon will hate me when I'm old?"

"It means you better be more than pretty – you need to be smart."

"So smart is better than pretty?" Brenna looked frustrated.

"Not necessarily," she smoothed Wyn's hair away from her crossed eyes, "It's more important to be good, and do good."

"Like angels?" Wyn asked.

Loni smiled and nodded.

Brenna looked as if a light came on behind her eyes, "Is that why my papah calls you our angel?"

Loni was touched at the unexpected compliment and horrified that tears began to form, "I didn't know he did."

"All the time," Brenna said with an air of non-chalance. "He says you're the angel of all orphans."

The compliment was her favorite gift that day.

"Come, let's go down with the others now. I want to show everyone my new clothes." Loni cleared her throat, smiled, and took the girl's hands and they went downstairs.

*

Taking advantage of the noise of the birthday festivities, Loni motioned to Mari so they could speak. She never knew when she would have another opportunity, so she had decided to tell her powerful sister what she was beginning to feel.

"It's time to show Brenna how to bend light."

Mari just stared at her.

"I feel like the sooner the better, in Brenna's case."

Loni seldom asked her for anything, but this was unexpected.

"Have you had a dream?"

Loni's dreams were sometimes clairvoyant in nature and Mari always trusted Loni to tell her the truth.

"Not really, but I just feel like Brenna needs to know. I keep thinking about the enchantment around Dyman breaking because…well, I think about it breaking. Knowing how to do it would maybe save Brenna."

It was common sense, if not wise. "Okay, Loni, I'll teach her later tonight."

Loni smiled and hugged her.

In light of the festivities, Mari decided to postpone her talk with Haddy. Loni had so few pleasures she wasn't going to ruin the day for her. In Mari's eyes, Loni was the most beautiful of them all and stood for everything that was right in the world. She was more than a sister, she was a friend and a second mother to Mari. Haddy and her troubles could wait one more day.

The party was wonderful, the children excited, the food delicious, and the entertainment endearing. The children who were old enough had prepared a play, with Zaya's help, about how each of them had come to the orphanage. The adults present found themselves brushing away tears of raw emotion and hysterical laughter. Loni clapped and kissed, laughed and cried. It was the best birthday, ever. When the party was dying down, Mari found Brenna and took her outside the house into the twilight.

"Aunt Loni asked me to teach you something very special."

Brenna smiled, excited enough to bounce on the balls of her feet, "To scry a pool?"

"Not yet." Her daughter had been curious about it ever since Mari told her that she could scry others in the sandpools. Mari suspected it was because Brenna wanted to watch Talon.

"Watch me." She disappeared and watched Brenna's mouth drop open.

"Now," her mother said, "reach out and touch me, I haven't moved from where you saw me." Brenna reached out and could feel her mother's arm. Her mother held her hand and re-appeared.

"It's called wrapping in light, although, technically, what we do is use the energy that surrounds us. All living things are made of energy."

"Energy?"

"Maybe it will help to think of it as the light around you."

"Like the sun?"

"Yes. Only, imagine the suns rays – not the sun itself." Mari didn't want Brenna to do something to the sun. "Think of how warm they are."

"Okay."

"Now think of them as a warm blanket, like you're going to use the blanket to cover yourself, your entire body."

Brenna closed her eyes to concentrate.

"Can you see the blanket?"

Brenna shook her head, "No, but I see the light, it looks like when you try to look at the sun, only it doesn't hurt my eyes."

Mari was grateful Brenna's eyes were closed. What they were trying to do was difficult for most people who held power. The fact Brenna picked up on it so easily was both provoking and disturbing.

"Everyone sees it a little differently, but as long as you can see it, you can use your mind to grab hold of it and pull it over…"

Brenna disappeared.

Mari stiffened, then forced herself to relax, "Very good!" *Astonishing.*

"This is fun!" Brenna's voice moved away.

"Stay here," Mari's voice trembled slightly. She was shaken. Not only did Brenna master something in minutes that should have taken years, she had taken the basic concept and without thought or extra effort, moved while wrapped in light. It should have been impossible.

There was something she needed to teach Brenna that was going to be difficult for her daughter.

Brenna suddenly re-appeared, beaming with excitement.

"You did an excellent job, Brenna," she complimented with a smile. "There is one more thing."

She looked into her daughter's long-lashed blue eyes, being sure that Brenna could see the seriousness in her own. "You must not show or tell this to anyone who is not a member of the family. Is that understood?" Mari knew she was going to have to leave no loophole.

Brenna nodded.

"That includes Talon."

Brenna's smile became less brilliant, but she nodded.

"Now promise me you won't reveal to anyone outside the family, what I've shown you."

Brenna paused, but whispered, "I promise."

Mari's brow arched at the slight hesitation and then touched her forehead, her daughter's forehead, and then Brenna's heart.

"If you break this promise, you'll feel you're palms sting as if they've been slapped. It will continue until I find you, or you find me, is that clear?"

Brenna's eyes widened and her smile was gone.

Mari went back inside, "Loni, go ahead and get some rest. Go to bed, do whatever you want, I'll take care of the dishes and cleaning up. Ketu will be here, so you can even sleep in tomorrow if you want."

Chapter 35: Indulgence

Loni closed her bedroom door, grateful Mari gave her a second gift: time. She would use it and allow herself to remember. Every year, on her birthday, she allowed herself this one indulgence. She pulled the hand mirror out of the drawer, which had been a gift from the man she still loved with all of her heart. She looked at her reflection by candlelight and recalled the only romantic glory she'd ever experience. It lasted a mere five months.

Her world, at 26, began and ended with one word: Dasan. Here, in her own room, she whispered his name. In the soft light, she looked at herself in the hand mirror. Wrapped in the softer light, she looked younger. She was still puzzled why he'd ever looked at her. Other men considered her too tall, gangly, or downright ugly.

She was honest with herself. Any comparison to Mari would have left other women wanting, but the fact Loni was plain never struck home as hard until someone inevitably compared her to her full-blooded Utakian sister. Even among other beauties, Mari stood out.

Loni's hair was so fine it looked thin, though she liked the reddish tint the sun gave it. Physically, her pale green eyes were the only feature she liked about herself and that was because they were such a different color of green.

Mari told her she had a beautiful smile and a more beautiful soul than any of the Ryn's. Still, Loni knew she wasn't the type to catch a man's eye unless it was to perform some menial task like cleaning, mending, or cooking, all of which she excelled at. That's why Dasan's interest was so puzzling at first.

Dasan was four years her junior when they met. In an unbelievable twist of events, he had ignored Mari and smiled at *her*. He picked some flowers and given them to her, offered to dig vegetables with her. He acted like he'd seen something special in her from the very first day.

Through five magnificent, glorious months he cared enough to walk several miles from his home to ask how she felt and what she thought. They spent hours in each others company. The third time he'd visited, he'd just casually taken her hand as if it were the most natural thing in the world. After that, he always took her hand. He didn't seem to care that one of her arms was stiffer and her face a great deal less than perfect.

The brightest day of her life was when he had kissed her, very tenderly, once. It knocked her breathless and light headed with the glory of love. The very next day he had not come as he had promised. She had not known he never would; that he was dead. All she knew was that there would be no other man for her.

In silence, she brushed her hair and paid him tribute. She never spoke of Dasan, though she thought of him every day for the last fourteen years. The memories were too sacred and she preferred to keep them close to her heart. It was enough to know, that for a short time in her life, there was a man who loved her for who she was soul-deep.

There were times when Dasan felt near. One day last week, she had been in the kitchen softly humming, getting her baking ready for the day. She looked up from the mixing bowl and froze when she found herself staring at him. Still young, still handsome, he was standing across the kitchen counter from her. He smiled and her heart thundered as she swallowed, afraid to move, afraid to do anything but stare. The moment she blinked, he was gone. She had slid down to the floor, hugging the bowl, and quietly sobbed for five minutes, shaking as the early morning light peeked in to witness her grief.

Right this moment, with her eyes closed, she had no trouble picturing him sitting by her side, telling her he loved her. Her imagination allowed her to hear him say he was sorry he had not said the words, but that one day they would be together. The fantasy was bittersweet and much better kept close to her heart.

Loni re-played that comforting scene in her mind, over and over, until she fell asleep.

*

As Mari helped Ketu and Pash clean the kitchen she realized the two of them were too quiet. "What's going on?"

Pash glanced at Ketu, who said, "You'll never know until you ask."

This seemed to firm something inside Pash and she whispered, "Why is Loni so sad?"

Mari glanced at Ketu, who already knew the story, but had not told. It was a measure of her devotion to Loni. Few knew that Ketu was Loni's first orphan.

There was really no reason to keep it a secret from these women. "When Loni was a young women, the man she was in love with disappeared and it broke her heart."

Pash paled. All of them were drying dishes except Ketu, who washed them.

Mari leaned on the broom she'd been using. "It took me months to find out what happened to him, but in the end, it was bad news. He had been murdered."

"Did you tell her?" Zaya wanted to know.

She nodded. "And it changed our lives."

Ketu solemnly added, "But it all turned out good."

Zaya looked skeptically at Ketu.

Ketu ignored her and said, "If Loni hadn't lost him in such a cruel way, she wouldn't have been free to save so many children."

They all knew Loni had a well-deserved reputation for her relentless quest to find and love the orphans in the world.

"I guess you could look at my efforts to find his murderer as the first mission of the Hi-Sha."

"What did you find out?" Zaya asked.

"That his mother worked in a brothel that Nez frequented. At the time, Nez was a promising diplomat. He set her up in a private house with a generous allowance and immediately abandoned her when he found out she was carrying his child. Mava vowed revenge when Nez denied paternity."

"You're telling me that Loni was in love with *Nez's* son?" Pash stopped working, blue eyes wide in astonishment.

Mari nodded. She understood the shock. It seemed like something Haddy would have done. However, it wasn't Loni's fault. "The boy was raised by his mother and kept ignorant of his father's identity. His mother was a twisted harpy that became accustomed to the luxury afforded her while keeping Nez company. She plotted her revenge and eventually she and her son traveled to Dyman. That's when we first met him. His mother's hope was to somehow blackmail Nez."

"Not very smart, was she?" Pash murmured, stacking plates in the cupboard.

"Anyone who sees something attractive in Nez should see a healer," Ketu said. "Or a priest, so they can confess their insanity."

Mari swept the floor. "Naturally, Nez saw his former mistress and illegitimate son as a kink in his bid for the office of Minister of Religion, and arranged their assassination."

"How long before Loni knew?" Zaya asked.

"Two months. Ketu and Haddy were in charge of the orphans while I took Loni to see the proof."

"I remember that day," Ketu's dark eyes filled with anger.

"Loni was under the impression that he just didn't like her any more and didn't want to bother anyone, but I knew Loni wouldn't accept the truth unless she saw the proof."

"How old were you?" Pash asked.

Mari sighed. "About seventeen. Loni was so mortified to be near a brothel that I went to the door and asked for his mother. I had to threaten to light the house on fire before they'd tell me anything."

"Seventeen?" Zaya was shocked.

Ketu's tone was proud and she smiled, "Mari was always bold and beautiful. Her courage is the stuff of family legends."

Mari felt grateful at the words, but not the memory. "We went around back and up some rotting stairs. No one would answer the door, so I …blasted it in. Loni was terrified someone would come and take me away."

"There was only an old woman there." She didn't tell them her own eyes had gone purple and the woman only told them because she was sure Mari was a demon coming to collect her soul. "It turned out to be his grandmother and she's the one that told us that he was dead. She said he and his mother were buried out back and that we could go see."

Mari wiped away the tears that came, even now, after all these years. She didn't tell them she had feared for Loni's sanity and watched over her older sister while she wept for three days over the grave of the man she loved. His death broke something in Loni and for that, in Mari's heart, there was no forgiveness.

"When she finished crying, we got back in the wagon and returned."

She left out the part where Loni had turned to her and in a dead voice, said, "I never told him that I loved him."

That was the point that Mari had cried and later she knew it was her own weeping that forced Loni back to reality. Her older sister had taken her into her arms and they had cried together. It was one of the few times Loni had ever seen Mari cry.

"I'm so sorry for her," Pash sniffed. "I know what it's like to lose the only man you'll ever love."

Mari had forgotten Pash was a widow. No wonder she and Loni had bonded so well. "From that tragedy, the Eyes were born. I had to do something about the things which ripped him away from her and I'm proud to say that the Eyes are finally at a place where we can ferret out almost any secret. By telling you this, it binds you all more fully to our family. It's a sign of my trust in you."

There was one piece of information that Mari had not divulged and Ketu remained quiet, waiting for Pash to ask. To her credit, she never did ask the name of the man Loni loved. There were some things, even among the Eyes, that were too personal for conversation.

Chapter 36: Sandbox

There was something about the scream that made Loni's hair stand on end. One of her three-dozen children was terrified.

She nearly tore the hinges off the back door getting to the source of the scream. It was Eli and he was running as hard as he could toward her. The other children had stopped their play, recognizing the tone of the scream. It wasn't the kind one gave because they were furious, or demanding their turn at some game. This scream was serious and the fact that Loni had shown up made it much more serious.

Eli trembled from head to foot and pointed toward the sandbox, wordless with terror.

Loni was relieved. Evidently, someone had buried yet another pet or something in the sand. Lately Chun had been curious about the process of decomposition. It was likely one of hers. Loni had never met anyone with such an insatiable appetite for knowledge or flare for chemistry. Twice this week she had removed books from Chun's sleeping form.

"It's all right," she told the rest, "it's just the sandbox. Brenna, keep them away from it."

Brenna dutifully headed toward the sandbox, forbidding the younger children to appease their curiosity. The older children had seen enough maggot-covered pets, so they weren't in the least interested.

It was very loose sand, perfect for digging. Several wagonloads had been brought in from the great Eastern Desert years ago. Mari had used her magic to dig the hole four feet deep. Several of their charges liked the idea of digging deep enough to get to the other side of the world, but seldom lasted beyond three feet.

Loni gave Eli a hug and took him into the house and gave him cookies and a glass of ice-cold milk. *Hopefully he won't have nightmares.* Wyn had followed them in and sat near him, putting her skinny arm around him and looking at the cookies longingly until Loni held up two fingers, and she understood that she would be allowed two and no more.

Loni went out the back door, picking up the shovel. She would take whatever poor little animal had been buried and put it to rest in the woods as she had so often before. Brenna stood at the edge of the sandbox, looking down. At Loni's approach she looked up, her face was sheet-white. Prickles of warning shot up Loni's spine and she hurried to Brenna, who did not scare easily.

"I couldn't scream," Brenna whispered and hugged her Aunt, burying her face in the apron that smelled of cookies and comfort. Loni stared at the sandbox, wishing she had been the one to see the gruesome sight first, instead of her niece or Eli. She had a queasy feeling about this newest horror. It was enough to tip the scales and get Haddy in more trouble than she had ever been.

Loni bit her lip. Haddy still wasn't home and that wasn't a good sign. Of course, neither was what she found looking up at her from the sandbox.

Mari would be back soon from the mercantile. Mari wanted to speak to Haddy this morning before she and Brenna left for home. Loni knew the conversation would center around the hit Haddy had made on her own. That alone would be cause for concern because her actions had lost the Eyes the chance to remove a dangerous man. She had the feeling that Mari had postponed it until after her birthday and she was grateful. It had given her a much needed rest from her cares and a chance to remember.

Loni mentally braced herself for Mari's return. Haddy was nowhere to be found. She had decided to let Mari talk to Haddy first, and while they were still all together, bring up the fact that there was a corpse in the children's sandbox. She ran the scenario through her mind and could not see one peaceable solution that would satisfy them all.

*

Haddy knew that Lyon would be coming today. She had overheard her sisters talking about it last night. Mari and Lyon usually rode a pair of stunning 'Hauzian horses that were very fast and difficult to tame. *Like Lyon.* She thought with a sense of excitement. He would be blessedly alone while he unsaddled his horse. She knew from experience it was hard to get him by himself.

She had carefully planned the moment she could declare her feelings for him, already telling the boys who worked in the barn that she would do their chores for them - as long as they promised to stay out of the barn until lunch. She hugged herself, shuddering in anticipation. She could finally tell her brother-in-law how much she loved him. She was nearly positive he would take her away from here. Mari was too busy to be a proper wife.

She heard the hoof beats long before she saw Lyon ride in. He usually rode fast, pushing his horses to their limit and smiling like a bandit who made off with the royal treasury. This time the horse's hoofbeats confused her. It was almost as if he had the horse trotting rather than at a full run, but that could have just been her nerves.

While hiding up in the loft, she wondered if he would like her new outfit. She had chosen it from the pile of discarded clothing from the brothel and modified it, but not too much. She would wait to reveal her presence until she heard him dismount and unsaddle his horse.

"Good ride, Meersa," he said softly to his horse. The beloved voice sent pulses of anticipation up her spine and she felt her stomach clench. *You've never been a coward. Tell him!*

It was time. She was getting ready to stand up when she heard a familiar voice, and all her hopes were dashed. She ground her teeth in frustration. *It isn't fair!*

"Hello stranger," Mari's voice called to Lyon from the barn door.

Haddy peeked from the space between the boards at Lyon. He looked a little weary but very handsome and his smile made her heart flutter in her chest. *This man should be mine!*

*

Lyon knew better than to stay the night at the orphanage with Haddy on the loose. Normally, he would have left the saddle on, but the mare he rode had miscarried months ago and he didn't want to push her.

His wife walked into the barn looking like a slice of heaven and he took some packages out of the saddlebags. The sun was a few hours from setting and it was peaceful. He couldn't see Haddy anywhere with her hot eyes and poisonous thoughts. He shook his head with relief.

"Something wrong?" Mari smiled knowingly. "I'm sure Haddy would be willing to bring you something for that headache."

Lyon squinted at his wife, "Now that you mention it, I do have a headache coming on…"

Up in the loft Haddy's eyes sparkled. *He does care!*

Lyon paused for effect, "…at the thought of what she'll do or say to embarrass me. I've seen saddles with thinner skin. I just wish she knew how she was embarrassing herself."

Stunned by his words, Haddy felt tears come to her eyes and she bit her lip. She could hardly breathe with the pain his words caused.

"If anything ever happened to me she could mend your broken heart," Mari said lightly as she wrapped her arms around his neck for a welcoming kiss.

"Under Achaite law, I can forbid you putting yourself in danger," he pulled her closer and kissed her soundly. Then he released her and put the saddle on its stand. "I always want you with me, but as long as you're willing to give me to one of your sisters," he winked, "I'd rather have Loni."

This statement nearly made Haddy gasp out loud.

"She's far more beautiful than Haddy. And you," he waggled his eyebrows, "are more beautiful than both."

"No need for flattery, just gold," she laughed at him as he handed her the pouch at his belt. "Loni isn't saying much, but I can tell she needs it. And hand me that brush I asked you to bring. If Brenna will brush Mee's fur once in awhile, maybe Mee will stop pestering Haddy."

Lyon fetched the required items and gave them to his wife. He wanted to reassure her about something, "Mari, just for the record, Hadasha *is* very beautiful."

"But?"

"She found out early how to get her way with looks alone and she hasn't had to face any challenges her beauty couldn't conquer," he said with frustration. "I feel sorry for her but I never know whether to put her across my knee and give her a well-deserved spanking, or to just ignore her and hope for the best. She could never hold a candle to you, or to Loni, for that matter."

"She's just young," insisted Mari. "She'll find her way."

"As long as it's out of my way, I'll be happy," he grunted.

"Please don't be mean to her Lyon," Mari begged him. "I love my sister."

"I'll gladly stay out of her way, if she'll just stay out of mine," Lyon growled as he offered his arm and they left the barn.

If Haddy didn't hate Mari so much right now, she'd be tempted to feel grateful. Right now though, the wound in her heart was too raw for her to do more than continue biting her lip to keep from sobbing out loud. Her world was crushed. Loni had obviously been right about Lyon. He didn't love her, not even a tiny bit. But for him to say he would prefer plain-faced Loni to her was an unimaginable lie. *It has to be.*

Her pain soon shifted to anger. She needed to make him suffer for that. *Mari too.*

She had no sooner climbed down the loft ladder when Loni found her. Loni's eyes widened at the outfit she wore and said, "Please change your clothes before you come to the kitchen."

*

Once the family members were gathered in the kitchen, the questions came up about exactly what had happened in town last night. Loni steeled herself for the blowup, grateful that Pash was teaching at the moment, so all the orphans were out of the house. Currently, Zaya was keeping a watch on the unhallowed grave and its sandy-eyed corpse.

"No one got hurt!" Haddy was truly angry and sent dagger-eyes Loni's way.

Loni supposed it was natural for someone as self-absorbed as Haddy to assume Loni had broken her word and tattled to Mari and Lyon about the attack on Brenna. The fact no one was hurt wouldn't change what was coming. *At least she had the sense to change her clothes before she came to the meeting.* No matter how bad it was at the moment, the revealing dress would have made it ten times worse; especially with Lyon in the house.

Loni had known it was going to be bad but she had never seen Lyon so angry. Perhaps it just seemed so much worse because she knew his anger was justified. She was hesitant at the moment to add the corpse into the conversation, because Lyon and Mari were already so livid.

"Brenna can't stay here any longer," Lyon said in a flat voice that brooked no argument, shooting a poisonous look at Haddy.

"Don't punish her on my account!" Haddy said hotly, facing him with blazing eyes.

"Your choice left me no alternative; she was seen."

Loni knew he was right. Brenna was extraordinary enough to remember. While Mari's enchantment encouraged the locals to forget the location of Ryn House, whenever orphans ventured out of it, they could be remembered.

Haddy seemed to remember this as well and stated, "As long as she's in the orphanage, they can't find her."

Mari fumed, "And make our daughter a prisoner here because of your mistake?"

That's not the point," Lyon glared at Haddy, who took an involuntary step back.

Loni placed herself between Haddy and Lyon and Mari gently pulled his hand so he would back away. He shook her off and his jaw tightened.

"I already told you, I took care of them – all of them," Haddy stubbornly insisted.

"I don't care how long you trained with Monus, you're an amateur in every way that counts," Lyon snarled.

Wanting to calm the tension and feeling Haddy still didn't understand the consequences of her impulsiveness, Loni said, "Can't you see how you put her into danger?"

Mari icily added, "If you won't be honest with us, at least be honest with yourself."

"I will if you will," Haddy shot back.

"What's that supposed to mean?" Mari folded her arms and her eyebrow rose.

"You're both just upset because you lost your babysitter!" she looked at Loni.

"No," Mari corrected, a hand on Lyon's chest to prevent him throttling Haddy. "We're upset because you love yourself more than Brenna." Lyon nodded his agreement.

Haddy went white with shock. "You know I'd die before letting anyone hurt her!"

"I want to believe that's true," Mari said evenly, "but I can't. You'd never have put her into danger in the first place if it were."

380 | Michelle Erickson

"I know the prophecies, Mari!" Haddy stood with her hands on her hips, "It won't matter where she goes, there will always be danger."

"But not *yet*!" Lyon re-entered the conversation like a lightning strike and Loni's eyes grew large when she recognized he'd taken second-form fighting stance. Lyon was an impressive man to look at. He could be, and usually was, silent. Right now he looked as if he was measuring Haddy for a casket and planning the method to arrange her future nailed inside of it, buried six feet down.

"Brenna leaves Ryn House today and as long as you're here," he jabbed his finger at Haddy, "she won't be. You're an endangerment to every child here because You. Can't. Control. Yourself." Lyon's eyes were cold as they went over Haddy's angry face.

Mari knew that Haddy usually acted the fool in front of him, but was bursting at the seams to do or say something to him that would hurt. Her youngest sister didn't know that he didn't care enough about her to be hurt by anything she could possibly say to him.

Haddy's eyes darted over to Mari. "Brenna loves it here. I'll leave."

"Lyon?" Mari had exchanged a look with Loni and knew it was time to speak with Haddy alone. "Loni and I need to talk to Haddy alone before we leave. Would you please get the horses ready?" Lyon left, his eyes still looking at the youngest Ryn sister with contempt. He left in search of his daughter.

"That's just like you Haddy," Mari hissed in disgust after he left, "running out and leaving the responsibility for Loni to carry the load."

"She has Pash and Zaya, she doesn't need me."

"That was always meant to be a *temporary* arrangement."

"That isn't the only thing she needs to claim responsibility about," Loni's eyes were sad and her voice a little hoarse. Wearily, she sat in her favorite chair. She felt like her family was flying apart. There wasn't anything she could do about it except pray Mari wouldn't kill Haddy, who was so self-absorbed that she didn't seem to realize how close she had already come to death. Mari's eyes had that faintly purple cast to them which spoke of the great power that was boiling within.

Haddy looked at Loni, defenses raised, "Now what? Did I forget to ask your permission to breathe?"

Loni looked at her like she would a spoiled child, "Actually, I was wondering if you could explain the corpse Eli found in the sandbox." She avoided mentioning Brenna.

This statement brought Mari's eyes snapping back to their younger sister, "While you're at it, you can explain why you made a hit without permission."

Haddy had the gall to look surprised and desperate. Loni wasn't sure if it was because of the body or the hit. "How did you…?"

"I'm Hi-Sha! Perhaps you have heard that before?" Mari was standing with arms folded, and the familiar lecture-stance was resumed. There was one difference. Mari was beginning to glow; a faint purple outline surrounded her.

Loni also stood and judiciously placed herself in front of Haddy, facing her powerful sister, "Mari, for my sake, please let her explain."

Loni turned to Haddy. "It better be good."

With a heavy heart, Loni felt it wouldn't be. She was right. There was one consolation, At least Mari didn't dissolve Haddy on the spot after the lame explanation and insulting justification.

"So…let's make sure I get this right," Mari was glowing again and this time Loni didn't blame her. She was appalled at what Haddy had confessed.

"You took out the second man on the list - without permission - because he was there at the time, and you felt it was as good a time as any to do so.

Further, you did this before we could remove Scive Fellstein, who by the way, has now gone into hiding," Mari shook her head at the impossibility of rectifying that mistake. Clear shots at a member of the Nine were rare.

"On top of that idea, you brought a man right outside the walls of this orphanage and later killed him. You did this after Loni told you he was talking to Delf, the Minister of Trade, who doesn't live here, and therefore is immune to the enchantment that keeps our exact location secret."

"You make it sound so bad when you say it that way!" Haddy's green eyes flashed, "The first one I took out had information about Lux and he was going to take her out! I was saving her life and doing you a favor!"

Mari's fists were clenched as tight as her jaw and she was literally trembling with rage. Lux was another one of their Eyes and currently living in Phoenix House, safe in Utak. Even if she wasn't, Lux was among their top Eyes and could take care of herself. "That was a setup! It was supposed to happen! You would have known that, if you had come to the meetings instead of running down to the Mercantile everyday to make cow-eyes at the clerk!"

Haddy had the nerve to say, "It wasn't my fault! I just..."

Loni held up a hand, her head beginning to ache again. "Enough. Haddy, I contacted Mistress Shu last night. You leave for Utak within the hour. Mari, take Brenna, I may send Wyn later. I've called an alert to all Eyes through the usual channel. I'll start preparations for an evacuation."

Mari knew Loni's "usual channel" meant the small marble boxes filled with sand and used for communication between the Eyes. Haddy didn't have one, and at this point, it looked like she never would.

Haddy snorted, "That won't be necessary Loni. I'm leaving, remember?"

Mari gritted her teeth, striving for patience. "For now, remain here, but put them on alert and we'll see if anything comes our way. I don't have anywhere to put the children yet." Her eyes narrowed at Haddy.

"Why don't you just close your doors? We have too many kids already," blasted Haddy.

Mari couldn't help it and Loni didn't stop her as she used her power to roughly lift Haddy up by the ankles and turn her upside-down.

Apparently, Haddy had forgotten she was still wearing the lingerie she had taken from the brothel's discards. Straw fell from Haddy's skirts. Mari looked with open-mouthed disbelief at Loni. Then Mari's bi-colored eyes sparked with anger and Haddy screamed as she felt Mari's invisible blow land across her backside.

Loni wasn't sure why Haddy had been in the barn, but it didn't seem too hard to figure out, considering Haddy's passion for their brother-in-law. If Haddy somehow overheard Mari's conversation with Lyon, something Loni only heard the last part of, that would explain her foul mood. On the other hand, it was probably a good thing if she overheard that Lyon didn't think of her that way and never had. If she had listened closely, she would realize he never would.

"I have been too lenient with you Hadasha Ryn." Mari's voice turned formal, "I strip you now of your office as M'sha and revoke all rights, privileges, and duties herewith." She gestured and Haddy was gently placed on the floor instead of slammed as Loni half-expected.

Loni ignored Haddy and worriedly spoke to Mari. "Are you sure that Phoenix House couldn't hold all the orphans?"

Mari shook her head, scowling at Haddy who angrily flopped on the old sofa. "I'm sorry Loni; maybe I can find another in the next week."

Loni's back stiffened. "I'll obtain the necessary supplies, if you'll find a safe place to put everyone."

Mari's mind was already attacking the problem, "There were quite a few farmsteads abandoned by the plague that broke out a few years ago.

I'll send Lux back to Shugahauze to scout along the Krymea river. I doubt she'll have to go as far as the west coast, I'm sure she'll find something suitable."

*

Lyon had come in the door, seen Haddy hanging upside down and turned away with a smile. His wife was handling things very well. From the little conversation he was able to hear, it sounded like Loni would be setting up a new orphanage and that was good. Wherever they set up an orphanage, he would generally set up a business and Shugahauze was far from Haddy.

It was comforting to know his wife could maintain her temper when disciplining family because if it had been him, her twisted harpy of a sister would be a sad memory. He didn't trust her and wasn't sure anyone should.

Chapter 37: Living Dead

The next morning, Brenna was quiet on the trip home. Aunt Haddy hadn't come home last night and her parents seemed to be upset over something. She felt uneasy, sure that it had been her fault for telling her parents about how brave Mee had been. Once she had said those words, the rest had followed, and as a team her parents had marched out of her room. When they returned, she was told to pack all of her things, not just some of them, and that was troubling. She had left a few things on purpose, giving them to Wyn to keep for her. Wyn started to cry when Brenna sadly told her goodbye and that made Brenna cry.

Risking punishment, she slipped down to the kitchen and got Wyn three cookies. That seemed to cheer up Wyn for a moment. However, the cookies sat untouched on the dressing table in Wyn's room, a sure sign that Wyn was seriously unhappy. She liked cookies almost as much as Mee liked crab.

Her parents told her that she would not be returning to Ryn House anytime soon. She felt a peculiar wrench at the loss. Wyn was like a little sister to her although Wyn was a few years older than Brenna. The cross-eyed Wyn looked and acted much younger and Brenna wanted to protect her. Some of the orphans had started to call Wyn a ghost, probably because she was so pale and quiet. They didn't call Wyn anything when Brenna was around.

"Will you come back?" Wyn's wet eyes were full of despair. Brenna couldn't help that.

"Yes, to visit." She tried to look positive as she quoted what her father had told her. She left off the rest he'd said – that she'd never stay for very long when they did allow her to visit, and she'd always have one parent with her. This was only problematic because her mother was much better at catching her in the act of doing wrong than Aunt Loni.

"Why?" Wyn's sorrowful question had no answer. In fact, it was the question Brenna kept asking herself since the grownups refused to answer. Was it because of the dead man? Was that why Aunt Haddy hadn't come home? The only thing keeping her from throwing a tantrum and bursting into tears was the fact they were going to pick up Talon from Tryk's place.

Tasut had forbidden Talon to come to the orphanage after his first visit. No explanation was given. Every time Brenna saw Talon after that, she told him all about Ryn House and everyone associated with it. She shared everything with Talon. In her mind there was no secret she would keep from him. Except now.

In spite of the stinging that would accompany breaking the promise she had given her mother, she was considering showing him how she could bend light. She reasoned that the stinging wouldn't be too bad if it was like a slap. Slaps didn't look like they hurt too much.

"Brenna? get Mee, we need to leave," her mother commanded.

Brenna called, but no Mee came. She didn't fret about it because she'd told Mee last night they were going to Tryk's. Brenna was certain her Shee hadn't been able to wait. Not with the prospect of a full crab cage beckoning.

The day was peaceful when they left Ryn House, even if her heart wasn't. Wyn refused to wish her goodbye from the door, but did wave from her window. Brenna could tell she was still crying. Brenna kept looking back at her Aunt Loni, who watched until they were out of sight.

The horse she was riding was content to stay at a steady walk. Her mother was still looking unhappy over something, but her father's eyes never stopped moving, even when he was talking. He told her that he looked around so he could enjoy everything. Brenna thought it was because he was looking for Mee and didn't want her to worry.

Brenna liked mornings. Everything was fresh and there was the smell of breakfast and a new day where so much fun could be had.

Today would be especially nice. She would get to see Talon and that was always a good day. She'd tell him about the nightmare she had last night. It was all about the dead man in the sandbox. She'd wanted to tell her mother, but it just didn't seem like a good idea when her parents were mad at Aunt Haddy. She wanted the comforting reassurance that all was well in the world and when she saw Talon, it would be. *I don't like dead things.*

They had ridden several miles when they caught a foul stench in the air. The natural supposition was something died, or as the stench grew stronger, perhaps several somethings. The stench wasn't uncommon in this area, where animals were slaughtered in fields for meat, skin, or horns. The smell grew so strong that they were soon covering their mouths and noses. As they came to a bend in the road, her father signaled them to halt just before they would see what was around the curve.

"Mari, you know what to do."

With that, her father went ahead of them. Her mother nodded and Brenna guided her horse as close to her mother's as she could.

"If we're attacked by anyone, Brenna, hide," her mother told her.

Brenna nodded her understanding, still pinching her nose and breathing through her mouth, "Where should I go?" she looked around at the unfamiliar countryside.

Mari also had her nose pinched, "Wrap yourself in light and ride back to Ryn House."

Her father was gone only for a few moments and came back at a run, he signaled her mother and they all went into the wooded area and he spoke quickly and quietly. "There's been a battle," her father told them. "There are casualties all over the road and meadow just ahead. I didn't see anyone move. I think they're all dead." He looked at her, "Brenna, keep your eyes closed until we say."

Brenna had seen one dead man and she had no desire to see more. She squeezed her eyes shut, but her stomach still felt like it wanted to crawl out of her mouth.

"Follow me," she heard her father say. "We'll do this at a run."

Kicking the horses up to a run, they came upon the results of the battle that had raged over both sides of the road.

Unable to keep her eyes closed because the smell seemed even worse, she saw corpses covering the nearby meadow her father had talked about and some bodies littered the road itself. For whatever reason, no one had bothered to bury the dead. The dead men all wore soldier uniforms and they looked bloated like they'd lain there for a long time in the hot sun.

Brenna couldn't help feeling horror at the butchery that lay in the field. The victim's gruesome faces flashed in her minds eye over and over in cadence to her horse's gallop as they left the scene behind.

They kicked their mounts to a full gallop. Soon the smell grew fainter so they could breathe. Brenna held on tightly as her horse flew along the road next to her mother's. She anxiously waited for Tryk's odd house to come into view.

The first thing she saw, however, was Talon. He stood at the end of the long drive, waiting. Before her parents could stop her, she jumped off her horse before it actually stopped and Talon had to catch her. As he put her on the ground, she began to sob. Baffeled, he looked up at her parents.

It had been a long time between visits and Lyon noted he had grown. He looked four inches taller and the chopping he had been doing had added bulk to his lean frame. He was a nice looking boy and it was obvious that Brenna adored him. It was obvious in Brenna's eyes, that Talon hadn't changed much from the last time she had seen him.

"I missed you!" she exclaimed, wiping away her tears. She took his hand. "Show me what new things Tryk has," she ignored her parents who were behind her, dismounting and taking care of the animals.

Mee, who had indeed been staying at Tryk's, was laying on a sunny rock with the empty crab shells littering the nearby ground. Her ears twitched and she sat up and sniffed, looking over at the pathway leading to the road. Brenna came into view.

"Bren!" the little Shee scolded, crossly kicking one of the crab shells off the rock. Mee placed her paws on her waist in a fair imitation of Mari, "You go with no Mee!"

"Sorry Mee, I couldn't find you," Brenna said with a smile, her slender hand petted the soft fur but she left her other hand in Talon's.

"Ran hard," Mee complained. "Bad Had! Her horse too fast. Came here."

"You mean Haddy?" Mari had caught up to hear the last of what Mee said and was now intent on the peach-and-cream colored Shee.

Mee nodded. "Had go. Take Mee big bug."

Brenna translated for her pet. "Aunt Haddy accidentally took Mee's pet bug when Aunt Haddy rode away from Ryn House."

Mee wasn't likely to forgive this thievery, but was curious, "Bad Had need bug?"

"No, but I'd like to be there when she finds it," smiled Lyon who had also joined them.

Mee nodded at him. "Mee too," her eyes went glittery.

Talon, who had spent several hours in Mee's company, said, "When Mee got here, she came into my room and demanded crab." He didn't tell them he was asleep and she pulled his eyelid up and called his name. "We've gone crab hunting twice already."

Tryk appeared at his front door. His craggy face with its scars was unpleasant in the daylight, but he was the grandfather that Brenna had never known. "Come in, my friends, lunch is waiting. This young buck," Tryk nodded in Talon's direction while he wiped his greasy hands on a not-too-clean cloth, "woke up this morning and told me that you would be here about lunch time."

*

After dinner, Tryk and Lyon rode out to the battlefield.

"Why here?" Lyon asked. His grey eyes traveled over the field. It hadn't been a large battle, but it looked like the men in Terisian uniforms had been ambushed. Whoever the victors were, they hadn't left any of their dead.

In spite of popular myth, dead men did tell tales. Bodies told only the basic tale, but certain cloth and stitching came from specific parts of the world. Jewelry could speak volumes to Lyon, who was an expert in the field.

After a thorough search, they found no survivors; only more questions. Tryk had just mounted his piebald mare when Lyon broke into a run and knelt by a man who lay spread-eagle near the road. Lyon hung his head for a moment and then returned to Tryk, who was holding their horses.

"You knew him."

Lyon nodded, not speaking. It hadn't been a question.

But there was a puzzle. Why here and now? What purpose did the battle serve?

Later that evening, listening to her parents discuss the happenings with Tryk, Brenna looked at her father. He told them what he thought happened and then he described a man he had found. To her surprise, his eyes were moist. She couldn't ever remember seeing him shed tears and it made her want to cry as well. She was sitting by Talon and she looked at him. He looked so sober, that she felt a tear escape her eye. If everyone was this sad, it must be very bad.

"Who was he?" Mari asked, quietly taking her husband's hand.

"He was a…" he glanced at Brenna, "…at the Guild." He finished, his voice hoarse, "Good man, good friend." Then he expressed his frustration, "I wish he were alive so I could ask him about the battle. It's too close, Mari, something isn't right. If he were alive he could tell me who ambushed them. It would help us plan our next step."

It was hard to get her father's pain out of her mind. As she went to bed, her father's voice came from the kitchen where the adults were still talking "I wish he were alive…"

*

In the deepest part of that same night, Talon was wrenched out of a deep sleep by a blood-curdling scream. With hair on end and trembling, he struggled to pull on his pants. He slammed his toe against the foot of the bed, sure he had broken it, and yelled at the unexpected pain.

Tryk, who was still awake and in the middle of testing one of his machines, hit a wrong switch and was thrown violently backward, knocking the fireworks he had been saving for Talon's birthday into the nearly exhausted fire.

Lyon, hearing his daughters scream, ran for her room at top speed without remembering he was in Tryk's house, missed the doorway, and ran into the wall, breaking his nose and knocking himself out.

Mari woke in time to see him falling to the floor covered with blood. He wasn't moving. Tears sprang to her eyes as she focused her staff into being, listening to the awful noise that surrounded her, and sending out her senses to ascertain who was attacking them. Outside the house, there was something that felt like men, but it was somehow wrong. Urches!

Staff ready, she knelt to check her husband as the fireworks exploded and added a new meaning to the word chaos.

In the meantime, Talon hobbled quickly and painfully toward Brenna's room, Tryk crawled out from under the ruined experiment, his hair singed, and Lyon moaned and tried to sit up, spitting blood and dazedly looking the direction of Brenna's room. Mari shushed them all, her eyes so fierce, Talon froze in place.

"Something's coming; it feels like Urches. Thank All they aren't in the house."

Talon remembered the knobby-eyed men and felt instant revulsion.

"Talon, go get Brenna and hide under the stairs while I fix Lyon's nose. If things go wrong, take her back to Ryn House."

Excitement and fear battled for victory in Talon's mind. What he was expecting, he wasn't really sure. He only knew that Brenna had been screaming. The sound of her shriek was still ringing in his ears as he opened her bedroom door, only now it sounded like... moaning.

He paused to listen for a moment. The sound wasn't in her bedroom after all. It seemed to surround the house.

Mee was hiding under the bed repeatedly saying, "Bad!"

Talon would have been relieved if all Brenna had been doing was tossing and turning, but she was glowing like she did the night they saw Father of All, perhaps even brighter. The feeling was different though, not exactly evil, but not good either.

Talon silently reached out and touched her, "Brenna?"

She sat straight up and her eyes opened. They were totally white and he backed away as she whipped her head in his direction. He wasn't sure she could see him.

"Brenna?" he asked, fearing for her. "Brenna?"

Lyon and Mari ran in and Mari shook her daughter awake.

The glowing ceased and Brenna's eyes turned back to the color they were supposed to be. She looked at Talon. "I had a nightmare," Brenna explained, "some bad men were coming to take you away from me and I called for help."

Talon could swear he still heard moaning.

"What in the name of all stone-fisted wonders happened?" Tryk entered the small room tucking his shirt into his baggy britches and blinking like an owl. His hair was fried on one side of his head and the ends were still smoking.

A heavy knock at the door made the grown-ups exchange glances.

Looking uneasy, Tryk took an oil lantern and went to the door. They all followed him out and he looked back at them to see if they were ready.

Mari went to the left with her staff. Lyon slipped into the shadows on the right and looked over at Talon and Brenna, who were still standing, frozen, in the middle of the room.

Talon picked up on the non-verbal direction and nodded, pulling Brenna into shadows under the stairs where they could see the front door between the slats. Talon thought he saw something shiny in Lyon's hand, but he couldn't be sure.

When they were hidden, Tryk opened the door and instantly gagged, backing away from the stench, his hand over his nose and mouth.

A corpse had come to call.

Stunned, Tryk said faintly, "It's for you," to no one in particular. His one good eye looked like it was bulging from its socket as the corpse entered.

Lyon, bare chest covered with his own blood, looked a bit macabre himself as he stepped into the light to meet the dead man.

First, Talon thought Lyon would take the man's head off because he was in sixth form, but then he stiffened.

Talon felt confusion – why wasn't Lyon doing anything?.

*

Lyon felt shock and horror. His hair tried to stand on end. There, standing in the waning moonlight, was the very friend Lyon had kneeled by in the open battlefield earlier that day.

"Jax?" His mind knew the man was dead, but his eyes refused to give his mind the peace it demanded on the subject.

Talon noticed the dead man's head was slightly tilted from the fatal slash he had taken across the neck. He even looked bloated, as if his corpse had baked in the sun all day. The smell was horrendous.

In a hoarse, desert-dry voice the corpse said, "We are here. Ask and we shall deliver that we might have peace."

The corpse pointed to where Talon and Brenna hid and moaned, "Ask. She must ask."

"Brenna?" Mari's voice was calm, but her eyes were a bit wild. "What did you do?"

"I…I don't know." Brenna was shaking like a leaf. Talon gave her hand a squeeze as he tried to shut out the horror he felt.

"Then release us!" demanded the corpse of the frightened little girl. His dead filmy eyes fixed on Brenna.

"I don't know how!" she wailed and buried her face in Talon's side. Talon was grateful that they were under the stairs.

"Bring her out here," Lyon ordered Talon.

Talon gently led her out. Hand-in-hand they faced the gruesome visitor. Talon put Brenna slightly behind him.

"You called! We came! What do you want!" the corpse seemed to have a temper.

"We?" asked Mari, stunned, as her mind tried to form the thought she didn't want to accept.

"My men are awaiting orders in the yard. I repeat, what do you want!" The corpse demanded angrily. "We were at peace."

"Jax, can you tell me who killed you and your men?" Lyon did not want to pass up this opportunity.

The corpse seemed to take in more than Brenna for the first time. It turned its head toward Lyon, as if the corpse had just seen him, "You were my friend in life."

"Who ambushed you?" Lyon ignored the maggots crawling on the corpse by looking elsewhere and he tried to breathe through his mouth to avoid gagging.

"Sogoian regulars dressed as Terisians. I did not know this until I crossed over," confirmed the corpse.

"What, or who, were they looking for?" pressed Mari, dreading the answer. She stayed out of reach, her hands on Brenna's shoulders. The smell was staggering.

"The One," the corpse fell silent but continued to look at Lyon. "Jax" or what was left of him was finished speaking and was now backing away from the doorway and out into the yard where groaning corpses staggered, crawled, and moaned.

Jax turned, "Lyon, I beg you, tell her to release us, we have great pain."

Lyon looked at Mari who turned to the pale Brenna standing hand-in-hand with Talon.

"Just tell them they're free," Mari coached, her face white at this show of power from her eight-year-old.

"Jax," Lyon was desperate for information, "When will it happen?"

"Before a score of years."

Talon had no idea what that was about, but he felt Brenna pull him forward until she faced the doorway. Talon could feel her shiver although it wasn't cold outside. He knew how she felt because every hair on his body was doing the same thing.

"You're free," she said in a quavering voice, her eyes huge with fright.

The corpses disappeared and along with them, the stench of death, decay, and the sounds of agony.

Lyon turned from the door and looked straight at Brenna. Her mother was doing the same. She peeked around Talon at her parents, her shivering continued.

"Don't you hate guests in the middle of the night?" Tryk said dryly, "Now I won't get a wink of sleep. What do you all say to a bit of breakfast?"

ABOUT THE AUTHOR

Michelle graduated from Children's Institute of Literature. She lives with her family in rural Idaho in a fun-size community where the silence is loud - *especially* after harvest. She enjoys writing, reading, hiking, family history, and photography.

CPSIA information can be obtained at www.ICGtesting.com
Printed in the USA
BVOW011108011211

277262BV00001B/3/P